FOR LOVE

Also by Sue Miller

Inventing the Abbotts
The Good Mother
Family Pictures

FOR LOVE

SUE MILLER

HarperCollinsPublishers

HarperCollins books may be purchased for educational, business, or sales promotional use. For information please write: Special Markets Department, HarperCollins Publishers, Inc., 10 East 53rd Street, New York, NY 10022.

FIRST EDITION

Designed by C. Linda Dingler

Library of Congress Cataloging-in-Publication Data
Miller, Sue, 1943–
  For love / Sue Miller. — 1st ed.
    p. cm.
  ISBN 0-06-017979-1
  I. Title.
PS3563.I421444F67   1993
813'.54—dc20   92-54422

93 94 95 96 97 CC/HC 10 9 8 7 6 5 4 3 2 1

For Ted Solotaroff

It isn't until several days after the accident that Lottie lets herself—makes herself—think about it. Think about how it was for all of them, for Cameron and Elizabeth, and for Jessica.

What she imagines is that Cameron must have been certain, right up until the moment he turned the car into the driveway, that he could get control again, that he could win Elizabeth back. She imagines him—her brother—shut up alone in the dark car, driving much too fast across the city, his whole intention bent toward Elizabeth, that terrible, lost, pumping sensation of pure will feeding on itself. Lottie has felt it too, she knows all those feelings: someone has told you it's over, but you can't begin to believe that, you simply want it too much. You're like a child in this: what you believe in, all you can believe in, is what you want.

Probably Cameron has barely noticed anything on the way over. Probably he doesn't even realize, really, that it's raining. No, he's living only in the moment he knows is coming, the moment when he'll claim Elizabeth, the moment when she'll turn to him and say yes. Because she has to say yes, he's sure she will. He can see her face, lifting, her mouth making the word.

Now Lottie pictures Elizabeth, the woman he's in love with. Lottie knows this about her: that she's just called Cameron. She's told him she's not coming over this evening, as they have planned. That she's not ever coming over again. Her husband has arrived from the Midwest, and he wants her back. She says something like she'll "remember forever this wonderful summer" with Cameron—oh yes! Elizabeth is quite capable of this kind of melodrama too—but now it's done. It has to be done.

They argue on the telephone. Cameron is unbelieving, unyielding, and this makes Elizabeth angry. Who does he think he is, after all? Her voice rises as she speaks, it's suddenly sharp and has an ugly edge. But maybe she hears this herself, maybe she lowers it, makes it sympathetic again. She must have gone to the back hallway or to the room that had been her father's study to make this call, and maybe now she's worried that her mother or her husband might have heard her raise her voice, might come down the hall or up the stairs to see what's wrong, why she sounds so angry. For just these few moments, then, maybe she's not focusing on Cameron, she's not being careful enough, not managing him well enough, not really listening to him; and so she's surprised, surprised and appalled, when he finishes talking and then says, "I'm coming over there now, Elizabeth." And hangs up.

She would have been frozen, Lottie thinks. For perhaps thirty seconds she might have stood there—Lottie sees her at her father's neat desk—looking out at the rain. The humming phone is still in her hand. The window must be shut, and the wind-driven rain hits the glass in long, particulate slaps. What is she going to do?

She sets the telephone down in its cradle, and what Lottie imagines for her, knowing Elizabeth as she does, is that the thrill of panic she feels is mixed with a peculiar joy. After all, she is at the center of this drama. Her husband has arrived unexpectedly this afternoon to claim her, and now her lover is coming over to make his claim too. Lottie suspects she might allow herself to feel it too, for a few seconds anyway—why wouldn't she?—the excitement of the most important role, the pleasure in being loved too much, by too many people.

Of course for Elizabeth there's no doubt or hesitation about which claim to honor. With her husband she has three children, a big house that looks out over a wooded pond, a life of mundane and compelling complications. With Cameron she has had an affair, a reenactment of her youth. For half of this airless, hot Cambridge summer, a summer of record rainfalls on the East Coast, they've pretended to be seventeen or twenty-two again, while Lottie has looked on, has been their witness—sometimes their excuse. She knows many of the details. Elizabeth has told her. They've sat in Cameron's car with rain drumming on the metal roof, the windows fogged, and talked and touched each other yearningly. They've sneaked out of Elizabeth's house at dawn after making love all night. They've taken long walks in the dark, stopping often on the brick-humped sidewalks to kiss. They've waked each other in the middle of the night with phone calls, with pebbles thrown against a screen just to tell each other again, I love you, I love you. They're both middle-aged now, but they haven't been able to invent other words, or more adult behavior.

And just as he did when he was younger, Cameron has believed in it, believed in it with the same conviction that's driving him now, gray-haired, slender and intense and worried-looking in his beat-up car, past the littered empty sidewalks near his apartment in the South End, across the rain-scoured streets in the Back Bay, along the blackened river, through Harvard Square, and back to the street in Cambridge they all grew up on, Lottie and Cameron on one side, Elizabeth on the other: the street Elizabeth has returned to this summer in flight from what seemed, until that afternoon, a ruined marriage.

Now Elizabeth goes out of the study, flicking the light off behind her. Lottie imagines her standing for a moment in the carpeted part of the upstairs hall. Perhaps her children are playing below. Yes, Elizabeth can hear that her daughter, the youngest, is too wound up, excited by her father's sudden appearance, confused and delighted that they seem to be a family again, that he's going to take them all back to Minnesota. Elizabeth stands very still and listens to the girl's shrill voice calling to her father to come see, come see. Elizabeth's husband is talking, in the kitchen, it seems, with Elizabeth's mother. He calls out to his daughter that he'll come in a minute. Maybe he sounds a little irritated at being interrupted, and maybe in the slight constriction that this would give to his voice, Elizabeth hears the reality of her marriage announcing itself, she hears the possibility of dailiness, of a life with only smaller joys, smaller heartbreaks. The life we all want more, finally, Lottie thinks, than the life we dream of at seventeen, or twenty-two.

And here it is, this is the way Lottie imagines Elizabeth setting it in motion, the unwinding of the event that will change so many things. She turns right, away from the wide hallway among the family's bedrooms, to the narrower back hall, where the floor is exposed, worn wood. She goes to the end of this hall, past the maid's tiny bathroom and a utility room, and knocks on the door to the room where the baby-sitter lives. Jessica.

And Jessica, who has been writing a letter to a college friend and drinking vodka bought with a fake ID, quickly caps the bottle and shoves it under the bed, then gets up and comes to the door.

As soon as she opens it, Elizabeth steps in past her, already talking, fast. Lottie has often seen Elizabeth like this: nervous, charming, confidential. She knows how to make people feel good, feel eager to be included, to be part of whatever the plan is.

The plan is that Jessica will intercept Cameron. She will wait for him outside, under the porte cochere; she will convince him that Elizabeth is not home, that she has left the house with her husband in order to avoid him. And that he must not come in and disturb the children, who are already very confused and upset.

"Oh, anything like that, Jessica," Elizabeth says. "I know you'll handle it brilliantly." Perhaps she's sitting on Jessica's bed now, and perhaps while she's been speaking, telling her story, her fingers have been alternately pulling at the loose threads in the faded blue bedspread and tearing at each other. Lottie sees a tiny bright dot of blood blooming next to one of her polished nails.

"The important part is, don't let him in. Take him out for coffee. Give him a shoulder to cry on. God, flirt with him if you want to. You have my permission. Whatever it takes." Elizabeth leans forward and lowers her voice. She's frowning now, and serious. "Cameron is a dear, dear person. You know that. But this is real life, and he must not be allowed to fuck. This. Up." She sits back and smiles again, her quick, electrically warm smile.

And pretty Jessica smiles back, the wide smile Lottie can remember only vaguely. "Got it," she says. She's been enunciating with a drunk person's exaggerated precision throughout this conversation, but Elizabeth hasn't noticed.

"Fantastic. Fantastic. But quickly now, dear heart, or I'm lost." They rise almost simultaneously. Elizabeth opens the door, and Jessica goes out past her.

"I'll stay up here a few minutes," Elizabeth says. She steps out into the hallway after Jessica. "Just tell them you're going to meet a friend, if they ask," she calls softly to Jessica's back from the doorway.

Jessica turns, her long dark hair swings, her smile at Elizabeth is conspiratorial and radiant, she's so pleased to be included, to help. And then she disappears around the corner, Elizabeth hears her muffled, quick feet move down the carpeted stairs. She hears, after a minute, the dulled thump of the heavy door to the porte cochere closing softly. She stands in the back hallway for a moment listening to the life that she can't, quite yet, relax into—the children, the alternating adult voices, the peaceful, ordinary clatter of dishes being rinsed down in the kitchen—and then she goes to her bedroom, at the front of the house.

Under the porte cochere, the light is off. Jessica has turned it off just before she stepped outside, wanting to take no chance that one of the family will look out and wonder what she's doing, standing here in her slicker, huddled against the wall, her long tanned legs bare below the black vinyl. She stands for some minutes under the porte cochere, and what Lottie imagines for her is that she takes it all in, the lush racket of rain on the leaves, the benevolent thickness of the heavy wet air, the complicated, rich mixed odor of water and earth. Imagines she stands and breathes deeply, that she slides the hood to her parka back to feel the air on her face and neck. Imagines that these moments are full of sensation, of life, for Jessica—the consciousness of all there is to feel and smell and see.

But now it seems that Jessica starts to worry that if Cameron drives up as far as the porte cochere, someone inside will hear the car, or see it. Or maybe she doesn't really know what she's doing, or why; she's drunk a lot of the vodka, after all. Or perhaps, filled with the very pleasure it seems she might be feeling, she wants to be out in the rain, to let it fall on her face. At any rate, she steps out now from under the sheltering roof and begins to walk down the long driveway toward the dark, deserted street.

But about a third of the way down, she stops. She stops, she takes her shoes off—they are little flats, almost ballet slippers, hardly shoes at all—and she steps up onto the wet lawn. And she's there, Lottie pictures her twirling slowly around there, in her bare feet on the grass, when Cameron turns the car into the driveway.

What he sees—all he would have seen at first—are his headlights raking the hedge on the other side of the driveway, and then the glowing windows on the second floor in Elizabeth's room, their light amplified and diffused in the rain. Lottie imagines him hunched forward over the steering wheel, keeping those windows in view, watching for the shadow he loves to move across them.

His own car windows are closed. There's the noise of the engine and of the rain, and he doesn't hear Jessica call him. He doesn't see her either, until she steps in front of the car. Until he feels, and then hears—it seems a heartbeat later—the dull, heavy sound of her body hitting metal. How quickly then she's in and out of his headlights! floating up somehow, up *and back, with a startled, almost pleased expression on her face.*

As he brakes, he's honking the horn. And he sits there in the car after he's come to a stop, honking the horn for perhaps thirty seconds, as though this could change something. He knew she was dead. It's just that somehow he almost imagined he could go back to the moment before he knew that. If he'd seen her in time, this is what he would have done, honked. She would have stepped neatly back onto the wet grass. Everything would have been the way it was.

And then he opens the door and gets out to go and see what it is he has done for love.

PART ONE

CHAPTER 1

Down the street, at the unfashionable end of the block, where the houses are suddenly smaller and clustered close together on their narrow rectangular plots, Lottie hears the honking; but she pays no real attention to it. She has opened some of the windows earlier, when it started to rain again, in order to feed her mood on the steady disconsolate noise, and that's what she's busy listening to. That, and the radio. The jazz station is featuring Billie Holiday with one suicidally masochistic song after another, and Lottie is singing along. She's had too much to drink too, as it happens, and she's taken up with one of those mindless tasks that leave you feeling empty-headed while you are also utterly absorbed in a kind of pseudo thought: she's hauled all the pieces of kitchen equipment out from her mother's nicked and battered cabinets, all the old dented, unmatched pots and pans and cookie tins and dishes, and she's sitting among them on the worn linoleum, trying to decide which is worth keeping—for herself or her brother, Cameron, or the Salvation Army—and which should be thrown away.

She's an odd sight, though there's no one there to look at her—a small, slender, middle-aged woman with a mass of curling dark hair just beginning to be peppered with white, sitting on the floor of the shabby kitchen in the cold fluorescent light of the circular overhead fixture. Her legs and bare feet are sticking straight out from under the very expensive gray satin nightgown her husband gave her as a wedding present. One by one she lifts the worn and obsolete utensils, gazes at each with frowning, drunken concern, and then places it carefully in what she has concluded is the appropriate pile.

This is part of her job for the summer, assigned to her by Cameron and willingly accepted. They're getting their mother's house ready to sell. Cameron had to put the old woman in a nursing home the winter before. She'd gotten more and more creepy and dotty as she moved into old age, and it was clear he had no choice when she was found for the second time meandering on Mass Ave wearing only a slip and her frayed pink mules.

At first he and Lottie had agreed to try to hold on to the house for a while; the mortgage had been paid off years earlier, and there were roomers living in it who provided a little income each month. But through the spring, Cameron—the one who lives in Boston, the one who has to do everything—has found it more trouble than it's worth. Two of the roomers began to complain that the third had a woman living with him now but wasn't paying any more rent. This wasn't fair, and they wanted something done about it. Many urgent messages about this accumulated on Cameron's answering machine. Then the toilet in the second-floor bathroom sprang a leak. By the time anyone noticed or called Cameron, the ceiling below was stained and puckered and had to be fixed.

What's more, the nursing home he's found for their mother is expensive, too expensive, really. He called Lottie a few months earlier in Chicago and suggested maybe it was time to sell the house. Prices in Cambridge, even for houses in the kind of shape their mother's is in, have skyrocketed over the past few years, and he told her he thought they might get enough for it so that the interest would pay the nursing home fees. By phone Lottie agreed. And she agreed to come and take charge of clearing their mother's things out over the summer. He could have asked her to do almost anything and she would have agreed. Lottie hasn't had much to do with her mother since she was in her mid twenties, and she's guiltily aware that it's Cameron's inexplicable loyalty to the old woman that has made this possible.

The fact is, though, that Lottie could do this particular chore anytime. Tomorrow, the next day; the rest of her life. "Love is just like a faucet," she sings with the radio. "It turns off and on." Oh, isn't it true. The reason she's doing it tonight, sorting through utensils and dishes—and drinking and singing—is in order to avoid thinking about just that, about the rest of her life. Her marriage, barely begun, is in trouble. Is over, is what she thinks. "It seems to me we have decided," she says aloud now, and then she sets the rusted eggbeater in the pile of things to be thrown out. She sips from a little jelly jar filled with white wine. She sets it back down on the floor and then listens a moment as the driven rain splashes and drips outside the rusted screens—and in the distance, a car honks and honks. "It seems to me *I* have decided," she corrects herself: her head nods in a schoolmarm's exaggerated insistence on precision, her hand rises and rests on her bosom.

She hadn't meant to get drunk. It was the chance result of her long, odd day. At a little after one o'clock, hours before Cameron made his drive across the city through the rainy dark, she was sitting with her son, Ryan, at the kitchen table, eating the pasta salad she'd fixed them for lunch, when she felt a portion of one of her back teeth—an artificial portion, it would turn out—gently slide away from the rest of it. This has happened to her sometimes in nightmares, this and hair loss by the handful, and she had an instant sense of mortal foreboding. *"Damn it!"* she said out loud. She began to shift the food around in her mouth with her tongue, selectively and carefully swallowing until she could extract the renegade piece. Little bits of it were crumbling off already; she could feel them between her other teeth.

"What? What's wrong?" Ryan asked.

"My tooth," she said, holding up a finger that told him to wait a minute, he'd see.

He started to eat again as he watched her, a steady in-shoveling that was the result of his morning's work. He was just back from a junior year abroad in England, and he was helping on the house for the summer—mostly scraping and painting and minor repair. He was tall and blond, and he didn't look anything like Lottie—except that right now they were both wearing paint-splotched work clothes and that the exposed flesh of their arms and faces was similarly freckled here and there with Benjamin Moore's semigloss Birch White. They'd been painting the trim in the stairwell.

Lottie finally extracted a sizable silver nugget. She set it by her plate and stared at it gloomily. Her tongue swung over the rough socket left behind, and she felt a little jolt of pain shoot skullward. "God, I'm going to pay for this," she said aloud. "I'm going to be so very sorry this happened."

Ryan made a sympathetic noise but went on eating. Others can never understand our pain, particularly dental pain. Where had she read this? It didn't matter. She knew it to be true.

Lottie cleared her place and went upstairs to the room that had been her mother's, the room she had been sleeping in while she worked on the house this summer. She sat for a moment on the bed, looking at her feet, encased in the paint-flecked old running shoes she wore to work in. She felt almost teary. She would gladly have lain back and fallen into forgetful sleep.

There was no reason why this—the tooth—should be so upsetting to her, she told herself.

But it was. Of course it was. Lottie was someone who believed in health. She'd had cancer seven years before. Mostly a bad scare: the doctor was sure they'd gotten it all. But now she took good care of herself. She ate carefully, she ran daily.

She had bad teeth, though, terrible teeth, and from time to time they reminded her of all she could not now control, of all the things that had been out of control in her past—dental care among them. She animated her teeth in her imagination sometimes, she thought of them as acting willfully on her. A set of bogeyman, half of them man-made at this point.

What's more, Lottie was upset anyway. She'd barely been holding herself together since her husband's visit the weekend before. He'd flown out from Chicago and stayed for two days, and by the end of the time it was clear that nothing had changed. They'd fought just before he left, and neither had called the other since. Lottie assumed his reason was the same as her own—that there was nothing she could say that wouldn't lead to another argument.

And now this. Then she laughed out loud at herself: yes, first my marriage goes, and now my tooth. She reached for the telephone. She called Elizabeth's house—Elizabeth, whom Cameron was in love with—and got Elizabeth's elderly mother, Emily, who fussed and clucked and gave her the name of the family dentist on Mass Ave. The receptionist there said to come over, they'd fit her in.

Lottie changed her clothes and washed the paint off her skin. She brushed her teeth carefully, so the dentist would believe she had good hygiene, that this was something unfortunate that had happened to her, rather than something she was in any sense responsible for. She reapplied her makeup. On her way out, she stopped in the kitchen. Ryan was doing the dishes. He'd cleared her place.

"I'm headed for the dentist, honey," she told him. "I'll be back sometime later. They said they'd fit me in between his other patients, so I'm not sure how long it'll take. I have a feeling I'm going to have read a lot of *People* magazines before you see me again."

"I hope I'm able to recognize you," he said.

It was raining out, a slow, soft rain at this point in the day, and when Lottie unfurled and opened the umbrella on the front porch, she saw that three of the spokes now stuck nakedly out from the fluttering fabric. Last time she'd used it, only one had. She sighed and stepped down the stairs into the gentle drizzle.

The dentist was a small, grave man with sparse hair combed carefully over the top of his shining head. He was appalled by Lottie's mouth; they always were. Most of the early work had been done at a cut rate in her impoverished childhood by dental students learning the trade at Tufts University. Lottie didn't bother to explain this; some part of her didn't wish to give the dentist the satisfaction of knowing what this suggested about her life. Instead she told him that she'd heard this many times before, that she'd never encountered a more competitive profession than dentistry.

When the dentist poked in the base of the tooth that had lost the filling, Lottie gasped. He said this would be a little more complicated than he'd originally thought, and sent her back to the waiting room until he had a longer gap between patients.

Lottie sat watching the gray rain fall on the shining cars, on the people moving from shop to shop along Mass Ave. She listened to the soft rock flowing gently from a speaker in the ceiling and thought of the dental clinic. God, where had it been? She couldn't even remember. Many subway stops, changing lines in the grimy, old-fashioned stations, the narrow escalators with slotted, sloping wooden steps. And then, once there, you waited and waited under the flickering lights with all the other mendicants, hoping you'd get someone who had some minimal competence, who didn't actually seem to like to inflict pain.

7

Mendicants. Lottie had used the very word in telling the tale more than once, making an amusing, exaggerated story of her life. Today it seemed grimly pathetic. It seemed true. She felt sorry for that girl-Lottie, that Charlotte, who traveled across the city alone to have her terrible mouth fixed in a way that dentists for years to come would shake their heads over.

Late in the afternoon, she stepped out into the rain again and began a slow walk back to her mother's house. Her mouth was benumbed and it tasted of peppermint, yet it still ached. Exactly the way she felt about Jack, she mused. Numbed, yet still in pain. She was glad for the numbness for the time being, though she wondered when it would hit her—the full sense that it was over, that there didn't seem to be a way for them to stay together. And then she pushed that thought, all these thoughts, aside.

Lottie subscribed to denial, the best defense, she said. She often claimed it was how she'd survived her childhood. And there was a way in which she was proud of rolling so smoothly through the days since Jack had been here, proud of how little anyone might have guessed of the pain she was pushing under. But she had also pushed under, with far less consciousness of feeling it, the sense of having had a *close call* with this marriage, the tentative pulse of relief that it might now be over. She'd pushed under the odd excitement about the blank slate that waited once she'd taken the last, final steps of extricating herself. Now, too, she had a glimmer of this; but she quickly thought instead of Ryan, of how much he might or might not have understood of what was going on. Not a lot, she suspected. And she was determined to hold it all together until he went back to college, so that he wouldn't have to witness the terrible details: the packing, the silence. Or, worse, the chilly politeness.

And what then? Whatever. Whatever came next.

Lottie started down the hilly street she'd grown up on, past the bigger, fancier houses where her childhood friends had lived. It was deserted today, in the steady rain. In the distance, though, she could hear children somewhere yelling—soaked, no doubt, and wilder and noisier on that account. Her eyes swept the houses. How many streets in Cambridge were like this, she thought. Streets where at one end lived the children of Harvard faculty, or lawyers or doctors; and at the other end—where the houses had peeling paint and wobbly wrought-iron railings on their porches, where ornamenta-

tion had fallen off, leaving black holes like so many missing teeth—
you had the children of janitors, or state employees; or, like her
father, criminals.

Abruptly Lottie remembered that counting game, "Rich man,
poor man, beggar man, thief . . ." The way, when the kids chanted
it in her presence, there'd be a peculiar pause before they got to
"thief," then a hard emphasis when they arrived; and she'd feel
them watching her for a response. Early, she'd learned to keep her
face perfectly blank; somehow the image in her own mind at the
time was of Little Orphan Annie with her empty white saucer eyes.

My father, the thief. *The criminal*, she thought as she passed
Elizabeth's big Victorian house and looked over at it. She said the
word aloud, and it came out "cwiminaw," along with a little drool.
She wiped her lip, swung her tongue over the smooth new filling.
The dentist had said it was a tooth that would "bear watching."
Lottie had told him that she'd have her dentist at home check it
when she saw him. *Home*, she thought. Wherever that was.

She heard the downstairs shower singing when she came inside.
The shower singing and Ryan singing too, chanting some bit of rap
in which "world control" rhymed with "soul."

She flapped the umbrella and left it puddling in the front hall.
She went upstairs to her bathroom, the bathroom she shared with
the one remaining roomer in the house, Richard Lester. She shook
her damp hair out and looked at her face. The skin at the corners
of her mouth was red, raw, stretched-looking. *What big hands you
have*, she'd wanted to say to the dentist. Her numbed lips drooped
on one side.

More than once, Jack had said he loved her mouth. He'd told
her he could sit across from her forever and watch her lips shape the
words as she spoke. Forever. *Fowevewr*. She remembered how he'd
looked when she'd driven away to come here to her mother's house,
standing in the dappled sun of the driveway with his old dog.

Ryan turned off the shower downstairs, and the pipes through
the house thudded implosively. The dinner bell, Lottie thought.
Make yourself useful. She put lipstick on her thickened and awkward mouth. She went downstairs, through the dining room, where
her books and papers lay strewn across the table. Lottie was a
writer. She had brought her work with her to her mother's house;

9

but she hadn't gotten much done. The messy dining room nagged at her each time she passed through it.

In the kitchen, she pulled several different kinds of lettuce out of the refrigerator and began to fix a huge salad, using some cold leftover chicken, some pecans, some sliced pear. She was starving, she realized as she tore off pieces of the frilly green. She'd only managed a bite or two at lunch before her tooth crumbled apart.

Ryan came into the kitchen looking scrubbed and fresh, two bloody bits of toilet paper stuck on his face where he'd nicked himself shaving. He started to set the table while they talked together in the mild and aimless way they'd grown accustomed to this summer. Lottie put the salad on the table, and they sat down. But as soon as she started to chew, she bit her tongue and the inside of her cheek. Shocked tears rose in her eyes; abruptly she felt precariously near the real thing.

She got up, went to the refrigerator, and uncorked the wine. "Would you like some?" she asked Ryan, waving the bottle. "It appears I have to drink my dinner, since I can't chew."

"I don't want wine, but I'll take a beer, if you've got it," he said.

She opened the refrigerator again and lifted out a brown bottle. She brought one of her mother's larger glasses to the table for him, one that had a picture of Fred Flintstone on it. He carefully poured the beer out, explaining his technique for minimizing foam, learned in England. When he'd emptied the bottle, she held her glass up and they clinked their glasses together.

"To dental health," he said.

"To fluowidation," she answered, exaggerating the Elmer Fudd stuff.

She had two glasses of wine while he ate almost all of the salad she'd intended for both of them. Between bites he told her that he'd called his father that afternoon and put him and his wife on alert that he'd be coming for his summer visit within a couple of weeks.

"That sounds fine," Lottie said. "Whatever you guys work out."

Then, because it always made him a little uncomfortable to talk about his father with Lottie, he moved quickly on to a movie he'd seen the night before, and began to tell her the entire plot. At every pause, Lottie said pointedly, "I'd like to see it."

"You should," he'd say, and then, oblivious to nuance, he'd

begin to describe the next episode. While this irritated her in one way, she also took such a simple, almost physical, pleasure in his enthusiasm, in his too loud voice, his laughter, that she didn't want him to stop. She felt the wine hit her midway through the second glass, but finished it anyway. The hell with it.

After Ryan left, she poured herself the definitive third glass. She dumped out the remaining salad. She turned on the jazz program and started to sing while she washed the dishes. When she was done she sat down at the kitchen table. In spite of the rain, or perhaps because of it, she opened the window wider. A mist strained through the screen onto her face and bare arms. She looked around the room. It was small and old-fashioned, a dingy riot, if there could be such a thing, of fluorescence and plastic and linoleum. They weren't going to do anything to it, as they hadn't to the bathrooms: Cameron's theory was that people always wanted to redo the kitchen and bathrooms anyway. With the painting of the stairwell done, she realized, they were finished inside. And when Ryan had finished the windows outside, it would be over—the job, the peculiar summer here. Nearly as soon as this thought crossed her mind, though, she began to think of the things—the odd, leftover chores— she still had to do. It was almost a kind of consolation, going over this list. Lottie sat at the table and reviewed it several times. A song ended; another one began. "Miss Brown to You": the moment the clarinet started, she recognized it. She decided, abruptly, that she would begin tonight. Yes, she would clear out the kitchen cupboards.

She went upstairs to change back into work clothes. But once she was stripped down to underpants, standing in front of the tidy stacks of folded clothes along the freshly painted wall of her mother's room—she'd sold the Depression-era bedroom set, the bed and bureau and night tables, the first week here—her eye fell on the gleaming strip of gray satin halfway down one pile, the nightgown Jack had given her those few months ago.

"Oh, wallow in it," she said aloud. She bent over and slid the nightgown out. She pulled it on, let it shimmer down wetly over her breasts and hips. Then she went back to the bathroom to see what she could of how she looked in the mirror there. But Lottie was short, and the mirror was high on the wall; she saw her face, encircled by the wildly curling hair, her regular features, the large dark eyes. She saw her narrow shoulders, the sheen of fabric over her breasts, the glowing dot of each nipple. That was all.

She went downstairs, and while Billie sang, she pulled everything out of the lower cabinets onto the floor, settled herself amid the junk, and started.

And so it's a little before ten when she hears the siren, its frantic cry choked off abruptly. Much too close, she thinks. She gets up and pads barefoot through the dining room, the hall, into the dark, almost bare living room. The furniture they've saved for the Salvation Army—so little of what was jammed into the house—is shoved against the windowless side wall of the room. She stands in the emptied bay of front windows and sees that the ambulance is stopped in the long driveway to Elizabeth's house. Her hand rises to her mouth. There are people milling in and out of its headlights, there are sharp voices. Lottie's quick thought is of Elizabeth's mother, Emily, in her early seventies and overweight. Through the sound of the rain, she can hear a child crying hysterically. She hunches against the sticky, cold glass. She sees that Cameron's car is hulked in the driveway, ahead of the ambulance.

For a moment Lottie considers getting her clothes on, going over. But while she is standing there, drunkenly weighing it, a police car drives up and squeals to a stop by the curb at the foot of Elizabeth's driveway. The men get out and move quickly up the lawn. The blue light slices rhythmically through the driving rain. Somehow this gives everything a dimension that frightens Lottie, excludes her. She looks up and down the street. She can see a few neighbors at their windows, like her, and one little cluster of three or four people on a porch halfway up the block. All keeping their distance. Then she hears the sudden explosive *whumps!* of the ambulance's doors slamming. She looks back quickly and sees it coming down the driveway and then turning sharply, driving away up the hill. Its wail starts again as it rounds the corner, and fades almost immediately behind the noise of the rain.

There's still a knot of people standing under the porte cochere, but now they begin to move slowly into Elizabeth's house. One of the men looks like Cameron, but Lottie isn't sure of that. She feels a sense of her own helplessness, her uselessness. She thinks of Emily again, and shivers.

She goes upstairs to get a sweater. When she looks out the bedroom windows through the quivering black leaves, it seems that everyone is gone. She comes down again, crosses the hall, and steps out onto the wet front porch in her bare feet and nightgown. Someone has turned off the swirling light on top of the police car. Cameron's car still sits two thirds of the way up the drive. It looks abandoned; the door on the driver's side hangs open, and the interior light is on. Lottie feels peculiar, knowing that disaster has struck so close by but not having any sense of what form it has taken or of how her brother may be involved.

And then suddenly she feels called back again, as she has on and off the whole time she's been in Cambridge, to herself as a girl. Herself—she feels almost dizzy with the sense of recollection—standing here in her nightgown, looking across the wide empty street at another mysterious drama unfolding at Elizabeth's house. There comes the image of all the surfaces plumped and whitened under a sheen of snow, the memory of the way her feet felt then, bare and burning on the icy porch as she uselessly whispered to Cameron to come home—Cameron, who stood calling outside Elizabeth's front door. He had sat down, finally, and huddled on Elizabeth's stoop, an almost invisible dark lump, and Lottie went back inside her house and stood, frantically watching him with numbed fingers and feet, from the dark of the living room windows. He stayed there for so long that in the end Elizabeth's father came outside with a topcoat on over his pajamas, and unfastened, jingling galoshes on his feet, and gently escorted him back down the street to Lottie.

She remembers another time, when Cam fell and broke his ankle climbing out Elizabeth's window at night. In that case, too, it was Lottie who had to take charge, who had to comfort him and arrange for help, even though she couldn't have been more than seventeen or eighteen at the time. Their mother was home, of course, but she was up in bed, blanketed under a thick fog of booze.

Now a damp wind kisses Lottie's face, flaps her nightgown around her legs. It seems to her that she's had this same sense of *watching* for the entire summer. A sense of her own life stalled, halted, while everyone else's—Elizabeth's and Cameron's, even Ryan's—rushes forward with a violence and energy she can't help being frightened of. Over and over she's had the impulse to say to

13

someone, "Maybe you shouldn't . . ." "Do you think you ought to . . . ?" It's made her feel elderly, elderly and pinched.

Standing on the porch now, she's vaguely aware of a vindictive pleasure rising in her at the idea of tragedy striking so close to Elizabeth and her brother: *That's what you get.* The thought is gone almost before she lets herself feel it, dismissed by a startled pulse of shame that makes her suck her breath in, that widens her eyes in the dark. She shudders and pulls the sweater tighter around her. With her heart racing, she goes back inside. "To work, to work," she says out loud. In the kitchen, she lowers herself to the floor again and looks absently at the ordered piles of junk. She picks up a rolling pin with a long swollen crack in it and sits motionless for some minutes, holding it, before she's able to make a decision about it.

At around eleven, she hears the front door opening. She looks up in time to see fat Richard Lester, the one remaining roomer, pass by the open doorway of the dining room. He sees Lottie in the kitchen, too, but instantly averts his eyes, moving nearly sideways in a crablike haste not to have to take notice of her. Sometimes she calls out to him when he does this, cruelly trying to force him to acknowledge that they have seen each other, that they do live in the same house; tonight she lets him go. She hears his muffled, modest noises in the bathroom upstairs and then the silence that means he's working at his desk or reading in bed. The bright line under his door often glows all night. He's a graduate student in linguistics. He's lived in Lottie's mother's house for eight years. In September he'll move to some other rented room. In Somerville, he's told Lottie sorrowfully one of the few times they've spoken, as though she were somehow to blame for this fall from grace.

Lottie works for about another hour. There's some crazy, drunken equation governing her behavior: since she can't help over there, she can at least be useful here. Every now and then, though, she's stopped completely by the image of Cam's car in the driveway with its door hung open; or of the cold blue lights whirling and whirling in the rain.

At around midnight she closes the windows and goes upstairs to bed. She falls almost instantly into a heavy, boozy sleep, cradled by the sound of the rain. It's close to two when she hears Ryan come in and go into the little bedroom on the first floor where she slept

14

as a girl. The pipes hum and bang in the downstairs bathroom as the water goes on and off.

For a while Lottie lies in the musty dark listening to the silence on the street outside. Suddenly she realizes: the rain has stopped. She gets out of bed and raises the shade. Through the heavy cover of the leaves, she can see that the lights are all off at Elizabeth's house now, and the door to Cameron's car has been closed. Everything looks normal, except for the odd placement of the car—almost all the way up the drive, but not quite. This seems somehow more ominous to her than the ambulance earlier, or the blue lights.

She braces her feet and pulls slowly at the window; Ryan painted these windows only a few weeks ago, and they're still a bit sticky when it's damp outside. As it jerks open, she feels the cool rush of air moving her nightgown against her body, and she thinks of Jack, his touch. She lowers the shade partway and goes back to bed.

She lies awake for a long time. And then she sleeps, or thinks she sleeps. Very late, she hears Richard Lester get up and use the bathroom again, then his door shutting, the sharp click of his latch. She dreams Jack is there, moving with her through the bare, unencumbered rooms of her mother's house. She can hear children somewhere crying, but they have nothing to do with her and Jack. Several times the breeze shakes the trees outside and leftover rain splatters against the house. The shade lifts and lightly whacks the window frame, the air moves across the room, and Lottie wakes partially at least once at its touch with a sense of deep pleasure in just being alive to feel it. And then she seems to remember that there's trouble, that something has happened, something is wrong; but each time, this thought is folded into her pleasure—thickens and weights it—and she falls back heavily into animal sleep.

CHAPTER 2

It's early the next morning when the telephone on the floor starts to ring, loudly. Lottie dangles one arm over the edge of the bed and pulls the receiver up. Elizabeth's voice is tight, low, and almost whispering.

"Char," she says. "It's Elizabeth. Listen, you've got to move Cameron's car."

"I don't have the keys." Lottie licks her lips and leans up on one elbow. "Isn't Cameron with you? Elizabeth, what happened? What's wrong?"

"No, no, he's not here. Never mind. Can't you get Ryan to help you push it? You've got to get it out of here."

"Ryan's asleep. But what's wrong? Is it—"

"Can't you get him up, for God's sake? This is important."

"Elizabeth—"

"Oh, Christ. I've got to get off. Do what you can. I'm begging, Char." The phone goes dead.

For a few moments, Lottie stupidly continues to hold the receiver against her ear. Then she hangs it up and looks at the clock. Six-thirty. Her head is throbbing lightly. She remembers the ambulance last night, the strange scene in its headlights. What could it be, she wonders, for Elizabeth to be up so early? To be sounding so urgent.

She has swung her legs down now, and her feet rest on the bare, nicked floor; she threw away the worn carpet weeks ago. In the open rectangle under the window shade she can see sun on the leaves across the street. Her mother's room is greenish and underwatery in the reflected light. They repainted the walls white when they redid the bedroom—as they did every other room in the house—and the only furniture they put back after the paint was dry was the box spring and mattress that Lottie is sitting on. There's something beautiful in the bareness of the room, Lottie thinks now, in the play of shifting light over the blank surfaces. She remembers her dream suddenly: moving with Jack through the open, empty spaces. It was happy, she realizes. Odd, when the waking thought of him is so hurtful. She stands up. And now this thing with Elizabeth, whatever it is. "The old vale of tears," she says out loud. That sounds to her like something W. C. Fields could have said, and she repeats it as she crosses the room, with his snide intonation.

She pulls on some jeans and finds a T-shirt in one of the piles against the wall, an old T-shirt of Ryan's with the name of what she thinks must be a rock group on it, Worms in the Earth. She slides her feet into her flip-flops. In the bathroom she uses the toilet and brushes her teeth. Her jaw is tender under the temporary filling, and she thinks again of the dentist, of the long crazy day yesterday. She runs a hairbrush through her hair, then her fingers, fluffing it up. Down the creaking stairs with the intense smell of fresh paint, and across the empty front hall. She's conscious of trying to move quietly. Richard Lester and Ryan, night owls both, routinely sleep late.

Outside, the air still carries the scent of last night's rain. The light lies slantwise in a buttery yellow against the houses opposite, and on the huge, old trees. Lottie crosses the street, out of the shadows and into the sun's warmth, and walks up the sloping, deserted sidewalk toward Elizabeth's house. Then up the driveway. There's no sign of life, no indication of whatever it was that might have happened the night before. Probably it was an ordinary accident, she thinks. Just a little pain. One of the children needed stitches, swallowed the wrong way, broke his arm. Not anything serious, surely, or Elizabeth would have said so. Not Elizabeth's mother, not Emily.

She opens the door to Cameron's car and lowers herself into it. The car smells of Cam—a bookish, leathery smell—and of its own old age. It's a '71 Volvo. The upholstery is worn to a kind of fleshy gray colorlessness on the driver's seat, though the passenger side is still a faded pinkish red. She releases the emergency brake. Nothing happens, in spite of the long slope the car is sitting on. She opens the door and pushes her foot against the driveway's rounded concrete edging. The car moves, slightly. She pushes again, then once more as it begins to roll very gradually backward down the drive. She shuts the door and turns quickly to steer. The car slows when it gets to the street, but Lottie cuts it sharply toward the gutter so that it's heading downhill again. After a few long seconds when it seems it will come to a stop, the car's momentum picks up ever so slightly.

Everyone on Elizabeth's side of the street has the same kind of long driveway to pull into, so the curb is free and Lottie can roll the car backward down the street's slight incline, choosing where she wants to park. She swings in nearly opposite her mother's house and brakes sharply. The grayish scaling trunk of one of the huge sycamores that overarch the street rises outside the window on the passenger side. She imagines that its bulk will partially block the car from sight at Elizabeth's house, if that's the point. Is it the point?

For a moment she sits, looking over at her mother's house. Ryan had pulled off the old fake-brick asphalt siding from the front of the house in his first week here. Then he sanded and patched the clapboards that had slowly weathered and darkened under it. They chose a light-beige paint, and as soon as he finished the front, the house looked more like the others on the street than it had in years.

In scale, it—like the two houses next to it in a tight row—is still completely different. Small, only two stories, without much ornamentation, all three seem like miniatures of the huge Victorians that dominate the rest of the block on both sides of the street. But Lottie remembers that when she was a child the house didn't seem so out of place as it had more recently. Tackiness was rampant then; no one yet knew about good taste. In those years even some of the largest houses had been covered in the same asphalt siding hers and Cameron's had, and perhaps a third were divided up into rooming

18

houses or apartments for graduate students and young faculty. One of the stateliest houses on the street was then a nursing home, wrapped in coiling fire escapes, which the children dared each other to climb. And all the kids of the block, no matter which house they came from, played wildly together, up to a certain age unconscious of the differences between them, unknowing about how much it would matter that one's father was imprisoned for fraud and embezzlement, and another's was a distinguished professor of anthropology—like Elizabeth's.

It occurs to Lottie now that maybe some of her failure to understand the differences among the families then was because when she first began to notice them, they seemed to work so strongly in her family's favor. There was a kind of Brahmin, academic parsimony that dominated Elizabeth's house, for instance—the Harbours. They used margarine instead of butter—disgusting, Lottie thought. Cheap, her mother had said. They never had food like hot dogs or packaged cakes and cookies. Their bread seemed dry and grainy, and sometimes something in it crunched in your teeth. Nothing that was supposed to be sweet—cookies or cocoa—was anywhere near sweet enough. And Elizabeth had to have piano and dance lessons, while Cameron and Lottie were left on their own to play, to do what they liked. The Harbour kids had chores they had to do, too, and a chart on the kitchen wall on which to check them off each day. At the time, this seemed a kind of lunatic slavery to Lottie; she couldn't understand how they could have consented to it.

They didn't have a television either, none of the academic families did, whereas Lottie and Cameron had one of the earliest ones, a fuzzy, small, glowing rectangle in a huge wood-veneer cabinet. One of Lottie's few memories of her father—who was sent to prison when she was five—is of his hauling that TV in. Cameron had helped him, and they carefully uncrated it and arranged it directly in front of the fireplace. It was with a sense of great ceremony and pride that her father made them all sit down in front of it before he turned it on. And it seems to Lottie that after that moment, it was always on, always part of what was happening. Part, even, of the way she thought, of her dream life.

Later, before she began to take on boarders, Lottie's mother sold off many things around the house. Her washing machine went, her mangler, the radio, the record player. She even gathered up all the books in the house—their father's lawbooks too—loaded them into her wire shopping cart, and lugged them down in repeated trips to the Harvard Coop to see what she could get for them.

But there was never a question about the TV. It was as permanent a part of the living room as the fireplace itself. When the afternoon shows were on, sometimes nine or ten kids from up and down the street would crowd into the darkened room to watch Howdy Doody, or Hopalong Cassidy, or Tom Corbett—or, later, the Mickey Mouse Club. Lottie's mother was always there too, smoking, drinking: beer usually; she didn't start on the hard stuff until after dinner. And she seemed fully as absorbed in what was passing on the screen as the children did. Sometimes she'd get up during a commercial to do some more ironing or fiddle in the kitchen, but she always came back in and sat once more in the sagging armchair that faced the television. No one else ever sat in that chair.

Often she would wordlessly place a bowl of small candies—Mary Janes, still in their yellow wrappers, or malted milk balls—on the coffee table. She never cared about the number of kids in her house, as long as they were quiet; she never said they ought to be outside on a beautiful day like this, as Elizabeth's mother did. Absentmindedly, she called everyone "dear." "You're so lucky," the other kids would say. Lottie felt, then, only that she was. "Your mother's so nice," they said. And she was, nearly all the time.

Her anger, when it came, was quick and violent, and almost always directed at Cameron, so Lottie felt free to ignore it, to pretend it wasn't part of her life or who her mother was. It wasn't until much later, after she'd escaped, that she could afford to think about it; and then the shameful memories came flooding back: The time when her mother locked Cameron in his room overnight and she and Lottie had supper downstairs and talked about the kind of hairstyle that might work best on Lottie, just as if he weren't upstairs hungry and scared, as if he were out at a friend's house. The time when her mother was slapping Cameron, banging his head against the wall in the dining room and shouting, "What's wrong with you! What's wrong! with! you!"; while Lottie and Elizabeth sat in front of the television in the shadowy living room and watched those cute boys, Spin and Marty. When their eyes occasionally slid toward each other, Lottie smiled at Elizabeth, a smile meant to say:

It's nothing; it'll be over soon. You don't need to pay any attention to it.

Years later, Lottie wrote a story about her mother. She was taking a creative writing course, trying to accumulate credits for a college degree at night school while she worked in the day. She and her first husband had recently bought a television set because it seemed so important to follow the news of the Vietnam War; and somehow its steady drone in the daytime, the way they existed in front of it, not speaking to each other, brought her childhood memories intensely back to her. Late one night, in a concentrated burst of energy, she wrote the entire story out. It was very minimal, very depressing, and the point of it was, as Lottie remembers it now, that after she's gone up to bed, the mother in the story can't recall whether her children are still awake watching television or whether they, too, have gone to bed at some point—she confuses them with the characters in a program she's been watching. But somehow she finally decides it doesn't really matter; and then she sleeps.

Lottie showed it to her husband. He was impressed and pleased with her. Their marriage had been a rocky one from the start, and the story offered them a way to feel a momentary affection for each other. Lottie understood as they discussed it that he was excited also by this evidence that she had finally realized the inadequacy of her upbringing: when she'd met him, she still couldn't see it clearly, she thought of it only as odd, a funny tale she could tell.

Of course, it seemed to Lottie that at first Derek liked the tale too. The crook, the drunk—it had all been exotic and therefore a little exciting to him. He'd grown up safe and solidly middle class in White Plains. But now it seemed the tale's charms had faded. It seemed that what he wanted from her was credit for rescuing her from her life, and the story she wrote seemed the perfect expression of all this—both the content and the fact of her writing it. Her husband taught comparative literature, and most of what Lottie knew about fiction she'd learned from him.

He sent the story to a friend who edited a literary magazine, and they were both tremendously excited when it was taken. The story didn't appear in print for almost a year after that, but when Lottie got her copies, she immediately sent one of them to her mother. Later she thought of this act as having been committed in a state of nearly willed unconsciousness of the pain it would cause her mother. All she allowed herself to feel at the time, though, was the

sense of conviction that her mother would be proud of her accomplishment.

Her mother didn't respond one way or another. The next time
Lottie saw her, months later, on a trip east, she asked her what she'd
thought of it.

She didn't look at Lottie when she said, "Well, if anyone had
accused you of being capable of writing such a thing, I'd have
defended you to the death. 'It couldn't have been Charlotte,' I'd
have said. 'This story's too full of hate.'"

Lottie had tried to talk to her then about its being fiction,
invented. She said she had thought her mother might be pleased.
They were working side by side in the kitchen, doing dishes. Lottie
had set the towel down, she'd turned to face her mother.

But her mother kept at her task, scrubbing, rinsing. "Pleased!"
she cried. Harsh lines pulled in her neck. "How could you imagine
such an idiotic thing! A girl of your intelligence! That I'd read an
article that shows me up to be a careless drunk? And want to say it
was well written? What can you be dreaming of?" When Lottie
persisted, unwilling to acknowledge the point, her mother simply
turned away and left the room, her wet hands leaving a trail of drops
behind her.

Lottie and her mother were angry at each other for a long time
after that, but they never spoke of it again. And even after Lottie
understood what a mean story it was—understood that she had in
fact intended it to be mean, intended the pain her mother had
felt—she couldn't find a way to talk about this to her mother. And
she wasn't sure it would make any difference anyway.

How strange it has been this summer, then, to step so directly
back into this old universe, to poke slowly through her mother's
stuff, to put a value on the junk that cluttered her house, her life.
Cam had wanted Lottie to sell everything at a yard sale, but she
refused. She told him it was simply too much work and that they'd
probably get as much benefit from donating anything of value to the
Salvation Army. But the truth was she didn't want the pathetic
leavings of her mother's life, the icons of her own early life, set out
for strangers to paw through and comment on. And she's been
astonished and pained by the cheapness of everything, by its hopeless trashiness. The imitation Hummel figurines, smirking and badly
painted. The grimed plastic fruit. The ancient, splitting squirrel

22

coat. Every pair of shoes her mother had ever owned, it seems, some cracked, some dotted with blue mold. Graying underpants with sprung waists, bras with shot elastic. Stockings with mended runs. Drawers full of caked and dried-out ends of makeup. Little packets of carefully clipped, long-outdated coupons. Aspirin so ancient it crumbles to powder when Lottie shakes it out. Stacks of magazines: *Ladies' Home Journal, Family Circle, Woman's Day.* And empty bottles hidden everywhere, of course, like some bad joke about a drunk.

This was what it was, her childhood on this block. With the other, very different childhoods going on just steps away. She gets out of Cameron's car and crosses the street slowly back to her house. Inside, after the freshness of the early morning air, she's aware of the smell of the chemicals they've been using all summer— paint, polyurethane, turpentine. As she passes through the dining room to the kitchen, she stops to open each of the windows, shut yesterday against the rain.

In order to make coffee, she has to push aside some of the stuff she left out on the kitchen counter last night. While she waits for the water to boil, she tries to call Cameron. Maybe he can tell her what's going on, what happened at Elizabeth's. His answering machine cuts in after the fourth ring, and his voice says simply, "It's Cameron Reed. I'm not home. Wait for the beep."

Lottie leaves a short message, asking him to call her back. Then she goes into the kitchen and clears a corner of the table for Ryan, so there will be a place for him to have breakfast when he gets up. When the coffee is done, she takes a cup upstairs and sets it on the rim of the sink while she showers.

At home, Lottie always takes baths, long baths. She likes to read in the tub. But the tub here is a claw-foot model with the drain hole installed too low to allow it to fill deeply enough for comfort. And it is stained brown with mineral deposits, in themselves harmless enough but somehow, in light of all the roomers who have shared the tub over the years, who've cleaned or haven't cleaned it after they used it, unwelcoming to Lottie. This is unreasonable, she knows. She's had roomers in her apartment in her poverty-stricken years and never felt such suspicions about them. In her youth, she was a roomer herself, in a boardinghouse in Cambridge. She's always been a good citizen, a scrupulous and lavish user of Comet or

Ajax or whatever was provided. No doubt her mother's roomers have been too. Richard Lester, for instance, with all the prescription bottles lining the medicine chest: would he have so many pills if he weren't careful about his health? Doesn't it argue that the tub is antiseptic?

It does, but that doesn't matter. Here, Lottie showers, touching the embrowned porcelain with only the soles of her feet. This morning she soaps herself vigorously. Her elbows whack the circle of cracking plastic shower curtain suspended from the chrome ring above her. As she's rinsing off, she remembers again the ambulance, the little helpless crowd of people left behind.

The betrayal in our bodies, she thinks, and her fingers rest for a moment on the white scar on her breast.

She imagines Elizabeth's mother, her frightened, plump face. Touching her own body, she imagines for a moment—she can't help it—Emily's naked, fat body. She has seen women's bodies in all shapes, all sizes, in the locker room at her health club. Almost all of them are pretty to Lottie. But Emily is too fat; something bad could have happened.

Surely not. Surely not, or Elizabeth would have said so on the telephone.

She steps out of the tub, she wipes the steamy mirror off and applies her makeup, sipping at the cooled coffee between foundation and eye shadow, mascara and lipstick. Then she pulls her clothes back on and takes the empty cup downstairs to the kitchen for a refill. It's almost seven-thirty by the clock on the stovetop, the time by which the newspaper delivery is guaranteed. She goes outside to sit on the front porch steps and wait for it.

At the top of the sloping street, one of the neighbors is out bending and moving in her garden. Lottie can hear music somewhere, what she hopes is a child practicing the piano, the same uninflected phrases over and over. And here he comes, the paperboy, cresting the hill on his bike, then drifting down toward her. At each house where he has a delivery, he makes a slow elegant loop, standing on his pedals, and tosses the folded paper vaguely toward the intended porch. When he gets to Lottie's house, he calls out, "Hey!" and rides up the walk to hand the paper to her. He's perhaps thirteen. His face is puffy and sullen with sleep. His head has been shaved at some point recently, and his hair has just begun to grow in. It makes a nearly invisible sheen on his skull, like a thin layer of something metallic poured on.

"You must be glad the rain stopped in the night," Lottie says, smiling at him.

"Yeah," he answers soberly, lifting his bike between his legs and turning it and himself awkwardly in the walk. "Rain sucks."

Lottie watches him wobble back down the walk and across the curb, then pick up speed again. When he finally turns the corner at the bottom of the block, she spreads the paper out on the porch next to her. Sipping her coffee, she scans the headlines and flips through the front section. Politics, mostly. Then she turns to sports to see how the Red Sox have done. She reads a long article about Wade Boggs. As she's closing the section, her glance falls to the page often reserved for deaths, and she sees it: a photograph of Elizabeth's au pair girl, Jessica—she recognizes her instantly—and the headline, STUDENT KILLED IN ACCIDENT.

The morning stops. She sets her coffee down. She reads it through.

Jessica Laver, a nineteen-year-old college student, was struck and killed last night in what police describe as a freak accident. Miss Laver, a student at Wellesley College, was in the driveway of the Cambridge home where she was working as a baby-sitter, when she was hit by a car driven by a friend of the family. "The car didn't even hit her that hard," said Sgt. Robert Benson of the Cambridge Police Department. "But there was a raised concrete edging to the driveway, and she was thrown back against that." The driver of the car, Cameron Reed, 49, was taken in for questioning and released. Police said they did not think alcohol was a factor in the accident.

Miss Laver was a freshman at Wellesley College, her family said. She lived in Lexington and attended Lexington High School. Funeral arrangements are incomplete at this time.

Lottie sits for a moment and feels the gentle stir of the morning air.

This is it, then. Jessica.

Lottie had met her several times this summer, had sat through a cookout in Elizabeth's backyard with her. And of course, Ryan had at one point slept with her, though Lottie understood nothing

25

about how to think of that. She'd surprised them in her bed one night, and it is that image of Jessica that rose in her mind as she was reading through the article, that lingers with her now: the girl's face, turning toward Lottie in the sudden light from the hall, frowning and confused, her long hair covering one shoulder. For a moment Lottie had seen her legs, elegant and tanned against the sheets, and her startlingly white buttocks; and then Ryan, in a show of what Lottie assumes was chivalry, threw the top sheet over her, and Lottie shut the door and stumbled back downstairs, out of the house. She was supposed to be visiting a friend on Cape Cod, but she had started out too late on a Friday afternoon; the traffic was already bumper to bumper. Then, when she heard on the radio that there was an accident on the Bourne Bridge, she decided to turn back, to wait until morning and start all over. She stopped in the square to eat and browse in a bookstore. She'd called her friend from the restaurant, but it hadn't occurred to her to call Ryan.

So far as Lottie knows, Ryan didn't take Jessica out again after that night, though Jessica telephoned him off and on for a few weeks. Lottie took the messages. "Could you have him call me?" "Did he get my other message? Could you tell him I'd like to talk to him?" Ryan's face never changed when Lottie repeated her words to him.

And now she's dead. Jessica. *Not Ryan*, Lottie thinks irrelevantly, and somehow feels a prideful comfort in the thought of him inside, asleep—as though she's kept him safe. As though it is through some virtue of hers, or his, that he wasn't the one in Elizabeth's driveway. Lottie looks over again at Elizabeth's house. She thinks of how it looked, the nightmare spotlights of the ambulance, the whirl of the blue police light, the child's wail, the siren. Cam's empty car in the driveway. The car, which had to be moved. Before the children woke up? Before Jessica's parents came to get her things? The house looks serene, immaculate, like those you see in advertisements for life insurance, or cigarettes.

And Cam! Poor Cam, who was driving. Lottie gets up and goes inside. She tries to call him at his apartment again, but again gets the machine. This time she speaks haltingly. "Cam, it's Lottie. I . . . saw in the paper about Jessica. About Elizabeth's sitter. And I'm so sorry. So . . . concerned. Please call me when you get in. As soon as you get in. Thanks."

Then she reads the article through once more, as though she doesn't remember almost every word. She climbs the stairs slowly in a queer state of exhaustion, and uses the toilet. From her bedroom she dials Cam's number again. Then she calls his bookstore and gets the message announcing its business hours.

She goes downstairs and pours herself another cup of coffee. She wanders uselessly through the blank rooms, sits for a while in one of the drooping chairs pushed up against the wall in the living room. She gets up and stands in the front doorway, looking over at Elizabeth's house again. When the phone rings, she starts so violently that she spills coffee down the leg of her jeans.

It's the police. They got her number from Mrs. Butterfield—Elizabeth. They're looking for Cameron Reed, understand he's her brother. Does she know where he might be? No? Well, then, can they come by and ask her a few questions? Maybe in half an hour or so.

Fine, she says. Fine; and gives them the address.

Almost as soon as she hangs up, the phone jangles again. It's Elizabeth.

"Char," she says. "You're there."

"I saw the news," Lottie answers. "In the paper. I'm so sorry."

"It's in the paper?!" Elizabeth cries. "Good God! They're like vultures." Then her tone changes. "What did it say?"

"Just . . . that Jessica died. That it was an accident. It said where she was from and that kind of thing. It gave Cameron's name. Not yours."

There's a brief silence. Then Elizabeth says, "This is an unimaginable nightmare, Char."

"I'm sure," Lottie answers.

"No; you don't know the half of it. And now Cam disappearing like this . . . Do you have any idea? Where?"

"No, I've been trying to reach him, but I—"

"Charlotte, I just gave your number to the cops. They want to talk to him."

"I know. They called."

"I thought he might be with you."

"No."

"Well. Char." Elizabeth pauses. "I don't know how to ask you this . . ."

27

"Whatever." Lottie imagines supervising the children for the day, driving someone somewhere, making a casserole.

"Could you . . . not mention? About Cam and me? To the police, I mean. I'll explain it all later. But it just doesn't have anything to do with what happened to Jessica, and I'd just rather it wasn't mixed up with the whole thing. If you understand me."

Lottie stiffens, wants not to say yes, not to do what Elizabeth is asking. It seems to her that there must be something important in Elizabeth's denial of Cameron's claim on her at this moment. But since she understands so little of what has happened, there seems no way, really, to refuse her; how can she refuse? "All right," she says. She can hear the reluctance in her own voice. "If that seems best to you."

"I know it's best," Elizabeth answers, grownup to child. And then, as though to reassure Lottie: "It was just a terrible, terrible . . . just one of those inexplicable, horrible things. We're devastated."

Lottie murmurs something.

"And no one, not even Jessica's parents, blames Cam." Lottie doesn't answer. "This is between you and me, Char"—Elizabeth's voice has warmed intimately—"but she'd been drinking. She stepped right out in front of him. There was nothing he could have done differently. Nothing. In a certain cruel sense—but you know what I mean—it was her own fault."

"I see." Behind her, Lottie hears Ryan's door opening, his heavy footfall in work shoes shaking the tiny house with every step. He turns on the radio in the kitchen—loud suddenly, manic violins sawing the air—and then adjusts the volume.

"I'd better go, Elizabeth," Lottie says.

"Yes; me too. Look, I'll talk to you later, then. I appreciate everything, Char. The car too, by the way. I'm just forever in your debt. You're an angel."

"Okay. I'll talk to you later."

When Lottie comes to the kitchen doorway, Ryan is standing in front of the stove, drinking his coffee in regular small sips, as though it were a necessary but distasteful drug. He's dressed in splattered paint clothes—torn jeans and a T-shirt he seems to be bursting out of. Printed on the shirt over the spots where his nipples might be, there are two large eyeballs with spiky lashes. "Hi, honey," Lottie says.

"God, Mom." He lowers his cup. "What is going on around here? The goddam telephone must have rung six times already, and it's not even eight-thirty yet."

"Come on out here, Ry." Lottie gestures behind her to the table in the dining room. "Let's sit. I want to talk a minute."

"What? Just tell me."

"No; come on out and sit down." She steps back into the dining room and sits at the table. Papers and books, materials for an article she's writing, cover it almost completely.

Ryan slouches into the kitchen doorway. He nearly fills it. He's tall, like his father. He gets the blondness from him too. Except for the shape of his face, you would never guess that he and Lottie are related.

"What?" he asks. He's irritated at her, she can tell. Too much melodrama.

"There was an accident last night, Ryan. An automobile accident. And Jessica? Jessica . . . Laver was killed."

He walks to the table and sets his cup down. "Jesus Christ, Mom," he says. He sits slowly, sideways, in the chair opposite her. "Oh my God, I can't believe this."

"I know, honey," she says, though in fact she can't imagine what he might be feeling.

"Are you sure?" he asks, absurdly. Lottie nods. They sit without speaking for a few moments. Lottie is intensely aware of the violins, thin and nasal-sounding on her mother's old radio in the kitchen.

"This is so horrible," he says at last. His voice is oddly high-pitched. He lifts his hands and covers his face. Lottie stands, but then she doesn't know whether to go to him and touch him. He jerks his head up abruptly, and shakes it. "Oh!" he cries. "God! She was just a stupid kid."

He gets up and quickly leaves the room. Lottie can hear him in the little back bathroom. For a while there's the sound of running water, of splashing. He blows his nose, loudly.

The announcer comes on the radio, and in his maddeningly slow, self-important voice, begins to recite the news. Lottie gets up, nearly tipping her chair over in her sudden irritation. She goes directly to the radio and yanks the button to Off. She stands breath-

29

ing heavily for a moment. Then she fills her coffee cup once more and goes back into the dining room, sits down at her place.

After a minute she hears Ryan blowing his nose again. When he finally comes back in and sits down too, his face is pink, his eyes red-rimmed. He clears his throat and then says nothing.

Lottie says, "There's something else, honey."

"How *could* there be anything else?" He slams the table and his cup jumps, slops coffee onto the scarred veneer. "Jesus, Mom," he says.

"Well, there is. It was Uncle Cam. He was driving."

His mouth opens.

"He was . . . It was a freak thing. He was driving up the driveway, and she just stepped out. He wasn't even going fast. Apparently she just stepped out in front of him."

"Oh, Mom." His voice sounds almost whiny, as though he were complaining about Lottie's exaggeration of something, as though he wanted her to stop now and tell him the smaller, less dramatic, truth.

"It's so awful, I know," Lottie says. "It's just . . . Well, it is."

He picks up his cup and holds it. After a moment he sets it down. He runs his finger through the spilled coffee, spreading it on the table's surface. Involuntarily, Lottie's hands lift a little, as if reaching to protect her papers. "I don't know what to feel," he says. "I don't." He looks up at his mother. He's frowning. "I never knew someone who died before. I mean, someone my age."

"Well," she answers, straining for any sympathetic response, "and you knew her too."

The way he's looking at Lottie changes abruptly. It sharpens. Something you could not quite call a smile lifts the corners of his mouth. He wipes his hands slowly on his pants. "I didn't *know* her, Mom," he says. "I hardly knew her at all. I know Uncle Cam about sixty times better than I knew Jessica."

"Oh, I understand that. I just mean . . ." She trails off.

He's sitting up straighter and staring directly across the table at Lottie. His face is closed to her in the way it seems he's grown expert at making it sometime in his teens. "You just mean I fucked her, right?"

Lottie looks back at him.

"Right? That's what you meant, wasn't it, Lottie?"

30

Lottie swings her head in confusion. "Look, honey," she begins, hoping he'll give her a chance to start over. "I know that I don't really understand how you felt about Jessica . . ."

"That makes two of us, then, thanks," he says. He stands up and carries his cup into the kitchen.

Lottie sits alone at the dining room table. She lets a rush of air out of her lungs. From her chair she can see the abandoned furniture in the living room. She has dropped the opened newspaper onto one of the chairs, though she can remember doing no such thing. It seems to float there, tented over the chair like a huge bird just landing on a nest. In a minute, she thinks, I'll have to get up and pick that up, start to work.

Abruptly she feels a tug of revulsion at herself for being this kind of person. For moving cowlike, thickly, through chores as she has all this summer—*puttering*—while real sorrows, real tragedies, play themselves out around her. How has she let this happen to her?

Then the kitchen explodes in a crash that dwindles to the sound of a few things rolling to the corners of the room. Lottie's heart has already seized as she moves to the doorway. In time to see Ryan turn and bend and clear the table too, everything flying and smashing. "Fuck!" he yells. "Fuck! Fuck!"

She crosses the room in two steps and grabs his arms from behind, speaking his name. He freezes in her grasp, waiting; she feels a muscle jerk spasmodically under her grip, and she releases him, lets her own hands drop. She's discovered in that moment that she's afraid of him.

He steps a few feet away from Lottie and stands there, his back to her. His breathing is uneven and loud. Then he drops suddenly to his knees and starts to pick up the junk scattered on the floor. Lottie looks down at him as he moves around, blindly grabbing stuff and putting it on the table. His shoulders are shaking. He coughs, and then sobs.

Lottie crouches quickly next to him. "Darling," she says.

"Don't comfort me, Mom," he says in a ragged voice. "I'm sorry. I'm sorry I did this. But I can't stand for you to comfort me."

For a moment more, Lottie watches him work. Then she shifts forward to her knees too, amid the broken glass and tins and plates and bowls, and starts to help him clean up. Silently they work together. Every now and then Ryan shudders or wipes his face with the back of his hand, and Lottie stops, helpless, and watches him. They've nearly finished, stacking all the things on the table, when she looks over and sees that his hand is bleeding, that he's smeared blood on his face and jeans.

"Oh! Ryan," she cries, and when he looks up at her, she points at the blood.

He looks down at his hand as though it bears no connection to him. "Forget it," he says.

"You need a bandage or something, though," she says.

He stands up and walks to the back door. He pulls the hem of his T-shirt up and wipes his face, then wraps the fabric around the heel of his hand. "Forget it," he says, and goes outside.

For a moment Lottie kneels there alone on the littered floor. She can hear her son outside, hear the bang of the big aluminum ladder, hear the metallic clatter as he raises it. She pulls herself to her feet and goes upstairs to the bathroom she shares with Richard Lester. There's a box of Band-Aids in the medicine chest, jumbled with Richard's many bottles of prescription pills. She carries it back downstairs, through the kitchen. She's just opening the wooden screen door when Ryan shouts from up on the ladder, "Don't come out here with any Band-Aids, Lottie! I told you I don't want a fucking Band-Aid!"

Lottie lets the door bang shut and turns around. She stands in the kitchen, uselessly holding the little metal box. The bright sunlight lies over the pots and pans, the ancient cookie tins and rusty flour sifter, the cracked rolling pin. The glass on the floor glitters, and reflected pinpoints of light dance on the walls. A minute passes, or more, she can't tell. She feels as though she were frozen.

But then the doorbell rings, and she sets the box down and steps across the bits of broken glass to go and answer it.

CHAPTER 3

"Well, come into my parlor," Lottie says, and she gestures into the living room. The policemen laugh. It looks, she suddenly realizes, like a derelict doctor's waiting room, the way the sprung, worn-out chairs are pushed in a row against the white wall. She snatches the newspaper up off the chair that was her mother's, and the policemen pull two other sagging chairs forward a little so they'll all be more or less facing one another. They're agreeable and loud, middle-aged, and Lottie appreciates their careful politeness to her, though she knows it's automatic for women her age. Even dressed as she is, she's "ma'am" to them.

"You're redoing things, then," says one of them, looking around at the freshly painted, bare walls, at the emptied rooms. He has a red face; the flesh of his cheeks is angrily cratered, seared by acne. A difficult youth, Lottie thinks.

"It was my mother's house. We're going to sell it. You interested?"

He laughs. "I might be if I didn't have a guess as to what you were going to ask."

They joke about real estate prices, about how outrageous they are. How that won't last. Lottie can't keep the nervousness out of her voice. When she laughs, it sounds like a whinny.

The other policeman is big too, but not as beefy. Tall and thick around the middle, like someone who played basketball in his youth and has gone to seed. Danehy, he said his name was. Lottie didn't get the larger man's name. Danehy shifts in his chair now, and the leather of his holster creaks. "Your brother," he says. "Mr. Reed?"

Here it comes. Lottie tenses. "Yes."

"You say you don't know where he is at the moment?"

"No. I've actually been looking for him too. I've called his work and his home. . . ." She turns her empty palms up. "Nothing."

"Anyplace else you can think of he might be?"

"No. I don't know. He's not in trouble about the accident, is he?"

"No, ma'am, nothing like that," the beefy cop says. "He did seem"—he pauses—"*distraught*, the officers said, last night."

This odd, elegant word leaps up at Lottie, and she imagines Cameron as she'd seen him a few times in adolescence: white-lipped, silent, his eyes moving too fast. He punched a hole in the living room wall once, in such a state. It was after he was too big for their mother to hit anymore.

"So we wanted to let you know that."

Danehy speaks up. "You know, that it might be good to kinda keep an eye on him when you find him. It's a terrible thing, a young girl like that. He must be feeling terrible. You have no idea where he is." It's a statement.

"No," Lottie says. And then because she suddenly imagines that this might cause them to go in search of him, she says quickly, "I'm sure he'll turn up, though."

"Oh, yeah," Danehy says. "Probably out driving around. Trying to shake it off, you know."

Lottie decides not to mention the car left in the driveway. "Yeah," she says. "I expect he'll be in touch."

"He knew the girl?"

Lottie nods. Then adds, "Well, not well, really. But yes, he knew her some. Elizabeth—Mrs. Butterfield? She was . . . well, we all grew up together. On this street, actually. She was a friend. And so we all knew Jessica a little. Just because she was around, essentially." Though none of this is untrue, Lottie feels somehow that

34

she's lying, and it seems to her a guilty heat must be visible in her face. She shrugs, stupidly.

The bigger man, the beefy one, takes over again. "Well, we just had a question or two that we needed to ask. Just routine stuff. Somebody screwed up the paperwork."

"Yeah," Danehy says. They're both grinning, as though this were a familiar story; but now he sobers. "And then there was the family—the girl's family?"

Lottie nods.

"They wanted to talk to him. And we wanted to clear that with him, giving them his number and all."

This alarms Lottie. "What do *they* want?"

"Oh, it's not that they think it was his fault," Danehy says quickly. "They understand that it was, you know, like the officer explained to them, unavoidable. But I think it's just he was the last one, really, to see her alive. And they just wondered, you know, the stuff we'd all wonder about: did she suffer, did she speak, was she conscious for just a few seconds? Those kind of things. The doctor already told them no, that the injury was massive. Death was instantaneous. But I think they just needed to know that, direct from him." His heavy hands lift from his thighs. "And then we just have these few loose ends."

"And you're the one to tell, I guess," the larger one says. "He's not married? He has no family?"

"No," Lottie says. "Just me."

"Okay, then, just so you know that he was . . . very upset. And he left his wallet too. His wallet and his keys. Just left without them, I guess, when they said he was free to go."

Now Danehy pushes himself with effort out of the deeply sprung armchair he's been in. He stands towering over Lottie, pulling the wallet out of his own back pocket. He hands it to her. It's brown leather, worn almost white around the edges, warm from his body. "If it's okay with you, we thought we'd just leave them here." He unbuttons his shirt pocket and pulls the keys out, hands them over too. "Assuming, you know, that he'd rather not have to come in and deal with us again."

"Yes; that's fine," she says. "I'll see that he gets them."

"So," says the bigger one, standing up. Together the men seem to fill the room. "I guess that's it."

35

Lottie rises too.

"When you see him, have him call the station, if you would," the bigger man says. "He can ask for me or"—he gestures—"my partner here."

Lottie walks behind them to the front door, feeling suddenly small and childish in the wake of their creaking, jingling bulk. They smell of cigarettes, of leather. She feels a peculiar relief when she closes the door after them.

She returns to the living room and pushes the chairs back where they were. She stands alone in the middle of the room, watching the men out on the street. They laugh at something over the roof of the car as they open its doors.

When they have driven off, she picks up the wallet from the threadbare arm of her mother's chair. She hesitates for only a moment before she opens it. There's about fifty dollars in cash, and some ATM slips—his checking account has seven hundred dollars, his savings account three thousand. More, actually, than Lottie would have thought. He has a license, a MasterCard and a Visa, a card for an HMO. He has business cards from another used-book dealer, in Fall River, and from an interior decorator in New York. This seems odd for a moment, but then Lottie remembers that he sometimes sells whole libraries of beautifully bound books to people who are furnishing elegant studies, who want that cultured, Ralph Lauren look. There are several other scraps of paper with names and addresses on them, but nothing that suggests anything to Lottie about where he might have gone or what he might be doing.

Distraught, the policeman said. A clear picture of him in his bathroom, cutting himself, rises quickly in her mind. Lottie winces and immediately dismisses it; but she also decides, at that moment, to go over to his place. Maybe he's there, just not answering the telephone; maybe he's asleep. Lottie feels she needs to know, one way or another.

She goes upstairs to get her purse. When she comes back down, she stands in the hallway for a moment, trying to make up her mind whether to tell Ryan where she's going. She can hear the noise of the paint scraper, pulling in hard regular strokes. Finally she decides to write him a note saying she'll be back at lunch. She props it up on the kitchen table, where they usually leave messages for each other.

Maybe after a morning of work he'll calm down and they'll be able to talk more peaceably about all this.

Her car, a dark-blue Saab she bought used four years earlier, is slow to start. It always is after a rain, and Lottie feels a kind of near affection for its predictability. When it finally catches, she leaves it in neutral for a few minutes, to let it warm up. There are people out on the street now: a man walking his dog, and two little kids on one of the wide lawns farther up the hill, throwing a big pink plastic ball back and forth. As she drives past Elizabeth's house, she looks closely at it, but it still has its sleepy, blank look.

Everywhere on the sidewalks and along the river, people are already out, jogging, walking dogs, lying on blankets in the sun. It's been raining for three days straight in a summer in which every week brings at least two or three days of rain; on sunny days like this, no one wants to be inside. The South End, where Cam lives, is quieter, though. More people work nine-to-five jobs; there are few students. Cam's apartment is at the southern edge of this neighborhood, next to the expressway. All around it are warehouses and abandoned buildings. In the littered entryways along his street, the alcoholics and homeless people from the shelter on the corner, turned out after breakfast, sit and smoke and tip their faces up to the sun, as grateful as everyone else for its healing touch.

The stairwell outside Cameron's apartment is ugly: dirty, covered with graffiti. Here and there, the stairs' metal railing has been hammered out of shape. With such great effort! Lottie thinks. What would make you want to take the time? She's a little breathless by the time she reaches the top, she's been going so fast. She knocks on the door, and waits. She knocks once more and calls out: "Cam! Are you there? Cameron!" She can hear a door open below, and someone is silent a moment, listening for her. She is frozen, listening back. Then the man's voice yells up, "He ain't home. Okay?" A door bangs shut.

Lottie takes Cameron's keys out of her purse. She tries several before she gets the right one. The scarred door swings open. There is an envelope lying on the floor a few feet in front of her. Even from where she stands, Lottie can tell by the bold, nearly calligraphic writing in the center of the envelope—*Cameron*, it says—that it's from Elizabeth. She shuts the door behind her and calls Cam's name again. Her voice echoes in the open space. The inside of Cameron's apartment is huge: he actually bought two lofts and knocked out the walls between. To Lottie it has always seemed beautiful. He did most of the work himself, years before. There must be twenty warehouse-size windows, spaced at regular intervals—tall, narrow, curved at the top. From the middle of the room, all you see outside is air. The floors are painted a light gray; there are skylights. In the far corner of the space, a green cast-iron Victorian spiral stair climbs to the opening for the roof deck. Though it's a completely different kind of place from the apartment Lottie lived in with Ryan in Chicago, it reminds her of it. Everything has the same quality of having been rescued, claimed from old age and heavy use with effort and care.

She bends over and picks Elizabeth's letter up. The paper is creamy, heavy. A letter she wrote at home, then, not something composed in haste here. Carrying it with her, Lottie walks through the open space that comprises the apartment, calling Cameron's name. The bathroom door is ajar. She pushes it, moves slowly forward. The room is empty, antiseptically clean. Lottie expels her breath so loudly it echoes in the tiled space.

She goes into the bedroom last, the only area besides the bathroom that's walled off in any way. The bed is made. There are full, fat red roses in an old pitcher on the nightstand next to it. Of course: he must have been expecting Elizabeth. Their erotic perfume floats in the room. The phone machine on the bedside table is blinking steadily. Lottie comes back into the living room and sits down.

After a moment she opens the envelope. She feels justified. She's worried about Cameron. She doesn't understand fully what happened at Elizabeth's house the night before or why he's disappeared. She assumes that Elizabeth doesn't know where he is either—what was it she said? "I thought maybe he was with you"—but Lottie hopes the letter will help her, will tell her something about what he might be doing and why. The paper is creamy too; it matches the envelope. There are four or five sheets covered on both sides with the big, bold letters.

"Darling Cameron," it begins.

I can only imagine what you're feeling, what you're going through right now. The most important thing you must hear is that it wasn't your fault,

38

and it's worth all the risk I'm taking now—to me, to my marriage—to try to let you know that. Jessica was very drunk, we have learned. I found several bottles under her bed, and the doctors feel the blood test will show it too. Dear Cam, she obviously wasn't thinking straight. I had asked her to stop you, to talk to you—and she was so drunk she somehow thought stepping out in front of the car was a not unreasonable way to do that. [There are several words crossed out here.] Forgive yourself, Cameron. You truly couldn't have prevented it.

And forgive me too, darling, for the choice I've had to make. Lawrence does want me back—me and the children. And I'm going to go. He is their father, he is my husband, and it's our life. We'll stay in Cambridge until after Jessica's service, and then we'll go back to Minnesota.

And I mustn't see you again, darling. You mustn't try to call or come over. You can understand, I'm sure, how hard it will be for all of us if you do, how upsetting to the children—to say nothing of me! And Lawrence mustn't know about it. Not because it would change anything. I honestly don't believe it would. But because it would needlessly cause him so much pain. You and I are in pain, darling—in my case, agony—but there's no reason to put him through this too. And so, when you speak to the police, when you talk about it to anyone else, even Jessica's parents, I must ask you not to mention our relationship this summer. It was beautiful, everything about it, but now it must be just ours to remember forever. There is simply no point served in making it public knowledge.

You must know how grateful I am to you for your silence so far. What torture it must have been—as it was for me!—to be silent last night through the questions, to sit across from Lawrence and me and talk to the police and say nothing of what was uppermost in your mind. That took a kind of generous courage I knew I could count on in you—that I did count on when they took you down for blood tests, etc. When you said, "family friend," I hope you could read in my face how moved, how touched I was that you weren't going to [here several more words are crossed out] say anything more. I want my marriage back, Cameron. I thought it was over, done, but it isn't; and I find I want it very much, for a whole variety of reasons. And I need you to be the loyal, true friend you've always been, and let me have it once more, by staying silent, by staying away.

It isn't anything like what you and I have—have had—but it has been steady and good and full of devotion in the past, and I think it can be again. And that's what the children—and I too!—need. Cam, you and I love each other in a passionate way, a nearly desperate way, that I'm not sure either of us could live with. And each of us needs to go back to living, darling, in spite of all the hunger we will always feel—I know I will—for what we have experienced together. I beg you to remain silent. I beg you not to ruin this for me. I wish I could come and comfort you. I wish our lives hadn't taken the course they've taken. And I also know we must stay apart and we must keep our secret. I implore you. With all my love, Elizabeth.

Lottie sets the letter down and looks out the window. This is the back view, across to the elevated expressway. Traffic headed into the city is still thick, but Lottie isn't seeing it. She's thinking about Cam, Cam and Elizabeth this summer. She's remembering the way his face looked when he watched her. She's recalling her own pang of hunger for what they seemed to have—and the anger she felt at Jack while she witnessed their falling in love. She looks again at the sheaf of papers. The writing gets bigger, sloppier, as Elizabeth works her way through, Lottie notes. Suddenly she is imagining the way the scene must have played out at Elizabeth's last night: the wailing, grieved children bundled up the stairs with Elizabeth's mother; Cameron, Elizabeth, and her husband in the living room with the cops. Mostly she can picture her brother's white-faced silence, his stunned cooperativeness with the police, with Elizabeth. They would have asked, "Now, you were pulling in the drive, Mr. Reed, right? Coming to call on . . . ?"

"I'm a family friend," he says, and Elizabeth probably nods. Lottie imagines Elizabeth's faceless husband looking from one of them to the other as the police move to their next questions: about the sequence of events, about what Cameron saw, what he noticed.

Lottie gets up, leaving the letter on the wooden trunk that serves as Cameron's coffee table. She strides across the big open room into the bedroom again. She goes directly to the answering machine and pushes the message button. How quickly, she thinks, she's gotten used to feeling she has a right to do this—to read his mail, to listen to his messages. She sits down on the bed.

The first voice is male, loud. "This is a message for Cameron Reed from the Cambridge Police Department. You left your wallet and keys with us, Mr. Reed. Repeat: we have your wallet and keys. And we have just a question or two we'd still like to ask you. Please get back to us. This is Officer Scott, at a little after midnight." A fumbling noise. Then a click, and the buzz of the dial tone.

Another beep, then Elizabeth's voice, husky and urgent. "Cam, it's me. It's . . . it's around five. A.M. Pick up, darling. I'll wait." A

40

long pause. "Pick up, Cameron." Then, "Oh, God, where are you?" After perhaps ten more seconds, she whispers, "Cameron: don't call me. I'll call you back, sweetheart."

A buzz, and then Elizabeth again. "Cam, it's sixish now. I don't know what to do. I'll keep trying, off and on, when I can. If you're there now, darling, please pick up the phone." She waits. "I'm so worried about you. I'll call again."

The next message, Elizabeth too. "Cam, Char moved your car for me, and I'm coming over, darling. Don't go anywhere, if you get this message. Stay right there. It's about six forty-five or so. In the morning. I'll be right over."

Then Lottie's own voice, sounding little-girl-like and slightly midwestern after Elizabeth. "Cam, it's Lottie. I'm concerned about what happened at Elizabeth's last night. Give me a call when you get back."

Then a male voice again. "Mr. Reed, this is the Cambridge Police. We have your wallet, which you left behind last night. We have your keys. And we have a few questions for you, of no real consequence. Paperwork. Please call when you get in. And ask for Officer Danehy."

Another call from her, the one she'd made after she read about Jessica's death in the paper.

Then several hangups, including one that she knows was her own. Finally a long, fuzzy silence.

Lottie turns the machine off. No news here, then. She gets up and drifts slowly back out into the open space. She crosses to the big wooden dining table. There's a long bookcase on the wall behind it, and for the length of one whole shelf, Cameron has arranged pictures and memorabilia: drawings by friends, notes, bits of pottery, poems, wind-up toys, photographs, postcards. Cameron's life, as he's constructed it. The first night she arrived in town, they had dinner here, in front of these objects, and they talked about their lives, how they both felt they'd been mother and midwife to themselves. Lottie remembers that he spoke of Elizabeth that night, a remote Elizabeth, an Elizabeth who was, for him, still just a distant memory—neither of them knew then that she was already back in her mother's house. He compared her role in his life to Derek's in Lottie's. "You use the tools that come your way, don't you?" he had asked. There were candles burning on the table between them, and his face seemed suffused with light. She was happy for him in this apartment, this self-constructed universe. "And they weren't bad tools, as these things go. They were interesting people, they had a lot to teach us about the world. You got Ryan out of it, and what else I can only guess at. And from Elizabeth I got a certain sense of life as . . . I don't know. I suppose a romantic thing, a rich thing, a complex thing. I'll never think of her unkindly, as badly as it ended."

"Did it?" Lottie asked.

He waved his hand over his coffee cup in a dismissive gesture. "You can't imagine."

Now Lottie looks around again at the elements Cam has chosen for himself. It astonishes her, actually, his life, his friends, his ease in a world so different from the one they grew up in. It's a little like the life she lived with Derek, full of talk of books, of music and art. In her case—in Derek's case—there was all the academic gossip too, another form of office politics. But it seems to Lottie that she and Cam have both reached for a life as different from the one they grew up in as they could. In fact, they've both tried to create in their own lives a world like that of the people who lived at the fancy end of Farmington Street.

Lottie, of course, never stopped feeling like an impostor in it, like someone having to scramble too hard just to stay two steps behind. She knows this is part of the reason she's chosen, finally, to write about medical issues—to work with doctors, whose intelligence is much more foreign to her but also by and large more concrete, less intimidating. But Cam, it seems, is at home in this life, this world.

There's a photograph on his shelf of a dinner party in this room. Ten or twelve people are sitting around Cam's table, their faces blurred and happy in the long exposure, the candles floating in their midst like so many small full moons. Abruptly she remembers the night she and Derek had Clive Leahy to dinner—a poet, a translator, and an old mentor of Derek's. She'd worked so hard—they had candles too, candles and wine—and she made some Julia Child dish that took her nearly all day. She grimaces at the memory. At dinner she was struggling to keep up with the literary references, the talk about people whose names she should have recognized but didn't. After one particularly ignorant question on her part, Clive smiled forgivingly at her and patted her hand. He had a sweet face, round and red and shiny in the candlelight—Santa Clausy, Lottie had felt.

"Derek told me about this," he said.

"About what?" she asked. Derek was out of the room, changing the music.

"How bright you were, but that there'd be these . . . lacunae with you."

Lottie felt slapped: at Derek's betrayal, at Clive's apparent unconsciousness of his insult to her. The blood rose to her cheeks, she hoped not visibly. She managed to say, "Well, it was kind of him to forewarn you, wasn't it?" before Derek came back in, his finger held up in the air to silence them so they could listen to an aria he'd chosen for them. Callas, she remembered, *La Traviata:* how life was just a fleeting joy.

Lottie picks up a photograph of her parents from Cameron's ledge. They are young in it, laughing at each other under a rose arbor somewhere. Her mother's hair is brutally permed, but still she's pretty: the dark, dark lipstick against her white skin, the short flared skirt, and chunky high heels tipping her forward in a potbellied, sensual way. Her father is in shirtsleeves, the cuffs rolled back. His tie is straight and fiercely knotted at his neck. He has Cameron's thick dark hair—though Cam, of course, has gone almost completely gray now.

Looking more closely, Lottie sees the shape of a house beyond the roses, the windows in a familiar pattern. She puts her finger on the photograph and traces the configuration. Then she sees: this is the house behind her mother's. This is their own backyard! She traces the flower beds. A wooden rail stands behind them where now there's the neighbor's stockade fence to take away his view of their weedy decrepit lot. But the flowers! Who was the gardener? Her father, before he went to jail? Her mother, before she took to drink and television? Lottie looks hard at the blurred jumble of blossoms behind the laughing couple, above them, looks at her father's face, a face she barely remembers. Can Cam remember them this way? she wonders. Can he remember this garden? How difficult it is for her to think of this labored-over beauty in connection with anyone from her childhood.

She sets the picture down and picks up the one next to it. It's framed, of Cameron, perhaps ten years younger than he is now.

He's sitting in an Adirondack chair. He's been reading, but he's looked up, frowning, at the interruption just before the picture was snapped. He's shirtless and deeply tanned. The wildly curling hair on his chest is still black and matlike. It must be the handsomest he's ever been. Who was in his life then, to love him? To admire that beauty? To take this picture?

She slowly walks the length of the ledge, picking the pictures up, looking. A costume party, with someone dressed as a number-two pencil, someone else as a carrot. A trio of stoned-looking people on a couch, staring thickly at the camera. A pen-and-ink caricature of a professorial-looking Cam with books falling out of his pockets, his pants legs. A framed poem in longhand about memory. A post-card of Dizzy Gillespie blowing his horn, his cheeks inflated and gleaming. Ryan's eighth-grade graduation photo—his hair far too long, a hostile and fraudulent smile on his face. A shingle cottage in a light-flooded clearing in some New England woods. Cam and a long-haired woman, both on skis, both smiling, a blur of people moving in the snow behind them.

What had Elizabeth made of all this? Hadn't she, in fact, mentioned the apartment once to Lottie? Yes: she said—Lottie remembers this abruptly—that it made her feel "ineffably bourgeois."

Lottie steps across the room, aware of the smart slap, slap of her rubber sandals against her own heels in the silence. She has come to a decision. She picks up Elizabeth's letter and shoves it into her purse. Whatever is driving him to wherever he now is—walking the streets, drinking in some bar, taking a train, a plane, to anywhere else—whatever that is will surely only be made worse by this letter. It does offer him the comfort of Jessica's drunkenness, her own responsibility for part of what happened; but then it takes away everything else that might still be keeping him going. And Lottie wants him to keep going. To keep going long enough to show up anyway—to come home to his apartment or to her or even to Elizabeth.

On a pad of paper she finds on the kitchen counter, she writes him a note. She says she's worried about him. That she has a letter to him from Elizabeth; she has several messages for him. She asks him to call her or to come over. She tears off the top sheet and sets it down on the floor in front of the door, where she found Elizabeth's letter. She weights it with Cameron's wallet and keys. Outside, she leaves Cameron's door open and goes to the electric box at the head of the stairs. She reaches on top of it. The spare key slides under her fingers and *pings!* on the floor. She replaces it. Elizabeth must have used it this morning to drop off her letter; Cameron will have it whenever he comes home. Lottie goes back and shuts the door. She turns the knob, pushes against it to be sure it's locked.

On the way down the stairs, she hears a man's voice from behind the door on the second floor. She thinks it's the same voice that called up to her earlier. He's speaking loudly and steadily in an uninflected, litanic tone, as though he's said this so many times before that by now he's completely bored himself: ". . . so god-damned tired all the time when all you fuckin do is sleep around here . . . never even out of the fuckin bed till nine, ten o'clock and you fuckin complain about it from the moment you're up . . ." Lottie stops and listens for longer than she wants to. Something holds her. And she can still feel her heart pounding after she's gotten out on the street—in fear? in anger? Some excitement that she can't label. She sits in the car for several minutes, regulating her breathing, before she starts the engine.

She drives to Cameron's bookstore. It will be open by now. It's at the lower end of Newbury Street, near Mass Ave. There are plenty of parking spaces at this hour. The young woman at the counter, Maeve, recognizes her and greets her with great friendliness. Lottie met her one afternoon when she came in with Ryan. Cameron had introduced them around, shown them the store. Maeve has long hair, black for more than an inch at the roots, and from there on down, an almost Day-Glo orange. Each of her nails is painted with a different intricate design: lightning bolts, stars, crescent moons, crosses. Lottie remembers that she flirted openly with Ryan that afternoon, that she called Cam "the big C" to his face. This had startled Lottie: she would never have been able to make fun of Cam; he seems so grave, so intense, to her.

Today Maeve is wearing a dark dress straight from the forties, with little cap sleeves cuffed in white across her sturdy biceps. She shakes her head: she hasn't seen or heard from Cameron. Her two-toned hair sways heavily.

She gets on the extension and calls upstairs to the used-book section. The guy up there says Cam called to say that he wasn't coming in today.

Lottie feels a surge of relief, a nearly physical sensation. "When did he call? Did he say where he was?"

Maeve repeats the questions into the phone and listens, nodding, afterward. Then she covers the mouthpiece and speaks to Lottie. "John says he called first thing, right at ten, and that he *didn't*. He didn't say where he was. Just that he had some stuff to do and would be out—" Her mouth and eyes round in Betty Boop surprise. "Wow! a couple of days." She listens to the telephone for a few seconds more and then covers the mouthpiece again. "But that he'd call in regularly to be sure everything was okay."

"Okay," Lottie says. She feels relieved at this; this sounds so reasonable. This sounds all right. He is somewhere, he plans to be somewhere.

"Thanks, Johnny-boy," Maeve says into the telephone. She laughs at something he says, and hangs up.

"I want to leave Cam a message," Lottie says. "If he calls?"

Maeve nods.

"That he call me right away. Tell him it's important. And maybe I'll write him a note too, if I can leave it with you."

Maeve's face is serious, eager to help. "Is it your mom?" she asks.

"No. Not that anyway. But I'm a little worried about Cameron. He's had a . . . shock. A bit of a shock. So if you see him, or he calls, I'd really like to be in touch with him. And try to find out where he is, if he calls."

"Will do." She's reaching behind the counter, and now she produces a pad of paper and a pen and pushes them across to Lottie.

Cam, Lottie writes. *Please check in with me. I have news. I have a letter for you from Elizabeth. Call. Lottie.* She folds the note, writes *Cameron* on the flap, and pushes it back over the counter to Maeve.

"Okeydoke," Maeve says. She turns and tucks it into the frame of the mirror on the wall behind her. "He won't escape my eagle eye, you may be sure."

· "Thanks, Maeve," Lottie says.

"De nada," the younger woman answers. And as Lottie starts to push the door open on her way out, "Hey, send that cute boy of yours around here sometime, okay?"

46

"Right," Lottie calls.

Maeve grins and lifts her hand.

Driving back, Lottie feels the adrenaline slowing in her body. *He will call in.* She chants this silently once or twice. My mantra, she thinks, and smiles. But she does feel safer about him. Reassured. She turns the radio on. A drag of dissonance bursts at her, and she quickly hits the Seek button. She lets the radio leap from station to station for a while, taking a kind of pleasure in the motion, in the *throop* of its track to a new program. She settles on a Brit, discussing the state of what he calls "the cinema" in England. It is sorry, Lottie gathers.

She stops at an expensive little restaurant and grocery store in Cambridge for two take-out sandwiches on French bread. While she waits for them to be assembled, she paces, she mindlessly picks up the elegant little packets and jars of marzipan, of imported bitter chocolate, of hoisin sauce, of anchovy paste and eau-de-vie. It would have been possible, she thinks, for her mother to have wandered into this store and found nothing she was familiar with, nothing she could use in the way of food.

The moment she steps into her mother's house, carrying the paper bag, she can hear that Ryan is still at it. She grabs a bottle of seltzer from the refrigerator and two glasses. She pushes the wooden screen door open and shades her eyes to look up at his dark shape above her on the ladder. "Come down," she commands. "I've got a picnic."

"Good. I'm starved," he says. He shoves the scraper into his back pocket and grips the side rails, starts to descend.

Lottie sets the bag, the seltzer and glasses, on the stoop and steps back up into the kitchen's sudden dark to get salt and pepper and a sharp knife. When she opens the screen door again, Ryan is just sitting down, opening the bag. Lottie lowers herself next to him on the stoop. Her knees creak audibly. "Want to go halvesies?" she asks. "One is roast beef and Boursin, and one is turkey and Swiss with mustard."

"Oh, upscale stuff. Trying to impress me, huh?" She nods. "Gimme the roast beef first."

The sun falls directly onto them, and they sit side by side and squint out into Lottie's mother's backyard. The arbor would be *there*, Lottie thinks. In its place now is a rampant patch of mint with a wild vine snaking through it. The vine has swallowed the tree back here too, so that it looks droopy and deformed. In the far corner of the yard, a few daylilies survive, but the rest of the growth and flowers are weedy and lanky. Lottie's filled with a sudden absurd yearning for the father she never knew. "Maybe I should clear out the jungle back here," she says idly to Ryan.

"No way. If you've got that kind of time, you ought to help me."

"Yeah, you're right. It's low on the priority list." She drinks some seltzer. "It's just that it's such a mess."

"Who cares?" he asks. He looks around. "It's green anyway. I like it like this."

Lottie shrugs. They chew companionably, and the seltzer fizzes with a steady, pleasing sound in their glasses. Lottie thinks of Cameron, in a phone booth somewhere, calling. She notices that little flecks of dried paint are sprinkled on Ryan's forearms, on his T-shirt and pants.

"Be careful not to eat that stuff," Lottie says, pointing. "I'm sure it's laced with lead."

"Now you tell me, after I've been licking the window frames all morning long."

"Well. Be careful, is all I mean."

"Careful's my middle name, Mom. You know me."

She snorts.

After a moment he says, "But I'm not doing this very carefully back here. I figure the front was what counted. Right? For selling the house and stuff."

Lottie shades her eyes and looks up at the bare, light patches on the wood trim. They haven't taken the siding off back here, or on the sides of the house. He's just scraping and repairing the wood of the windows. "No, it's fine. When they take the siding off, they'll have to do a lot of repair anyway. Just make it look okay for now."

After a little silence he says, "If it'll just stay dry for a day or two, I think I can finish up." And then: "I'm sorry I yelled at you before, Mom."

"You were upset," she says. "How's your hand?"

"It hurts a little." He holds it up. It's a clean slash across the pad at the base of his thumb. The skin has whitened and curled a little around the edges of the cut, and the blood in the middle is blackened and solid-looking.

"But it's huge! Maybe you need a stitch."

"I don't want one, though."

"A stitch in time saves nine," she says.

"Bad rhyme, Mother Goose." He shakes his head. " 'Nine' and 'time.' "

"Nonetheless," she answers. They munch in silence. Lottie can feel the pressure of the new filling as she chews. She shifts the food to the other side of her mouth. She is busy looking out over the backyard, trying to see it as it was, trying to imagine that world, and her parents in it.

She thinks of her mother as she is now, in the nursing home. Lottie has seen her only once this summer, in the second week she was here, and Ryan and Cameron were both with her to buffer it. She has told herself several times she ought to go again, alone, but she has put it off. She wasn't sure her mother even knew her on the first visit. But more than that, her mother's confusion, her incoherence, had frightened Lottie, repulsed her. Each time she's thought of driving out there again, she's pictured the empty, watery eyes, the slack mouth, and found a reason not to go yet.

"Is there going to be a funeral?" Ryan asks abruptly.

She looks at him. He's frowning. His eyes don't meet hers. "I don't know, honey. I assume so."

"Do you think I should go?"

"I don't know, Ryan." Then, because he still looks unhappy: "No one will object, certainly. If you want to, then you should."

"Well, I know I want to. I just mean, do *you* think it's okay to go?" He points at her with what's left of his sandwich. "Not, some-how, false."

Lottie looks at him. "Why false?" He shrugs and takes a big bite. "Because you slept with her but didn't care for her?"

"God, Lottie!" He can barely speak with his mouth so full. He finishes chewing and swallows, hard. "Be more direct, why don't you." Lottie laughs. He frowns again then, and says, "Actually, maybe that's it, I guess. I just wasn't . . . I don't know. I wasn't particularly nice to her."

"Were you actively not nice? Do you think you were cruel?"

"I don't know. I didn't ever call her back, all those times she called me. But I thought it would be more . . . cruel, yeah, I guess, to call or let her think she was, like, special to me. But also, hon-

estly, it was selfish. I didn't want her hanging around that much."
He sets his sandwich down. "God, how can I be saying this about
someone who's dead?"

Lottie reaches over and rubs his shoulders and neck. He lets her.
"Why would you want to go to her funeral, then?" she asks softly
after a minute.

"I don't know." He shrugs again. "A kind of penance, maybe.
That I was that close to someone I didn't want to bother to really
know as a person." He looks sharply at Lottie. "I mean, I'm not
saying I would have loved her or anything. Or even that I would
have liked her. In fact, I don't honestly think I would. But just that
I should have, like, noticed her more. Her *personhood.* I should
know what I fucking felt for her, and I don't."

"So the funeral would be the equivalent of tying a string around
your finger to remind yourself not to do that again?"

He chews slowly. "Well, no, actually. That's not what I want.
It's just that the people there will know her. *Will have known* her.
And I, maybe, should watch—should have to watch—what she was
to them."

"Honey, you shouldn't *have to* anything. You don't have any
guilt in this thing."

"No, I know that. But I want to. I just feel I have to mark this.
To, somehow, acknowledge her death."

They eat in silence for a few minutes. "Are you ready for some
turkey?" Lottie asks. He nods and reaches for the half sandwich she
passes him.

"I remember my father's funeral," Lottie tells him. "It was the
first one I ever went to, and I think I felt a little the way you're
feeling—that somehow I could get to know him, or something
about him anyway, by watching the grownups grieve."

"You didn't remember him?" Ryan knows that her father died
in prison.

"No, not really. I was only five when he went to jail."

"God, I remember a lot of stuff from before I was five."

"Well, I just don't. About him anyway. Maybe when someone
is gone like that, and you don't have their presence to trigger earlier
memories, they just fade gradually. It's really true that I have a total
of about three images of him."

"Which are?"

"One: that he wore a green, see-through visor when he worked—I suppose cellophane or something. His office was in the little bedroom you're in, the one I had later for my own. It was crammed with books and papers, it was really a mess, and he sat there and worked on wills or estates or medical claims—"

"And doctored the numbers." Ryan's grinning. He's proud, in a perverse way, of this part of his own history. That his grandfather went to jail for embezzlement and fraud. What he hasn't taken in, what Lottie has always known, is how small-time, how pathetic, even, the criminality was. A two-bit lawyer, chiseling two-bit, marginal clients. Nothing to be proud of.

"Whatever. But that visor just terrified me. I don't know: something about its *greenness*, something about the way his face looked under it." She stares out over the shadowy yard, remembering.

"And?"

"And what?"

"The other memories?"

"Oh. When we got the TV. When he brought the TV in, how pleased he was. I loved him then." A breeze stirs the trees, gently bends the lanky weeds. "I got the crate too, the crate it came in. I had it back here, for a house, a playhouse, for the longest time." Lottie's voice has slowed. "There was something magical about it that I connected to him.

"And I remember that he used to dance me." She smiles at Ryan. "I did it with you too. You know, when you're little and you put your feet on the grownup's shoes, and suddenly you're taking giant steps and twirling as though you're part of them. Moving in great . . . arcs!" She gestures broadly with her sandwich. "It felt wonderful. It was . . . heavenly. I can't explain it."

Ryan has been watching her face closely. Now he says, "Was he a lush too?"

Lottie sets the hand holding her sandwich down on her thigh. "I don't know, really. And people felt differently about booze then anyway. It was just a boozier time. I don't know. I just can't remember it. Maybe she wasn't even as bad when he was still around. And after all, he *did* work. So he must have been sober some of the time." Lottie thinks again of the picture of them together back here, looking at each other, the secret of what was between them. She lifts

51

her shoulders. "If he was a lush, he was more part-time than Mother anyway. She was a pro."

After a moment, Ryan says, "So anyhow, the funeral?"

"Oh! I don't know. It didn't help, that's all, as it turned out. So few people came. And I didn't know a soul, and they didn't seem inordinately sad either. And then they all came here and had drinks, and Cam and I went out and played in our good clothes and got in trouble. Not even so much because we left the collation as that we'd played wearing these special clothes that had been bought just for the funeral."

Ryan shakes his head. "I have to say, Mom, that you had a really weird upbringing."

"No weirder than yours."

"Christ yes, it was. Are you kidding me?"

She looks at him. He believes what he's saying. "Well, actually I'm glad you think so. I used to feel guilty about how bizarre yours was."

"Mine? Mine was normal compared to yours."

Lottie decides just to laugh. Not to bring up or list for him all the things that make her feel uncomfortable about how he grew up—the sometimes strange baby-sitters she had to arrange for him while she worked, his unbuffered exposure to her short temper and weepiness when a love affair or money was a problem. Even some of the good things have come to seem liabilities. Their tremendous early closeness seems to have turned him into this edgy, sometimes slightly chilly young man. And compromised her life too: she feels that no adult intimacy will ever approach in either comfort or clarity the feelings she had for him when he was small. *Everyone feels that*, she has argued to herself. But she knows that she was more deeply solitary than most people then—no family, no husband, for some years no close friends. She clung to Ryan.

What's more, she knows that she was healing herself with Ryan's childhood. For it wasn't that with their closeness she asked him to be grown up, to be the little man of the house. No, instead she took the opportunity to be young again herself. She appeared to be a loving parent, she knew. And she was. But she was also a child, reliving in the things she did for Ryan and gave to him what might have been done for her, given to her, but hadn't been. And no matter how much she tells herself that she didn't, after all, take anything from him with all this, his occasional coolness to her now is like a rebuke to that notion—as though he understands there is something suspect and finally self-serving in the very depth of her attachment to him.

Though who knows? Maybe he feels none of this.

"I've got to get some more paint," Ryan says now. "Can I take the car?"

"Sure. Maybe I'll work a little up there while you're gone. Priming, I mean. I don't want to scrape."

"Great. Do as much as you want. I'll work from the ground up when I get back if you're still at it." They both stare over at the windows, appraising.

Lottie sighs. "Well, we'll see how long I last. I need something to calm me down, though."

"Why? 'Cause of Jessica?"

"Yeah. Not just the accident, though. Though that's bad enough. But Cam too—I feel so bad for him. And I can't find him to tell him so."

"What do you mean?"

"Just . . . no one can find him." Ryan frowns at her, a sharp adult furrow between his brows. Lottie explains: "He left his car at Elizabeth's last night, and it was still there today, and no one can find him. He did call the store, it's true, so he's around somewhere. But I'd like to talk to him, just to be sure he's okay."

"But isn't that, like, illegal? Like leaving the scene of the crime, or something?"

"No, no, no. He didn't leave *then*. He stayed and talked to the police and went and had his blood tested and everything. All those things. But as soon as they gave him permission to leave, he vanished." She lifts her hands, her shoulders. "I've called his home, I went over there, I went to the store—"

"Doesn't Elizabeth know? Where he is?"

"No; she's all muddled up in her own mess. Her husband turned up, I guess. And she's going back to him. With him. That's part of it, I'm sure, with Cam. He knows that. I'm sure he's upset about that too." She starts to pick up the plastic wrap, the empty seltzer bottle.

"But I thought he and Elizabeth were, like, in love. For real, or something."

Lottie half grins. "I would have thought so too. I'm sure Cam did."

"Christ. Uncle Cam." He shakes his head. "First Jessica, then Elizabeth. Bummer."

"Good Lord, Ryan: *bummer?*" Lottie says. Her voice sounds pinched and affronted, even to herself. "It's a little more than a bummer, I'd say." Neither of them speaks for a few moments. He doesn't look at her. Finally she tries to make a joke of it: "And to think I worried that you'd come back from England with a vocabulary too highfalutin for me to keep up with."

He turns to her, and here it is, the suddenly blank face, the eyes a little more hooded than usual: *Do I know you? Have we been introduced?* After a moment he says in a small, tight voice, "It's just a wee figure of speech, Lottie." He stands up and brushes crumbs off his jeans. "A figure of speech, is all. Keys inside?"

"Yes. On my worktable in the dining room."

"Okay. Later. Thanks for lunch," he says coldly.

Lottie moves out of his way so he can open the screen. "Okey-doke," she says.

After she hears the door shut behind him at the front of the house, she picks up the rest of the lunch debris and goes inside. She throws the paper away, sets the glasses and bottle down, and then she stands, looking around the kitchen. Suddenly it seems pointless, all this sifting through what is, after all, trash. The broken bits of dishes and glass still lying on the floor make it seem especially so. She gets out a big trash bag and begins wiping the counters and table clean, sliding everything in. She fills two bags. She sweeps the floor free of the glistening bits of glass and china and ties the bags up, sets them in the living room until trash day.

Then she goes upstairs to change into painting clothes. Richard Lester has left his door open, and she can't help looking in as she passes his room on the way back down. He's begun to pack for his move, she's glad to see. There are liquor cartons filled with books and papers lined up against the wall.

Outside again, as she opens the bulkhead and begins getting the primer and brush out, she's thinking of Ryan's face when she chided him, his sudden coldness. How quickly he can change!

Didn't she start it, though? If it were anyone else, would "bummer" have offended her so? Didn't she, after all, act like a mother first? Of course he resented her tone, her telling him what to do. *I own you*, that tone said. And what he was saying with his coldness was simply: No, you don't. Why should she feel hurt when he acted like a grown-up son, too big to be told what to do? He was, after all.

But hadn't she spoken—she's stirring the primer now—as she would to anyone who chose such an inadequate word? who used language so callously? "Aaah!" she cries suddenly. "Murk!"

She climbs the ladder carefully, carrying her hook, her little bucket of primer, her brush. She hooks the handle of the can to a rung of the ladder.

She starts to paint the patches of wood trim Ryan has scraped bare. The primer is creamy and thick as she strokes it on. Its sweetly chemical smell combines with the odor of the sanded wood and the sound of the leaves shifting in the moving air to soothe her. Her mind begins to slide loosely over the events of the last day and a half. After a few minutes, she's thinking of Jessica again. Picturing her. Jessica, as she imagines her in the ambulance, wrapped in white, the bloodstain widening under her head. Then Jessica as she looked that night when Lottie turned the light on—the blindly frowning face, the long, beautiful body.

Later she and Ryan had argued about it.

"But in *my* bed?" Lottie asked. She was sitting at the dining room table. She'd been trying to work.

"Have you looked at my bed?" Ryan asked. "It's about a foot across."

"Still," Lottie said. "It is my bed. It bothers me. A lot."

"Should I have asked?" he said sarcastically. "Or maybe we should have talked about it when we chose rooms. 'Who do you think's gonna get laid more this summer, me or you?' " Lottie flinched, and he lowered his strident voice. "Come on." He shifted his weight. He was standing in the doorway. "You just took the big bed, Mom. No discussion."

"Well, I'm the grownup."

"Mom, you're not *the* grownup." She didn't answer. "I could argue that I'm bigger," he said. "I could argue that I'm sexually active and you aren't." He shrugged. "This summer anyway."

Lottie fiddled with her papers. Then she said, "This isn't the point, Ryan. You hardly know this girl, that's the point. The night before, you were out with someone else."

"*This* is the point? Listen to yourself, Mom. Listen to what you're saying."

She didn't answer him.

"Do you know how old I am?" he asked more gently.

"Of course I do," she said.

He lifted his hands as if there was nothing further to talk about. But she didn't look at him, so he started again. "Let me ask you, Lottie: you've never slept with someone just to have some good old meaningless sex?"

She stirred uncomfortably. "What I've done or not done is none of your business."

"Why not?"

She looked over at him sharply. "Because I was discreet. Because I didn't do it in front of you."

"Mom." He rolled his eyes. "You were away for the weekend. And you didn't bother to call me. To say, 'Oh, gee whiz, Ryan, I'm coming home.'" His face was like a nine- or ten-year-old's in his eagerness to make his point. She saw that yes, he was right. But wasn't she right too?

She has finished the area within her reach. There's just a little bare patch beyond it at the upper edge of the window frame, and then she can lower the ladder. She yanks the ladder away from the house, leaning slightly to the right, to walk it over a few feet at the top. Ryan has showed her this trick, this way of saving trips up and down when you want only a little more reach. Under her hands the ladder slides; and then goes on sliding. Lottie squawks, her body convulses, she jerks the ladder back violently, and it stops, it stops almost as soon as it started. She stands clinging to its side rails. The bucket swings wildly on its hook below her, the yard blurs to a green shadow down there. *Not me!* she thinks. She rests her head along the side rail. Her heart drums irregularly as she shoves the picture of herself, the fall, the damage, out of her mind. *Not me.* And with the cold metal on her cheek, she closes her eyes and suddenly sees Jessica stepping forward into the headlights, so young, so sure the car must stop for her, of course, for her.

Then slowly, carefully, her foot blindly caressing each rung before she shifts her weight lower, she climbs down the ladder to the squalor of her parents' teeming, overgrown garden.

PART TWO

CHAPTER 4

It was late in May, almost two months before the accident that killed Jessica, when Cameron had called Lottie to ask if she could come and help with the house. He was apologetic about his request, and it might well have seemed to him that the timing was bad: Lottie had been married for only five months. As it happened, though, she was grateful, glad for the possibility of getting away. And Jack, who knew her by then very well, seemed to hear that in her voice. At any rate, his eyes never left her face as she told him she was going; he looked as though he was trying to read through her words.

They were still in the kitchen at his house—their house together now: Lottie had given up her apartment the previous December, a few weeks before the wedding. Megan, Jack's daughter, and the only one of either of their children still at home, had gone to her room after dinner, in all likelihood to talk to some friend on the telephone about how stupid her stepmother was and what she had done or said tonight that proved it. Jack had cleared the table, and they were sitting over cups of decaffeinated coffee. "Well, of course," he said when she'd finished talking. "If Cameron needs you."

She blew on her coffee. "It's not so much even that. It's just I feel I owe it to him. After all he's done."

"Is that it?" He was smiling slightly now. His eyes were a strange color, a light brown that was almost gold, and to Lottie they made his face, which was deeply lined, seem always youthful too. There was nothing about the way he looked, in fact, that wasn't a source of deep satisfaction to her, and even in these difficult months since they'd gotten married, she often found herself watching him—even while he did something as ordinary as clearing the table or lowering the shades in their bedroom—with an intensity that seemed to startle him if he caught her eye.

She didn't say anything now.

"I know it's been hard, Lottie."

"Nothing we didn't expect," she said. She gestured vaguely upstairs to where Megan had shut herself in her room, away from them. They had been in family therapy, all three of them, for several months, and only the day before, Megan had announced that what really bothered her about Lottie was her habit of clearing her throat repeatedly in the morning. She'd imitated it, sounding like a motor trying to turn over: *hrmm, hrmm, hrmm.* That, Megan said, and the perfume she wore. "Gross," Megan had called it. Then her eyes had swiveled wildly toward her father: had she gone too far this time? "It's just, you know, a bunch of small stuff like that, really." She raised her narrow shoulders. "No big deal at all. I don't know why we all have to keep coming here," she said.

For once Lottie was in agreement with Megan. The family therapist had an office on Michigan Avenue, where they all met weekly. He kept the venetian blinds closed, presumably so they wouldn't be distracted by the view out over the lake, and they sat in the artificial dusk and leveled this kind of charge at each other over and over. The therapist seemed unable to move any of them beyond these petty gripes. But it was just this kind of complaint that pained Lottie most, of course. And it seemed clear that Megan somehow knew this. How much more easily, Lottie felt, she could have confronted accusations about being a liar, or an adulteress. Why couldn't the therapist force them to talk openly about that stuff? she wondered.

"I don't mean just Megan," Jack said. "I mean me."

"Ah!" Lottie said.

"Ah!" he echoed. He looked sternly at her. "*Don't* say 'Ah,' please." Lottie smiled. Jack was a doctor. "Say yes, Lottie," he said gently. "I know it's true."

And of course it was. Lottie looked at him. She thought of him as beautiful. Beautiful, and inaccessible to her. "Okay, yes," she said.

He twisted his head away as though she'd struck him. She swallowed some of her coffee and, over the rim of her cup, watched him compose himself again. *You said it first,* she thought.

Jack's wife had died almost a year before, after what is called "a long illness." In her case, a major and catastrophic stroke about ten years earlier, when the children were all young, followed by periodic smaller strokes. Lottie had been involved with Jack for six years before his wife died. The night of Evelyn's final stroke, Megan had called Lottie's apartment.

"Is my father there?" she asked. Lottie knew instantly who it was, though she'd never talked to Megan on the phone. She had waited a beat before she could answer. And then she made a terrible mistake. "I think you must have the wrong number," she said.

"Look, just get my fucking father on the phone," the girl's voice had said. "This is an emergency."

Jack hadn't called Lottie for more than a week after Evelyn's death. He hadn't been able to make love to her again for more than a month. They had waited seven more months to be married. The night of the wedding, Lottie woke up and heard him pulling on his clothes in the dark, then leaving their hotel room. She looked at the bright numbers on the digital clock. She watched them change through the long hours. Each digit made a nearly inaudible click as it shifted its shape, became a new number. He hadn't come back until five-thirty.

And he'd continued to get up at night through the months of their marriage, often staying awake for two or three hours. At first Lottie would get up, too, and sit with him in the living room, sometimes with the lights on, sometimes in the dark. Always he smiled when he saw her, always he apologized. Once, early, he talked about it. He told Lottie he'd been so relieved when his wife died, for her as well as for himself, that he didn't feel he mourned at all. "And now," he said, "I feel as though her death has given me back some earlier version of her. The way she was then. And I feel so . . . tender for that person. I'm mourning that person now, I guess." He had looked at Lottie with pouched, tired eyes. "On your time."

Finally Lottie had stopped getting up with him. Often she didn't even wake now when he slid carefully out from under the covers, when he padded across the carpeted bedroom floor, the clicking of bones in his ankles the only sound he made.

He looked at her again across the kitchen table. His eyes seemed deeper momentarily, a darker color. "Poor Lottie," he said.

She shook her head. "Poor Jack," she countered.

He smiled. "In general, a sorry group."

Lottie drank some more coffee and set her cup carefully in the saucer. The china was Jack's—Jack's and Evelyn's—like almost everything else. It was elegant, formal, some Wedgwood pattern with intricate little dragons chasing each other round and round the rim. Nothing Lottie would have chosen. "I don't know what I expected," she said.

"But it wasn't this?"

"No." She looked at him. "It was this: I knew it'd be . . . hard. I knew you'd still be feeling terrible about Evelyn. But I didn't expect it to feel the way it does to me. I thought *I'd* be different, honestly."

They were quiet for a moment. Faintly they could hear music, what Megan called music anyway: the steady punch, punch, punch of rap. "You've been a trouper," he said.

Instantly her eyes filled with tears. "Don't say that. Don't say a stupid thing like that. This isn't something I'm enduring."

He watched her as she grabbed a paper napkin and blew her nose.

"When will you go?" he asked after a minute.

"Mid-June or so, I guess. Cam has to get the roomers out of the house, and that'll be the hard part. They've been there forever. They're entrenched. They're working on *theses*. And Ryan wouldn't be able to come till then anyway. I'm going to try to reach him in the morning to see if he's interested. Cam says Mother's estate can pay him, and I know he'd like the money. He loves money."

"Well. It'll be nice for you to have some time alone together with him."

"Yes. In all honesty, I was dreading this summer here. The two of them in the same house." She gestured vaguely up at the distant pulse of Megan's music.

But this wasn't the truth. The truth was that Lottie hadn't been able to imagine Ryan living here with them. Jack was used to a more public life with Megan and his other children. For years there'd been a housekeeper and a daytime nurse for Evelyn, and the shape of their life together seemed connected to that: they were all polite with one another. She would have called it *distant* if she couldn't feel the affection too.

She and Ryan had always had a messier relationship, volatile and intimate. They fought loudly and often, and he sometimes swore at her; but he was also capable of a rough affection—wrestling holds that loosened to a kind of embrace, occasionally a visit to her bedroom after a date or an evening out, when he sat by her feet and earnestly and self-importantly explained his feelings about some girl, or a political event, or something he'd read, liberally sprinkling all his comments with profanity. How could any of that become part of her life in this house?

"Megan likes Ryan," Jack said. "I thought she even had a crush on him during the wedding stuff."

"She hasn't had to live with him yet." Lottie got up and took her empty cup to the sink. From here she could see across a wide patch of grass and low bushes to their neighbors' house. The lights were off in their kitchen now, but all the upstairs windows blazed. Homework, Lottie thought.

"You think it'll be most of the summer, then?" Jack asked behind her in a cautious tone.

She turned and looked at him. "No, no. But maybe a month, I'd guess. You can't imagine the way she lived. Bottles, bottles everywhere. And lots of drops to drink. It'll take a while to clean it up."

He nodded. He knew all about Lottie's mother, though he'd never met her. "Will you drive?"

"Yes. I should think having a car would be convenient." She came back and sat at the table again. She'd left already in her mind; she was thinking ahead—to the house, the work. To Ryan. To her freedom.

"If you could leave on a weekend, I could drive out with you and then fly back."

The pinch of claustrophobia Lottie felt at this suggestion startled her and made her feel sad for both of them. It made her remember, too, how often they had sneaked off together while Evelyn, Jack's wife, was still alive. Lottie would be working somewhere, interviewing someone, and Jack would join her for a night or, occasionally, a weekend. She could suddenly see one of their crummy hotel rooms, the bed, the orangey drawn curtains that didn't quite close. She remembered the rush of erotic weakness in her spine at the thought that he would be there with her that night. The things they would do.

"Oh, no, sweetie," she said. "I'll stop halfway or so and have a motel night. I'll be fine."

Bader came in stiffly, his toenails clicking on the tile floor. He was Jack's family's dog, named by his sons so they could call him Master Bader, a joke they were sure their parents were too out of it to get. The dog was elderly now, grizzled from the bottom up, as though he'd been dunked partway in white paint. He had fallen in love with Lottie, perhaps because she was the one who was home with him all day; and now when he saw her, his mouth fell open in a foolish panting smile and his tail swung steadily back and forth in a low arc.

He came and put his muzzle in Lottie's lap. She bent over him, grabbed his ears, and moved his head back and forth. "Ohhh, I'll miss you, sweet old Bader. Bader. Old Bader."

She patted him in silence for a minute, and when she looked over at Jack again, she saw he was watching her, as she'd known he would be, with a pensive, almost stricken look on his face. The thought had obviously occurred to both of them at the same time that she'd been able to say to the ancient dog the very thing she couldn't say to Jack.

In the night, Lottie was the one who woke. Jack was on his back, breathing heavily next to her, his mouth fallen open as though something shocking had happened in his dreams. She sat up and slowly got out of bed. Bader met her at the foot of the stairs—he no longer climbed them—and followed her to her study, off the kitchen. In Evelyn's time and before Lottie married Jack, this had been the housekeeper's room. Idalba's. Megan had liked Idalba's cooking. "Why can't you get some of *her* recipes?" she'd asked one night as she scraped most of her dinner into the disposal.

It was the one room in the house now where Lottie felt completely comfortable. She had painted it herself, a deep ocher color. "We can hire someone who'd finish it up for you in a day," Jack had said the second night she came to the table with paint in her hair.

But she had wanted to make the room hers the same way she'd always laid claim to the spaces she'd lived in before she married him: by doing it all herself. She'd kept the pretty iron bed Idalba had slept in and had bought a big square table she painted white to put her word processor on. There were overflowing bookcases against two of the walls, and more books piled on the bed and the floor. Photographs and clippings were tacked on the walls in no apparent order.

From the windows of this room you looked out over the deep backyard to the alleyway. Lottie had driven slowly down that alley more than once when she was still Jack's secret. *His paramour*, she thought. She had driven by and seen the light on late at night in Idalba's room and thought it was Jack, in what must be his study. Alone in her car, she had thought of him as being as restless, as sleepless as she was, in his tragic house. She felt connected to him when she looked up at the glowing rectangle in the night.

Instead, though, it was Idalba, Jack told her when she finally confessed to him. Idalba, who drank thick black coffee through the evening and stayed up late every night reading cheap American romances in order to perfect her English. Lottie had made him laugh, she remembered now, playing out a balcony scene between a lovesick version of herself and a confused Idalba imagining one of her paperback fantasies had come to life.

Now she turned the light on and looked over the clutter on her desk. She had to decide—it must have been this, she thought, that had waked her—how much of her work she would try to take with her. She sat down and flipped slowly through her notes, the odd multiple starts she'd made on an article she was doing.

Lottie specialized in medical issues, explaining them simply in short essays usually published in the health or beauty columns of expensive women's magazines. She'd done several books too. It was how she had met Jack. She was writing a book on cancer at the time.

She had just recovered from it then—breast cancer: they'd removed the lump and given her radiation. The result was only a small, smooth dent in her right breast that her hand restlessly fluttered back to over and over in the first months after it was removed; and a roughened patch of skin that was supposed to return to normal slowly. Her own doctor was reassuring, said it was contained and small, with what he called "clean margins." He was certain they'd gotten it in ample time. But Lottie had been scared for months, scared in the way that wakes you at night dry-mouthed, scared in the way that had her calculating how she would arrange for Ryan's growing up. And her method of coping with that had been to begin to read, to read everything she could about the choice she had made, then about the rationales for all the choices, then about the history of the rationales, then about the wackier, less researched, less respectable choices: coffee enemas, macrobiotic diets, reinjecting your own washed blood, crystals. Somewhere in the middle of all that, she'd decided to write the book—or she'd decided that she was, already, writing it.

Jack was an oncologist, and he was willing to talk to her. A lot of doctors weren't, she'd discovered over the years of research on this and that. They didn't want their work popularized. They felt that it led to hypochondria, to people diagnosing themselves, medicating themselves, questioning the doctor's wisdom.

But Jack had seemed to like their conversations. They had met at first several times in his office, among his diplomas and the pictures of his family. Lottie remembered clearly the photograph of Evelyn on his desk, strong and young-looking in tennis whites. It wasn't until after the first time they met for dinner that he explained what his life with Evelyn was like now—what she was like.

From the start Jack had enjoyed playing with analogies that he thought would make the medical intricacies clear to Lottie. It was only very slowly that it dawned on both of them that all of this was an elaborate analogy, itself, for courtship. A courtship he felt he had no right to, in literal terms. But by the time they discovered it, it had done its work. In spite of the invalid wife, the children at home— Lottie's son at her home—they were in love.

Although love was not what Jack offered her, or chose to offer her. In fact, he scrupulously avoided offering it. "I need to believe," he said to Lottie, "—no, I *do* believe—that in some sense or another I still love my wife."

And Lottie, who thought of herself as big and tough and having been around the block a few dozen times, had said yes, that was all right, she could manage that. She was, after all, a grownup, with her own life. She had felt, actually, that this might be almost ideal for her, to have a lover who wouldn't want to see her all the time, who couldn't focus very much of his attention on her.

The first time they made love, Jack was passionate and thorough. About ten minutes after they were finished, his beeper went off. He had rented a room for them in an expensive hotel near his office, and as he dressed, he told Lottie she should just drop the key off at the desk on her way out, it was all taken care of.

"Including me," she said. "You thought of everything."

He'd smiled and bent over to kiss her, a tall, lanky man whom she'd been completely pleased to see naked earlier. Now he pulled a tie through his collar and slid his long arms into his jacket. "I'll call you, about the middle of next week, okay?" he said. "The weekend's full of sports and lessons and kids for me."

"I'll be waiting," she said.

After he left, she'd put on one of the hotel's thick robes—it probably cost three times what she paid for the robe she had at home—and opened the curtains. Out to her left she could see the lake, gray and swollen-looking, and, far below her, shoppers streaming down Michigan Avenue amid the first pale blossoms of a chilly spring day. She stayed in the hotel room for several hours. She ate part of a jar of cashew nuts from the honor bar and drank a little bottle of white wine. She ran a bath full of scented gel and soaked in it. She applied her makeup carefully in front of a magnifying mirror and dried her hair with a fancy little dryer. She was alone and she felt perfectly happy.

She felt happy shopping for Ryan and herself later that afternoon, and happy still cooking dinner and talking to him; and then sitting down at her desk around ten or so to begin her evening's work. On her skin she could smell the scented gel from the hotel. She thought of Jack's touch, of the graying hairs on his chest, of his sleepy, strong erection, his gentle fingers. And she was glad he wasn't with her.

Everything worked, beautifully, for about a year. She saw Jack for lunch once or twice a week, and they met to make love once every two weeks or so. Occasionally they had what he called "a date." Sometimes they drove to a seedy pool hall to the west of the Loop. He taught her to play cowboy pool, and they sat in the big scarred wooden booths and drank beer and dropped quarters in the jukebox. Three or four times he took her to a crowded dance hall in a Polish neighborhood, where every third number was a polka and they seemed to be the youngest people present. They listened to jazz in black bars on the fringes of the ghetto; once they actually went roller-skating. They never spoke of it, but Lottie assumed that one reason for the peculiarity of these evenings was that they weren't likely, in these settings, to run into anyone who knew Jack, who'd known Evelyn. It didn't bother her. They were things she would have liked to do with him anyway.

She talked to friends about it sometimes, about how made-to-order for her busy life this relationship seemed. She finished the cancer book and began to work on a book she'd actually gotten a good advance for—the first real money she'd made writing: a book about fad diets and the medical realities and ramifications of them.

And then Evelyn had another stroke. Jack called her at home and told her. He said he wasn't sure how soon he could talk to her again. He was at the hospital, and it was touch and go. Evelyn's parents were flying in and would be staying at the house for a while.

Lottie was understanding, completely sympathetic. But for the week or so until Jack called again to say Evelyn would survive, she was appalled to find herself sometimes lost in a waking dream of Evelyn's death, and of herself married to Jack, living with Ryan and Jack's kids in the big house she'd driven by once or twice when she was in his neighborhood.

They didn't see each other for more than a month that time, and Lottie didn't seem to be able to stop herself from thinking of Jack over and over. Of his angular body, his lined face. Of his hands with their knotted knuckles and joints. Of his odd-colored eyes. She was traveling a good deal, interviewing the originators of various diets, and often she couldn't sleep in the strange cheap hotels she stayed in. She sat up late watching TV, listening to arguments or lovemaking on the other side of the Sheetrock walls, and thinking of him. In airports, in restaurants, driving over unfamiliar terrain in small rental cars, she would see his image in front of her. His hands, his hoarse voice. She remembered the moment he'd reached over and turned off the tape recorder she'd set on the table between them while she asked her carefully researched questions. Startled, she'd looked up from her notes and noticed his eyes for the first time. "This is something you can't use in the book," he'd said. "I'd like very much to make love to you."

She remembered the slow mock-medical exam he'd performed on her once, in a hotel in Cleveland—his stylized professional distance, her increasing frantic arousal. He'd still had all his clothes on when they made love that time, in a position he said was recommended by the AMA.

One day, driving, picturing him, she was suddenly aware of tears streaming down her cheeks, into her open mouth.

Finally they met for lunch and an afternoon at their hotel. Everything seemed the same. They sat in the bar. He had seltzer and she had wine, and they laughed and talked about what they'd been doing at work, about the children. She told him about Ryan's dyeing his hair green, the running spots all over the bathroom walls. He told her that Megan had gotten her period, that he'd had to help her with it.

"Same idea," she said.

"Not even in the ballpark, madam." He shook his head. "In the great Olympics of parenting, it's gold to your, maybe, lead."

They didn't speak of Evelyn. When Lottie had asked about her on the telephone, he had said, "It's very bad. She'll live, but it's very, very bad." They went upstairs and made love, twice. Lottie didn't come, and when he was finished the second time, Jack moved down between her legs and lapped and stroked her gently until, with an act of fierce concentration, she managed a small, shuddering convulsion.

Afterward they showered and dressed together, talking in a desultory way. Lottie was unbearably tense, but she tried to imitate Jack's rhythm, his relaxed tenderness with her. He walked her to her car, leaned over the open window, and touched her cheek as he said goodbye.

"Two weeks okay?" he asked. "Life is still nutty for us."

She smiled. "It's fine."

As soon as he turned and walked away, cutting into the crowd, she rolled her window up and was shaken by ragged sobs. She bent over, as though she were looking for something on the floor of the car, and kept her head down until she was calm again.

In the next weeks, she called his home repeatedly, and hung up when one of the children or the housekeeper answered. It was during this period, too, that she began driving down his alley, looking up at the room that would later be her own study. She was so absentminded and irritable at home that Ryan asked her one night, "Is this that menopause thing you're having?"

She'd gotten control of herself after that, in front of Ryan and her friends anyway. She'd always been in control when she was with Jack. And slowly the most intense of the feelings seemed to pass. But still, several times a year up until Evelyn's death, she would feel so shaken on leaving him, or so abruptly in need of him in the midst of something she was doing, that she'd drive to his office at the end of a day and double-park across the street just to watch him set out for home—a tall, skinny gray-haired man, his head bent down, his hands in his pockets, his topcoat open and swinging from side to side behind him in even the coldest weather. Or she would make the slow drive again, down the alley behind his house, her headlights off. As though she were some criminal, she thought. A house-breaker. A *homewrecker*.

And the first time she was alone in the house after they were married—her house now too, just as she'd dreamed—she had gone through Jack's things, looking for a sign, any sign, that he might have some parallel feelings about her. And found none, not a thing, unless you counted the reviews of her books he'd clipped and tucked inside the covers.

Instead, to her dismay, she found a box full of photographs of Evelyn and letters they'd written to each other. She forced herself not to read the letters, though she couldn't help taking in phrases, words: "so shaken, to my roots," "all my thoughts, my dreams, of you," "darling, darling Jack." She allowed herself the photographs. And then was sorry she had. Most of them were fairly standard snapshots: Evelyn with the children on a beach somewhere; Evelyn in the background at Christmas, wearing a bathrobe; at some big party, balancing a plate of food while she talked. But several stayed with her long after she'd closed the box and slid it back on Jack's high shelf in the closet. One of Evelyn in a wide-brimmed black hat, sitting at a table covered with half-filled glasses somewhere clearly in Europe, laughing. She was big and dark and very beautiful. And one of her staring intensely into the camera, her eyes nearly out of focus with feeling, her hair in disarray, her shoulders and one large breast bare while she nursed what was clearly a newborn on the other.

In the days and weeks following, whenever one of the images rose in Lottie's mind and her world lurched sideways, she would chant internally, *You deserve what you feel, you deserve what you feel.*

70

Now Lottie hunched over the table in her room, Idalba's room, looking at her papers under the bright light. In the deep stillness of the sleeping house, the refrigerator began to whir, and Lottie stopped for a moment to identify the sound and then went on reading. She was writing a series of articles on emotions, and the distortion of medical terms used in discussing them popularly. She had started thinking she'd simply write an essay about the process of grief, wanting to understand Jack, what he was going through. She'd read a wealth of self-help books, some trashy, some serious, about the subject. But all of them infuriated her with what she saw as prescriptive, shallow accounts of the "healthy stages" of the feelings involved. She had begun to seek examples of sick and healing extravagance in literature and biography. She discovered, for instance, that Flaubert, devastated by his mother's death, had asked a maid to wear an old dress of hers; that he would burst into tears at the sight of her moving around the house. She wrote about this. She wrote about the nineteenth-century preoccupation with séances, she wrote about people wearing jewelry made from the bones, the hair, of the dead. She described voodoo ceremonies in which people had intercourse with the dead, a culture in which they disinterred the dead annually for celebratory reunions. She talked about the comfort available in what was taboo, in what was extreme. She closed with a paragraph gently chiding the fear behind the particularly American need to normalize emotion by using medical language to describe it.

None of this helped her with Jack, of course, with his private, understated sorrow. But it did bring a very nice fee from an elegant women's magazine that often published Lottie's work. And the editor said yes, they would be interested in a series on various emotions. It was this series Lottie had begun to jot down ideas for now. Love and hate, to start with, she thought. Then fear. Anger. Jealousy.

She was looking now at her notes on love. Bader, whom Idalba had forbidden entrance to her room, lay on the threshold with his paws crossed under his chin. Under the glare of her white lamp, her ideas seemed sketchy and inadequate. She had just begun to read the psychologizing literature and had been struck with the consistency of opinion on things. Romantic love was obsessive and childish and couldn't last. Mature love was trusting, friendly, more relaxed. Part of the function of marriage, sociologically speaking, was to transform one into the other.

Over the past weeks, Lottie had begun to feel that doing this reading and making these notes had reawakened in her all those feelings about Jack she thought she'd suppressed. She had started to cry one night recently after they'd made love—their sorrowful grownup love—wanting back the feelings they'd had before they lived together, before Evelyn died. Megan had been at a sleepover, and Lottie took the opportunity to be as histrionic as she wished, weeping, accusing Jack of having withdrawn from her.

That in itself repulsed him; he wasn't used to this kind of thing, especially not from her. He had put on his bathrobe and left the room. She had washed her face and followed him to the kitchen, determined to stay calm, but also to make him hear what she had to say. She stood in the middle of the room, barefoot and wearing only one of his T-shirts, her face swollen, her hair snarled after sex, and started in again.

He was standing at the sink holding a glass of water, and he looked over at her coldly. "I simply don't know what you mean or want, Lottie," he said. "This"—he swung the glass toward her— "seems adolescent to me. It's like some holdover from your single life."

Lottie was stung, furious at the smugness in this. She felt a pure rage at him, who'd lived so safely, utterly sealed off from emotion by his wife's illness for years. It made her want to rub his nose in the disorder of her sexual life before him, of most people's lives *out there*, as she thought of it.

"How dare you lecture me?" she shrilled. "You had to have your kind of marriage—sad, and full of patience and kindness. But don't pretend you know what it has to be for other people. What it is."

He turned and looked at her. His voice was sharp. "I know it doesn't have to be melodramatic. That's not what marriage is about."

"This is *our* marriage," she said. "How would you know more than I do what it's about, you asshole?"

They looked at each other, both full of the wish to injure, to hurt. "Do you hear how you sound?" he said. "How ugly you sound? If you were Megan, I'd send you to your room."

"How inconvenient for you that you can't. That you have to listen to someone for once."

"I don't. I don't have to listen to this . . . garbage."

He started from the room, and she grabbed his arm. Something gave, stitches popped audibly in his sleeve. They stopped. Lottie was aware of a pang of confused feeling having to do with his size—how much smaller she was than he, like a child—and with how badly she was behaving. She thought, suddenly, of her reading about love, and she was swept with a sense of the absurdity of their argument, even of their dilemma.

They stood still, looking at each other for a moment. One of his eyelids was pulsing erratically with fatigue. She wanted to end this, somehow. She stepped back and said, in a little girl's voice, "You're not the boss of what love is."

If they hadn't both raised children, if they hadn't both been middle-aged, it might not have worked. But his face opened in relief, his shoulders dropped, and he laughed. Half an hour or so later, when they were side by side in bed in the dark, he spoke suddenly, intensely, as though they'd been in steady conversation all along: "We can get through this, Lottie. I know we can. It's just time. Just give me some time."

Lottie was dizzy with sleepiness, but she reached over in response and touched his shoulder.

She turned the desk lamp off and got up and went to the window. It was almost five, and the sky was turning a papery white. The rectangular backyard was deep, black with shadow. Jack had told her Evelyn had had a flower garden, which he'd tried to keep up for a few years after her first stroke, so she could sit in her wheelchair and look out over it; but that it had slowly become overgrown and weed-choked, and finally he'd had a yardman tear everything out and plant yew bushes. He said Evelyn didn't notice at that point.

Lottie thought of Evelyn looking blindly out on the yard; she thought of herself driving down the alley, looking in with all her frantic passion. Bader yelped suddenly, painfully, from his exile on the threshold, and she looked over at him. He tilted his head, he moaned in love.

"Yes, just like that," she said, and laughed out loud.

In the weeks before Lottie left, she and Jack were, if anything, even more careful with each other than they'd been. Sometimes Lottie had the sense of herself being an invalid in Jack's eyes, he was so solicitous with her. *This was the way he must have treated Evelyn,* she thought. And then she'd wonder again whether the problem might not be more Jack's than her own. Whether he simply didn't remember how to have a wife who took up room, who was whole and wanted something from him. At other times, though, when she had to stop herself from picking up the telephone to call his office in the middle of the day, or felt herself yearning for him in the night, even though he was lying next to her, she was aware of how easily she could slip again into her crazy, shameful desperation.

The morning they packed the car, the air was clear and cool. It felt like a fall day in New England, and Lottie sang of distance as she carried things out to the driveway: ". . . across the wide Missoooou-ri." She was familiar from her free-lance days with the rising excite-ment in herself. She'd driven off to do research or an interview often enough with the same eager heart.

Bader followed her on her trips in and out. The last time in, she went to the kitchen to say goodbye to Megan, who was still in her shorty nightgown, having breakfast. She looked up at Lottie, star-tled. She had cut her hair recently, in a kind of elongated flattop, which she kept in vertical spikes in the daytime with gel. Now it was matted from sleep. It looked artificial, like a cheap toupee made of some clumped synthetic fiber.

"God, you're leaving so soon?" she asked, as though she'd been unconscious of the bustle of preparation around her for the last hour or more. Then she stood up and crossed to Lottie. Awkwardly and with her eyes swung to a far corner of the room, she pressed herself momentarily into Lottie's arms. Lottie could feel the girl's small high breasts, could smell her sweet breath—she'd been eating pancakes with maple syrup. This was the first time Megan had voluntarily embraced her stepmother, and Lottie found herself sud-denly tearful. When Megan stepped back, which she did very quickly, Lottie turned away too, so the girl couldn't see her face. At the doorway, though, she stopped. "Have a good month, Meggie," she said.

74

"Oh yeah, like I *can* with summer school breathing down my neck."

"Well, maybe you can manage a good moment or two, though," Lottie said.

"Yeah. Well, you too," Megan said, and sat down again at the table, where the funnies were spread out next to her plate.

When Lottie came outside, Jack was hauling Bader out of the front seat of the car. The back seat was full of her bags and boxes of books. She'd put her computer in the trunk.

"He's been misinformed. He thinks he gets to go," Jack said.

"No way, Mister Master." Lottie bent over the dog and let him lick her chin. Then she stood and turned to Jack. She reached up and set her hand on his face. "I hate goodbyes," she said. "I'll call you when I get there, and we can say hello."

"I love you," he answered. He reached for her. His hand spread across the small of her back and held her in the way it always did, a way that reminded her of dancing, that made her feel fitted to him, part of him. Then Bader barked and nosed her butt jealously, and they pulled apart, laughing.

As he bent down over her open window, Jack said, "Have a good rest from us, and then come home and let's get on with it. Or get it on, or something."

"I can't wait," she said. She ran her hand up his forearm to where the veins corded in a greenish knot inside his elbow. Then she turned quickly to back down the driveway.

Before she reached the corner she had the radio on, and she kept it on across Indiana and Ohio and into Pennsylvania, where she spent the night—all the oldies stations catering to people her age who yearned back to the time when they were twelve, or fifteen, or twenty. She sang along at the top of her voice, she pounded the steering wheel to Fats Domino, to Little Richard and the Beatles. It was quite possible that Jack would have enjoyed this too, but she chose to imagine him disapproving, changing the station.

She stopped at a Holiday Inn. After dinner, she went to the lounge for a drink. Everywhere in the public areas the floor was carpeted in a dark-red plaid, as though they wanted you to believe you were in some private British club, she thought. There was a large-screen TV hanging over the bar, tuned to the NBA playoffs. She had a slow dark beer and talked easily to the bartender, a kid a few years older than Ryan, wearing a clip-on black bow tie.

When she went back to her room, she opened the window and lay down on the one of the two king-size beds that was closer to it. She could hear some children using the pool; she could hear the whine of the highway. She placed her hands on her breasts and moved them slowly down her body. She felt at home, she realized. Relaxed in her body. Relaxed, in this ugly, junky motel room. The feeling frightened her, and she tried to think of Jack, of what he might be doing at that moment: cleaning up after dinner, or reading, or talking to Megan. Or maybe he was watching TV, the playoffs too. He liked basketball.

But the world she shared with him seemed far away from who she felt she was at the moment. It was hard to picture him. Outside, a man laughed; she could hear the drone of someone's TV. She looked up at the sky, which opened over the motel, an untroubled, improbable pink. She turned on her side, bent her knees, slipped her hands between them. Inside her, a door shut firmly against any thoughts, and she felt a dizzy, empty happiness at being here, no-where, alone at last.

CHAPTER 5

Lottie arrived in Cambridge in mid-June, thinking she might stay at the most for four or five weeks. Certainly she would have said then that she'd be back in Chicago by late July, which was when the accident occurred. Sometimes, later, she would wonder: if she'd left earlier, if she'd taken Ryan and gone when she originally planned to, would it have changed anything? And then she'd try to dismiss the thought.

Her first five days in Cambridge were sunny and hot, and Lottie had her mother's house almost to herself—only Richard Lester, the last tenant, crept in and out like a frightened fat ghost. Actually, Lottie felt a little like a ghost, or a shadow, herself as she moved alone through the cluttered rooms. She slept in her mother's bed, she sat in her mother's chair, she ate from her mother's chipped, stained dishes—even drank from what was left of a cheap bottle of her mother's gin.

The first evening she was in town, she had dinner with Cameron in his apartment, which lifted her spirits temporarily. But when she opened the door to her mother's house that night and the familiar musty, sour smell rose to greet her; when she flicked on the light in the dining room and felt the room, noisy with doodads, with heavy, outdated furniture, with violently patterned draperies, press in around her: then she felt as trapped and yet somehow as emptied as she had as a young woman planning her escape. She went immediately to the telephone and called Jack. He was in bed, reading. They spoke for ten or fifteen minutes in halting, hungry phrases, like new lovers.

The second morning she woke in her mother's airless bedroom, the heavy faded curtains closed, and stared at the collection of dinky glass figurines on the bedside table a few feet from her face. There were a chihuahua, a poodle, a mother dachshund and three tiny pups. Next to them, irrelevantly, stood a shepherdess with a broken crook, so badly painted she was cross-eyed. Lottie felt a momentary pulse of confusion, not just about where she was, but who. Reflexively, her fingers floated up her body, rested on her dented breast.

Her first act after dressing and brushing her teeth was to unhook the bedroom curtains. They fell in a heap on the floor, releasing a swirl of dust motes into the leaf-filtered light that entered the room. Next she swept clear every surface, dumping the figurines, the decorated Kleenex container, the dusty, faded, and dirty cloth flowers, into the wastebasket—itself painted with a bucolic scene. And all that day she moved through the house, scooping things off shelves, out of drawers, piling everything into any container she could find—a bucket, a trash can, a plastic bag. That evening, before she ran, she dragged all this, plus all the small pieces of furniture that she didn't think anyone would want, out to the curb.

She jogged slowly through the hilly streets, making her way by feel down to the river, emerging finally onto Memorial Drive from a narrow dark street of tall apartment buildings. The light was still a yellowy pink in the western sky over the water, and a last power boat was making its way slowly upriver. It threw a wake, which lapped at the weedy banks as Lottie ran along. She could hear it over her own deep breaths.

As soon as she started back toward her mother's house, the shadowy, tree-lined streets engulfed her in darkness. The streetlights above her were flickering on, and here and there, windows were lighted in the apartments, the houses she passed. She walked the last block home. On her mother's street, she could see her neighbors moving inside houses that were so altered from her childhood days she wouldn't have recognized them individually. In front of her mother's house, the curb had emptied a little; some of the furniture had been hauled off. After she'd showered, she unpacked her books and notes and sat for a while, reading, in the transformed bedroom, telling herself she already felt better.

Over the next few days, she drove around Cambridge and Boston, locating junk dealers, the Salvation Army, Goodwill, hardware stores, rental tools, paint stores. In this, too, she had a sense of dislocation: everything was approximately the same but also deeply changed. Mostly spruced up, made expensive-looking and spiffy. Houses were repainted in tricolor pastel schemes. Yards that had been dirt-packed playgrounds in her youth were full of perennials and roses. The A & P was gone and the old five-and-ten, replaced by gourmet shops, elegant little clothing and fabric stores. Even the old yellow-brick Sears, where she'd gone hoping to buy a fan the second day, was transformed, its ugly factory bulk turned into an unconvincing mall with a few stores sprinkled through it in lonely, upscale splendor. She found herself grateful for the rudeness of the man at the hardware store; for the seediness of the secondhand-furniture dealer, who left the lingering stale odor of a fat black cigar floating in the rooms of her mother's house as he moved through them, pointing out to his assistants whatever he thought he could sell. Lottie sat on the front steps and watched the sweaty young men haul her mother's possessions out to his flatbed truck in a light, warm rain.

On Saturday, Ryan arrived from London. Lottie was twenty minutes or so early to pick him up, and she sat near the door to customs and drank two weak cappuccinos as she waited. She was nervous. She'd dressed casually, in a denim shirt, blue jeans, and little heeled sandals. Still, she'd put on her makeup carefully, she'd been aware of wanting to look pretty.

Jack had always teased her about her relationship with Ryan. He called it their "romance." And when Lottie had met Jack, that had seemed especially apt. Ryan was just thirteen then, and Lottie had barely finished her treatment for cancer. They'd always been close, but Lottie was aware of feeling even more focused on him after her lump had been diagnosed. Actually, a small part of her initial eagerness to get involved with Jack had to do with her feeling that it would help her not hold on to Ryan, not get in the way of his trying not to be her little boy anymore.

What she'd felt in recent years, though, particularly since Ryan had gone off to college, was how absolute the ending to that mother-child romance was. It astonished her, given how central it had been in her life, given how much of her emotion had been taken up by Ryan—by love for him and anger at him and sadness with him and pride in him—how suddenly *gone* he was. All of that world was. She'd had a sense, the last few times he'd been home for a stretch, that there was some new relationship unfolding, something that, with luck, might look finally more like a kind of friendship. But mostly what she felt was the absence in herself of the old mothering emotions. Not that she loved him less. Not that at all. But that the kind of love was different. Less consuming.

She was, on the whole, glad for this. But she missed the other too. She missed *him*, the person he had been and wasn't anymore. The younger Ryan, the little Ryan—all the little Ryans—who might as well have died, really. Sometimes she dreamed of him as he was at three, or six; and woke with a mixture of gratitude and bottomless sorrow, the same feeling she had when she dreamed of one of the few close friends she'd had who'd died.

They were coming in twos and threes through the customs door now, most of them pushing carts stacked high with luggage. Lottie had moved over to the waiting area and was quickly shoved up against the barrier with the crowd. She saw Ryan before he saw her. He was messy-looking, unshaven, but tall and blond and very adult. An enormous backpack towered behind his head, and he walked toward the edge of the barrier, lugging a big duffel bag in each hand and scanning the crowd for her. When she broke free and stepped toward him, she saw his face open in pleasure.

"Hey, my ma!" he said. He set both bags down and held his arms out. She stepped forward, into his embrace, and he held her hard against his chest. He smelled funky, and Lottie laughed and hugged him back, her arms trying to circle his waist, fumbling against the frame of the backpack.

All the way home in the car he chattered to her. He had stuff to show her, tapes she had to hear; he'd met the greatest people, it had been an amazing time.

In the next days, he seemed to expand and fill the little house with his energy, his noise. Everywhere Lottie turned, there were the signs of his presence. He trimmed his hair and left the pale curved wisps in the sink. His abandoned shoes were waiting to trip her in almost every room. He left his dishes all over the house. He stood in front of the refrigerator with the door open and drank milk directly from the cardboard carton. He claimed the very air. He played the radio from the moment he got up, rap and blues, the music he'd missed most, he said. He was on the phone for hours each evening, calling people from school who lived in Boston or Cambridge, calling friends in Chicago, calling his father in Connecticut.

Lottie felt restored to some earlier, familiar version of herself. It made her aware, abruptly, of how long it had been since she lived with a daily sense of ease with herself, of belonging in her skin. Since before she married Jack, since before she moved in with him. This seemed a dangerous line of thinking to pursue, and she put it aside. But it rushed over her as *feeling* several times a day—when she heard Ryan making his noises somewhere else in the house, or outside; when she was fixing a meal she knew he liked. And she didn't fight it then, in that form.

Ryan had begun the work project with characteristic energy too, peeling back curled corners of the ancient wallpaper the very first time he walked through the house. His first full day of work, he had rented an extension ladder and completely removed the siding from the front of the house.

Today, four days after his arrival, he was stripping wallpaper upstairs; outside, it was still wet from last night's rain. Lottie was hauling trash out to the street. She'd been in Cambridge almost ten days now, through two trash pickups at this point, and both times she'd filled the curbside and the little strip of lawn in front of it for the width of her mother's property with bulging green plastic bags, sagging stained furniture, and cartons of rusted or moldy junk from the basement. The bag she was pulling behind her now was heavy— bottles—and her back was bothering her. She was thinking about taking a hot shower as she dragged the bag, clinking and shifting weight, down to where everything else was heaped.

A car honked and swung over close to the lumpy bags already lurching this way and that on the curb. It braked with a sharp, animal squeal, and Lottie turned to it, annoyed; and then she saw the henna-red hair, the oversize sunglasses. "Elizabeth!" she said, mostly to herself. She stepped over the bags and leaned into the car's window on the passenger side. "My God, Elizabeth! How are you? What are you doing here?"

In the kind, dimmed light of the car's interior, Elizabeth looked young still, even beautiful. Lottie was abruptly aware of the frayed T-shirt she herself was wearing, the baggy work pants, the paint-dotted bandanna covering her hair. No makeup: *naturally*, she thought.

"Charlotte! This is utterly amazing!" Elizabeth cried. "How wonderful to see you!"

"But what brings you here?" Lottie asked. "This is such a coincidence!"

Elizabeth waved a dismissive hand. "Oh, I'm visiting. Kiddies too. Marital trauma, et cetera, et cetera. It's a boring tale if ever there was one."

"Oh," Lottie said. "Well, I'm sorry."

"Oh, don't be," Elizabeth said. "After all, it happens to everyone. Why should I be exempt?"

"Still, it's hard, I'm sure," Lottie fumbled.

Elizabeth shrugged. Her blouse was silk, expensive, and it shimmered with the gesture, made it more elegant, more dramatic than it would have been otherwise. She wore a bold, Indian-looking pendant, and cufflike silver bracelets on both wrists. "And you?" Elizabeth asked. "Visiting too?"

Lottie gestured behind her. "We're getting the house ready to sell. My mother's in a nursing home."

"I'm so sorry," Elizabeth said. She whipped off her sunglasses as if to show the compassion in her eyes. Lottie noted the careful, unfashionably thick black eyeliner, drawn as though the sixties had never ended, with a little wing at the outer corner of each eye. "How long are you staying?" Elizabeth asked. "I've no idea, myself."

"About a month, I think. It's a tremendous mess in there."

"But you're not doing it all by yourself? Surely someone . . . ?"

"My son is helping me."

"Oh, that's right," Elizabeth said. "I knew you had a son. God, he must be gigantic by now, you started so young."

How was she meant to take this? Lottie wondered. But she answered only, "He's twenty. Almost twenty-one."

"Twenty-one! Weren't you smart! Smarter than any of us. By

the time my youngest is twenty-one, I'll be geriatric." She snorted. "She can *wheel* me around."

"Oh, come on. You look fabulous, Elizabeth."

Elizabeth laughed. "I wasn't fishing, I promise," she said. "But how nice you were to say so." She leaned forward. Her voice dropped, became warm and confidential. "Look, we should *do* something together. Let's have lunch. Let's be nice suburban ladies who lunch."

"That'd be great," Lottie said. "I'd love a break from all this."

"Me too," Elizabeth said. "Not that I'm doing a damn thing to take a break from. I can't honestly tell you even what I have been doing since I got here. Bored does not begin to describe it. A nice, winy lunch would be just the thing. We can catch each other up on all these years. Some of which I'd rather forget."

"Yeah," Lottie said. "I've got about a decade like that."

Elizabeth laughed. "Well, the nice thing is, we can just edit out whatever we want. Or don't want."

"Well, great," Lottie said. She tapped the car with her open hand in preparation to leave. She was aware, suddenly, of a desire not be looked at as she was any longer. "I'll look forward to it."

"Me too," Elizabeth agreed. She slid her sunglasses back on. "So, you'll call?"

Lottie smiled. "Why don't *you* call *me?*" she said in a voice gone suddenly cool and dry. She straightened up and stepped away from the car.

But Elizabeth didn't seem to notice being corrected. "Of course, of course," she cried. She put the car in gear, waved as if she were going on a long journey, and then she drove the little distance up the street to her house.

Lottie stood, massaging her back under the arching trees. She watched as the big new station wagon turned silently up the long driveway. She waited until it disappeared under the elaborate porte cochere at the side of the house. Then she stepped over all the junk she'd carried out and walked slowly up to her mother's house. She was still smiling. All the old feelings, she thought.

She shut the door behind herself and stood for a moment in the empty entrance hall. "How humiliating," she said aloud. "How can it possibly be?"

"Ah, ah!" Ryan's voice floated down from upstairs. "You're talking to yourself again, Mom."

"Oh, leave me alone. You'll do it too one day," Lottie called back.

"Hey, you talk like I'm going to get old, like you. When you know I never will." When she didn't respond after a moment, he started to sing along with the radio again, his voice pathetically faking funk: "I got a black-eyed bone. I got a mojo too . . ."

In the kitchen, Lottie was pouring herself a glass of wine. But instead of heading for the shower upstairs, where Ryan might want to talk to her, she opened the back door and stepped outside. She sat on the stoop. Elizabeth, she thought. *Shit.* Lottie hated the past; she was sorry she'd ever consented to come home. A gnat buzzed by her forehead and she caught at it. The backyard smelled of dirt, of the summer's rain, of weedy blossoms. She felt mugged by memory, suddenly: God. She gulped some wine and closed her eyes.

It was in high school, when she and Elizabeth were no longer friends, although they still stopped and talked in what would have seemed a friendly way if they saw each other on the street. But the kids who played together outside on the street now were younger than they were, and the kids their age had separated out, went to different schools, had different friends, different hairstyles, different ways of talking.

So Lottie should have been smarter when Elizabeth called. She should have known something was wrong: there was whispering in the background, laughter. Elizabeth's voice was strange too, secretive, lilting with a pleasure Lottie couldn't understand. But Lottie was foolishly eager, hopeful. She saw a whole new social world opening to her. She said no, no, she wasn't doing anything Friday. Yes, she would come to the party.

When the game was decided on—Fifteen Minutes of Heaven—Elizabeth and her boyfriend had gone first. "To show the rest of you how it's done," he said, and everyone laughed. There were about twenty kids, none of whom Lottie knew. They all talked to one another while Elizabeth and her boyfriend were in the closet; they made sly remarks, sniggered. Lottie stood smiling in what she hoped was a friendly way, but no one spoke to her. When it was time to open the door, Elizabeth and her boyfriend stumbled out, blinking and flushed and laughing in embarrassment and pride.

And then it had been Lottie's turn, and she was shut into the muffled dark with a boy she didn't know, a boy who hadn't bothered to speak to her or look at her while Elizabeth was in the closet. He was supposed to be able to do whatever he wanted until the strangers outside called "time," that was the way the game was played, and Lottie had seen from his expression as he stepped into the little room behind her that he had been promised this, that she had been summoned by Elizabeth as a gift for this boy. Her notion of a new life shriveled, and she felt exposed: here it was, the camphor-smelling dark, the funny, ugly boy the other girls didn't want but thought they could give her to. Probably he was "nice." Probably everyone thought he had a good sense of humor. As soon as the door was shut, he pressed against Lottie. She said no.

"C'mon," he said. "What will it hurt?" He smelled of onion dip.

Thinking of this now, Lottie set her wineglass down on the mossy wood of her mother's back stoop. As she looked out over the overgrown backyard, her face was clenched in anguish for that younger Charlotte. Why hadn't it been possible, she wondered, to open the door? to step out of the closet? To walk out of the house, to cross the street back to where her mother sat in the darkened living room, the TV turned too loud, the bottomless drink balanced on the arm of the chair.

It just wasn't, it wasn't. He pushed a knee between hers. His breath was in her face. Lottie was backed into a space Elizabeth and her boyfriend had cleared by shoving the coats and hangers to either end of the bar.

"Get away from me," she said.

Her back was against the wall. She bent her knees and slid down until she was sitting on the floor.

"Hey," he complained softly in the air above her. The empty hangers clicked as he fumbled around where she'd been.

Lottie set her hands on the wooden floor of the closet; and felt, under her fingers, something cottony and wet and warm. Sticky. A string at one end. She knew before her brain said the word: *Tampax*. And it had to be Elizabeth's; she was the only girl in the closet before Lottie. The boy squatted by her; she could feel him.

"C'mon, please," he said.

She folded her fingers around the Tampax. In her mind were

clear, sharp images of how it had come to be here. What she could say! Casually: "Does this belong to you?" What she could *do* to Elizabeth! She carefully pocketed it.

"Please," he said again.

She felt sorry for him, suddenly. "I can't," she said. "I've got a boyfriend." This was a lie. "Elizabeth never asked me, or I would have told her."

"Ahhh, *hell*," he said. Then there was a long silence. He stood up finally. Next to Lottie, his feet shifted every few minutes.

She stood up, too, before they called "time." She stood up and in a generous impulse rumpled her own hair, rubbed her lipstick off. What did she care what anyone here thought of her? And when they opened the door, she staggered out with the boy, looking the slutty way she was supposed to look.

She left a short time later. Elizabeth was in the kitchen. She hadn't spoken to Lottie since the game started. When Lottie came in, Elizabeth looked up. There were two girls standing with her, and they all smiled at Lottie. Lottie said she had to go, and Elizabeth answered with heavy sarcasm, as though the last thing she would ever really want to do was ask Lottie to stay: "Oh, are you *sure?*" She and her friends exchanged smirking glances.

She closed her hand around the Tampax in her pocket before she answered. Just knowing it was there was enough. She smiled right back. "Yeah," she said. "I've got stuff I have to do, actually."

It was the summer after this party, the summer when Lottie and Elizabeth were both between their junior and senior years of high school, that Cameron had started dating Elizabeth. When Lottie found out, she felt a sense of intense betrayal. Cam should have been in love with someone like her, she thought. Though if he'd asked her what that meant, she would have said only someone who'd gone to Cambridge Latin, not the Winsor School. She wouldn't have been able to label, or even describe, the other differences: someone whose family rented rooms, someone who had to have a job, someone who wasn't going to Martha's Vineyard for three weeks in August. Someone whose life had tighter corners, a smaller fence, a shape Lottie could imagine. Someone who wouldn't have thought Lottie was a cheap, stupid girl she could donate to some drip.

Lottie was working afternoons and evenings that summer at an ice cream parlor in Harvard Square—Brigham's—so she didn't see much of Cameron. He was gone by the time she got up; he had a job downtown at a bookstore. He never told her he was taking Elizabeth out, but one night when she came home from work, she heard laughter and, looking over, saw them on the glider on Elizabeth's front porch. After that she began to see them together everywhere. They were down on the weedy riverbank of the Charles one Sunday afternoon when Lottie went there with a towel to sunbathe. She pedaled right past them on her bike and turned back up Boylston Street. She saw them walking in Harvard Square, she saw them sitting together on a bench on the Cambridge Common. They came into Brigham's once; she looked up from the register and they were seated at one of her booths. She asked another waitress, Jan, if she'd take them.

"Unh unh. Can't. They asked for your station."

Lottie walked over to them, conscious suddenly of the servile-looking uniform, the apron, the clunky white shoes, like a nurse's, or an old lady's. She pretended that she was very busy, that she didn't have time to talk. Cameron teased her; he said if she wasn't nicer she wouldn't get a tip. After she'd brought them their order—he had iced coffee, Elizabeth had a frappe—she noticed when she passed their booth that he was reading aloud to Elizabeth, that she was rapt, intent, watching his mouth, his hands holding the book. Lottie had thought of the closet, the homely boy, the Tampax. It made her most angry, oddly, at Cameron.

After Elizabeth left for Martha's Vineyard, Cameron was home a lot more, and he suddenly focused his attention on Lottie. Where was she thinking of going to college? How much money had she saved? Why was she wearing so much makeup? What were her board scores? Did she ever go out? Who did she go out with? He was five years older than Lottie, and he often began his sentences, "You know, Char, it's time you thought about . . ."

Well, she'd thought about none of it. She'd gone through the motions with the college-track kids at school, but she'd assumed that when the time came, the counselor—someone—would tell her where to apply, what to do. When Cameron began asking his questions, she saw that she might have been thinking differently, that she should have been thinking differently. That Cameron must have thought differently to be where he was; that Elizabeth, of course, had thought differently all along. She felt suddenly thick, stupid. Absurdly, she missed her father. Maybe it was something he'd said to Cam, given to him before he went away, that made her brother so different from her. She hadn't worked hard in school at all. Her grades were mediocre. She had almost no money saved up. She'd used it to buy clothes, records, makeup. To go to movies. To have her hair straightened.

Cameron had advice for her, lots, and Lottie didn't want to hear any of it. They fought. "Oh, leave her alone, will you?" their mother would say. "For God's sake, let's have some peace in the house."

But he didn't. One night he followed her into the kitchen when she got home from work. While she stood at the counter in her uniform, eating a bowl of cereal—her dinner—he brought up rumors he'd heard from Elizabeth that she'd been going out with an older guy, a guy who had dropped out of high school, who was known as a troublemaker.

"So what?" she said. She said, briefly.

"That's all you'd need," he said. "To get knocked up by some guy who's going to end up driving a bus for the MTA."

"Elizabeth's much more likely to get knocked up than I am," Lottie said.

"What's that supposed to mean?" he asked.

But Lottie turned away. She dumped the cereal into the sink, rinsed the bowl. She couldn't have told him what she knew. She couldn't have confided it, the secret that had given her a sense of power over Elizabeth. Besides, she was angry at Cameron for trying to change her. *Not telling him* made a barrier between herself and him that she could use to ward off his advice, to keep herself deaf to his good sense. She was relieved when Elizabeth came home a week or so later and Cameron left her alone.

That winter, of course, everything changed between Elizabeth and Cameron. At Christmas he fell from her porch roof as he climbed out of her room at night, and after that Elizabeth was forbidden to him. At the semester break, there was the drunken scene when Elizabeth's father walked him home across the snowy street, and then it seemed to be pretty much over. And Lottie was glad. Glad for his pain: he thought he was so much better than she was! And glad for the possibility that Elizabeth had been hurt too.

All this without once really examining the differences between her life and Elizabeth's. Because to have thought about them would have been to acknowledge the lack of choice in her own life, the way in which money and class and circumstance had shaped her sense of who she might be. And that was something she wasn't ready to think about, that she wouldn't be ready to think about for years. Instead she conceived of herself then as hating Elizabeth for purely personal reasons. The differences in their lives reflected only the differences in who they were. She thought of them as simply being Elizabeth, Charlotte, willfully and freely making all the choices that they made.

Lottie did go to college the next fall—to the University of New Hampshire. She remembered those two months before she dropped out as being among the most miserable of her life. She missed home, she missed the city, she missed her mother and the dark, stale-smelling living room. She missed the shy greetings of the roomers as they went in and out, the blare of the television still going as she dropped off to sleep at night, the solitude of the little first-floor bathroom in the mornings. It was easy to leave school, to say she couldn't afford it anymore, because this was at least in part the truth.

But when she came back home, she felt somehow unfitted for that life too. She never argued with her mother, but she saw things differently. The house was shabby, dirty. The silent boarders seemed suddenly like shadowy grotesques. She noticed, for the first time, not just that her mother drank—she'd known that—but that she got shit-faced, as they'd called it at college, just about every evening. Sometimes Lottie would wake in the night to hear the television still shouting in the living room. She'd go in to turn it off, and her mother would be asleep in the chair, the bottle she'd fetched after Lottie went to her room within reach, her mouth shaping a slack rictus, her knees flung wide in what seemed to Lottie a hideous parody of sexuality.

When she'd saved a little money, Lottie moved out. She rented a room in a big boardinghouse on Mass Ave and began a new life. She had a job at the Midget, a deli and restaurant where students and faculty met for breakfast, for lunch. She made good tips. Sometimes she picked people up, slept with them. She bought herself a hot plate, an Indian bedspread, fat scented candles she burned when she was alone. She signed up for night courses at the Extension School.

She saw Elizabeth occasionally, heading across Harvard Yard on her way to class or the library in one of her eccentric outfits—sometimes peasant clothing from Turkey or South America, things her father might have brought back for her from his journeys. Sometimes all black. Always pale lipstick and dark eye makeup. Once Lottie glimpsed her in a rainstorm wearing what clearly was a flowered pink plastic hair-dryer hood over her dark-red mane. But even then there was a young man walking with her, as there usually was, though he looked—they all always looked—as though he were following a few paces behind. And what Lottie felt then, what she felt whenever she saw Elizabeth, was no pang of envy for her or for the life she was leading, no impulse to compare what seemed to be their fates. Just the sense of hateful recognition: "Ah, *Elizabeth.*"

There was a coach house behind her boardinghouse, rented to a group of graduate students, all men. Lottie met them when she was sunbathing in the side yard the next spring. They invited her to a party where everyone got very drunk, where someone rode a bicycle in and out of the house, where someone else attacked the police with a squirt gun when they arrived to break things up. It was 1964, 1965, and a brave new world was just beginning, the great romance everyone decided to have with everything that was different. A few years earlier, Lottie couldn't have made it happen even with enormous effort, but now she was interesting to several of these men; she represented a half-formed idea that would come to full flower later as the counterculture. They had posters on their walls of Malcolm X, of Mao, of Che Guevara. Lottie was another, different species of exotic.

She dated Walter a few times. Then she had a long affair with another of them, a graduate student in biochemistry, Al. She virtually moved in with him. But it was Derek she ended up with, Derek Gardner. She moved in with him, and Al moved out. And then she married him and they began their itinerant life as graduate student and working wife, and then junior faculty member and working wife, and then assistant professor and working wife with baby. And then she was a young divorcée with a small child. This all happened before she was twenty-five.

She'd ended up in Chicago, far from all thoughts of Elizabeth and Cameron and what had happened in their lives. Cameron wrote to her perhaps twice a year, sketchy, short letters, news of their mother, his jobs, his plans for the future; but she hadn't seen him in two years, and they hadn't really talked since before her marriage to Derek, when he called one day from the highway. She could hear voices, Muzak behind him, the binging of a cash register or maybe a pinball machine. He said he was in Ohio, he was driving to the West Coast, could he stop and stay with her overnight?

She was glad to hear from him, mostly in the way a single mother living alone with a very young child is always glad for company, for stimulation. She put Ryan in his carriage and went out and blew her food money for a week on a jug of wine and some steaks, even a handful of chrome-yellow daffodils, an unspeakable luxury for her. Shortly before Cam was due to arrive, though, while Lottie was frantically picking up, her downstairs neighbor, who had a little girl six months younger than Ryan, knocked on her door. Nadine baby-sat for Ryan in the mornings while Lottie worked, so it was necessary to be gracious. Lottie asked her in, but said that her brother was about to arrive. Nadine said she'd only stay a minute, if she could just have some coffee. They were out, she was desperate.

But while Lottie was dripping the cup through, she saw Nadine bend down and take off Chloe's sweater. She realized this was to be the standard visit, in spite of Nadine's promise. She was talking about Chloe's cold now, about milk products and mucus. Lottie sighed and put on some water for a cup for herself too.

Twenty minutes or so later, the bell rang. When Lottie answered the door, Cameron took her breath away, he was so changed. It was that era when everyone was allowed to change abruptly. Men grew beards, shed ties and jackets, and suddenly looked like different people, different *kinds* of people. Women wore costumes: beatnik, mod. Lottie herself was wearing a long flowered skirt. Her hair was parted in the middle and caught into a fat wispy braid, which rested on one shoulder. She had golden hoops in her ears. She looked like a gypsy girl.

Cameron's change wasn't extreme, but it made him more attractive, arresting-looking. His hair lay across his shoulders, thick and black and straight, longer than Lottie had ever seen it. He was clean-shaven, but he wore jeans, his shirt was open at the neck, and she saw a dark cloud of curling hairs in the V below his collarbone.

Unsmiling as ever, he seemed intense, dramatic. A Method actor, say. His embrace was quick and didn't involve their bodies touching. He set his suitcase on the floor in the living room and looked around, taking in all that was seedy and worn, Lottie was sure: the bookcases made of milk boxes and boards, the mattresses on the floor, the toys scattered everywhere. Suddenly the very flowers, in their glass jar, looked shabby—looked fake.

"And where's my famous nephew?" he asked when his eyes had made their careful circuit of her life.

She brought him into the little kitchen where the children were banging pots and pans, where Nadine sat up straighter now over her coffee. She introduced him to Nadine, to Ryan, who swung his body shyly behind Lottie's long skirt. Cameron said yes, he'd have a cup of coffee.

Ryan was silenced, staring in admiration at his uncle, and Cameron turned his chair so he could watch the children. Nadine's conversation grew livelier, more pointed, for Cameron's benefit. Lottie tried to ask about the trip, the drive, but Nadine kept reclaiming the floor. "The doctor said there was nothing to be done, nothing. With that kind of fever, you just wait it out."

Lottie served Cameron his coffee and stood with her butt resting against the sink, watching the scene, wondering how to rescue them all.

"Anyway," Nadine was saying now, "when I got back, I saw that Chloe's spit-up was all over me, all the way down my back. No wonder they'd been staring. And I'd thought they might be admiring me. Foolish." Her eyes always flickered back to Cameron, who sat glum, sunk in stupefaction, Lottie imagined, to have arrived off the roar of the highway to this.

"Maybe you'd like to stretch your legs, Cam? Take a walk?" she offered when she could, and watched the gratitude lighten his face.

He carried the stroller downstairs for her, while Nadine trailed them, telling Lottie where she should take Cam on the walk, as though Lottie were a stranger, too, to the neighborhood. She was still calling after them as they set off toward the schoolyard a couple of blocks down. It was late spring, cool. The bright-green shreds of leaves on the trees shook with the wind. Once they'd crossed the last street and stepped onto the patchy grass, Lottie braked the carriage and set Ryan free. He ran ahead of them up the slow rise, and stopped dead when the playground equipment came into his view. When she caught up to him, he pointed, awestruck. "It's the swingss!" he said. "It's the big kids' swingss!" he told his uncle. Cameron smiled and reached for his uplifted hand.

For a while they took turns pushing Ryan on the swing. Then Lottie spread a blanket on the grass, and she and Cam sat down. From a distance, she thought, they must have looked like a pretty, young quasi-hippie couple with child. Ryan meandered in a wide circle around them, bringing back treasures he found—a rock, a dandelion—and depositing them worshipfully in Cameron's hand. Lottie's eyes followed him, and every now and then, when he wandered too far or seemed to be putting something in his mouth, she'd get up and run to him; but within this punctuation she and Cameron were attentive to each other, busy accounting for their lives, for the years that had passed.

Lottie went first. Her story was still new to her then, and she brought a fresh and venomous energy to it. Later she would learn to tell it differently, she would see how she'd used Derek to escape what was becoming of her life in Cambridge, to open certain doors, to be a new family from which she could launch herself less fearfully into the world. But what she described that day to Cameron was Derek's never having time to take care of Ryan when she was both working and trying to go to school. His desire for an open marriage. Their competitive, joyless series of affairs with other people. She recalled for Cam a party a few months before Ryan was born, at which, coming downstairs from the bathroom, she met Derek on his way up with a woman she knew. She'd turned sideways to let them pass, and they'd both had to slide along against her big belly.

Lottie was sitting very still on her mother's back stoop now, remembering all this. Remembering herself pregnant, her unhappiness. Thinking with shame how often she'd used that detail—the twin touch of her belly—as the final brush stroke in the portrait she painted of Derek for anyone who'd listen in the years after her divorce.

She noticed abruptly that Ryan's music had changed inside the house. It was classical now. Lottie sipped her wine. As she thought about those long-ago days of her first marriage, it seemed just possible that it hadn't really happened that way at the party. There'd been the stairs—oh, yes!—and the pretty young woman. She could call up even her name, Barbara Doyle. But she seemed to remember now that the two of them had been ashamed or embarrassed to see her, that she'd turned away from them, coming down, that there hadn't therefore been that doubled caress of her pregnant belly, the detail that made it all so much crueler.

How much else might not have been true? It was so long ago. She remembered that she'd chronicled for Cam a few of her ugly fights with Derek, the days of not speaking. And after the divorce, the troubles getting child support, the infrequent visits. And Cameron had nodded and agreed: Derek was a bastard. He asked at least several of the right questions.

But once he began to talk, to tell his story, his voice seemed suddenly tuned differently; and Lottie realized he'd simply been enduring everything that came before. That for Cameron, hearing her story was like her having to listen to Nadine go on about Chloe's achievements—her progress in toilet training, say. It was the first time it occurred to Lottie that the intricate shocks and pains of her life could be of no interest whatever to someone else.

Cameron said he was going to marry Elizabeth.

Lottie had felt yanked back to a country she'd forgotten the shape of, the climate of. "*Our* Elizabeth?" she asked after a beat.

"Elizabeth Harbour. My Elizabeth," he said.

"But when did this happen? You guys haven't been together in years." From twenty feet away, Ryan called to her, and she waved.

"Oh, but we have. Off and on, off and on. We always come back to each other."

"This is since high school? This is, like, when she was in college too?"

"Yes. It's why I came back to Boston." Cameron had worked in publishing for a year in New York after college, then gone back to Boston and started working again at the bookstore he later bought a share in. "She always had a key to my apartment, all through college. She wanted to be free—like Derek, I suppose, with his open marriage stuff, only we weren't married. I mean, I agreed with her. We both knew she was too young, that she needed time and space. And I wanted to give that to her. But just every now and then, I'd open the apartment door and she'd be there. Like a gift." His face was stamped with a commanding awe: *Imagine this.*

And Lottie had imagined it then, Elizabeth with her long red

94

hair, her big pale-pink mouth, waiting in the sunstruck apartment. Lottie had been in Cameron's apartment a few times; it was in Cambridge, on Mount Auburn Street, near the post office, a brick building with lots of windows and a tiny weed-choked courtyard. She saw Elizabeth in a chair, a Modigliani figure, the sunlight glinting through the vine-covered window behind her. She saw Cameron in the open doorway with just this eager gratitude rising on his face.

"Didn't it ever interfere?" she asked. "Other relationships and stuff? It must have."

"Oh yes. Lots of times. But those were the rules. Once, actually, I remember I came home with a woman I'd been involved with for a couple of months, and she was there—Elizabeth—asleep in my bed." He grinned quickly. "Goldilocks. She was wearing a shirt of mine. And that was it with that woman. I mean, I took her home and all, but she didn't even speak to me on the way. That was it."

"It would be, wouldn't it?"

Ryan had staggered up to them and fallen into Lottie's lap. Now he flung his head back against her breast, under her chin, and reached up idly to explore her face and hair with his hands while he watched Cameron talk. Lottie leaned forward and closed her lips over his fingers, sucked them gently for a moment. "And what about now?" she asked finally. "I thought she was at Berkeley?" How did Lottie know this? She just did, she couldn't remember.

"Well, I've flown out a few times. And of course, she comes home a couple of times a year to see her parents."

Lottie shook her head. "I can't believe I never knew any of this."

"Why would you? I never said anything about it. And you and I haven't exactly kept close watch over each other the past few years."

"True," Lottie said. She rested her head on Ryan's. "And now you're going to marry her. The famous happy ending." She felt a quick pang for her own failure. She held Ryan tight for a second.

Cameron was looking away, off over the top of the ugly flat school building to the scudding clouds. "Well, Elizabeth doesn't know it yet."

"Oh. You mean you're . . . what? Like, proposing?"

"I guess. Or more like carrying her off or something. She's *supposed* to be marrying someone else."

"I beg your pardon?" A phrase Derek had used when she said

something that displeased or shocked him: *"If you ever do that again, I'll leave you." "I beg your pardon?"*

Cameron was smiling now, grimly. With his strong profile, the longish dark hair, he looked like an American Indian. "Oh yes," he said. "But that's not going to happen. It's all a mistake."

"Well, but you're not getting married, then." Ryan had stood up again, and now he lurched off after a big, dirty-looking pigeon, crying out in excitement.

Cameron watched Ryan for a moment and then turned to her. The breeze lifted his hair suddenly. "Yes I am, Char." He spoke to her as though she were a very young child. "That's exactly what I'm going out there to do."

Lottie felt a sense of dismay; this seemed so wrongheaded. "But . . . well . . . It sounds like Elizabeth has other plans, Cam."

"Elizabeth just needs to see me. She needs to listen to me. I shouldn't have let her stay out there this long. It was too long, apart. She just needs to be with me again."

"But . . . I mean, it really sounds like she's moved on, in some way." *"Let her stay out there"?* she was thinking.

"You don't understand this, Char. I don't think you and I should even be talking about this." His voice was chilly, suddenly.

"Well, I do understand that you can't force someone to love you again if they've stopped."

"She hasn't stopped. That's the point. And it's not a matter of force. We just need to be together. We were meant to be together."

Lottie was wishing they had stayed home and drunk a lot of the wine she'd bought. She would have liked to dismiss all this as wine talking.

"But, Cam," she said. "If she's met someone new, someone she's planning to marry . . ."

He got up quickly. She had to shield her eyes to look up at him, a tall shadow in the bright, thin sunlight. "You don't understand this, Char. You've always settled for things. You've given up, you've compromised, you've settled. For what you could get, for what came easy. And Elizabeth and I have lived a different way." He turned abruptly and walked off a little distance.

Lottie was stung. Her eyelids felt suddenly swollen, and she looked out, unseeing, after Ryan. After a few minutes, Cameron came back and said more gently, "I'm sorry, Charlotte, but I don't really want to talk about Elizabeth with you."

Lottie didn't say anything. Silently she rose too. As they folded the flapping blanket, they walked toward each other once, twice, three times, without meeting each other's eyes. Lottie pushed the blanket into the back of the carriage. Then she went to retrieve Ryan from his circular, futile pursuit of the bird. Later—often, later—she would think back to Cameron's remarks about her that day, to his comparison of his life with hers, and feel outraged. But at the time—with Ryan so happy to be around a man, any man; with her own sense of her defeat as a lovable person so recent in her life—she had thought only that Cam might well be right. That real love might just be a universe she'd never been part of.

The next morning he was gone, even before Ryan's gay crowing woke her up. There was a note on the kitchen table. "I'm off. Thanks for dinner and the bed. I'll write when things settle down. Kiss Ry for me."

And that was all she ever knew of it. The next time he wrote was on a Christmas card. He was in Boston again. There was no word of Elizabeth. Somehow later—maybe through her mother—Lottie knew of Elizabeth's marriage, to a different man entirely, of several children. Nothing more until now. She'd assumed, she supposed, that Elizabeth had gone on to have the kind of life they'd all imagined for her when they were young together: accomplished, distinguished, full of glamour and excitement. Because everyone had understood, of course, that Elizabeth was special. Even when Lottie had hated her most, she had believed that. And it seemed, in some way, that now, long after she'd stopped thinking in these categories for anyone else, she still did for Elizabeth. Or how else could she explain the senseless pant of envy she'd felt, leaning into Elizabeth's car?

Ryan was calling her now from inside, asking her something she couldn't quite hear. She stared at her wineglass for a moment, then poured what little was left out onto the ground and went back in the house to see what he wanted.

Elizabeth telephoned a few days later. They arranged to meet at the Harvest—the best thing to happen to Harvard Square for years, Elizabeth said: a bar for grownups. Lottie got there first. A sullen waitress with spiked black hair and a deadly-looking crescent of earrings dangling from one lobe led her to a table. It was outside, on a shadowed terrace at the bottom of a well of tall office buildings. When Elizabeth arrived, Lottie watched her cross the terrace in her sunglasses and high heels, watched the middle-aged men trail her with their eyes.

Elizabeth kept her sunglasses on through the meal. Sparrows hopped at their feet eating crumbs, and in the office windows hidden by the tree arched above them, all the air conditioners hummed with a sound as steady as rain.

Elizabeth talked freely—astonishingly so, Lottie thought—about the problems in her marriage, the details of her husband's infidelity, of how she had found out about it. He had been unable or unwilling for the moment to give his lover up. But he'd wanted to hold on to his marriage too. "I told him forget it," Elizabeth said. "I told him there was no way I was going to cooperate for a minute in wrecking the children's lives, in letting him wreck my life. And then I left town. Let him see how it feels to live alone with his bimbo. Let him understand the damage he's doing." Elizabeth's dark mouth pulled down at the corners when she spoke of her husband, and Lottie could see now that behind her sunglasses, there was a fan of delicate lines, fine as paper cuts, around each eye.

"He's the kind of person—I'm sure you know this kind of person—who simply won't acknowledge the effect his behavior has on other people."

Lottie was much more careful when she spoke about her life. She felt oddly protective of everyone in it, as though Elizabeth posed some danger to them all. She said nothing about her difficulties with Jack, about his grief. She made it sound as though Evelyn had died years before, as though the folding together of their families had been smoothly accomplished.

Elizabeth sighed and lifted her hands to her heart. "A newlywed. How nice." Lottie noticed that the cuticles around her polished nails were ragged and torn. She was wearing the same heavy, cufflike bracelets. Elizabeth smiled. "And all that success too. I love your articles. Whenever I see there's one somewhere, I buy the magazine instantly."

Lottie smiled too. "That's awfully nice to hear," she said.

Elizabeth flung herself back in her chair, dramatically. She had drunk two gin and tonics with lunch. "God, who would have thought, all those years ago, that we would have ended up like this?"

"What do you mean?"

"Well, positions reversed, as it were. *I* was the one who was supposed to go on to fame and glory, wasn't I?"

"Oh." Lottie nodded. And then she asked, with deliberate innocence, "And what was supposed to become of me?"

"Well . . ." There was a pause as Elizabeth saw what she'd stepped into. "You were sort of going somewhere else." She laughed, nervously. "And look at me now," she said rapidly. "What a mess I've made of everything." She leaned forward and tapped the table with a polished nail. "Much good it did to spend all those years studying Keats and Shelley. I might as well have made my way to some *stud* farm in Kentucky and learned how to be a brood mare. And how very appropriate." Her splayed hands gestured wildly, as though she thought she could distract Lottie with enough activity. *"Brood* is of course precisely the word. . . ."

But as she talked, Lottie was feeling a pulse of confused anger left over from so long ago that she might have been holding the sticky Tampax in her pocket. She watched Elizabeth's bright calculated smile flashing at her as she spun her apologetic fantasy, and she thought of that sadder, stupider Charlotte who lived inside her still.

Elizabeth had barely finished speaking when Lottie set her coffee cup down and said, in a friendly tone, "You know, Cameron still lives in town." Elizabeth's expression behind the dark glasses didn't change, but her body quieted abruptly. "I'm sure he'd love to see you. Maybe you should call him."

Before they left the restaurant, Lottie and Elizabeth went to the ladies' room, a tiny box with two stalls wedged into it. Lottie finished first. She stood in front of the mirror over the sink, looking at herself in the bright overhead spotlight. Behind her, Elizabeth's modest trickle seemed pathetically human, her story suddenly so sad. Under the harsh glare of the light, Lottie looked older than she was; the lines at the corners of her mouth were fierce and embittered. Why had she said what she'd said about Cameron? How could it possibly serve her leftover anger for Elizabeth and Cameron to come together again? She would remember this moment weeks later, when she heard about the accident; but even now she felt guilty, thinking of Cam. She felt she'd sacrificed him to some ancient, childish need of her own. Something she should have outgrown long ago.

Elizabeth flushed, began talking loudly over the gurgling water. Lottie leaned toward herself into the shadow and applied her lipstick. She shrugged. Well, they were both adults now. And they almost certainly would have bumped into each other anyway. Whatever happened between them at this stage of their lives, surely none of it was her responsibility.

CHAPTER 6

Lottie was making a plate of deviled eggs for the cookout. She had boiled them early in the morning, a dozen of them, and all day the kitchen had held that gassy, sulfuric odor. While she was working at the counter, still in her bathrobe after her run and a shower, Ryan came in from the backyard to get cleaned up. He had warned her he wouldn't stay at Elizabeth's for very long, that he had friends he was meeting later in the Square.

"Now who is this dame supposed to be again?" he asked, standing by the open refrigerator with a glass jug of Gatorade in his hand. The cold air around him was visible, a faint, smoky mist.

"Shut the door," she said. Half the eggs were finished, and Lottie picked up another oval, rubbery white and began to fill the perfect little hollow with stiffened yolk.

The door whumped. "Okay, it's shut. Who is she?"

"She lived across the street when we were growing up. Elizabeth. Née Harbour. It's something else now. Elizabeth Something-or-other. She's married. Though actually she's separated now. I had lunch with her last week."

"So she was a friend in the old days?" He was smiling at her, a teasing smile. "So very long ago, when you were young?"

She made a moue. He was like an old man in the way he kept

reworking the same familiar jokes, she thought. She remembered Derek's grandfather, who'd told Derek every time he met Lottie that Derek better watch out or he'd run off with her himself. "More Cameron's friend than mine," she said. "An old lover of his, actually."

"Aha!" He set the jug down on the counter.

"Aha, what?"

"Aha, the plot thickens. Aha, the story becomes more complicated. Aha, perhaps we watch them rekindle their romance." He was walking by her. As he passed the plate, he picked up a stuffed egg, popped the whole thing into his mouth.

"Ryan! Come on!"

He grinned, a disgusting eggy grin, and then he was gone.

Lottie continued to work. Then she stopped and laughed out loud. She'd suddenly realized she was humming "The Second Time Around."

Because Elizabeth had called Cameron, of course. Probably thinking only that Cameron's was a devotion she could count on having lasted all these years, and that she could use a good dose of devotion. All she'd told Lottie yesterday when she called to invite them to the cookout was that she and Cameron had been "having a lovely time."

Lottie got ready for the party at a leisurely pace, trying on first one dress, then another. Though she wore the scruffiest of clothes around the house to write in—she was often still in her bathrobe at noon, at two or three o'clock; or wearing faded jeans, old shirts of Ryan's—she liked fine clothes. Even when she was her poorest, she'd worked hard for a worn elegance, anyway, when she went out. She'd bought things secondhand then, or at antique-dress shops. And she had drawers of scarves and jewelry she liked to experiment with.

Tonight she finally decided on a loose black cotton-knit dress with a scooping back, and therefore shoulders that occasionally slid a little way down her arms—a dress Jack had once said made her look "eminently fuckable." She belted it with a bright, narrow scarf and slid into a pair of low-heeled sandals. She hooked long, filigree-delicate earrings into her earlobes and applied a lot of shadowy eye makeup.

As they crossed the impossibly wide street, Ryan said to Lottie,

"I feel weird. I feel like we're the slaves being invited up to the massa's house for some completely irrelevant celebration. His birthday. The acquisition of another hundred acres."

Lottie smiled. "That's probably apt," she said. "In fact, I bet the little houses were built for servants of people in the big houses."

"Think so?"

"Well, a very different class of people anyway. Just look."

They stopped in the middle of the street and looked back at Lottie's mother's house, crammed in a row next to the other two miniatures; and then over at Elizabeth's house, with its wastefully deep, curving porch, its sloping lawn, its porte cochere, its turrets and elaboration of ornate woodwork.

"Say no more," he said, and started for the curb. He had dressed up a little too, in baggy cotton shorts and a clean black T-shirt. He wore European sandals on his feet, sandals that oddly looked almost exactly like the ones he'd worn as a little boy. He seemed, to Lottie, unbelievably handsome.

"When I was a kid, though," she said, trailing him, "it was all invisible to me, these differences. Up to a point, of course."

"Yeah. Kids don't care, do they? Until they do care."

"That's about it," Lottie said.

As they walked up Elizabeth's driveway, they could hear her children's shrill voices out in the backyard, so they continued under the porte cochere and came out behind the house. The backyard opened before them, huge and slowly sloped uphill to a row of tall evergreen trees at the property line. The children were playing badminton on a net set up just in front of these trees. In the corner of the yard loomed a carriage house that was probably larger than two of Lottie's mother's house. Elizabeth waved from the flagstone terrace off the kitchen. She and her mother and Cameron were sitting in wooden chairs there. Cam got up and strode barefoot across the grass to them. He shook Ryan's hand, kissed Lottie on the cheek. Loose blades of grass clung to his white, arched feet. He wore slacks and an old shirt with the sleeves rolled up. His collar was so frayed it had split along its top edge. "Thanks for coming," he said, with a gratitude that seemed proprietarial to Lottie. As they all walked back to the terrace, she filed this away mentally.

Emily Harbour, heavy and slow, was struggling up out of her chair. She had sturdy sandals strapped onto her swollen, bruised-looking feet. Her varicosed legs were partly covered by an unfashionable wraparound skirt, and her doughy white arms looped out of a wrinkled sleeveless blouse. Her face was still pretty, though, the way fat women's faces can be as they get elderly—plump and unlined. And she still wore her hair exactly as she had in Lottie's childhood, in a wispy bun low on her neck. It was a pure yellowy-white now.

She greeted Lottie warmly, was pleased, pleased indeed to meet Ryan, and effusive about the eggs. She asked Lottie to help her, and Lottie followed her into the house, into the cavernous old kitchen, unchanged in twenty-five years it seemed, except that the gray walls had darkened—the higher, the darker—with greasy soot. Emily spoke in a steady, unpunctuated, and gentle stream, with a light, girlish voice. "It was just so kind of you, Charlotte, to bring over deviled eggs, and I can't begin to thank you, they are beautiful, I've never been able to make a reasonable deviled egg myself, they always run a bit and they're not supposed to do that, of course, so I just confine myself—*here* you go," she said, handing Lottie a plate from the refrigerator, "—to slicing things, it's much safer and it takes much less of a knack, you know what I mean, just whack whack whack and you're finished." On the chilled platter under the plastic wrap there were tomatoes, radishes, celery, carrots, flat glistening circles of Bermuda onion. Lottie unwrapped this and set it on the big square table in the middle of the old-fashioned room.

Someone would certainly redo *this* kitchen, Lottie thought, as she followed Emily's instructions for finding additional bowls and plates in the Hoosier cabinet. There were no countertops, just a series of separate pieces of kitchen furniture set against the walls—a sink with a drooping grimy skirt of faded blue gingham, an old electric stove, the Hoosier cabinet, painted a pale green, and another cabinet, a hutch, really, stacked with plates. There were also several wooden tables of various heights, and a huge, bulbous refrigerator with bright strips of shining metal on its door in an art deco pattern. It reminded Lottie of the Chrysler Building.

Emily was lumbering painfully back and forth from the pantry to the big table in the middle of the room, bringing jars of pickles and olives, mustard, mayonnaise, talking all the while. First about picnics: ". . . some Latin derivation for the word, I believe, but it's charming, nonetheless, when you think of it, isn't it? pic, nic, pic, nic. But basically such a wonderful idea too, just to escape from the necessity for all that fancy folderol at the dining room table, especially with the children here, don't you know . . ." She ripped open several bags of potato chips and dumped them into one of the bowls Lottie had found. "Here they come now, tumbling out, pure salt, pure fat, dreadful for you, I'd never allow myself to have them if I didn't pretend I was getting them for the children, in fact I adore them, and the children are such a wonderful excuse, aren't they?"

Lottie murmured her unnecessary responses. She was remembering how proud she had felt as a girl of her mother's kitchen when she compared it to the Harbours'. Her mother's kitchen was *modern*, that was the point. The linoleum counter with the gleaming aluminum strip along the front edge, the fluorescent bulb overhead, the marbled plastic table with matching chairs: these were things you saw in magazines. This room, by contrast, had seemed pathetically dumpy and old-fashioned to Lottie, and her mother had confirmed that for her. "I don't know what they think they're saving it for," her mother would say after one of her rare visits to the Harbours. "You can't take it with you."

When Emily had everything ready to her satisfaction, Lottie went in and out several times, setting the food, the plates and napkins and bowls, on the large wooden picnic table on the terrace. Cam helped too, bringing out candles in colored glass jars, and then a plate of uncooked hamburgers the children had apparently shaped earlier in the afternoon.

Ryan had joined the badminton game—Lottie saw there was a girl his age playing, a girl with long dark hair tenting her shoulders—and Elizabeth was at the net too, talking to the youngest child, her daughter, who was upset about something. Cameron had started some coals earlier, in a round metal grill. ("I don't know why one feels a man has to start the coals, but one just does, I suppose, and anyway it's such a messy job, if there's a man around I'd just as soon foist it off on him in the name of whatever—male superiority, fine with me.") Now he began to cook the hamburgers. Elizabeth drifted back down from the game, carrying her daughter. The child was so big Elizabeth seemed engulfed, wrapped in the girl's long, skinny arms and legs. Emily, she said the child's name was. After her grandmother. "This is Charlotte, sweetheart. Can you say hello?"

The girl turned her face for a second to look at Lottie and then buried it again in her mother's neck, tightened her limbs' clutch on Elizabeth. She was a pretty girl, with a long oval face and Elizabeth's red hair. She'd been crying.

Now Lottie sat down by Emily Harbour, as instructed, and as the older woman talked, she kept offering the requisite supporting murmurs and comments. But she was watching Elizabeth and Cameron together. Normally Elizabeth had an exaggerated, stylized animation, but she was even more dramatic tonight than usual. You could hear where the italics would fall when she spoke. She laughed often, a bright, gay laugh that made Cam's head swing toward her, even when she had wandered off again with little Emily, even when he began talking to Lottie and Elizabeth's mother.

Finally the meal was cooked, and the sweaty children and Jessica, the au pair girl, trooped down to the terrace. They all sat on the long wooden benches at the sides of the table. Big Emily, as they were instructed to call her—horrible, Lottie thought—and Cameron were on chairs pulled up to the ends of the table, but Lottie was squished among the children, between Jessica and one of Elizabeth's boys. There was a frenzy of questions: what grade, what school, what sport, what major, and so on. They were eating too, of course. There were plates, condiments, pushed and passed up and down the table along with the conversation, and people had to raise their voices to be heard.

"Well, I think Cambridge is sucky," Elizabeth's smaller boy said.

"Oh, Jeff. What do you even know about it? Nothing. Have you ever even been to Harvard Square at night? No, you haven't." This was Michael, the oldest. His eyes skipped around the table, asking the adults to notice how much more like them than his siblings he was. He was fourteen or so, Lottie guessed. Both boys were dark and stockier than the little girl. Little Emily.

"Sucky is an awful, awful word, darling. I won't even discuss its meaning with you. Just do not, please, do not ever use it again in my hearing."

"Where is the mustard? Or did big fat Jeffrey eat it all?"

Now big Emily's voice floated down the table toward Lottie, and Lottie leaned forward to hear. "Elizabeth tells me you're a writer, Charlotte. Now there's a hard job, so solitary, inner strength, it just

106

befuddled me how long my husband could just sit alone all day, writing, writing, writing."

"I suppose so," Lottie answered. She had to pitch her voice above the squabbling children next to her. "But I suppose if you do it willingly, there's a part of you that likes to be alone."

"Yes, I can see that, one gets used to solitude." The old woman's head bobbed thoughtfully, and she was off: "I enjoy it myself, finally, though I never thought I would when I had a houseful of children and my husband, oh, that was lovely, and of course"—she lifted a fat hand in a circling gesture meant to include her daughter, her grandchildren—"this is always wonderful too, but I know what you mean, it can be very satisfying, though of course I don't claim to do anything much of use with it, just putter around, keeping busy, but one does like it . . ."

Lottie kept nodding in the swirl of voices around her. She saw Elizabeth smile radiantly past her at Cameron. He had been describing what sounded like a convention for booksellers, Lottie thought.

"So, Ryan, when do *you* start?" Jessica's voice, behind her. This was Jessica's third or fourth question to Ryan, Lottie noticed. He was sitting on the bench across from Lottie and Jessica.

"Classes? I guess the seventeenth or something. Registration is a little earlier."

Elizabeth got up and went into the house. Lottie had begun to talk to Michael about school. He was polite and thorough in his answers. She was learning more than she'd ever wanted to know about the cutoff ages for junior high and high school, and how much you could and couldn't manipulate them to get maximum playing time on the basketball teams. But she kept sneaking glances at Cameron, and she could tell without looking up when Elizabeth was approaching again, his face was so altered, so lifted—though he too was talking, politely, to Ryan and Jessica.

"Oh, I adore them," Jessica was saying. "I went to one of their concerts last year and we had great seats, so close that their sweat actually fell on me."

Elizabeth had set two more bottles of wine on the table before she sat down again. Lottie reached forward and poured herself another glass. Then she sat back a little and listened to the babble of the multiple conversations. In every silence she could hear the whirring saw of crickets, the distant horns on Mass Ave.

"I *never* get to wear my purple dress," little Emily complained.

"Darling, it's much too fancy for tonight. Look at us all, eating with our bare hands, dripping blood and ketchup all over ourselves."

Big Emily launched herself. "When I was little we weren't allowed to eat with our hands, even hamburgers . . ."

"Why do you have that earring?" Jeffrey asked. "Earrings are for weird guys."

Lottie turned quickly to Cameron.

"I'm weird," he said, and shrugged. Then he smiled at Elizabeth, and Lottie had to turn away, his gaze was so intense. It seared her.

It had grown dusky, and the candles' yellow light had begun to cast upward shadows on their faces. Elizabeth looked tawny and beautiful. She was wearing a light, flowered sundress of some gauzy fabric. Her collarbones were deeply shadowed. Her long arms, cuffed again with the wide silver bracelets, were in constant motion. Now she bent toward her daughter to say something.

Across from Lottie, Ryan was talking. "They say 'bloody this' and 'bloody that' all the time, and you forget they're fucking swearing." Then he looked around the table, suddenly shamefaced. "Oops."

"But these are real deviled eggs, dear," Emily was saying as she held the plate out to Jeffrey. "Not mine."

"Nary a book in the house," Cameron was saying. "Well, hardly a book. God, what a way to grow up. That's why it's the perfect profession for me."

"But *why* can't I stay up as late as the boys?"

In the flickering light, everything was happening either too fast or too slow. When Elizabeth came around the table, pouring wine, Lottie put her hand over her glass.

"It's eeny, meeny, miney, mo', catch a *tiger* by the toe, stupid. Isn't it, Mom? Mom?"

"We have our little volunteer uniforms, you know: blue-striped, middle-aged, genteel ladies of mercy."

"Oh, I never get to New York," Lottie heard herself say. "You do everything by phone and Fed Ex. You could live in Nebraska for all they care."

"I was, like, oh *no*, do I have to go through this again?"

"Well, at home we have lots of pets, plus I get to go horseback riding once a week."

Little Emily began to cry, and Elizabeth leaned over and said to Jessica, "I'll get her set and then you . . . ?"

Next to Lottie, Jessica nodded, and her hair moved in a watery shimmer.

The boys began to rise too. It was dark, and Lottie had been swatting mosquitoes for a while, she realized.

At the kitchen door, Elizabeth stopped to call to her sons. "Plates to the kitchen before you go anywhere." The lights inside went on in successive windows as she trailed little Emily through the kitchen and then upstairs.

Lottie stood too, and Cameron and Emily, and there was a friendly clattering of dishes as they stacked them. At the kitchen door with her heap of stuff, Lottie turned back. Ryan and Jessica were still sitting at the table in the candlelight. The au pair girl was half lying across it, actually, seeming to reach toward him, resting her chin on her arm. This would be at least the second girl already this summer, Lottie thought. Maybe the third.

Emily came outside, passed Lottie on her way back to the table. "Oh, bless you, dear," she said as she floated away.

In the kitchen, Cameron was at the sink, scraping plates off into a garbage bag, then rinsing them.

Lottie set her stack down and watched him for a moment. He moved neatly, rhythmically, and she thought of his years of careful bachelorhood, his tidy apartment. She said, "Boy, the pheromones are fierce tonight."

"Ah, Lottie the romantic," he said. He didn't break his rhythm, but he was smiling, that quick, surprising smile that lit his somber face, that made you want to keep him happy.

She laughed. "Well, as it happens, I am."

"Who, you?" He looked at her, as though he hadn't really noticed her before.

"Did you think you had the patent?" she asked. "Yeah, me."

"It never struck me that way."

Lottie lifted her shoulder and popped a radish into her mouth. "Nonetheless." The radish exploded noisily between her teeth. "What's going on with you and Elizabeth?" she asked after a moment.

He looked over at her and squinted his eyes. He smiled again. "Pheromones," he said.

"Ahhh!" She went outside for more dishes, passing Emily once more. Emily had an empty wine bottle in each hand. She held them carefully, as if she were using them to balance herself.

"Charlotte, dear," the older woman said.

"Yes!"

"I just wanted to thank you and Cameron, dear, for all you've been doing for Elizabeth. It's so good for her to get out, to try to just put it aside for a while, till things come around, and I'm sure they will, these things happen, don't you know, even in a very solid marriage, but you've been lovely, just lovely to her, and I'm very grateful."

"I haven't done anything, really."

"No, no, no, no, my dear, you must let me say it, I'm old enough not to be contradicted, and I know it's not that much to you, a few movies and dinner and the like, but she's been so despondent, and it really has absolutely transformed her—so!" She bobbed her head up and down, up and down, in a diminishing series of dips. The reflected light moved from plane to plane in her bifocals, and she smiled warmly and leaned too close to Lottie.

"Well, it was nothing," Lottie said. How very interesting, she thought.

"Poo," said Emily. She patted Lottie's arm once, twice, and Lottie felt the cold touch of the bottle glass. Emily went inside.

Lottie stood alone for a moment in the dark. The light from the kitchen cast her own shadow in front of her. Across the terrace, Ryan and Jessica still sat, blurry in the candlelight and her middle-aged vision. Behind her, she heard Emily start up with Cam, his tight, small voice giving monosyllabic replies to the steady, watery lapping of her conversation. It was like sitting in a warm bath, listening to her, Lottie thought. Across the dark lawn, the white shirts of Elizabeth's boys moved like giant moths.

She had the odd sense of having somehow disappeared. She could walk across the street now, back to her mother's house, she could get in the car and drive off, and no one would miss her, no one would come for her. It was like the feeling she'd had once as a little girl when she hid under the front porch, behind the broken lattice, because her mother had yelled at her. She'd waited on the packed

dirt through the long summer afternoon and into the evening—
perhaps actually no longer than a few hours, but it had seemed
endless to Lottie then—and no one came. Her mother called her
once, at dinner, but then not again. Finally Lottie had crawled out
and gone inside. And though it wasn't until much later that she was
able to articulate the resolve she took from this event, even at the
time she somehow understood the feeling, the knowledge that there
was no one *out there* for her. That her mothering would have to
come from someplace in herself.

The feeling she allowed herself now, though, as she started again
across the terrace, was a sudden pulse of anger at Ryan and Jessica,
sitting here together in the dusk, as though the world, the adults,
had been invented to serve them, to arrange for them to meet, to
score. As she came up closer, she heard Ryan saying, "I was really
little, only about two or so, so I don't even remember it when they
were together."

Perfect, she thought. Tales of divorce. He was using the sorrow
of his life, of *her* life, to seduce this girl.

"Ryan, my dear," she said.

He turned. His face in the moving light was frightened, as boyish
as Michael's or Jeffrey's.

"Maybe you could be helping too." There was acid in her voice,
and Ryan and Jessica both quickly unfolded and stood up. Looking
almost sheepish, they began to gather the last glasses, the leftover
silverware and napkins, from the table.

A little while later, Lottie and Cam were sitting on the front
steps of their mother's house. It was dark, and Lottie could barely
make out Cam's face in the shadows. He'd asked her if she was going
out to see their mother again, and she'd said she wasn't sure.

"It isn't easy, I know."

There was something Lottie heard as condescending in this, and
she answered quickly, "I don't expect it to be easy, Cam."

He didn't answer.

"But she doesn't even know me."

He shifted on the step across from her.

"And it's not as if we were ever what you might call close."

"I wasn't either."

The thought of how true this was, of how much more he had to

111

forgive their mother for than she did, shamed Lottie, and she was silent.

After a minute Cam asked her how the article was coming.

Gratefully she answered, "I don't know. I'm at an impasse." She sighed. "Maybe I should do hate next, instead of love. Or anger. I mean, I think I keep reading and reading because I really have no notion of what I think about it all. And every time I hear a popular song on the radio, just some sappy thing—especially some sappy thing—I change my mind."

"What have you been reading?"

"That you gave me?"

"Or whatever."

"Well, *Romeo and Juliet* for starters. Stendhal. Turgenev: 'First Love' and then 'Clara Milich.' But I'm sick of death. Everything I read has death in it. You love, your lover dies. Or *you* die. Or you *think* about her dying. I already wrote the article on grief. I thought I was done with that."

"Well, of course, they did die more frequently then. Mortality was much more . . . a familiar, I suppose you should say."

"I suppose, I suppose. And I suppose a lot of female deaths must have been in childbirth, or from childbirth. So love was, literally, I guess, more dangerous. All tangled up in the anticipation of grieving and sorrow. Maybe that's part of what made it romantic."

The dark swirled a little around Lottie. She'd drunk too much. After a minute she said, "That 'Clara Milich' is a strange story—do you remember it?"

"I'm not sure I've even read it."

"The main character falls in love with a woman—Clara—after she's died. After she's killed herself on account of her unrequited love for him. Because—it seems, anyway, at least partially because—he's in love with the idea of himself that she's revealed. Of himself as someone worth dying for."

The living room light came on at Elizabeth's house. Lottie saw Cam's head lift in that direction. His voice, when he spoke, seemed tense. "But that would be compelling, of course."

"I think it's sick."

He turned to her in the dark, his face a light blur. "You can't have it both ways, Charlotte. I thought you were arguing *for* sickness. For what we call sickness." He turned away. "*In* our sickness."

112

"Oh, I don't know. I suppose I am. It's just . . . it all seems so drearily unhappy."

"Well, the happy ending isn't popular in literature. It isn't dramatic enough."

"Or maybe real enough," she said thoughtfully. "Because how could you say, 'They lived occasionally happily ever after'?"

"There's my cynical Charlotte." She could hear that he was grinning. "Romantic, my ass." He laughed.

"Why do you keep laughing?" she asked. She was pretending to be irritated, but she felt a quiver of the real thing too. "You're altogether too happy."

"You can't be too happy."

"That's not what my reading is telling me."

"You've been reading too much, then."

"The pot calling the kettle black."

Neither of them spoke for a long moment. The trees rustled with a sudden, cool breeze. Rain was predicted in the night.

Lottie said, "Mrs. Harbour—big Emily—thinks they're going to get back together, that this is just a temporary little blip in their happily married life."

"Emily is sweet, but she's completely in the dark."

"Well, here we sit too."

Across the street, a door banged shut. Elizabeth emerged in the light under the porte cochere, quickly became just a shape in front of it, then disappeared into the black lawn. They both waited in silence for her to reappear. After a moment she did, stepping forward onto the sidewalk, crossing the street toward them. Her skirt billowed around her long legs.

"Hi," Cameron called as she stepped onto the curb.

Her hand slapped her chest. "God! You startled me."

"Char and I are stoop-sitting."

She hesitated a half second, then walked toward them. "May I join you?"

"Of course," Lottie said. When had this been arranged? she wondered.

"We were talking about love," Cameron said.

Elizabeth laughed her bright, nervous laugh.

"And laughter," Lottie said.

"Love, laughter, and the sorrow that comes after," Elizabeth said. "Isn't that in some song?"

"We were just voting on the sorrow-that-comes-after part," Lottie said.

Elizabeth stopped, facing them. Her mouth made a dark O in her face. "You're too quick for me, Char," she said. "I don't get it."

Cam's arm lifted toward Elizabeth. "Come sit," he said.

As though he pulled her by a string, she stepped forward with the inward motion of his arm and sat down on the step below his. Her perfume floated up toward Lottie.

"But I want you to cast your vote, Elizabeth," Lottie said. "Do you think sorrow follows love? That's what we were debating."

"What an odd thing to be talking about."

"I'm writing about it. An article."

"Oh."

"So, what about it?" Lottie could hear the nervy, persistent edge in her own voice; and she realized how cruel this question was. What was wrong with her tonight? No one spoke for a few seconds. "Well, it's probably a dumb question," she said. Then: "All's well at your house?"

Elizabeth nodded. "For the moment," she said. "Emily's asleep anyway. Little Emily. The boys pretty much take care of themselves. How's your other project, Char? The house, I mean."

"Oh, coming along. Coming along."

"You're so admirable, to do it yourself. If it were me, I'd just throw money at it."

There was a silence. Lottie waited for Cam to speak, and finally he did. His light voice was polite, moderate. "Well, of course, Charlotte could do that. But I couldn't, and that's the problem. I'm afraid I'm in a way responsible for keeping her in chains this summer."

Elizabeth had spun around to look up at him. "Oh, I'm sorry, Cam, I didn't mean . . ."

"As a matter of fact," Lottie said, "I can't afford it either. I mean, Jack can, but that's Jack's money." He had offered at one point, had said the estate could pay him back after the house was sold, if Lottie felt uncomfortable about taking the money.

The estate couldn't afford it either, Lottie pointed out. And for Jack to donate it, in light of Cameron's financial situation, was awkward—impossible, as Lottie saw it. Jack had backed off, in the end. In part, Lottie knew, because he couldn't tell how much of her argument was reasonable delicacy on her part about Cameron and his finances; and how much might be connected to her wish to escape him and his sorrow—the sorrow of their life together.

"Besides," Lottie said to Elizabeth, "Ryan likes earning the dough, and he's cheaper than anyone else we could hire. He and I together are a very cheap team."

After a moment Elizabeth said, "You seem to have a very nice relationship, you and Ryan."

"Do we? Well, we do sometimes." And then, because that sounded so tepid, she said, "It's always lovely to be with him for a while. For about . . . five days. And then we discover why it wouldn't work indefinitely."

"But why wouldn't it?" Elizabeth said. "That's so hard for me to imagine. I feel in some way that my kids—at least one of them anyway—will always be there."

Lottie smiled. "All I can say is, you'll see." They were all facing the street; they were quiet for a minute. Lottie thought she could feel resistance to this idea. From Elizabeth? From Cameron? "It's the way it's supposed to be," she said. "They have to push away. They have to find you . . . *wanting* somehow."

Cameron said quietly, "I imagine it's different for different people."

Lottie was about to answer, sharply, when a car turned onto the street at the top of the hill. They all looked up at it. It descended slowly, then turned into Elizabeth's driveway. *Her* car, Lottie realized. It was Ryan. She could hear the pulse of the radio playing. Some reggae beat.

"Hey, look at this," she said. "Speak of the devil."

"Oh, yeah," Elizabeth said. "Ryan's taking Jessica out."

The car pulled under the porte cochere and parked, most of it hidden along the side of the house. They could see only its taillights, and Lottie noted that one was missing. She'd need to replace it.

"God, this is like déjà vu," she said. "Like watching you guys start up in high school."

Elizabeth cleared her throat.

Lottie looked over and saw that Cam's hand was resting, a patch of light, on Elizabeth's dark hair. Lottie felt brittle and worn, suddenly, teetering on the brink of some outburst. She slipped her sandals off and massaged her bare feet. It was just that she'd drunk too much, she told herself, like a mother to a cranky child. She leaned her cheek against her bare shoulder.

After a few minutes, the car backed out. "And they're off," Lottie said. She could see Jessica in the passenger seat. "You should warn her," she said to Elizabeth. "He's a bit of a rake and a rambling boy."

"Oh, I don't worry about *her*," Elizabeth said. "She gets about three calls a day from different men herself."

"And do you tell her what time she has to be in, Elizabeth?" Lottie asked. "Are you *in loco parentis?*"

"I hardly dare," Elizabeth said. "I've been staying out so late myself. And you? With Ryan?"

"Oh no," Lottie said. "No. That part of the mom act is over too."

"Do *they* believe in love, you think? Does Ryan?" Cam asked after a moment. Elizabeth was leaning back against his opened legs.

"I suspect so," Lottie said. "He takes himself tremendously seriously, and that's the bottom line, isn't it? That high seriousness that we weren't allowed."

"What do you mean, we weren't allowed?" Elizabeth asked.

"Well, I mean, really, do you think? Didn't you feel, the moment you felt *anything*, that it was inauthentic? I mean, weren't we the first real post-Freudians? The first ones to live with that understanding of life? It was impossible to take yourself seriously. Every single thing was a dynamic. We knew everything was neurosis. And love in particular was made suspect forever, don't you think? Trivialized." Lottie was warming to it. "See, in the nineteenth century, people could *feel* their emotions without second-guessing themselves all the time. They didn't have to realize that there was something ridiculously predictable and culture-bound—mundane—about even the most grand of them. Now no one can even write about love anymore." She saw Cam's hand move in protest, and said, "It's true! Where are the twentieth-century love stories? They're not allowed."

"I don't think your . . . post-Freudian feeling is as universal as you claim it is, Charlotte," Cam said dryly. "And after all, weren't you the one who called yourself a romantic earlier?"

116

"Well, maybe I did," Lottie said. "But surely I know better. After all, we can't believe in romantic love anymore, can we?" She was asking permission. She was asking them what they were up to.

"But we do," he said firmly. Then he laughed. "We suspend our disbelief and we do."

"But that's hanging by the proverbial thread, isn't it?" she asked.

Cam turned his blank face to her. "But as Cheever said, it's hanging by a thread in the moonlight."

Elizabeth spoke suddenly: "As Woody Allen says, we need the eggs."

Cameron laughed again. He bent over Elizabeth for a moment.

Encouraged, Elizabeth continued. "And don't you think we all believe—in our hearts anyway—that our emotions are enormously serious? Just the way they do?" Her arm swung toward where the car had disappeared.

Lottie felt exhausted. "Oh, who knows?" she said. "Maybe they don't take themselves so seriously anyway. I mean, do you know what they call it? Having sex? Among other things they call it, I presume."

"What?"

" 'Doing the nasty.' Isn't that strange? Here they treat it as though it had all the moral weight of . . . aerobics. But they label it as though it were powerfully evil. So maybe they don't believe in love, after all." No one spoke. "I'll ask him, tomorrow," Lottie said. "And get back to you."

"Well," Cameron said, after a long silence. "I guess I'd better be hitting the road."

"Oh, okay," said Elizabeth casually. And then she stood up along with him. "Well, maybe I'll join you for a while."

Someone could have pointed out that this made no sense, but no one did. It was awkward as they left, but they accomplished it, calling good night to Lottie in hushed voices as they walked toward the Volvo, which was parked farther up the street, at the foot of Elizabeth's driveway. The doors slammed, the engine went on, then the headlights. Lottie heard Elizabeth's piercing laugh just before they drove off.

She sat by herself for a while after they'd left. Had this summer been invented to teach her something? Was there some purpose to her solitary witness to all this romance? This *love*, if love it was. She thought of what Cameron had said about hanging by a thread in the moonlight; of what Elizabeth had said about eggs. Two utterly different notions, she thought suddenly. She should have said so. *Those are two very different ideas. One is concerned with perilous beauty, and the other is about lying to yourself.*

She thought again of Ryan, driving off with Jessica. Then of his reeling the girl in with his story, his sad story, in which she, his mother, was just the backdrop, a minor character.

Perhaps, after all, that was what was making her angry—being relegated to a supporting role. Didn't she have a story too? a story in which Ryan's role was significant but definitely minor?

The difference was, Lottie thought, that she was old enough to understand the nature of the story: that everyone had one, but that it was thrust upon you, as often as not. That what counted was what happened after that, the combining of the aftermath with the original story. Your mother is an alcoholic. Yes: and then? Your mother is an alcoholic, and you live at home and take care of her as she sinks into early dementia. Your mother is an alcoholic, and so are you. Your mother is an alcoholic, and you leave home and reinvent your life. Your mother is an alcoholic, and you never, ever let yourself touch a drop.

Jack's story was Evelyn, of course. But then there was what he'd made of his life, of his family's life, while he somehow kept Evelyn at the center of it. It was a good story, an interesting aftermath, and it had helped her fall in love with him.

Of course, when they met, Jack also had the knowledge she was seeking. That was powerful, Lottie thought. Sexy. That certainly helped it get going, that same thing that allowed middle-aged professors to hit on nubile young students with such ease—women who a few years later, when they'd become investment bankers or lawyers, would wonder at their choices. At the clunky brown shoes, the hair artfully arranged over the bald spot, the food spilled down the lapel.

With Jack, though, after the knowledge, the power, other things unfolded. His story, and what he made of it. And if Lottie were honest about it, she was the one, anyway, with the physical and sartorial liabilities: the closetful of secondhand clothing, the inevitable run in her panty hose. And, of course, the dented breast, a mild lateral scoliosis, terrible teeth, a tendency to spill when eating. Their first dinner out, when the waiter cleared her place and then fastidiously swept the crumbs from the tablecloth in front of her, there was a silence as they'd taken it in—the smears, the bright dabs of color. They didn't know each other well yet. When the waiter had left, Jack leaned forward and looked more closely. "It's really worthy of de Kooning, Lottie." Lottie smiled at the memory and went inside.

She wandered through the rooms, flicking the light switches. In the kitchen, she turned on the radio. The Red Sox were losing. She changed the station—jazz—and went into the living room, sat down in her mother's chair. She liked the way this felt. This was better. Light fell in from the dining room, pooled on the floor. Lottie turned away from it and looked out the window at the dark street, the odd porch light up and down the block a melancholy beacon. She could hear the music, dim and tinny on the cheap radio, but it wasn't where she was. She was at a remove, she thought. "At a remove," she murmured.

What about Cam's story? Was there a narrative to his life? She had no idea, she realized. There was the one he'd seemed to make— the clutter of books, friends, the beautiful apartment in the derelict neighborhood, the store. But she didn't really know how he fit in. There was something disjunctive, not clear, about it all. About him. His history with Elizabeth, for instance. He'd said to Lottie that it made him what he was. But what was that? How did that go with the bookish Cam? or with the Cam who stayed and took care of their mother? And who was the Cam who had passed through Chicago those years ago so full of romantic will?

Could there be such a thing as romantic will?

She remembered the visit they'd made together a few weeks earlier to their mother, how oddly uncomfortable she was watching his patience, his attentiveness to the old woman. She had thought then that it was because she felt he shouldn't have forgiven her for being the kind of mother she'd been. She'd tried to get him to concede that, in fact, in the car on the way back that day. But now it occurred to her that she'd felt even then that there was something false in his devotion, something that had to do with his need to see himself as a certain *kind* of person, when his truest feelings—she would have sworn this—were quite different.

She heard footsteps on the front porch—Richard Lester!—and

she froze, every muscle tensed. The front door creaked open, then shut, very carefully. Richard appeared, moving slowly across the hallway. As he passed in front of the lighted dining room doorway, he turned to where he thought she was, in the kitchen, where the music rattled. Lottie was holding her breath, absolutely motionless, watching him, his exaggerated high steps. When he made it to the foot of the stairs, she heard him gasp in excitement and scamper up, careless now of his noise.

In her mother's chair, invisible Lottie sat, still frozen. And then she was aware of how rigidly she was holding herself. She inhaled, slowly. Exhaled for a long count. She forced herself to relax, she let her muscles drop, her head loll back. Her legs bent open at the knees, her arms slid down and rested, curled fingers turned up, on her thighs.

She closed her eyes. How absurd they were, she and Richard: the two celibates of the tale, hiding from each other in terror. She imagined describing this night to Jack, making a foolish story of it. "A non-bedroom farce," she'd call it. She imagined Jack's lined but youthful face, the intense light eyes, the curve of his mouth. *The palsied waltz of the wallflowers,* she'd say.

Then someone was shaking her shoulder. She was cold, it had started to rain, she could hear the hard pelting drops outside. It was Ryan.

"Jesus, Mom," he said. His voice was tightened in judgment and disgust. "What're you *doing* down here?"

CHAPTER 7

As the alternately rainy and muggy days of the summer wore on, as the time when the accident that would change their lives drew nearer, Elizabeth began to hang around Lottie's house for a little while almost every day. She'd arrive sometime after breakfast—Lottie would hear her on the porch, her light, quick step—and then she'd knock at the open front door, call, and come in as far as the empty hall.

The first time she came, she seemed almost shy, hesitant; and Lottie contributed to the awkwardness since she couldn't figure out why Elizabeth was there, standing with her hands on her hips, surveying the work Ryan and Lottie were doing as though she were the contractor in charge of the project. She'd left her paintbrush lying across the open can too, and the image of it, its bristles hardening slowly in the damp air, kept recurring in her mind's eye as she slouched against the doorjamb, talking uncomfortably to Elizabeth for about ten minutes. Finally Elizabeth left.

The next day, when Elizabeth showed up again, Lottie thought to offer her coffee. They sat opposite each other at the kitchen table. Elizabeth leaned forward and set her elbows down, and suddenly she looked so completely settled—relaxed—that Lottie realized that this was the point, that she simply wanted to talk.

And so it started. Sometime usually around ten or ten-thirty, Lottie would hear Elizabeth's voice echoing in the open hallway, the question mark in the "hello," and she'd come from whatever she was doing to make a fresh batch of coffee and sit in the grim little kitchen with her for a while.

Her subject was Cameron, Cameron and herself, and virtually nothing else. She'd repeat various things he'd said to her, she'd describe how he looked when he said them. At first Lottie could scarcely believe how bored she was. She barely needed to listen, really, she knew the basic themes so well. She remembered behaving just this way when she'd been so intently focused on Jack. Her closest friend then, a magazine editor Lottie had met through her work, had heard the same kind of details. "Mmm," Lottie would say to Elizabeth—as her friend had said to her—and pour herself another cup of coffee. "No kidding," Lottie would offer, and unbelievably, that was enough to keep Elizabeth going. Once she actually made a note to herself while Elizabeth spoke, a note she thought might be useful for the article she was still working on: *Exhibitionism*, she wrote on a folded paper napkin. *The early stage of love which requires an audience.* Elizabeth's eyes had followed Lottie's hand as she uncapped the pen, as the spidery vertical script bloomed on the napkin; but she never stopped talking. Lottie's behavior clearly didn't exist on the same plane of consciousness with her preoccupation with Cameron, with her need to speak of him. She watched Lottie sit up straighter and push the napkin into a pocket of her jeans without her attention's ever appearing to waver from her own train of thought.

Slowly, though, over the course of ten days or so, Lottie was drawn in. She found she actually began to look forward to Elizabeth's arrival. She realized that at least part of the reason this could happen was the curious blankness of her own life in Cambridge and the way in which what was going on between Elizabeth and Cameron seemed a comment on it. But some of it, too, was the glacial but inevitable course of the drama, the steady slow flow of information shifting just slightly over the days. It made Lottie remember the period just after she had separated from Derek, before she finally gave her television away, when she had religiously followed the soaps. She was working mornings then, and she'd pick up Ryan from the baby-sitter after lunch and put him down for a nap almost as soon as they got home. Then she'd lie down herself in front of their tiny, blurry TV and watch the self-destructing love affairs, the bitter rivalries, the medical and legal entanglements, as they played themselves out incrementally.

Now, against her will, her better judgment, she felt the same eager fascination for Elizabeth's slow-moving narrative, her tedious piling up of mundane and yet—to Lottie—compelling detail. And as though she sensed Lottie's appetite, Elizabeth began to elaborate her stories, began to reveal more and more intimate aspects of her falling in love again with Cam—though she never gave it that name. "Our little romance," she called it. "Our recycled affair."

And so Lottie came to know that Cam had wept the first few times they made love again. She knew when Elizabeth gave Cam the key to her mother's house so that he could sneak in and up to her room after everyone had gone to bed. (After that Lottie had to will herself not to watch for the Volvo at night, had to keep herself away from the front windows.) Elizabeth told Lottie about the rainy night when they'd turned into a dark passageway between buildings in Central Square and made love against a wall there, how she'd just stepped out of her panties when they left, how she'd looked back as they reached the sidewalk and seen them lying there, a flag of white in a black puddle.

Lottie knew that Cameron's body hadn't changed much, she knew that he had what Elizabeth called "a lovely fat penis." She thought she had probably flinched when Elizabeth told her that, so startled was she that this could be something Elizabeth would want someone else to know. It occurred to her to wonder when this kind of discussion had become possible among women. Had the women's movement done it? She thought about it and recalled herself in one of the three groups she'd belonged to over those years, talking explicitly—yet never, she was certain, without a sense of at least *overcoming* a kind of embarrassment—of Derek, of what he had liked to do in bed; and then, she remembered, of new lovers too. Yes, of penis size, of varying styles of pumping, foolish things said, postcoital behavior. And this was exactly the kind of thing it seemed Elizabeth needed to tell Lottie, again and again.

And gradually Lottie dropped her guard too, at least partway. She began to tell Elizabeth about her life. Never about the situation with Jack, never about her fears in that regard. And she was always

123

vague about Evelyn's death. But she revealed at least some of the particulars of their courtship. She told Elizabeth, for example, about the first night she'd spent with him, when someone had taken the opportunity to leisurely tear her apartment up, taking only two things in the end—an electric can opener she'd gotten as a gift when she married Derek, and her very beat-up stereo. Jack had bought her a new stereo to prove this wasn't God's judgment on them, and its sound reproduction was so good she'd had to throw away most of her records. "They went ga-thunk, ga-thunk," she told Elizabeth. "Or they'd get to a certain gluey part and just scrape over it to the end. We used to weight the old player arm with a nickel to push it right into those gummy grooves, but we knew we couldn't do that with this machine; it wasn't somehow ours in the same sense."

She told Elizabeth about therapy with Megan, about how Megan had said she didn't need another mother, the last thing she needed was another mother. "So I said to her, 'What can I be to you, then?' And she truly didn't know what to answer. I think she hadn't thought that far ahead, that I would have to be *something* to her. She hadn't reckoned on it, poor thing."

She told Elizabeth about having cancer.

Elizabeth's braceleted hand clutched her own throat. "Cancer! Oh God, I'd be so terrified. And you must think about it all the time, ever after."

"Oh no," Lottie said. "It's been years now. And even at the time—I mean, you just deny like crazy. It's an argument for the usefulness of denial, actually. I've never admired an unhealthy psychological phenomenon more."

"But never to *know*. When it might recur!"

"Oh, that's not true," she said. Elizabeth was a wonderful audience, really. Lottie was almost regretful she couldn't tell her about Jack and Evelyn. "You get into these statistical pools. I'm in a great one now, having survived for seven years. In fact, I'd bet money I'm in a better pool than you. But see, you probably don't even *know* your pool." Elizabeth shook her head. "And I do, so there you have it."

They even talked a little—gingerly, carefully—about their growing up, their parents. Lottie told Elizabeth of the permanent silence that had fallen between her mother and herself, of the sense she'd had of being orphaned from very early on.

124

"But it was precisely that that I envied you for," Elizabeth said. "I mean, I'm not saying I didn't also think your life was difficult, because I did. But you were also so *free*. Everything I did was simply . . . miraculous to my parents, was their possession. I suppose it was partly after having all those *boys*, that I was unique, just a different kind of creature to them. But I couldn't do a thing, not a thing, without its being held up and turned this way and that for the most minute and careful examination."

"Yeah, but the unexamined life is not worth living," Lottie said. And though she meant it as a joke, she felt it too, in a twinge of familiar pity for her old self. "Sad but true."

When Elizabeth didn't come, Lottie missed her. Were they friends, then? Lottie wouldn't have said so, exactly. But on the days when Elizabeth didn't show up, Lottie often stopped what she was doing anyway at about the time she usually arrived, and sat restlessly over her solitary coffee, daydreaming.

It forced her to acknowledge, finally, that she'd been using Elizabeth too. To be exact, that she adapted Elizabeth's accounts to feed her own fantasies of Jack. To transform them, so that she often pictured herself and Jack doing the things Elizabeth told her she and Cameron had done. Alone in her mother's room, she had imagined herself and Jack in the rainy passageway in Central Square—imagined the soaked clothing, the wet hair, the desperate need, the fogging pants of breath, the rough brick scraping her shoulder blades. Elizabeth's story of herself and Cameron nearly getting caught by her oldest son making love downstairs in the living room became, in Lottie's imagination, herself and Jack yanking themselves upright, hurriedly rearranging clothes, wiping stains, shoving underpants under the striped couch, as Megan returned from an evening out. For Cameron's light, pressured, curiously expressionless voice saying that he hadn't really been alive until Elizabeth returned to him—that she was the love of his life—Lottie substituted Jack's hoarse one, promising her the same things as they, too, sat in a car and heard the drumming rain on its metal roof.

Several times a week Jack called, or Lottie called him. Though his voice never failed to thrill her, there was something awkward and unsatisfying about their conversations. They were too polite. Lottie concluded that both of them were probably afraid of confronting what was most central in their thoughts: the idea that somehow it might *not* all work out over time.

But all the while Lottie was struggling so unsuccessfully to talk to the real Jack on the phone, she was allowing her fantasies about him to grow ever more elaborate, ever more concrete, nourished by Elizabeth's indiscretions. From time to time she thought about all this and was momentarily disturbed; and then she performed a kind of mental shrug. Really, what was the harm?

Because Lottie was used to giving herself permission to have fantasies—perhaps most women who have lived alone for long periods of time are. When Ryan was very small, the length of time between lovers would sometimes stretch to eight or ten months— occasionally longer—and her answer to this had been to conjure lovers in fantasies constructed around men she worked with or friends' husbands, or even movie actors, singers. Her rule was that she couldn't let the fantasy spill over into her life, she couldn't get *crushes*, for God's sake. But that as long as she was in control, she was free to use whomever, whatever she wished. So now she made no effort to stop herself either, without thinking about the damage she might be doing to what was, after all, her very real love.

One night, about two weeks or so after Elizabeth's cookout, Lottie invited her and Cam over for dinner. Partly it was a polite wish to return Elizabeth's invitation, but partly it was that Lottie was curious to see for herself how they behaved together, how they looked. She planned the dinner carefully and spent a good part of the afternoon in the kitchen.

Lottie was a fine cook when she felt like it. It was true that she had served Ryan oatmeal and fruit for dinner at least once a week when he was growing up, but that was because she didn't feel like it all the time. Nothing was worth being claimed by, she felt, particularly not kitchen work.

Tonight she'd made a seafood stew, a lemon tart for dessert. She had to serve it, though, on her mother's stained plastic plates, with her mismatched and bent utensils. When Ryan drifted into the kitchen, he stopped at the oddly set table and said, "Cute, Lottie. It's like you're playing house, or something."

Elizabeth and Cameron arrived together, both with damp hair and the pinkish yet sleepy health of people who've spent the afternoon making love. Before dinner they all sat in the sagging chairs in the living room, the fan Lottie had bought in her first days here resting on the floor in their midst, turning its benign wire face from side to side as though listening politely to all of them. Alternately it rippled Elizabeth's skirt, then Lottie's, against their bare legs.

Elizabeth was bangled, she had on three or four beaded neck-laces, one with a carved pendant. She was talking about the day camp she was sending little Emily to, the premium put on creativity, how Emily worried every day that what she made, or thought up, would be ordinary. "They have *activities*," Elizabeth said. "Dress-ups, for instance, is an activity."

"And it's possible to be inferior at dress-ups?" Lottie asked, incredulous.

"Apparently so," Elizabeth said.

"Robin Hood," said Cameron censoriously. "Dreary."

Lottie grinned. "The Fairy Godmother," she offered. "How . . . banal."

"That's how she feels, I'm afraid," Elizabeth said.

Lottie gave her opinion: children's imaginations ought to be predictable and boring.

"C'mon, Mom. You don't think that," Ryan said.

"No," she insisted. "It's like the brain patterning that occurs through learning to crawl before you walk. There's a need for it. Nobody wants a baby who rolls over, stands up, and begins to move like . . . Isadora Duncan."

"Charlotte." Cam was shaking his head and grinning at her. "This is what we call left field, I think."

"Poor Em," said Elizabeth. "She's such a mope anyway. I thought camp would be fun, but this is just so hard for her."

Ryan began talking about the YMCA day camp he went to in Chicago, how he learned mumblety-peg there and various kinds of pool. "It was like a program in gang-banging or something."

"Excuse me: gang-banging?" Elizabeth said. "What a disgusting term."

Lottie went out to the kitchen to get things ready. Ryan's loud voice dominated from the other room, talking about his peculiar childhood. She was thinking of him as he'd been at Emily's age. He'd loved to dress up, in fact. He'd had a collection of costumes he'd assembled out of odd bits of her old clothing, out of hats he made her buy for him at secondhand shops, out of cast-off jewelry of hers and "treasures" he found put out in the trash up and down the streets of their neighborhood. The ideas came from various sources—films, illustrations in books, television programs, comics. He was in some ways a socially powerful kid: he'd get others to participate, to play complementary roles. Sir Gawain to his Sir Lancelot—wearing an old snoodlike hat of Lottie's, a huge necklace worthy of Mr. T, a "tunic" made by cutting a hole in the middle of an old towel, a bejeweled belt holding it in place.

As she remembered it, though, most of their playtime had actually been spent in the planning stages. "I'll come in and I'll say, 'Avaunt,' and then you say, 'What is your name?' and I'll say . . ."

"No, first I come in and I say . . ." It never got settled; and by the time it might have, they would have passed onto another universe, another interest—prisoners of war planning an escape, football heroes. Yes, Robin Hood. Such cheesy dreams, so passionately embraced. But Lottie understood it—that wish to create a world, to control every detail, to be in charge, always, of what was coming next. She shared every one of those impulses, she thought.

When everything was set in the kitchen, Lottie called, "Chow time," and they slowly meandered out, still talking. Lottie went back for the fan and set it on the kitchen counter. Through the meal it blew the hot kitchen air across their faces, lifting Elizabeth's hair from her neck at slow regular intervals. They talked about food, about diets. Lottie described several of the more bizarre ones she'd discovered while doing her diet book. Elizabeth told them about a cooking school she'd gone to, briefly. Ryan complained about English food. It grew darker outside, and Lottie lighted the candles.

Ryan was finished. He stood up. "I'm history," he said. "I'll be late, I think, Ma. Don't worry."

She made a face, and he grinned at her and shook his head.

Lottie had caught Ryan with Jessica by this time, and she had to will herself not to think about what the rest of each evening would hold for him when he disappeared routinely at ten-thirty or eleven o'clock. In fact, she realized, she really had no idea. Two nights earlier, driving to the Square at around eleven-thirty to make a last-minute run for a book, she was waiting for the light to change at the Porter Square subway stop, when suddenly a group of kids she'd paid virtually no attention to, kids who'd been quietly seated on the circle of benches in that little urban park, jumped up yelling and sprang into a dancelike motion. They did a kind of elaborate do-si-do, their skinny legs kicking loosely around, and ended up, within about five seconds, each sitting opposite the place where he'd been sitting before. Ryan, she saw abruptly, was one of them, was bent over now with the rest of them, laughing; and when the light changed, Lottie drove on in such befuddlement about the innocence and humor of this, that within a block it seemed to her she must have imagined the whole scene.

Now the three adults pushed their chairs back and stretched out. For a while they sat at the littered table, talking and moving the empty plates and glasses around. Lottie noted that they'd drunk three bottles of wine among them, though she hadn't had very much. Someone had been working fast. Suddenly Elizabeth pointed to the huge bright-orange canister sitting on the floor in a corner. "What is this immense, lethal-looking machine, Char? The hair dryer from hell?"

It was the steamer, Lottie told her. Rented for the weekend. Ryan had been doing the upstairs hall and the living room, stripping wallpaper. "I'll finish tomorrow, if I have the stamina."

"But why don't we work on it tonight?" Elizabeth asked. "Cam and I will help you. We should do something constructive with all this drunken energy."

Lottie tried to put her off, mostly because she was tired after her own long day; but Elizabeth insisted, and in the end, they separated to change into work clothes, Cam going to Ryan's room to find some of his, Lottie and Elizabeth heading upstairs.

Elizabeth began pulling off her clothes as she stepped into the room. Lottie was slower, embarrassed to be wearing no bra, especially when she saw Elizabeth's underwear. It was silk, a sort of café-au-lait color, with creamy lace trim. The bra and underpants matched. Unthinkable to Lottie. She crouched, holding her own fat, small breasts, the one scarred white from surgery and the radioactive rods that had laced through it for the last treatment. Awkwardly she pulled out a baggy T-shirt and a paint-stained pair of white work pants with a elastic waist, and handed them up to Elizabeth.

Elizabeth even got dressed with sweeping, bold gestures, Lottie thought. She herself turned away, pulled her work clothes on quickly, hunched over with a schoolgirl's embarrassment. When she looked back at Elizabeth, she laughed out loud. The pants and shirt were much too small, and Elizabeth looked gangly and preposterous, her midriff showing, the pants barely as long as pedal pushers on her. "Your dress-up," Lottie told her, "is not as good as mine."

Elizabeth looked down and laughed too. Then she said, "If you're not nice to me, I'll tell Cam you're teasing again."

When they came downstairs, Lottie moved the steamer to the living room and fired it up. They took turns wielding the pad and scraping. Cameron brought the radio in, and they listened while they worked to *Little Walter's Time Machine*, all the old rhythm and blues, the early black groups Lottie hadn't even guessed at the existence of while she bought forty-fives by Pat Boone and Johnny Mathis.

There were three layers of wallpaper. The bottom one was probably original with the house—faded bouquets of flowers. Over that was a garish plaid, probably from the thirties. And on top of that was the wallpaper Lottie had grown up with, a sort of fake Pennsylvania Dutch motif, patched here and there where it had been torn or scratched. "This is like peeling back the layers of family history," she said, pulling off a long, satisfying strip.

"Only you never get anywhere," Cam said. "Just down to this blank wall." His voice was, surprisingly, bitter. His face was turned away from her, but Lottie glanced at Elizabeth and saw that she was startled too. It made Lottie remember his loving-kindness to their mother and wonder at it again.

Elizabeth had taken off her jewelry upstairs and left it on Lottie's bed. While Lottie was scraping above her on the stepladder, she looked down at Elizabeth's hands. They were holding the steamer pad pressed against the wall just below her. Elizabeth's head was thrown back—she was laughing at something Cameron had said— so she didn't see Lottie's face as Lottie took in the scars drawn across the insides of both wrists. Old scars, white, and maybe not that deep, not that serious. But an unexpected sign of her capacity for sorrow, for pain. *Elizabeth!* Lottie thought. And felt, for the first time, a sense of compassion for the other woman, of connection to her.

It was after two when they finished, and they sat in the nearly empty living room and had more wine to celebrate. Cameron was talking about the bookstore, about the difference between the used section and the new. "It actually works about the opposite of the way you'd romanticize it. Or the way I'd romanticized it anyhow. It isn't wonderfully erudite, educated people who care about used books. On the contrary, by God. Because used books, finally, are collectible objects—like, let's say, snuffboxes or walking sticks. As opposed to books as content—as ideas, language, story. *Words*, which is what people buy new books for. I mean, there are always a few people looking for an out-of-print book, or an old one, because they read it a long time ago and remember it and want to own it. Or because they need it for scholarly work or something. But most people upstairs just want to know what edition, what year, what binding, what endpapers—that kind of thing. The content is utterly immaterial. And the worst, of course, are the decorators. 'What do you have seven feet of in deep maroon?' "

" 'A kind of dried-bloody color, preferably,' " Elizabeth trilled, and they looked at each other and smiled. It occurred to Lottie that they were in the process of working up some of those set pieces that couples who've been together a long time develop.

Richard Lester came in—from where? Lottie wondered; where did *he* go until this time every night?—and Cam insisted he join them. Lottie got him a little glass too and poured him the last of the wine. They made an odd party, sitting in the half-dark living room with their jelly glasses on the floor by each chair. Little Walter squawked and blew horns on the radio between songs. Cameron and Elizabeth and Lottie were drenched with sweat and steam. Their clothes stuck to them, along with bits of old wallpaper and clots of glue. Elizabeth's makeup had steamed off, her hair was limp and straggling. All her elegance was gone, but she turned her charm on Richard anyway, and he seemed to expand in its bright light. He confided in them about the progress of his thesis, his job hunt. Lottie felt ashamed of all her small meannesses to him, the judgments she'd passed. And she clearly saw Elizabeth's flirtatiousness not just as compulsive behavior, not necessarily as a way for her to get something, but as a gift too, a generous gift that she made to others.

A slow song came on, and Elizabeth cried out, "Oh, Little

Anthony!" She leaned forward in her chair abruptly and said, "Let's dance," to Richard.

He flushed deeply, he tried to fuss and demur—small noises, murmurs and ticking in his throat. But in the meantime Cam had stood up and pulled Lottie to her feet. Now Elizabeth rose too and held out her hand to Richard. He struggled to heave himself up out of the chair. Cam reached down and jacked the volume up on the radio, and they all began to move slowly around the room. Cam felt strange to Lottie, so much closer to her own size than Jack. Cam and Elizabeth and Lottie sang loudly along with the lyrics. ". . . and tempt! the hand of Fate . . ." Richard held Elizabeth out in a formal, ballroom posture and moved awkwardly, but his face was opened in a foolish, sweaty smile.

It only lasted for perhaps ten minutes—through two or three songs—before the music got fast again and they stopped. Cam turned the volume lower, and Richard stood painfully thanking them for the wine and excusing himself for several minutes before disappearing up the stairs. Cameron and Elizabeth said their good nights too. Just as they walked into the front hall and were about to leave, though, Rosie and the Originals came on, singing "Angel Baby." Cam said, "The last dance," and put his arms around Elizabeth. They glided back into the living room together, and Lottie trailed after them and leaned against the bare, damp-smelling plaster wall to watch. Elizabeth's eyes were shut, Cam held her in the way they'd danced in high school, pinning one arm against her waist in back, the other held low, along their legs. They seemed bolted together at the pelvis, and their upper bodies swayed with a rolling, sexual motion.

It was nearly three o'clock. Even in the dim, reflected light of the living room, they both looked tired, they looked their age. Elizabeth seemed a plain, forty-fivish woman, carrying on her face, too, the scars of the things that had hurt her in life. But they moved smoothly together, they moved like the teenagers they'd been when they learned to move this way; and their worn faces were imprinted with such an intense pleasure that Lottie felt rising in herself a belief in their foolish happiness, a wistful hope that it might hold out against all the odds.

*   *   *

132

By now Lottie had all but stopped working, though she would have had sufficient solitude in Cambridge and enough time to do whatever she liked. She might have accomplished a great deal. Indeed, she had planned to. She had started to. In the first few days after she'd sold the dining room table and chairs to the cigar-smoking dealer from Widespread Depression—the store specialized in furniture of that era—she'd moved a small drop-leaf table from the hall into the dining room, opened it up, and set out all her books, her notes. And at first she had lost herself, that's how she thought of it, in reading, in making more notes. Even after Ryan arrived, she had most evenings to herself since he was so often out. Occasionally she worked on the house project, but more of the time she sat in the dining room at her makeshift desk, her legs hooked around the legs of a chair, her eyes moving slowly down the pages of print under the bright gooseneck lamp left behind by one of the tenants who'd moved out.

She'd already read the popular literature. That had been the easy part, the boring part—the books on love addicts, self-destructive love, men who can't love, women who can't stop. Earlier, in Chicago, she'd read some Freud, some legitimate psychology, some sociology. Now she'd begun the random circling though fiction, biography, letters, poetry, that was almost always part of what she loosely termed research. This was the aspect of her work Lottie usually loved best. She thought of it as her true education; the B.A. she'd finally gotten from Roosevelt was simply too hard-won, too much an issue of scraping together whatever it took—time, books, pages written, money—either to have left her enough energy to absorb much of what she was learning or to have been pleasurable, except as an unlikely achievement. No, this slow meandering-with-something-in-mind that had started after she began to specialize in medical issues, this had taught her more than all those years of earnest scholarship wedged between Ryan's feedings and baths, between PTA meetings and Little League games, between her job and the occasional bit of social life. Sometimes she felt a nearly erotic pleasure in the simple, physical piling up of the books to be gone through, a kind of thrill as she sat down at a desk or table strewn with them or with pages of notes, or articles clipped from the paper or Xeroxed in the law library or the medical library.

She'd done stories on jogging, on birth control, on pregnancy.

On anorexia, on the changing images of perfection in women's body types. On the politics of midwifery. On breast implants. On the spurious medical labeling of beauty products. On women and mental disease. When she was in the middle of an article, the apartment would be littered with splayed books—texts, poetry, novels—and with Xeroxes, with scraps of paper, notes she'd gotten up to make to herself in the middle of the night.

When Ryan had asked her once how she could stand it, she'd been honestly surprised. She'd looked around and seen it, momentarily, as he did: a terrible mess, a problem. She'd made an effort to keep it more contained after that. She'd actually bought herself a worktable and tried not to let her books and papers stray too far from it. But the truth was that she loved it, she loved the mess, she loved the sheer mass of paper and words and ideas.

Quite a few of the books stacked at her mother's house were on loan from Cameron. That first night she was in town, when they'd had dinner together in his apartment, she'd explained her idea to him. "I'm working on the article about love now. What I want, I think, is somehow to defend excess. To find examples of emotion that would be termed aberrant and talk about their importance." She didn't mention Jack, or the conflict between them. "Who should I read? Who do you recommend?"

"Well, run like hell from Flaubert this time," he said. She'd told him about Flaubert's extravagant grief.

"Yeah. I guess old Emma gets her comeuppance for romantic thinking, doesn't she?"

"Emma's the least of it. The only romance he allows is with Art." He'd gotten up from the table and turned on the spots that shone on the bookshelves. Blinking in the brighter light, they'd both moved in front of them. Lottie watched Cameron's hands slide lovingly, quickly over the spines of the books, as though he were reading the titles through his fingertips. He'd pulled out five or six volumes for her. *Romeo and Juliet*. Stendhal. Shakespeare's Sonnets. John Donne. A collection of short stories by Turgenev. C. S. Lewis.

Some of them she'd read before. Some she read for the first time at the table in the dining room or curled up in her mother's bed. But the more she read, the more it all seemed part of the argument in her head. Everything stalled her, threw her back into her own confused life, just as watching Cameron and Elizabeth falling in love did, just as hearing a schmaltzy song on the radio could. "Memory," for instance. Or even—God help her!—Barry Manilow.

It was as though Lottie had forgotten how she used to spend her days. She made herself recall it, she instructed herself about her habits. But as she thought about it, she realized that it had been a while since she'd worked well. She saw that even during the months at Jack's house she'd been off her stride.

What's more, she didn't know now how to recapture her sense of focus, of energy, about this article. She had thought it would write itself, really, so eager was she to expose the folly of current prescriptions about love. *Oh yes!* her heart had sung when she read of crazy Turgenev, attaching himself permanently to the household of his beloved Pauline: the third wheel of all time, with a speaking tube connecting his apartment to the music and conversations in her study below. *Heaven!* she thought when she discovered Aristophanes' theory about man as originally a four-legged, four-armed, two-headed creature, divided and set to search forever for his missing half.

But nothing came of all this. She just went around in circles.

One night—this was about ten days before the accident—she was reading Donne's love poetry. Just a few of them before she dropped off to sleep, she told herself. She was propped up in bed, and the circle of light fell on the worn white sheets and across the yellowed pages of the old book. A musty smell rose from it as Lottie turned the pages, a smell that weighted the words with physical meaning for her. "For, not in nothing, nor in things / Extreme, and scattering bright," she read, "can love inhere."

She thought of Jack, of course. In what did her love for him inhere? She rolled back on the bed. His goodness, it seemed to her. And then she laughed out loud. Excellent, Lottie. Hardly extreme, hardly scattering bright. "Come on," she said. And she made herself remember his unavailability at the time she met him, reminded herself that that was then the *sine qua non* for any of her relationships. And of course, she had rather liked certain hotels he took her to. Now she was getting extreme. His rangy body and big hands, she thought. His voice. His fidelity, as she saw it—Megan surely wouldn't—to Evelyn through all those years.

And then suddenly Lottie was remembering a conversation she'd had with him one night in her old apartment, several years before they were married, when Evelyn was still alive. He was talking about Evelyn; he told Lottie that what he'd missed most immediately about her after her first stroke was the way she did her hair. "She has beautiful hair," he'd said. "Heavy and dark and full, and she used to wear it in what I think you call a French braid. Do you know what I mean?"

Lottie said yes, she knew what that was. She had asked about Evelyn. Though Jack was almost never willing to speak of her, tonight he had started, and Lottie felt she had to be very still, very blank, in order not to make him stop. The room was dark: maybe this was some of it—what allowed him to drift into memory. And Ryan was away at a friend's house for the night. It felt to Lottie as though she and Jack were alone on an island in her bed; she had invited Evelyn to join them, and for once he had allowed it.

"Anyway," he continued, "she braided it and then coiled it in back and pinned it somehow, very elaborately. Every day. Only, of course, after the stroke she couldn't. And she looked so . . . unadorned, so ordinary without it, that I felt *grieved*, sometimes, just looking at her. I actually fired the first nurse because she didn't know how to do it—how to braid Evelyn's hair that way." He laughed, hoarsely. His head was resting uncomfortably on Lottie's stomach, but she didn't move. Outside her windows, she heard a car pass in a muffled, distant rumble over the snowy street. The flakes had been falling thick and lush for four or five hours. She hadn't pulled the curtains when they came to bed, and both of them were turned to watch the whited air.

"The agency really let me have it," he said. "They were nurses, not hairdressers, and so on. And of course that was right." A puff of wind hurried the snow sideways, and then it seemed to halt, momentarily suspended in air, before it began to float down again. "I knew that." He cleared his throat. "I called a hairdresser after that, to come to the house, and he tried it a couple of times, but it never looked the same. So for a while she wore it just in a braid down her back, something the nurse could easily do. And then, later, I had them cut it." His head moved just slightly from side to side on Lottie's belly. "I can't tell you the feeling of loss. I actually wept. I wept over her hairdo, of all things. What a betrayal of her. Of who she was. Because she wore it like that to get it out of the way, so she wouldn't have to bother with it through the day."

Lottie had lain there, breathing evenly and quietly, and added the French braid to what little she really knew of who Evelyn was: she'd been a good cook, a good tennis player, a slapdash housekeeper. She hadn't been able to quit smoking, and Jack felt guilty about that—that he hadn't somehow forced the issue. He thought it had probably contributed to her stroke. "I don't know that you would have liked her," he had said once to Lottie. "She was, I suppose, an old-fashioned sort of woman. Just enough older than you to have believed that marriage and a family were it, were enough."

What was left, Lottie wondered now, that Jack had loved, when these things—extreme and scattering bright—weren't part of Evelyn anymore? She lay in her mother's bed, in her mother's house, and she would have liked to ask him this. "When Evelyn was strapped in her wheelchair all day, when she signaled her pleasure—in food or your arrival home—with an animal cry, what then did you love in her?"

And then Lottie thought of a lover she'd had—the only serious, long-lasting love in all those years between Derek and Jack. He was a funny man, a wry man, and Lottie had been incredibly fond of him, though they never lived together. Sometimes she had let herself imagine that one day they might. Maybe after Ryan was a little older, easier for someone else to be around.

The second winter they were involved, there was a terrible snowstorm in the Midwest. The roads out in the suburbs where Avery lived weren't cleared for several days, and he was stuck. In addition, Lottie's telephone was out of service. To talk to Avery, she had to walk down to the deli a few blocks from her apartment and use the pay phone. She had to stand in line behind other people whose phones were also not working, who were all trying to conduct the urgent business of life armed with a pocketful of dimes. While you waited, leaned against the wall with take-out coffee, you could hear arguments, business arrangements, tears, vows of love, drug deals. When Lottie's turn came, she'd dial Avery's number and feel that they had nothing worth that much effort or passion to say to each other. And somehow because of that it occurred to her that he was a foolish man, more than anything.

And nearly as abruptly as that, her love for him began to diminish. All the things that had charmed her, interested her, simply lost their magic and were absorbed into his foolishness, as she saw it. When he asked her what was wrong—and he did, of course—Lottie didn't know how to respond. I don't like to look at you anymore? I'm not interested in you anymore? Impossible. Slowly they separated, though understandably he made one or two quite ugly scenes before it was finished. In what had that love inhered, that it could be over so abruptly?

Maybe what Lottie was feeling now, with Jack, was the end of her love for him in that same way. She remembered her relief in the anonymous solitude of the Holiday Inn in Pennsylvania. Even now, restless and miserable as she was in her mother's house, wasn't there a kind of pleasure in reclaiming herself? Perhaps her substituting fantasy for who Jack really was constituted a kind of infidelity to him, a way of escaping his love. Maybe she'd never truly been in love with Jack. Maybe she'd never truly been in love at all. Maybe part of what had made her angry when she found Ryan and Jessica in her bed the weekend after the cookout was that Ryan was behaving just as she so often had. "Haven't you ever wanted just some good old meaningless sex?" he'd asked her. Yes. Oh yes indeed, she surely had. And for years, that's all she'd had, even when at the time she'd thought of it as full of meaning.

Perhaps this was what she was suited to, was all she was suited to. Perhaps her mean growing up had unfitted her, finally, for deep feeling, for the kind of love that could last years, as Cameron's and Elizabeth's had; or through hard times, as Jack's love for Evelyn had; or through the kind of distance she felt between herself and Jack now.

Lottie hiked herself up again in bed; she turned over to rest on her elbow, bent over the book. She flipped through the pages. "Love is a growing, or full constant light," she read. "And his first minute, after noon, is night."

As soon as she felt her throat tighten at this, she made herself get up. She put on clothes—a loose long T-shirt, a short skirt, her heeled sandals. She picked up her purse and went outside. The street was deserted. She got into her car, and for some minutes she sat there clutching the steering wheel like a child pretending to drive. She couldn't think where to go, what to do, but she was outraged at herself for feeding her own melodramatic instincts in this way. John Donne as the *I Ching* of love! It wouldn't do!

When she started the car, the radio came on too, at tremendous volume, a station of Ryan's. She slammed the Off button. In the silence left behind, her wounded heart was jumping wildly. Slowly she drove to Garden Street, then headed roughly for the Square; and then, just because there was a parking place opposite the Common, she parked. She got out, locked the car, and walked through the open gateway into Radcliffe Yard, into the wet-smelling dark. Here and there a pretty, inadequate lantern twinkled.

She came out on Brattle Street and headed into the sound of music, of several different bands, actually, playing at the same time. As she got closer in she could see the groups of pedestrians stopped in clusters here and there—in open doorways, in the well in front of a clothing store just below street level, on the brick-paved traffic island. Stopped to listen, to watch the odd magician or juggler, to drop a quarter or a dollar into an opened guitar or violin case.

She stood in the back of a group listening to some Andean music, the mournful sprightly pipes over the rhythm of the drums and the guitar. The closed, grave faces of the Indians commanded respect, and Lottie, like the rest of the group, stayed until they'd finished their set. She left a dollar, though it was beneath any of them to take notice of this; they had turned to each other in a circle and were tuning their instruments.

Lottie went into one of the bookstores. The lights were bright in the store, and people sat cross-legged on the floor in the narrow aisles to read whole chapters for free. You had to be careful not to kick them, to trip. At first Lottie was just browsing in paperback fiction. But then she thought of Tolstoy, "The Kreutzer Sonata." She'd never read it, but she knew what it was, and it occurred to her it would be the perfect antidote to all her moony love reading. A little bitter pill. A brittle little trill. She went to the T's and found it in a collection of Tolstoy's short fiction. On the cover of the book was a photograph of the homely man himself in his middle age, scowling sternly back at Lottie as though he hadn't had, too, the occasional foray into meaningless sex. Then, on an impulse, she pulled out *Anna Karenina* too. Maybe she'd reread it.

She carried both books to the cash register. When she'd paid, when they'd been put in a plastic bag, Lottie walked out, happy again. She ambled slowly back through the couples with ice cream cones, through the straggling groups of summer school students who made it necessary for people to step off the curb, to hug the storefronts. The bag swung against her leg, the books slapped her rhythmically as she walked along in the cheerful carnival atmosphere.

Past Appian Way the street was abruptly darker, quieter. Lottie turned back into Radcliffe Yard, feeling the air shift, welcoming the sense of dampness, of dark. She first heard, then saw, a group of young men two thirds of the way across the black grass, clustered around an old, tentacled fruit tree. Their voices were loud and flat. There was a laugh, then someone said, "The *fuck* you say . . ." *Bad boys*, Lottie thought. And then reassured herself: Ryan might be in such a group. She kept walking, but without thinking of it, she made her step brisker and more businesslike. She could hear the slapping, tarty scuff of her sandals on the sidewalk.

And then they noticed it, she could feel them noticing with a kind of doglike attentiveness. There was a pause, and one of them called, "Hey, baby, over here"; and they laughed again.

Just keep walking, Lottie thought. She clutched the bag and her purse against her chest.

Now one of them angled out from under the tree, across the grass toward her. Unless she turned, she would encounter him.

She wouldn't turn. This was just their idea of a joke. Scaring her, talking a little dirty maybe: just fun, for them. She concentrated on keeping her stride even, but she stepped to the right side of the walk, toward where she would turn off quickly when she got to the little side path that led to Garden Street.

He was tall, the boy approaching her, he had a predatory strut. He passed under one of the dim lights, and she saw him grinning.

She was almost up to him, and she braced herself for it: the comment, the ugliness, the claim to some part of what made her female.

But he stopped before she did. No smile; then a wider one, amused. He turned and called over to his friends. "Hey, man, she's *old!*" He started to walk back to them. "She's fucking *old*, you assholes!"

CHAPTER 8

It was the third week in July when Jack called. Lottie had already been gone longer than she'd told him she would. "You're learning to get along without me, aren't you?" he asked in his hoarse voice. "I think I'd better come out there and remind you of what you've left behind." He told Lottie that Megan was going to a friend's house in Michigan for the next weekend. He had arranged coverage and booked a round trip to Boston. "Will that work for you?" he asked, and Lottie could hear all that was tentative in his tone.

Her own answering voice was shaky, but they arranged it quickly, getting to the point without much conversation, like the flurried undressing for hungry sex. Lottie would get a hotel; who needed Richard and Ryan listening in? Jack would come there by cab from the airport. The plane got in at eight. He ought to be with her by nine or so.

For the next days, Lottie was distracted, repetitively reviewing the history of her love for Jack, her life with him, as though she'd been asked to decide, in this short span of hours before he arrived, whether to stay with him or not. She felt a kind of heartsickness as she remembered the way they'd lived together in the days before she left: so careful with each other, so polite. "I can't go back," she thought she might say to him. "You have to understand, I was dying." But how could she say such a thing to him, who knew what dying truly was.

That was part of the trouble, surely: how could she say such a thing to him? There were too many things she couldn't say to him. She had no right.

Instead, then, she thought of the house itself, Jack's house, as the problem. It was too thick, too heavy, an impossible burden their marriage had to carry. She imagined it again and again with a kind of dread: brick and enormous, set far back from the street on a neat lawn in a neighborhood near the university. The front terrace had a huge cement urn at each corner. Lottie had peered into one once. It was filled with gravel and a few ancient cigarette filters. Inside, the rooms were all large, gracious, the windows heavy, with leaded panes in the top halves. You could be in Lottie and Jack's bedroom and not know whether anyone else was home, whether Megan and her friends were talking in the den or the living room. There *was* a den. A den, a living room, a study, a kitchen, a dining room, a maid's room. That was just the first floor.

The streets around the house were solid with other silent, digni-fied homes, just like Jack's. There wasn't a café, a bar within walking distance. There wasn't a laundromat—why would there be?—or a bookstore or a bulletin board. When Lottie left the house, she never walked. She got in the car and drove to Hyde Park. Often, actually, she drove to the North Side, where she'd lived with Ryan, and she cruised the crowded bungalows in her old neighborhood, stopped at places she'd gone to then.

This was unfair, she'd told herself. This was just a kind of homesickness for her old life that she was blaming Jack for. And she made herself number the reasons she'd come to love him. The fact that he could play the clarinet part to "Miss Brown to You." How once in making love, after she'd carefully lowered herself onto him, adjusting her hips a little this way and that, he'd said, "Prettily arranging her skirts." How his exuberant gray hair, which he combed down so tidily each morning, gradually rose and took on a life of its own over his long workday. Yes, of course, how he'd taken care of Evelyn.

But then she remembered, too, the time he'd come to join her at a hotel in Seattle when she was on the road doing publicity for the diet book. When he'd called that time, he didn't ask if he could come, his voice was not hesitant. "I'm coming out," he'd said. "I'm going to lavish money and sex on you whether you like it or not."

That was what she wanted, Lottie thought. That ease, that honesty. That need. She wondered if she could conjure it, if she could set them both free from the spell they seemed to be under. This weekend, this weekend, she swore, she'd make it happen, she'd make it be the way it was before between them.

The room at the hotel overlooked the Public Garden. Through the thick veil of leaves Lottie could see the drooping willow fronds over the rain-pocked water, and white glimpses of the tethered swan boats. The light by the bed was too bright, so she went downstairs to the lobby and bought a very expensive red silk scarf in the little shop there, which she thought she could drape over it. There was still more than an hour until the time Jack might be expected to arrive. Lottie stood in the shop and leafed through a magazine or two, and then she walked outside into the rain, across the street and down a winding path into the green of the garden. It was getting dark, the rain was light, and the air smelled of the sea. The living swans, as motionless as their giant wooden replicas, slept, floating close to the grassy banks, their heads tucked under their wings. Halfway around the pond, she passed a couple, laughing and jockeying for position under a small, collapsible umbrella. She realized abruptly how wet she was getting, and turned back. At the hotel, though, she didn't feel ready to go up to the room. Instead she found the lounge and had a glass of wine, sitting by a window looking out into the rain. There was a young man in a tux at the grand piano in the center of the room, playing Gershwin and Cole Porter tunes. He had on black, high-cut gym shoes, Lottie noted. Outside, the streetlamps had come on.

Finally she went upstairs. She tried the scarf over the lamp. A bit bordello-like, but better. She turned the light off. She opened the narrow, moveable portions of the window, welcomed in the heavy air, the faint sibilance of the rain and wet things stirring in the slight breeze.

She called the airport. The plane was on the ground, just arriving. She was nervous, as she'd been with Jack in only the craziest times. She went into the fancy bathroom and brushed her teeth. She fussed with makeup, covering a blemish. Then she decided that the

143

cover-up itself was too visible, washed her face, and started all over. By the time she heard his knock on the door, she had actually changed into the nightgown he had given her, and then, when it occurred to her he might want to undress her, into street clothes again.

She was at the door within seconds. His embrace engulfed her— the length of him!—her throat clogged, and she couldn't speak. She'd forgotten him, the way it felt to be held by him, his doctor smell, as she thought of it, the solid flat of his back under the fabric of his shirt, the long muscles of his thighs. It was at once familiar and completely strange, and it suddenly occurred to Lottie how little she knew him, that his touch could shake her this way.

Lottie pulled him over to the bed. "C'mere, c'mere." Her voice was rough and strained. They fell on the fancy coverlet, grappling, laughing.

"But it's lovely to *see* you," Jack said, artificially formal. He pushed the dampened hair back from her face.

But Lottie didn't want to be looked at, didn't want to make jokes. She pulled his face to hers, mouthed his jawline, his cheek. Then his lips, her body convulsing against the length of his. Her fingers clutched at his shirt buttons and worked them open, pushed frantically at his belt. He rolled away and reached down to undo his pants, to push them down, his hips arching up. Lottie hoisted her skirt to her waist, and he helped her with her panties. She was stroking him already, pressing against him, bucking rhythmically.

"Shh, darling, it's all right," he said. "It's all right."

She felt him try to slow her with his weight, but that wasn't what she wanted. With her teeth, her tongue, she stroked his chest, then his shoulder. Her mouth made senseless pleading noises, "Hnhh, hnhh." She lifted herself against him, her legs rose, opening her-self—she thought of this as a gripping, a reaching too—and then he was in her, she pumped violently, she bit down hard on his shoul-der's flesh and heard him gasp.

He pushed up, he arched away from her desperation and moved them now to the slower rhythm he chose. It was twilight in the room. He was a dark shadow humping over her, her own feet and legs like wings rising above his shoulders. The cars rushed past outside in long sighs. Jack cupped his hands under her buttocks and lifted her against him. His thumbs pushed her thighs down open, more open, and he shifted her to please them both so easily that she forgot her greed, she forgot her body as the dense form she lived in daily—it was so light, so insubstantial that it was only feeling, a space, a beautiful dark room with the doors opening out on sun, air. "Darling," he cried, and then more urgently.

"Oh, say *Lottie*," she whispered, and he did.

They lay heaped together for a while, panting, then side by side on their backs, watching the reflected light from outside slur across the ceiling. They began to talk, slowly. His voice floated over Lottie. "That was lovely."

"I was too hungry for you," she said.

"You were pretty scary," he said. She didn't answer. "We have lots of time, you know. All the time in the world."

"Mmm," she said.

His hand moved over between her legs and she opened to it. His fingers slid down her, then pulled up, cuplike, and spread the warmed syrup, rubbed it in cooling circles on her belly, in her coiling hair. His hand rested on her belly. Their talk idled along. He told her about the summer with Megan, about a visit from his oldest son, Charley. Lottie talked about Ryan, about the house and her pleasure in that work, about her inability to write. It was quiet for a few minutes. Lottie reached over and touched him. "I want to do everything."

"Baby steps first," he said. He rose above her again, unrolled her damp skirt, pulled it down. He eased her arms out of her blouse. He moved his hand over Lottie's belly, down between her thighs again, where it was still slick and warm. Lottie opened her legs, and his fingers moved onto her, into the folds of her flesh with a light, wet sound. "Mmm," she said. "Clickety, clickety."

"My fine hen." He'd already found the right slow rhythm.

Lottie laughed, mostly to herself, and held her knees open at her chest while he knelt back to watch his fingers on her.

Later they decided to get dressed again and go downstairs for a drink and maybe something to eat. "Let's live in a hotel," Lottie said as they walked down the wide silent hallway to the elevator. "Forever and ever. The hell with our children. The hell with houses and jobs."

He laughed, but when she looked up at him in the big mirror above the console opposite the bank of elevators, his face had already tightened, she saw he was unhappy. She had hurt him. Lottie felt a quick irritation. She glanced quickly back at herself, now blurred her eyes to take them in, Jack-and-Lottie, as a couple. She was startled by their appearance. So respectable. So oddly matched. Next to Jack she looked tiny and delicate, and it always surprised her to see this version of herself, diminished, made so feminine. Mutt and Jeff, she called them to Ryan once. "Who?" he'd said.

Lottie asked to be seated by a window again in the dimmed, plush lounge. The rain was heavier now; it stroked the glass audibly. There was only the odd pedestrian, moving fast. The nuts in the little silver bowl the waiter brought were so good they decided not to have anything else to eat. They each had a glass of wine, then a cognac, and the waiter kept filling the bowl with nuts.

"He disapproves of us," Lottie said. "Moochers, is what he thinks." She was conscious of flirting with Jack now, of trying to win him back.

"I can live with it," Jack said.

"I'm humiliated." Lottie shook her head and smiled across at him. "For both of us."

But Jack was looking out at the steady rain. After a minute he said, "So, Lottie mine, how soon do you think you'll be done?"

Lottie knew he was saying she'd been gone long enough, he wanted her back. She made her voice light. "Murphy's Law: The job expands to fill the time allotted to it."

His light eyes had shifted to her. "I guess that should be my question, then. How much time have you allotted to it?"

Lottie lifted her shoulders. "You talk as though I'd chosen to go away. This is my summer job, remember?"

He watched her face. After a moment he said, "We miss you; that's all I mean to say."

Lottie laughed, and then stopped. "We?" she asked. "Is that the royal we?"

"Megan and I." Then he smiled. "Bader."

"Well, I'm sure Bader does anyway," she said.

He leaned forward. "Lottie, I miss you. I want you home."

Lottie stirred uncomfortably. "I'm not finished here."

He sat back again. He reached for his cognac but just held the bowl of the glass in his long fingers. Lottie shifted uncomfortably.

"We're not talking just about your mother's house, are we?" he said finally.

Lottie didn't answer. For a while longer she didn't want to talk about their marriage, or Evelyn, or anything difficult. There was a little decorated matchbox on the table, and she picked it up now and shook it, opened it. Inside, the matches were wooden, long and white. "Look," she said. "How fancy."

"Lottie . . . ," he began.

"Shh, no," she said. "Please. Let's not. Please, let's be happy. Let's play a game."

He relaxed back in his chair, and she looked over at him. His face had fallen somehow; he looked defeated and sad.

Lottie had made her voice light again. She was explaining the rules as she laid the matches out on the table in expanding rows. They played a sample game. She won.

"Marienbad. It's an odd name for a game," he said as she was laying the matches out again.

"It's from the movie," Lottie said. He looked blank. "Don't you remember that old movie? *Last Year at Marienbad?*"

"I don't think I do. Probably it came out one of the times Evelyn was ill."

"Oh no, it was long before that," she said irritably. Why did everything have to connect to Evelyn? "I think I saw it with Derek. Of course he loved it. Very mysterious. Maybe very pretentious too." She paused. "I should probably see it again now, actually. It was about love. I *think* it was about love, so maybe I could use it."

"What happened in it?"

"Oh, it had no plot. Or no recognizable one. It was just a series of visual images, as I recall, repeated over and over, like memories being formed. One was—I think I'm not making this up—this woman in a sun-filled room, falling back on a bed, and then falling again. And then again. Elegant woman. Some French actress, Simone or Delphine or Monique Something-or-other. She had a boa."

"Is *that* the way memories get formed? By repeating images, you think?" He seemed genuinely to want to know.

"For me, yes. Pictures I call up. In life, of course, you can change them a bit. Or you do, I think. You see different things at different times, or you see them in different ways." She frowned. "They might have in this movie too, actually. Done it differently each time. It might not just have been exactly the same frames being repeated. I can't remember. That would be more interesting, of course." His eyes were steady on her, but he seemed to be smiling, and this pleased Lottie. "I go first this time," she said, and she picked up two matches.

"There's a trick here," he said.

"Of course. And I know it."

"And I don't." He lifted up a whole row. "Would you like a boa, Lottie?"

She looked up at him quickly, grateful. Maybe everything would be all right. "If it'd make you remember me over and over, yes, I would." She picked up four matches from another row.

"It might, as I think about the possibilities."

Lottie laughed. "You're a dirty, dirty man."

"Thanks," he said, and shrugged with stylized modesty.

She was about to win again. Abruptly she scooped all the matches from the table. She began to put them in the box.

"What?" he said.

"Let's stop," she said. "I'm tired of whupping you. It's too easy."

"I'll remind you later that you said that."

"What?"

"That what's too easy is tiring, boring."

Lottie felt the pulse of irritation again—at his seriousness, at the return to the same theme. "That's not what I said," she told him. "I make no such rule. You want some things to be easy. And even if it makes things boring, I wouldn't aspire to difficulty on that account."

He signaled the waiter for the check. Then he turned to her. "You never have to aspire to difficulty, darling. It arrives, uninvited. Then it stays for dinner." He was looking at Lottie with his light eyes. Suddenly he was smiling again, his broad easy grin. "Remember that stripper in the bar near the Loop, Lottie? She had a boa."

"I remember her, God knows. Not the boa, though."

"Now that's funny. I remember the boa. Over and over."

Lottie laughed.

The bed was made up when they returned, the coverlet removed, and the requisite chocolates wrapped in gold foil floated

148

on the pressed pillowcases without making a dent. When Lottie came out of the bathroom, Jack was standing by the closet, taking off his clothes, hanging them up. She crossed the room to turn on the lamp with the scarf over it, then came back and switched off the overhead light. Just then Jack bent to pull his shorts off his long legs, his big feet. His body suddenly looked storklike and unwieldy to Lottie. How much work he had in life, living in such a body! The entire length of each articulated limb to worry about, those enormous hands and feet. She felt a rush of love for him, and remembered a passage from one of the books she'd read this summer: Edna Pontellier in *The Awakening* defending her love for Robert, defending it on the grounds that his hair was brown, that he had a little finger permanently bent from a baseball accident. *Just so*, she thought. She ran her hand down the long, shaped muscles of Jack's buttocks. "Just so," she said aloud. He laughed.

While she peeled her clothes off, he lay back on the bed in the pinkish light. "Ah." His penis rested sideways, heavy-looking, slightly stiffened, across his thigh. He gestured at the lamp. "This is as good as a boa, almost."

Lottie crawled onto the bed, bent over him on her hands and knees, took him into her mouth. After she was finished, and had lain back too, he rose up and slowly, sleepily, returned the favor. She watched him for a few moments down what seemed the long slope of her body: the shock of gray hair, the kind, worn face moving between her legs as though he wanted to nuzzle his way inside her. And then she dropped her head back and drifted away, everything eased inside her. She could feel herself flailing around, bucking, moving sideways across the bed. When they stopped, she was wedged into a corner by the headboard, her head nearly at the bed's edge. "My pink, pink Lottie," he said after a while, and she felt his breath on her, and shuddered once more.

"Oh, this is heaven, Jack. I could go on doing this forever."

"Mmm. We'll have to get a few other men in, dear."

"Let's. Let's just stay here forever, having meaningless sex."

He laughed and moved up beside her. "I love a woman who says 'Let's,' " he said. But she thought she heard in his tone the pinch of disapproval again. He lay still next to her, not touching her. Lottie rolled to her side and turned off the light. Later she heard Jack in the bathroom, then over by the windows, closing the curtains. He came back to bed and pulled the covers over Lottie, he lay down next to her again. She listened to his breathing thicken, finally the long slow pulls of sleep. She was glad for his peacefulness; but now she was wide awake.

Meaningless sex, she had said. Why had she said that? It was not what she meant at all.

She was restless; she could have cried out or begun to sing, she felt so wild. Her hand slid down between her legs. She began a slow circling motion. She held her thighs wider apart, pressed her fingers in a smaller, tighter circle. All her muscles were tensed, her heels dug into the mattress. In the dark she bared her teeth, she gasped, she shuddered once, twice, then stopped.

When she lay quiet again, there was silence in the room. Jack's breathing had stilled to its waking rhythm. Her blood slapped in her ears. She listened, as she knew he was listening, to her own breathing come slowly under control. *I won't say anything*, she thought. *There's no need to say anything about it.* And then she fell asleep.

"*There* he is," Jack said, and banged the table with his hand as he stood up. Lottie had seen him too, her own son, but hadn't for a second recognized him in this place, a handsome blond man in an unfamiliar linen jacket and pressed slacks. She hadn't even known he had such a costume. She watched them as Jack reached Ryan across the restaurant, their greeting half handshake, half embrace. She watched them as they weaved back to her table, their faces moving animatedly at each other. Jack was the taller by several inches, but Ryan was larger, more solid. Who were they, to her? These two enormous men. It seemed impossible her life could be so connected to them, so defined by them. She felt almost dizzy with dislocation as they came to claim her.

Over lunch, Ryan talked about himself in response to Jack's questions, and Lottie learned more about what he'd done in England and what he hoped to do than she had in all the weeks they'd been working together. She leaned back in her chair and looked at them. She thought of Jack's sons, Charley and Matthew, and his friendly ease with them too. How good he was! How much she loved him. What was wrong with her that she held her heart so bitterly away from him?

Later in the afternoon, as she and Jack walked slowly to Cameron's apartment, they talked about Ryan, about how differently Lottie felt about him when Jack was around. "I like it," Lottie said. "I like the distance from him. I think of it as the way he'll be with me someday. I like how polite and grown up he is." She sighed. "Why isn't he like that when he's alone with me now?"

"I suppose he's busy creating that same distance in other ways now."

"I'll say. His *eyes*, sometimes. If looks could kill."

They walked down Dartmouth Street, past the skateboarders banging around in front of the Public Library, past the jazzy new Amtrak Station. "I like Boston," Jack said. "I didn't think I did. It used to be such a dour, prissy town."

"I like it too," Lottie said. "But it isn't as though I know it any better than you do. I never came over here when I was growing up. I really knew nothing about it. It was like living in the provinces, then, to live in Cambridge."

"Ah, poor Lottie," he said.

"I'm not complaining, I promise you. Now that I've grown up and seen Duluth, I know better than to complain of my childhood in Cambridge ever again."

Cameron had set out a tray on the trunk in front of the couch, with cheese and fat black olives, big wineglasses and bread. There was a blue bowl full of lemons next to all this, just for beauty, Lottie supposed. He opened a bottle as soon as they'd all greeted one another, and they clunked the heavy wineglasses together and congratulated themselves on this occasion. Cameron and Jack hadn't met before. Cameron was saying now that he was glad Jack had come out, as much on his account as Lottie's. "Though Char certainly deserves a break. Have you seen everything she and Ryan have done?"

"No; we haven't gone over yet."

"Actually, you'd need the Before and After for full effect. It wasn't until after it was cleared out that I realized how horribly Mother lived."

They talked about the house, about the legal process, now almost complete, of having their mother declared incompetent. Cameron and Lottie talked about Richard Lester, about other roomers they remembered over the years. Cam told a story about one of them who'd lived in the house for six years before their mother discovered he was a cross-dresser. "Not full time, you know. And not extreme. Apparently there are subtle gradations. He was, I guess you'd say, a tasteful transvestite. But one night Mother looked up"—here he imitated her blurry lifting of the head—"and sees this . . . dame! this floozy she doesn't know, heading up the stairs. 'Excuse me!' " he said, imitating her high-pitched, indignant tone. " 'Oh, Mrs. Reed, it's only me, it's Stan,' the poor guy says. The upshot was that I got a call the next day, and had to go over and throw Stan out. That was *it*." He shook his head. "I hated to do it to him; he paid his rent regularly and he was very quiet, very neat. But she was adamant. Wouldn't have such a thing in her house, et cetera, et cetera." His face was animate with a kind of anger or disgust that surprised Lottie. Then he looked directly at Jack and smiled, wryly. "This happened four or five years ago. If it was today, he would have sued for his civil rights and stayed forever."

Jack laughed.

"I'm surprised," Lottie said. "I thought Mother was more open-minded than that. Or maybe that she didn't have that much mind left, or something."

"Oh no. She was definitely offended. You'd be surprised at the number of things that offended Mother. Still do. It seems to be a response that outlasts cerebration."

"Uselessly," Lottie said.

They had relaxed by now, they had nearly finished the first glasses of wine, and there were bread crumbs sprinkled over all their laps, olive pits sitting on the plate. Jack had started to talk about his parents, who'd died within months of each other a few years before; when someone knocked on the door. Lottie looked at Cameron's face as he stood up to go and answer it, and knew instantly it was Elizabeth. When he opened the door, she stepped toward him, kissed him lightly. There was a murmured exchange, and his hand rose to her face. Then she came into the room, her wide blue skirt swirling around her. Just like Loretta Young, Lottie thought unkindly, as Jack rose.

"And this is Jack!" Elizabeth said eagerly, her hand extended. "I've heard so much about you!"

This was not true; Lottie had deliberately told her hardly anything; but Jack smiled warmly and let her hold his hand in both of hers as they shook. Lottie looked up at them. Jack and Elizabeth were both tall, leggy, and they looked good together, much better than Cam and Elizabeth did; or than he and Lottie had in the mirror last night. Lottie had a friend who used how people looked together as a gauge of their potential for success as a couple. She and Jack would flunk, Lottie thought now. She should give him to Elizabeth.

"I knew Charlotte would try to keep you to herself," Elizabeth was saying. "So when I heard you were coming to Cameron's for a drink, I wheedled an invitation."

Cameron was fetching another glass from the cupboard above the kitchen counter. "It was beautifully done," he said. "I thought for a while she badly needed to be with me." He came back across the room, holding out the glass, just as Elizabeth dropped into the butterfly chair. "You want wine," he said to her.

"Of course!" she cried. "Tons of wine! No, gallons!" She laughed. "I need to catch up with all of you!" She was wound even tighter than usual, Lottie saw.

Jack had sat down on the couch again, and Lottie leaned toward him a little. He spread his hand on her thigh, as though he felt her need for assurance. He was asking Elizabeth how long she'd been in Boston, and she began to tell him an abbreviated version of the story she'd told Lottie at the beginning of the summer, the story Jack had already heard from Lottie. While Elizabeth was speaking, Lottie looked at Jack's hand on her leg, at the long flat fingers. She remembered once looking down at them spread across her own abdomen and asking him idly whether he thought he might have Marfan's syndrome. He'd snorted. "That's about as likely a diagnosis," he'd said, moving his finger up to the whited dent in her breast, "as my concluding that this is the result of a broken heart."

Lottie's hand rose involuntary to her breast now, and then quickly down.

Cameron's eyes moved from Elizabeth's face to Jack's and Lottie's as Elizabeth talked, assessing their response to her. She's mine, she's mine, they said: what do you think?

They started to talk about the Democratic convention, held the week before, and Cam was being expert about Dukakis, his unlikeliness, his chances or lack thereof. The sun had moved directly opposite Lottie now, and she had to squint to look at Elizabeth and Cameron, so she didn't, for the most part. It made the conversation feel distant and unreal to her, as though she'd taken a powerful drug. "I don't know," Cam said. "Neil Diamond supplying the emotion. It seems a new low to me."

Elizabeth began to reminisce about the politics of the sixties. She'd worked in the McCarthy campaign. "Remember? Get clean for Gene? I bought these little cotton blouses with Peter Pan collars. I eschewed eye makeup. This, in context—well, in my life generally—was a macrosacrifice. I had a circle pin." She clasped her hands to her bosom. "Oh, I behaved so beautifully! And all for naught, of course. But it just felt—well, you remember it, Cam—so cosmically important. And every march! Remember the one in Washington? Cam and I went together," she explained to Lottie and Jack. "What a time!" She shook her head, dazzled by her memories.

Lottie remembered the spring of '68 too, hearing that King had been shot, that Bobby Kennedy had been shot, while Ryan careened and fluttered his way around inside her. She'd felt she'd made a terrible mistake, that she shouldn't be bringing a child into such a world.

"I'm just enough older than you to see it differently," Jack said. "I think it was a terrible and divisive time. I had friends who literally lost their children for years. Other friends who, it seems to me, compromised everything not to lose them."

"What do you mean?" Elizabeth asked. She'd sat forward in her chair, and she was watching Jack's face. Lottie turned to him too. The bright sun was in his eyes as well, and he was squinting, seeming to look far into his past. He talked about parties in Hyde Park and Kenwood, parties where adult children, stoned, offered critiques of their parents' lives, the lives of their parents' friends, while the parents themselves nodded, passionately agreed. "It was delusional, finally," Jack said. "I think those who crossed over thought they could make themselves young again. They paid a high price later. But those who resisted, who argued with their kids, paid a high price too." He shook his head.

"What was the price?" Cam asked.

Jack's shoulders rose. "They lost their children. Quite simply."

"No, I mean the price for those who—how did you put it?— 'went along'?"

"I think I said 'crossed over.' And that varied. Sometimes they were just foolish for a while. Sometimes the foolishness became a permanent condition: I still see some of them around, unable to let

154

themselves become . . . well, elderly, which is what they are at this point, really. Sometimes they lost their marriages—good, stable marriages—for some brief fling with what they saw, I suppose, as youth and passion."

"Why brief?" Cam's voice had a still, dangerous quality. "Why?"

"Yes. Why isn't it possible to conceive of someone really starting over, really discovering something that changes him, that makes a whole new universe of experience possible? Why should that be beyond imagining, just because you're a certain age?"

"I'm not arguing it is."

"You seem to be."

"I'm not. I'm sorry if I sounded that way. I just meant . . ." Jack looked at Lottie. She was watching him and Cameron. "Look, it was a wholesale promise that way, the sixties. I think individual change is possible, can be permanent. But any . . . movement that promises we can all find happiness, any way—love, drugs, whatever—is just wrong. People become what they are over time. There's a kind of cumulative meaning to a life—don't you think?—that isn't so easy to sweep aside." He turned to Lottie again. "It's like what Lottie is working on, this impulse to prescribe emotion, emotional health. People don't live that way. And if they try to, they lose something, something central, I'd say. And the sixties, during that whole Vietnam era, that's what people were trying to do."

Whatever it was that had piqued Cam seemed to have been resolved. He had relaxed back in his chair. And Elizabeth, as though she'd sensed the tension too, began to chatter again—about the war this time, about friends who resisted, friends who fabricated medical deferments, a few friends who went. "God, the endless moral arguments. Was it moral just to evade? Did you have to take a stand? Were you sacrificing enough if you gave up everything to go to Canada?" She shook her head. Her smooth hair swayed. "I actually ended a friendship because the man cheated his way out," she said. "Got a doctor to say he'd been a heavy drug user and was therefore, I don't know, psychologically unreliable, or something. When I think of my own sense of superiority—I, with this much"—she held her forefinger and thumb pressed together in front of her face—"to lose myself, of course."

Jack cleared his throat. "Yes, my first wife and I had those discussions. She was passionately antiwar." Lottie knew this about Evelyn. "She couldn't forgive me for my lack of involvement. Which was a matter of degree, really, because I did agree with her, on one level. But I came from a different life, a small-town life. I had a younger brother who went, who emerged from that same life and went, and what I was uncomfortable with was the venom that seemed to be directed toward those who bought in, as he did. We had some pretty lively discussions at home." He grinned. "She could be pretty high-toned, morally, herself."

Elizabeth laughed her high, excited laugh. They were all silent a few seconds in its wake, thinking, Lottie suspected, thoughts as disparate and self-involved as thoughts could be.

Then Elizabeth slumped back and heaved a thorough sigh. And here came hers: "God, to say—so easily—'my first wife.' Will I ever reach such a stage?"

Lottie felt Jack's fingers tighten momentarily. The equivalent of a flinch. She cleared her throat.

But Cameron was leaning forward and touching Elizabeth's knee. He said, in a too intense voice, "Yes, you will."

Lottie felt she was drowning; she didn't know why she hadn't been able to talk, but she didn't want to listen anymore, either. She tapped Jack's wristwatch through the cuff of his shirt, their signal, and then she stood up, dusting bread crumbs off her pants. "Excuse me a minute," she said. "And then we're going to have to go to dinner, Jack."

She stepped across the painted floor, her footsteps sounding thunderously loud to her. Once inside the bathroom, she could hear them begin to talk again, then she could hear other footsteps. They were up, walking around, beginning to say goodbye. The casement window in the bathroom was open. When she sat on the toilet, she could see out, over the brick buildings to the Prudential Tower and some other high-rises. She wished she could just step out the window and materialize outside on the street. "Step out the window and turn left," as Fats Waller said. She didn't want to have to pass back through Cameron's living room, to make the chitchat necessary to get them out. She surprised herself in the mirror, she looked so composed. She felt frazzled and adolescent.

When she went back out into the big room, though, she saw that Jack had done most of the work. The three others stood by the opened door to the hall, and when Jack heard her, he looked over and held up her purse, to show her they were ready to go.

As they came outside, Lottie took his arm. "God," she said. "I couldn't wait to get out of there."

"Yeah, what was it with you?" he asked. "Why were you so silent?"

Lottie shrugged. After a minute she said, "I don't know. I think I felt threatened by her with you around. I felt suddenly exactly as I had around her as a girl."

"Ridiculous Lottie," he said. "She's a nice enough woman. But also a particular version of a pain in the ass, darling."

Lottie laughed. "Well, how lovely to hear you say so."

They were walking down a derelict street, in the direction of the fancier part of the South End. Across the street from them, there was a towering hill of dirt behind a chain-link fence. A fat orange moon was rising from behind it in the still blue-domed sky. "This is a fine idea." Jack gestured. "Day and night simultaneously."

As they walked along, Lottie began to sing "Night and Day." Her voice sounded little and breathless in the open air.

When she was finished, they walked in silence for a while. Lottie heard the rhythm of their steps together, hers a beat and a half to his one. Jack said, "It's interesting to see you and your brother together."

"Really? How?"

"Oh, just to see how you're alike, how you're different."

"How are we alike?"

He put his hands in his pants pockets. His elbows winged back. He looked at Lottie intently. "You're both terribly willful. Strong."

Lottie was silent a moment, adjusting to this. Finally she said, "And the difference?"

He smiled, and his eyes seemed to lighten. "You wear it better, darling."

Lottie laughed, then sobered and sighed. "Well, I sure hope this works out for him."

He looked at her sharply. "Oh, come on, Lottie."

"What?"

"You're talking about Elizabeth and Cameron?"

"Yes."

He shook his head. "That's not going to work out."

157

"Why shouldn't it?"

"Because. It's an infatuation, on her part. She's biding her time, that's all. She's not, finally, going to be interested in the kind of life they could have together. Believe me. I know her type."

"Her type!" She was offended: on Elizabeth's account, of all things. "What a thing to say, Jack." She thought of mentioning the scars, but didn't.

"Nonetheless," he said, "I'm afraid I do."

"I won't ask you how," Lottie said.

"How what?"

"What who?"

He laughed, and Lottie decided to laugh too, to drop it.

They came through Union Park, and Lottie pointed out the house she thought they'd used in filming *The Bostonians*. Their stride had slowed now. They stopped at a restaurant Cam had recommended. It had big plate-glass windows on three sides; it seemed to sit out on the street. They unfolded their napkins and watched the waiter pour water into their glasses. They perused the menu, ordered, had a bottle of wine brought over.

"Not that we need it," Jack said, after the waiter had poured it.

"I need it," Lottie said. "I want to get throughly wasted." She saw his face tighten, but decided to ignore it. Just then a black woman and a white woman walked by on the street, holding hands. The black woman had intricate beaded braids dangling around her face. She was wearing clumsy-looking black leather boots, and frayed shorts, and a T-shirt that said, "How Dare You Assume I'm Straight." The white woman was coming from an office job. She had on a pastel suit with a straight, short skirt over pale, nurse-colored stockings.

"Check it out," Lottie said. "Talk about your mix of class and race."

"To say nothing of hairdressers," he said.

"And sense of chic," she offered. She sipped some wine. "Well, sisterhood is powerful."

After a moment he said, "You and Elizabeth seem unlikely friends."

"Well, we're not, of course. Friends."

"What would you call it, then?"

"Oh, I don't know." She shrugged. "We have spent a fair

amount of time together. But that just happened somehow. Proximity, I guess." She watched him for a minute. Then she said, "How do you, in fact, know her type? Elizabeth's, I mean."

He looked out the window, then back at Lottie, frowning. "Evelyn, I suppose." He seemed reluctant.

"Was Evelyn like *her?*"

"In most ways, no, she wasn't. She was steady and calm, almost reserved, I'd say, and Elizabeth is anything but. But they both have that patrician air, that smell of the upper class." He smiled. "That sense of themselves. It's hard to shake, growing up that way. And Elizabeth oozes it."

"But it's the first I've heard that Evelyn had it too."

"Oh yes. Oh, very much. A slightly different version. Lake Forest to Cambridge. And she struggled with it, to her credit. But it prescribed a great deal about our life together. Behavior and rituals. What kind of gift was appropriate, when. Who came to what kind of party. What kind of letter to write. And on and on. It drove me mad, sometimes."

"Really," she said. She couldn't help feeling some pleasure in hearing this. It seemed the first chink in the armor of Evelyn's perfection, a touch of realism in his grief-stricken idolization of what she'd been years earlier. "I've never heard you say any of this before. I'm surprised, I guess."

He shrugged. "I'm probably more aware of it right now, since her parents were in town."

"Oh, they were in town?" Lottie echoed.

"Yes. To see Megan, really. And that part was fine. But it was tough in other ways. The fussiness about what she was wearing. How she ate. Knives and forks at the dinner table." He drank some wine and set the glass down, carefully twirling it. "They leave me alone, of course. They know better. But it's as though they think someone needs to be in charge of Megan. To pass along the heritage, as it were."

"But . . . they didn't stay with you, did they?"

"Yes. Of course they did."

"In the house?"

"Yes. That's what we usually mean by 'stay with,' isn't it?" He stared at her, frowning. "This isn't some kind of problem, is it?"

159

"I don't know," Lottie said. It was a problem, of course, but she wasn't quite sure why yet.

"It seemed like a good time, Lottie. You were away . . ."

"Well, but that's my point. Or part of it, I guess."

"What? What is the point? I'd really like to know."

"Just that . . . I don't know. That I didn't even know they were there. In what is, putatively, my house too."

"But it's no secret, Lottie. I'm telling you now."

"But you should have told me before."

"Why?"

She couldn't answer.

"You mean, I should have asked your permission?"

"I suppose." Was this what she meant? She didn't know. "Isn't it my house too?" she asked.

"Lottie, look. If I'd gone away for a month or more, wouldn't you feel comfortable having . . . I don't know: your mother? or Cameron? someone like that stay?"

"Forgive me, but I don't think Cameron or my mother is in the position vis-à-vis you that your dead wife's parents are to me. And I should point out, too, that your wife has loomed very large between us. In particular, lately. In particular, since she's been dead."

"Lottie, you can't, you can't be jealous of poor Evelyn. Of my relationship to her parents."

The waiter came with their appetizers. Jack had made Lottie feel ashamed, and she sat silently while the waiter set their plates down, while he refilled their glasses. The light outside the windows had fallen. In what had been a church across the street, apartment lights had come on, figures moved in the tall, narrow windows, doing domestic things. When the waiter left, Lottie changed the subject. She asked after two of Jack's patients, ones he'd been particularly concerned about. Pedestrians strolled by, and Lottie commented on them all. She talked again about her work. And then, again, they discussed the children. All the safe topics. They finished the meal, the wine. They talked about films, about Dukakis, about Bush. They made a substantial bet on the outcome of the election. They ordered decaf. Lottie felt herself go into a kind of social overdrive, trying to avoid what seemed the chasm of all that lay unexpressed between them. She told him three jokes she'd heard, watched him laugh, and felt her heart would break.

They decided to take a cab back to the hotel. When they made love in the pinkish light, it seemed to Lottie that all of the routine of sorrow and obligation she'd been fighting so hard against had crept back in. She had to concentrate to try to come. She shut her eyes once, conjuring an image to release herself—but it was the dark passageway in Central Square that came to her, the rain, the dirty puddle. She was shocked; she opened her eyes quickly and stared at the patterns on the ceiling while Jack worked.

After breakfast, they packed and took a cab along the river and back into Cambridge. Standing in the street after Jack had paid the driver, Lottie pointed out the important sights of her childhood: Elizabeth's house, the houses of other kids she'd told him about, the elegant salmon-pink house that had been the nursing home on the corner, on whose roof she'd had her first kiss. When they turned and started up the walk to her mother's house, they could see the tilt of the ladder against its side. "It's Ryan," Lottie said, and they angled across the crabgrass in his direction. As they turned the corner, they saw him above them.

"Hey," Lottie said.

"Hey too," he said. He grinned down at them. "Don't stop me now. I'm going to finish this side today. Check it out."

Lottie stepped backward into the privet that separated the houses and looked up. All the windows were scraped and primed. He'd gotten two of them painted.

"Is this it?" Jack said. "Are you done when you finish this?"

"Nah. No way. I've been doing one side at a time, and I still have to do all the windows out back. Another couple of days, if it doesn't rain. And it will rain."

"What'll you do then?"

"Help Lottie inside. Actually, that's close to being done too, since we don't have to mess with the kitchen or Richard's room."

"Yep. Cameron will do that after Richard's gone in September. Come in and see, Jack."

They went in at the back door, leaving their bags in the narrow kitchen. Lottie led him through the house, showing him what they'd done, explaining what it had been like before. Upstairs, she held her finger to her lips as they passed Richard's door. "The roomer," she whispered. "He's in what was Cam's old room."

161

In her mother's bedroom, Lottie twirled on the bare floor. "Isn't it beautiful?" she asked. "You can't imagine how junked up it was when I got here. And now . . ." She held her arms out and curtsied slightly.

"Now it's empty," he said.

"But I love this emptiness. Doesn't it remind you of my bedroom? In my old apartment, I mean. Just bare wood and a bed."

Jack was silent a moment before he answered, looking around. "Actually, it was full of things, Lottie. Only they were your kinds of things. Books. Papers. Your pictures. Once, if you recall, I had to remove the typewriter from the bed to get at you."

"Well." She laughed. "Maybe you're right." She sat down on the mattress.

He moved to the window and stood looking out. Lottie knew all he could really see were leaves, that he wouldn't know the bits of color and shape that were Elizabeth's house to her, Elizabeth's yard and driveway. He turned back to her. "I'll say this again, Lottie, in case you didn't hear the first time." His tone was businesslike. "Anything you want to do to make the house yours . . ."

"Oh, Jack. How could I? It's Megan's house. It's your house."

"And not yours?" He was looking sharply at her. The light from the window fell sideways across his face. He looked old.

Lottie shrugged. "Not really." The silence scared her, and so she said, "Not yet."

"You feel more at home here, don't you, than in my house?"

Lottie shrugged. "Well, of course; this was home, once. So it comes freighted with a kind of perverse nostalgia. Those glorious bad old days." She tried smiling at him.

They both turned as they heard a door open, as sliding footsteps moved down the hall away from them. The bathroom door closed, hard. Richard.

Jack crossed the room quickly and shut her mother's door. He stood with his hand on the knob, looking down at Lottie on the bed. Then he said, "I hate the way we've been living together, Lottie."

"Jesus, Jack!" She recoiled.

"No, let me say this. I know that some of it is my fault, that I've been closed off. And I am trying. And I think it will get better if we both want it to. But looking at this"—he gestured around the room—"at all the effort you've expended here: this makes me aware of your share in it too. All this," he said, and his mouth went hard. "There's something about it that really pisses me off, when you've managed to leave your imprint on exactly two rooms in my house—our house. And one is Ryan's, and one is a room you use by yourself."

She breathed deeply several times before she answered. She didn't look at him. She said, "I don't know what you would have me do, Jack. I honestly don't. And whatever I might want to do, it's so clearly not the time." Now she met his gaze, the hard, light eyes. "You're in love with Evelyn. More in love with her than when she was alive."

He stared back at Lottie steadily.

"Are you not?" He gestured, a dismissive gesture that made Lottie angry. "And it's her house. How could I—now—even take a picture she chose off the wall? What am I supposed to do—rip up all the wall-to-wall carpeting? And what's more . . . I mean, what is my style, after all?" She lifted her hand to offer the room. "Nothing! Or junk. That's what I like, in fact." She shrugged. She was picturing her old apartment, furnished with oddments, with secondhand stuff she'd lovingly repainted. "I have terrible taste. Impoverished taste. I like old, beat-up crap. And I know it's crap. But I like it. Am I supposed to get rid of all your very, very comfortable, very well-made, very good stuff, so I can go out and buy crap to replace it with?" Only when she stopped could Lottie hear how shrill her voice had become.

Jack waited a moment, and then he spoke softly. "This feels very much like an accusation, Lottie. Against me. Against what I've made of my life."

"God!" she cried. "No! That's not it. That's not it. But you will admit, won't you, that we've lived differently? That my life has been . . . I don't know. Whatever. Marginal, sloppy. Bohemian— economically anyway. And yours has been solidly middle class. Neither by choice, really. By accident. But that doesn't make it easier now. I mean, I *am* the one whose life has suddenly changed. Utterly changed."

"What are you saying, Lottie?" he asked. "Are you saying you're sorry we married? You're sorry you moved in?"

"Oh, Jack. Those are two different questions."

"Answer them one at a time, then."

163

Lottie looked at him. His face was closed, stern. "I'm not sorry we married," she said after a moment. "And in fact, I'm not sorry I moved in. In themselves, those were the right things to do. The only things to do. But *I* had a life before too, Jack," she pleaded. "I had a real life, as much as you did." His face didn't change. "I don't know. Somehow in all your . . . grieving over Evelyn, it's as though I hadn't lost anything." She waited for him to say something, but he didn't, so she started again. "I'm *not* sorry. I'm not. But somehow there's been this . . . I don't know. Backlash, or something. And I feel it's you, Jack. Who's sorry. Apologetic. To Evelyn, really. Even to her parents. That you had them stay when I was away, for God's sake—as though you were all pretending I didn't exist!" His mouth opened slightly, but he didn't speak. "And I feel that way often, actually. As though I don't exist anymore. So yes, it's true, I guess, that in some odd way, I have felt more alive, more comfortable here this summer. Even though I've been in this weird kind of limbo, watching everyone else be sexy and in love."

Jack snorted, and his head swung to the window.

"What?" she said. "What is it?"

"Are you talking about Cameron and Elizabeth again?" He looked back at her, a dangerous half smile lifting his face. He looked mean.

"Yes. And even Ryan and his string of ponies, to a lesser degree."

"That strikes me as pathetic, Lottie."

"What?"

"That in any sense you should see Cameron and Elizabeth as embodying something you'd like. It makes me very angry."

Lottie picked up a pillow, swung it onto her lap, punched it. "And it makes me angry that you should so easily dismiss them. They are foolish. Of course they're foolish. But they're in love. That looks foolish, from the outside. I wish we looked so foolish, instead of so . . . fucking mature. I wish people said that about us, that we were ridiculous, that we were fools." Lottie was near tears, and it made her voice wobbly.

Jack's voice, on the other hand, was too soft. Hoarse, and dangerously soft. "That's like wishing we could lock ourselves in the hotel room, Lottie, and fuck ourselves blind. That's what children

164

want, Lottie—adolescents. But life doesn't work that way. That's a holiday. That's a weekend. But that can't last."

"*There* we go," Lottie said with bitter exultation. She was glad for his contempt, furious. And glad for the freedom it gave her. "You know what your trouble is? You've been on a beeper too long."

"What's that supposed to mean?" There was so much ugliness in his voice that Lottie was suddenly scared. What were they doing? How could they end this?

"Oh, I don't know," she said. She shook her head quickly. "You've been too dutiful. Too good and devoted. You haven't locked yourself up enough. I mean, wasn't that the power of what we used to have, really? In your life? We were the secret, dark, locked-up part of it."

"And you'd like to have that back?"

"God, wouldn't you? You loved that, Jack. You loved me then." She realized that her hands were gripping the pillow with enormous tension.

Jack was looking at her, and in a voice with no love at all in it, he said, "I love you now, Lottie."

Down the hall, through the two closed doors, they could hear the toilet flush mightily. Richard hawked once, twice. The shower was turned on.

Lottie let her breath out in a rush. "I don't know. Maybe these things will be better when Megan goes off," she said. She had meant this in a conciliatory way, but she saw instantly that she'd made a mistake.

"Why do you say that?" His voice was sharp.

"Oh, just that she's sort of emblematic. I don't mean Megan herself, really. Though God knows I wish she liked me a little. And there have been times I'd gladly have dunked her in cold water." He didn't smile. "But Megan, Ryan, whoever. All the detritus of our previous lives."

"We are the detritus of our previous lives, Lottie. By now we are. I would love you less, in fact, if you hadn't been Derek's wife or Ryan's mother. Because it made you who you are." He was speaking to her slowly and carefully, as though she were either very young or very thick.

"Oh, I know. I know. I know all that."

He walked back over to the window and stood, his back to her, looking out. He said, "And if it comes to it, Megan has tried harder than you have, I'd argue, to make things work."

"Oh, Jack! Now *that* pisses me off."

He turned. "It's true, Lottie."

"What complete bullshit!"

"Didn't she embrace you when you left?"

"One embrace. One stiff, awkward embrace. Is that supposed to make up . . . ? Okay, yes, she did, I'll grant you. Why? She reported to you on it?"

"We'd talked about it ahead of time. That's what I mean. She's been consciously struggling with herself, with her feelings, her behavior, in a way that's very touching to me."

"So *you* suggested that Megan embrace me."

"In a sense. She had said how disconnected she felt from you, how she wasn't sure she could ever come to care for you. And I made an analogy with Evelyn after the stroke. That I felt, really, nearly frightened of her in that condition, and that it wasn't until I forced myself to touch her again, to hold her, that I had a sense of love, or the possibility of love, for who she had become."

"I see," Lottie said. She was horrified.

"What is it? You're upset by that."

"I sure am."

"Why?"

"Oh, Jack. Surely you can see that there's something frightening, and deeply offensive too, I think, about your comparing me to Evelyn."

"I didn't—I hardly compared you to Evelyn, Lottie. You're distorting what I said."

"I know what you said. You said you made an analogy. I know that. Between me and an invalid, really. A vegetative person. A partly dead person."

"Lottie." His voice was dangerous. "You're looking for problems here. You're inventing them."

"No I'm not. I'm absolutely not. Because you'd prefer me that way, I think. That's what I feel, Jack. I think it's no accident that that analogy sprang to mind. Because your behavior, your way of dealing with me in your life since we got married, has been connected to that. I don't know. Maybe you feel guilty that I'm whole, I'm well.

166

Because everything that's most passionate, most alive, most insistent, in me—most in love with you—is to be pushed away." She stopped, but he didn't answer. She lowered her voice. "I'm in love with you, Jack, in some funky, low-rent way that embarrasses you. That you've forgotten how to feel, nearly. Or you think you don't deserve. Or something. I don't get it."

Richard had begun a tuneless, muffled humming in the shower, like a sorrowful bagpipe playing in the distance.

Jack's face had whitened. He shook his head. "I'm not sure how we got here, darling. From furniture or home decoration or whatever to . . . this. I'm sorry we did, though. I'm truly sorry."

He strode past her, he opened the door and left the room. Lottie heard him going down the stairs, going back through the house. A moment later, his voice sounded outside, muffled through the walls. His voice and Ryan's alternated in short sentences. False. Upbeat. Saying goodbye. Then he came back into the house. She heard his footsteps, she heard him pause at the bottom of the stairs. "Lottie," he called up.

"Yes," she said.

"I think I'll head out to the airport now." His voice was mild and polite. Public. This was the way they spoke to each other at his house, in front of Megan. "It's only a little early. There's no need for you to drive me. I'll call a cab."

"Don't be absurd," she called back. She blew her nose. "Of course I'll drive you."

She came down the stairs. Jack stood by his bag, watching her descent. "I really can manage," he said quietly. "You don't need to bother."

"Of course I'll drive you, Jack. We had an argument, but I'll drive you to the airport, for God's sake."

He shrugged and picked up his bag. Lottie walked ahead of him out to the car. At the curb, as Jack put his bag into the back seat, she shouted back to the house. "Ryan!"

His voice floated to them. "Yeah?"

"I'll be back in an hour or so. I'm taking Jack to his plane."

"Got it."

They drove in silence through the leafy streets of Cambridge and then slowly began to move east, into the land of triple-deckers, of bodegas and storefront churches. They descended past the courthouse and crossed the river. Lottie could hear her own nervous pulse in the silence that hung over them. She was terrified that they'd leave it like this, terrified about what this might mean.

"You'll be an hour and a half or so early," she finally said.

"I'll read the paper," he said coldly.

"*Will* you?" she asked, and felt a return of her anger. Was he trying to insult her, to suggest how easily he could dismiss all this?

He didn't answer. They drove past the Boston Garden, and Lottie thought about another universe, in which she would have pointed it out to him. He was a basketball fan. His oldest, Charley, had played it well in high school and college.

As they emerged from the tunnel, she said, "We both have a lot to think about."

He stared straight ahead. "I'm much too angry to think now."

"I know," she said. "Me too."

After a few minutes she said, "You're not used to people making you angry."

"I don't hold this kind of . . . discussion in as high a regard as you do. I don't see what's gained."

Lottie shrugged. "Depends on what you do with it."

He let her listen to his silence for a moment. Then he said quietly, "Don't be so fucking smug, Lottie."

She was stung; Jack never swore, and that alone had shocked her. But then she recognized that she had sounded smug, that she didn't know how to talk to him, what to say, what she felt.

When she pulled over at the departure curb, she reached out and touched his sleeve. "Jack. I'm just as confused as you. I'm not being smug, I promise you."

"I'll call you in a few days," he said.

"I'll be waiting," she said. She leaned forward and kissed his cheek.

He held her arm, hard, looking at her, and Lottie waited for him to say something. If he spoke to her now, if he asked her to come home, she felt she would break apart, she would yield. But he seemed to change his mind. He let go and got out of the car. And when he opened the back door to get his bag, he didn't look at her or speak to her. She watched him stride across the crowded sidewalk and in through the revolving door. He turned and looked at her once from behind the darkened glass windows, and then he

168

stepped back, and his pale face was lost in the reflections on its surface.

She had just come out onto Storrow Drive when she realized she couldn't go back to the house, to Ryan's cheerful noise, to the long afternoon in front of her. She drove into the Back Bay and parked on Arlington Street. She walked into the Public Garden again, amid the mix of Sunday strollers—the tourists with camcorders, the handsome, well-dressed couples pushing those expensive fold-up strollers, the punk kids, the odd homeless person. The high white clouds moved quickly across the sky. She sat on a bench near the water. There was a child under two with her mother, feeding the ducks with mixed terror and delight.

A wedding party entered through the iron gates, from the Ritz-Carlton, Lottie assumed. They crossed onto the grass and gathered in front of one of the arching willows. They were all small, with dark hair. Japanese, she saw. Their uniformity to her eye gave them a nearly emblematic quality; they reminded her of the little bride and groom statues on the top of a wedding cake. The larger, Caucasian photographer, wearing a brownish ordinary suit, lurched clumsily among them, directing them this way and that. They grouped themselves in response to him in various ways, various versions of perfection.

Lottie thought suddenly of a quote from Twain; not a quote she'd read for this new essay, the one on love; but the one about grief. He was talking about marriage and death. He called marriage the supreme "felicity"—the word had struck Lottie—and also the supreme tragedy. The deeper the love, he said, the surer the tragedy and the more painful when it came. Felicitations, she thought, looking at the doll-like couple; and get ready.

She thought of her own imperfect wedding, at City Hall—Megan's resentful tears, their loud, embarrassed trio of sons, only Charley really able to help them, to smooth things for them a little: he'd brought rice and streamers, he had champagne waiting in the car. There had been tears in Jack's eyes, too, as he'd watched her echoing his vows, and it had occurred to her, even then—even before she'd read the Twain—that perhaps Jack was seeing her through the scrim of his experience with Evelyn, that this ceremony marked for him, in some way, the beginning of her dying, her going away from him.

Suddenly all the tiny perfect figures—the fairy women in lilac gowns and wide-brimmed hats, the stiff small men in tuxedos—moved away from the wedding couple, and the photographer took three, four, five shots of them alone.

Now somehow a signal was given and it was finished. Everyone loosened and milled together; and then slowly, led by the beautiful bride and groom, they walked across the grass again to the ornate iron gates and out of the garden, across the street.

PART THREE

CHAPTER 9

In the confusing aftermath of a tragedy, of any terrible event, we sometimes try to make sense of it by finding a way to blame ourselves. It seems to Lottie in the afternoon after Jessica has died that Ryan is feeling something like this—responsible, and miserable on that account. After he's come back from the hardware store and they're working mostly silently together at the back of the house, she remembers abruptly a time when he was three or four and she was grocery shopping with him. Someone had spilled coffee beans in a corner of the store, and he kept wanting to return to that spot, to look at the mess. Finally he had asked her in a hushed voice, "Did I do that?" She had felt such a sweep of compassion, such an aching familiarity with this sense of oneself, that she knelt and held him tight for a moment before she could tell him, "No, of course you didn't."

It's only more slowly as the long afternoon wears on that she realizes she is doing it too. That she is calling up again and again those few moments when her actions might have had something to do with what happened. She remembers her anger when she told Elizabeth she ought to call Cam, that he still lived nearby. Perhaps that was what had set it all in motion. Or perhaps if she'd left when she was supposed to, she thinks, some element in the equation that added up to Jessica's death would have been different, and the girl would still be alive.

When she catches herself, she makes herself stop. It's absurd. She knows this.

But she does keep calling Cam through the afternoon. He's never home or at the store, but she talks to Maeve twice more. The second time, he's called there again, and Lottie feels the same sweep of lightness, of relief, she felt earlier at this news: he is safe, he is all right.

It's only a few minutes after this call that Elizabeth comes over to ask Lottie to drop by her house later in the evening; and this may be why Lottie so readily says yes.

It would help them out, Elizabeth says. She's breathless, apologetic, and confusing in her attempts to explain everything. If Lottie hadn't read her letter to Cameron, she might not even be able to understand what Elizabeth is saying. But what she gathers, after Elizabeth has explained about Lawrence's call from the airport, his sudden arrival in the afternoon the day before, is that Elizabeth has used her, Lottie, as a kind of cover for Cameron's appearance last night.

"Lawrence said, 'What was he *doing* here anyway?'—you know, late in the evening, long after the accident. And I said that one or the other of you popped over all the time, that we'd done lots of stuff together this summer."

She's standing with Lottie in the front hall. Ryan is still outside. "So it would just give me some credibility if you'd come over tonight and have some coffee and dessert or whatever." Elizabeth is dressed up again, Lottie notes. She's wearing slacks and a vibrant purple silk shirt. She has beaded sandals on her feet. "Plus, of course, it'll just distract us." She runs her hand over her head, down her hair. "It's been a ghastly day, Char. I've been so worried about Cam. I managed to get over there once, but of course there was no sign of him. And poor Jessica's parents came by this afternoon. The children, of course, are frantic. Basket cases. And in the midst of all this, I'm trying to hold on to some sense of reunion with Lawrence." He's leaving the next day, Elizabeth tells Lottie. He needs to get back. Elizabeth will stay on until after the service for Jessica, and then she'll fly home.

"You understand, don't you, Char?" Her voice is nearly pleading. "I wrote Cameron a letter and tried to explain it to him, but what I couldn't say, of course, was that as soon as I heard Lawrence's voice on the phone, it was over. It was decided. After all this happiness this summer . . ." Tears fill her eyes. "I just feel so fucking . . . shallow, I guess."

Lottie doesn't say anything.

"What was it?" Elizabeth whispers. "I don't know. I didn't mean to hurt him."

"Maybe you needed a little ego food," Lottie says. Her voice is drier than she intended.

"No," Elizabeth answers firmly. She shakes her head. "I think I do love Cameron in some way. And maybe if he were more, sort of, settled . . . I mean, if I'd felt he could have, somehow, taken us on. Maybe. But the way he *lives*, Lottie." She holds her hands out. "I mean, he's almost fifty, and I don't even think he has life insurance. Realistically, I guess I must have known all along there was just no way he could have had the children and me. I mean, what would I have *done*? Taught freshman comp somewhere?"

"A lot of people do. And even more horrible things. Hell, I worked as a secretary once."

Elizabeth's head tilts. "Don't be hard on me, Char."

"I'm not being hard, Elizabeth. It's the truth. Besides, I feel for Cam. How could I not? I know it's been stressful for you. But Cam's the one I feel for." Lottie shrugs. "You can understand that."

Elizabeth says she does. She's sorry. "But can you come over?" she asks, after a long silence. "There's just this one more night to get through, with Mother hovering, and the children, and Lawrence just . . . perplexed, I think. And I think if you came it would answer some questions he's got, first of all, and then simply help us get through a few hours. Please."

And so Lottie says yes, in part because she has the hours to get through too. She fixes dinner for herself and Ryan, and they both eat, ravenously. Then he goes out, and Lottie showers and changes and crosses the street to Elizabeth's house.

And now she's walking home—she's being walked home—by Elizabeth's husband. Lawrence. She stumbles on a dent in the lawn, her ankle bends, and he reaches over in the dark and cups her elbow with his hand.

"I'm all right now," she says. "Really." His hand on her flesh is warm, moist; and he doesn't let go. "You really don't need to be doing this anyway. It's not New York, or something. I go out all the time by myself at night. Here, and in Chicago. I *run* after dark."

They step off the curb, into the wide, black street. There's no light on at Lottie's house. Ryan has gone out with a friend from college who lives in Boston. He said he would be late. Lottie is aware of Lawrence's physical presence, like a heat that travels in the dark beside her.

"Well," he says, "I was hoping, actually, you'd offer me a drink." Lawrence has a quiet voice, an insinuating voice, Lottie would have said. But what is it insinuating? She can't tell. She looks over at him again, but his face is turned away and obscured in the shadows.

"I'm not really sure what we've got in the house," she says.

"Really? From what Elizabeth said, I would have guessed you inherited a sizable liquor cabinet."

Lottie laughs. "Now that wasn't nice of Elizabeth, was it?" she says. "And it's not true. A bottle at a time was Mother's motto. Waste not, want not. The New England virtues."

"Still, how 'bout it?" he asks. There's something urgent in his voice. "I'd settle for a beer."

They're standing now at the bottom of the porch stairs. Lottie suddenly has no wish to go into the dark house alone. "Well, we'll see what we can dig out," she says, and he follows her up the stairs.

In the kitchen, she leans over the refrigerator door, the Ryan pose.

"Okay, there are two beers, Anchor Steam. And part of a bottle of white wine. A California Chardonnay. But a cheap one, about four bucks a bottle, so you know what that means. And"—she turns to the counter—"some red, though it may be vinegar by now. And I think . . ." She opens the freezer door. "Yes. Some vodka. But no tonic or anything."

Lawrence is standing in the kitchen doorway. "I'll have vodka. Neat."

Lottie pours him some in one of the little jelly jars, and pours some white wine for herself. "Why don't you go on into the living room? Such as it is," she says. "I have one call I need to make."

She can hear him in there, shifting. She feels she can see him looking around. The rotary dial on her mother's phone seems

176

slower, noisier than ever, and she hangs up as soon as she hears Cameron's recorded voice start his message again.

When she comes into the living room, Lawrence is sitting, leaned back in one of the chairs—the first person, it occurs to Lottie, to somehow manage to look comfortable in here. His feet are stretched out in front of him, crossed at the bare ankle. His shoes are light-brown loafers of a leather so soft-looking it seems a dully shining fabric. Lottie can see the shape of his toes through it. He drinks, a long swallow, and sets his glass on the floor under his dangling fingers. He rests his head against the chair back and looks around. "Your son is helping you in this . . . enterprise?" he asks.

"Yes. Ryan."

"And then you're back to Chicago?" She nods. "To your husband too," he says.

"Yes," she answers. She slides one of the chairs across the floor and turns it, sits down almost opposite him. The light from the dining room falls in a long rectangle that slices across his pants legs. Lottie rests her toes exactly at the rectangle's edge on the other side of the room.

Lawrence is watching all this carefully. After she's settled herself, he says, "So. It was an unhusbanded summer for you and our Liz."

Something in his voice makes Lottie feel uncomfortable.

"She seems to have flourished," he says.

Lottie doesn't answer.

"For you, of course, I have no way of knowing. No baseline, as it were." His face is back in shadow, but Lottie can see he is smiling again. He has improbably white teeth.

Lottie shrugs. "She has, I think. Flourished."

"Not you, then."

"It's been a different kind of summer for me."

"How's that?"

"I'm not sure. I don't want to talk about it, really." Outside, behind Lottie, a car drives by. "Hard," she says. "It's been a hard summer for me."

"And not for Lizzie?"

Lottie smiles across the band of light at him. "Well, she got you back, in the end. And I think that's very much what she wanted, all along."

He lifts his glass again, raises it slightly as if to acknowledge Lottie's point, and drinks, a quick, small sip. He sets the glass down once more, his fingertips resting on it. He says, "And you were all . . . great friends, as children."

Lottie makes a face. "I don't think children have 'great friends,' do you?"

"Elizabeth is someone who *did* have great friends as a child. You can't believe the numbers of them."

"Yes. Well. That is Elizabeth. What I'd say, I think, is that we played together and loved each other and hated each other in almost equal measure. Certainly, at any rate, we knew each other well."

"And this summer you've sort of picked up where you left off."

Lottie laughs. "Oh, it's been lots better than that, I hope."

His bright smile flashes. Then his head lolls again, left, right. Lottie sees his eyes slowly measure the room. He says, "You guys had no dough."

"Zilch."

"See, I hadn't got that part. Your brother . . . confused me, last night. I saw him as a kind of tweedy, academic guy. I saw him the way I saw Elizabeth's father."

"Well, he is a tweedy, kind of academic guy. You're not frozen forever the way you were when you were ten. Thank God."

"But he's not an academic."

"No," Lottie answers. "He owns a bookstore. Part of a bookstore. I think it's pretty successful, actually."

He nods. "He's an interesting character."

"I suppose. It's not quite how I think of him."

"But you'll grant . . ." One hand swings up toward Lottie.

"Well, I'm not sure what you mean: 'interesting.' "

"Oh, just a guy like that, driving a car like that, at his age. Our age. Intense. A little humorless. Sort of on the fringes."

"But there are lots of people like that. Particularly in big cities, or near universities. He's not really that unusual. You know that Randy Newman song."

"No, I don't."

"It's about people who hang out in bookstores, as he puts it. Who work for the public radio. Who carry their babies around on their backs." She lifts her shoulders. "Mostly, it's about people who just don't know how to make money."

He seems amused. Then he regards Lottie for a moment. "He's different from you in that regard."

"I wouldn't say so. I've never made much money either."

"Haven't you? That's not the way Elizabeth tells it."

"Elizabeth doesn't know."

"I thought she did. I thought you and Elizabeth were great friends. Had become great friends, this summer." He sits up a little bit; his knees bend, and his legs slide apart.

"She misunderstands. She thinks to be published in certain slick magazines is to have a certain slick amount of money. And that's not the case."

"But your husband has a dime or two, I guess." Lottie shrugs. "He's . . . what? a cardiologist?"

"No. Cancer. An oncologist."

He nods. "Elizabeth thought heart. Cardiologist. But there you go. Everything comes back to the heart, with Lizzie." He taps his chest, and then he smiles at Lottie. "Not like you, eh?"

"What do you mean?" Lottie asks.

"Just, that you seem tougher, I'd say."

This is so unexpected that it takes Lottie's breath for a moment. Finally she says, "I find Elizabeth tough. Tough as nails."

He laughs. "Do you? Well. I'd have to disagree."

Lottie gets up to refill her glass. On the way across the room, she looks over at his. He appears to be nursing it. As she leaves the room, then as she returns too, she's aware of his eyes on her, on her legs and hips.

After she's sat down again, she says, "Isn't Elizabeth going to be worried about you?"

"Should she be?" He's smiling at her.

"Oh, come on," she says. She's not surprised, she realizes. "Don't start that stuff."

"But this is fun, isn't it?" he asks. "Lots better than the Harbour parlor, at any rate. You and I, we understand each other, I think."

"Do we?" Lottie asks. "I think you think you understand me. And maybe you partway do. But I don't much understand you. Why you're here, for instance."

"I'm here for Elizabeth."

"No, I mean here, in my mother's living room."

"I'm here so I don't have to be there." He nods his head at the windows, the street. "Elizabeth and I need to get off her turf. Her family's turf. Her mother's turf."

"I like Emily."

"I like Emily too. I like her a lot. But to be around her and Elizabeth together . . ." He shakes his head. "It's like drowning to someone like me." Lottie grins in recognition. She feels this way around Emily too. "So I'm here," he says. "And I'm curious."

"About what?"

"About you. About your brother. About what's been going on here this summer. I though maybe you'd care to enlighten me."

"I'm not sure I could."

"Oh, come on, Char."

"It's Lottie."

"Lottie?"

"Yes, Elizabeth and my brother and mother are the only ones who still call me Char. I prefer Lottie. By a country mile."

"All right then, Lottie. And I'm Larry, by the way. Elizabeth is the only person who calls me Lawrence. Elizabeth and Emily."

"Larry," Lottie says.

"Right." He lets a little silence fall. "So, *Lottie.* Clue me in."

"As I said, I'm not sure I can."

"Why not?"

"Well. I'm not sure what you're asking, for starters."

"Who's zooming who? That's all. What's been going on? Your brother, for example: he was involved with the baby-sitter?"

Lottie is startled. "What makes you think that?"

"You don't think so?"

"I *know* it's not so."

"Interesting."

"Why?"

"Because Elizabeth thought he might have been."

Lottie laughs, a sort of admiring laugh. *"Did* she?"

"Yes. You're surprised by that."

"I sure am. I think Elizabeth knows better than that too."

"Well, as I read it, there was *something* funny going on." He tilts his head. "Could it be he was involved with my wife?"

Lottie looks levelly at him.

"Or maybe there's some other possibility I'm not picking up on.

But I think you know. So I'd like to know." Lottie shifts in her chair. "Is all. Fair, don't you think?"

"He wasn't involved with Jessica."

"What about Elizabeth?"

She sips some wine. "Why don't you ask Elizabeth?" His eyes are steady on her. She crosses her legs, aware of the sound of her sliding flesh. "You know, I probably wouldn't tell you he was sleeping with Elizabeth, even if he was."

"But you'd tell me if he wasn't, I bet."

Lottie recognizes that this is true, and she's uncomfortable. "Why *don't* you ask Elizabeth all this?" she says.

"Why would Elizabeth tell me the truth?"

"Why should I?"

"You seem to me like a truthful kind of person."

Lottie feels confused, suddenly. It's a few seconds before she answers. "I don't think I'm the right person for you to talk to. To talk to you. If you have doubts about Elizabeth's . . . fidelity. Though I'm not sure you've got much of a leg to stand on. So to speak."

"No, no. You're certainly right, there. But I love Elizabeth. I do." He smiles. "And I understand her so well. I understand what she needs, maybe more than she does."

"What does she need?"

"Romance. For life to be romantic. She has to have things very . . . intense, all the time. In a way, she's kind of a phony, you know what I mean, but she's *alive*. I get a genuine kind of charge out of her. I always have. So maybe you're right. Just drop it. Be glad she's coming home. That life is back to normal." He sits up suddenly, hunches forward over his knees in the chair. "The thing is, I gave up a lot for her. To get her back."

"Your girlfriend."

"It was a lot of girlfriend."

"Hmm."

"You've been there, I suspect, haven't you, Lottie? You seem like someone who likes to fool around a little bit." He waits. His voice, when he speaks again, is intimate, urgent. "I couldn't keep away from her. She was a wonderful, a very dirty girl. I liked that a lot."

Lottie doesn't say anything, and after a moment he sits back.

181

He pulls out a cigarette. "Do you mind if I smoke?"

Lottie shakes her head. "No. Go ahead."

"Thanks." He lights the cigarette and inhales deeply, as though he's been rationed for a while.

Lottie walks in front of him again, enters the band of light. She goes through the dining room and fetches a chipped saucer for him from the kitchen. She squats to set it on the floor by him; and then feels uncomfortable, servile, as she gets up again. Stepping back to her own chair, turning, sitting, she is suddenly ashamed and angry. Is he doing this? Is she? He watches her across the shadowy space for a long time, smoking. Lottie notes that he holds the cigarette between his thumb and forefinger, with the lighted end turned in toward his palm; like the tough guys, the hoods, in high school. What is she doing? Lottie thinks. What is this man doing here?

Emily—big Emily—had answered the door earlier this evening, and her plump face had puckered at the sight of Lottie. "Oh, Charlotte, my dear." She stepped forward and embraced Lottie on the porch. "I'm so sorry," she whispered in Lottie's ear. She smelled of talc, and her hands were damp on Lottie's arms. She stepped back after a moment.

"Well," she said. Lottie saw that her eyes were glittering, but she'd clearly decided they were to have the usual chirpy conversation. She launched herself, her watery, lapping voice: "Elizabeth said you might drop by, and I'm so pleased to see you, just come in, come in, we're all sort of drifting around aimlessly, postprandial I guess you'd say, but we're about to have coffee and tea and that sort of thing . . ." Lottie was following her into the gloomy front hall. ". . . and little Emily and I made some dessert this afternoon. My dear!" Her voice lowered abruptly. "How is Cameron?"

They had paused on the threshold of the living room. Lottie could hear voices, adult voices, in the kitchen. "I think he's fine. I haven't actually been able to reach him, but they've talked to him at the store."

Her head bobbed. "Poor man, that's Elizabeth's experience too, and I want you to know that I am so sorry for him, if you speak to him please tell him so." As Elizabeth emerged into the long hallway from the kitchen, Emily squeezed Lottie's elbow again, for emphasis.

They had sat in the immense, cheerless living room, decorated in its faded, liver-y colors. Lawrence was a slender, compact man, with shining flat hair and smooth skin. He was beautifully dressed, Lottie noted, in loose, crushed-looking clothing Lottie guessed to be ridiculously expensive. He and Lottie were drinking decaf, Emily and Elizabeth tea, and the children had soft drinks.

The children seemed chastened to Lottie, scared. They sat silently and listened to the adults. Little Emily pulled her legs up onto the couch—you could fully see her white underpants—and leaned against Elizabeth, sucking her thumb.

For reasons that were unclear to Lottie, Emily was explaining at great length about the flowers on the living room rug, which had come from her family. That they had been part of a punishment ritual when she or her sisters misbehaved: they had to sit silently on a rose for a designated number of minutes while their father read the paper. "Oh, I remember him as clearly as if he were alive today," she said. "The way the paper would *drop* as soon as we began to wiggle or be the slightest bit restless, and Father would say, 'Emily, hold that rose.' *Emily, hold that rose*," she echoed. "I used to say it myself later, still do, sometimes, when I'm impatient or have to endure something: 'Emily, hold that rose.' "

Was there any situation, Lottie wondered, that Emily couldn't talk her way through? She took another bite of the cake the two Emilys had made. Her portion was iced in a violent purple, little Emily's choice for half the frosting on the cake's top. Others had a yolky yellow. She wondered if her teeth were staining.

Now Elizabeth was telling the children about how she had been disciplined: her father had set her to memorize passages of poetry, the more serious the infraction, the longer the passage.

"Bummer," Michael said; and Lottie thought instantly of Ryan earlier this afternoon, his anger at her, hers at him.

"How 'bout you, Daddy?" Jeffrey asked. There was shy eagerness in his voice, a remnant of his summer's sorrow. "What was your punishment?"

Lawrence had an odd smile on his face as he looked from one of his children to another. "My father beat us," he said quietly. "With his belt." He looked at Lottie then. It felt to her as though her eyes must be open too wide, and she looked away quickly. The room seemed to have lurched slightly.

"Oh, Lawrence, how terrible!" Emily cried. "Surely it isn't true—that lovely man, I so enjoyed him, to think of his raising his hand to you, to any of you. It just breaks my heart, dear, I wish you hadn't told me."

"I'm very sorry," Lawrence had said; but Lottie could see that he wasn't, not a bit.

Now he pulls on the cigarette, and Lottie can hear the air slide between his lips. "You knew the sitter," he asks quietly, finally.

"A little. Her name was Jessica."

"It's a tough thing. For your brother too," he says. Then, lightly, "How's he taking it?"

"I don't know, really."

"What do you mean?"

"Just I haven't been able to . . . he hasn't been home since last night. I'm a little worried, actually. I've tried him on and off all day. Right up until I came over to Emily's house tonight." Lottie had left another message just before she crossed the street. "And the call I made here. When we first got here." She lifts her helpless hands to indicate that he wasn't there. "But he's called in at his bookstore. So I have to assume he's just walking it off. Or drinking it off. Or avoiding me. Or all of the above."

"He'll turn up. He'll turn up."

Lottie feels, oddly, a sense of comfort in this. "What makes you think so?"

"Just . . . there was something last night. There was lots of nervous tension in the room. Lots of life, in some way, when the cops were there with your brother and so forth. He was upset, sure, but not . . . not depressed. I thought, to be honest, he might have been on something. But Elizabeth said no, he doesn't. That's when I asked her whether he was balling the sitter, actually."

"And she said he might have been."

"She said she didn't know, but that he might have been. Right."

"Well, he wasn't. That's all. He wasn't."

"He wasn't." It's a question.

"He wasn't 'balling the sitter.' Okay?"

"Okay, I believe you."

He puts the cigarette out. A long but somehow comfortable

silence falls in the oddly lighted room. Lottie is startled when he speaks again. "Tell me the hard part."

"What?"

"Of your summer. You said it was hard."

Lottie lifts her hands. "Won't this do?" She means Jessica, Cameron.

"But you implied it was hard before this."

"I suppose. But I think I also said I didn't want to talk about it."

"It's funny." He waits for her to respond, but she doesn't. He purses his lips and then continues anyway. "Elizabeth portrayed you as so happily married. But I don't think that's the case, is it, Lottie?"

"I *really* don't want to talk about it."

He holds up one of his hands so Lottie can see the palm. "Okay, okay." After a minute he asks conversationally, "How old's your son?"

"He's twenty."

"You look young to have a son that old."

"Well, thanks. I was twenty-three when I had him. Not so young, actually."

"You married young, though."

"I suppose so. I was twenty. Is that young?"

"I don't know." He shrugs. "How long?"

"How long what?"

"How long were you married?"

"Oh, only a few years. We split up a couple of months after Ryan was born."

"So you were single awhile."

"I was single for almost twenty years." Lottie has said this in a loud voice that surprises her.

"You seem single now."

"Oh, come on."

"No, you give off single vibes."

"Are you coming on to me now?"

"Maybe." He laughs, a bitter sound. "Maybe I'm just pissed."

"Why?"

"Because everyone's being so mysterious about what's been going on here." He moves his feet in the patch of light. "So maybe I'm just needling you, Lottie. Maybe coming on a little, but just trying to get to you, basically. You can ignore me. Not—you should know—that I don't find you attractive. I've always liked your type."

"I suppose I should say thanks."

"I would understand if you didn't."

"I suppose I should ask you what you think my *type* is."

"You don't have to."

"What the hell," she says, trying to make her voice light. "I can take it."

He's smiling at her, as though they've agreed to something. "You're one of those small, high-energy women," he says. "Narrow body, wide hips, loves to screw."

Lottie is shocked, though she shouldn't be. "That's a *type?*" she asks finally.

"You tell me," he says. "You were single all those years, you must know yourself pretty well. Am I right?"

Lottie is smiling back at him now. She shakes her head. "You know," she says, "this feels to me like one of the more cynical interludes I've participated in."

"I'll go, anytime you tell me to."

"That's what I mean: I haven't told you to." She lifts her hands, gestures. "This beautiful young woman is dead, my brother is out there somewhere, somehow suffering with it. And you and I are sitting here, toying idly—maybe toying theoretically is more like it—with various quasi-sexual ideas."

"Why do you suppose we're doing that?"

"I don't know, exactly. Well, you, I'd guess, because you're pissed, as you say, about what you don't understand. But maybe you're angry too, just that you've come back." He is smiling again. "She left you. You chased her. On the great seesaw of love, she's up now, and you're down."

He nods. "All right. I'll say all right to that. But how do you explain yourself? Why are you playing the game with me?"

Lottie sighs. "I don't know. I suppose I'm riding my own see-saw. With my husband, I mean. The stuff I'm not going to talk about. Plus . . . well, wouldn't it be a kind of revenge on Elizabeth, to fool around with you?"

"Revenge for what?"

"For having had an easier life. For any number of small moments of pain. Insults. For living across the street from this house in that house."

"You don't need revenge on Elizabeth for that."

"Oh, I know. Water over the dam, under the bridge. Spilled milk, and so on."

"Plus she's already in agony over your success."

Lottie realizes abruptly that she has known this about Elizabeth.

"You are aware, of course, that that's the biggest fuck-you you've got going?"

"Yes." She nods. "Yes, I am aware of that. As a matter of fact, it's given me some real pleasure this summer, I admit it. And I do feel that, some quiver of that, every time I see my name in print. Succeeding is an angry thing to do. For some people. For me. For you too, I suspect. I suspect, in fact, that that's one of the few ways you and I do understand one another."

They sit looking at each other for a long moment. Then he stands up abruptly, steps across the stripe of lighted air, bends over Lottie, and kisses her. Lottie lifts her face to him, she kisses him back, but she does not stand up, she does not move her hands, which are enlaced around the jelly jar full of wine. His tongue comes into her mouth.

Which of them decides it first, that it won't happen? It would be hard to say. If she had responded. If he were more insistent, if he'd touched her body. If Elizabeth weren't waiting across the street. If Richard Lester or Ryan couldn't come through the door at any minute. By the time he lifts his face from Lottie's, though, they both know it won't. But they smile at each other in a kind of complicity even about this.

He steps back across the room, picks up his glass of vodka from the arm of his chair, and gulps it. Then he holds the glass out to Lottie. She stands up and takes it. It seems the final part of some exchange. "I should be getting back, I guess," he says.

"Yes, I suppose you should," she answers.

But at the door to the dining room—to the light—he pauses and gestures at the messy table, the books, the papers. "You working on some new story?"

"An article; yes," she says.

"What's it about?"

"It's about love, actually."

"You're reading *books* to learn about love?"

"Well, that plus extensive man-in-the-street interviews, of course."

He leans against the doorjamb. "Ask me. I'll be your man in the street."

"Umm. Okay. *Love*. Sir: A: Do you think it's yearning, love? Or fulfillment? B: Is it knowing someone, or not knowing them? C: Is it having someone, or not having them? Then we come to the subquestions. Can you know someone? Can you, as it were, have someone?"

He is shaking his head. The gleaming, polished hair stays perfectly in place. "These are not useful questions."

"Why not?"

"Because they don't get at the real issue, and the real issue is, do you want love at the center of your life, or do you want it just to be a part, a part of your life? And I think women want it to be at the center and men don't. That's all." He holds his small, pretty hands out.

Peculiarly, Lottie is disappointed. Did she think he was going to reveal something to her, then? She did, in fact, she realizes. She thought he might have brought her *news*. She feels a jolt of contempt for herself; and then for him. "But weren't you, in fact, putting it at the center when you held on to your girlfriend?" she asks. "When you forced Elizabeth's hand?"

"Not at all. I told Elizabeth it wasn't going to last forever, that it was just a kind of craziness. I never forced her hand. I never said I loved the woman. I didn't love her, as a matter of fact. And if Elizabeth had been able to believe me, she'd never have gone through—she'd never have put the children through—what they've gone through this summer." He sounds angry for the first time, and Lottie feels strangely as though she's scored some sort of victory over him.

"But she sure would have gone through something else, wouldn't she?" she needles. "Sitting at home, waiting for it to be over. Maybe, in fact, she speeded that up by leaving. Do you think?"

His lips purse in a dismissive expression.

"I mean," she says, "let me put this situation to you: How easy would you be about being just a *part* of Elizabeth's life, if another

188

part of her life happened to be someone who was fucking her into oblivion daily?"

"It means something different."

"Say what?"

"It means something different to a woman. For the very reason, specifically because, women put love at the center of their lives, it means something different when they have an affair." He believes this, Lottie sees.

"Lame," she says. "I'm not even going to hammer you over the head with the overwhelming number of examples that can be offered of men who absolutely put love, want love, at the center of their lives. I'm just going to say that your argument is circular. And lame." She turns and steps into the darker part of the hallway, toward the front door. "Pathetic. Retrograde." She opens the door, and he comes and stands opposite her in its frame.

He is grinning. "You didn't buy it, I take it."

"I wouldn't even bid on it," Lottie says.

He bends close to her; his breath warms her face. "Well, thanks for the information, Lottie," he whispers.

"What information?"

"Exactly," he says.

His hand slides across the back of her neck, inside the fabric of her dress. He pulls her forward and kisses her again, roughly this time, maybe because it has been decided nothing more will happen, maybe because she's been snotty to him. Then he's gone, the slip, slip of his fancy shoes crossing the porch, going down the stairs and across the street. The night air makes Lottie's hair tremble; she catches her breath. He's disappeared onto Elizabeth's lawn when she shuts the door.

She goes back into the kitchen and looks at the clock that is part of the rounded back panel of the stove. It makes a constant, effortful, grinding noise, which Lottie has come to think of this summer as the very sound of time passing. Only ten o'clock. She planned to run after the evening at Elizabeth's, but now she's had the wine, she'd better not.

She feels a wave of self-disgust. She blames it immediately on drinking when she hadn't intended to, on not running for two nights in a row. And then she laughs out loud. "And how 'bout

189

almost *balling* Larry?" she says. "How 'bout almost *doing the nasty,* honey bun?"

Lottie rubs her neck and frowns. What was it? What could it have been that brought her so close? Maybe some wish to seal the end of her love for Jack? Because it would surely have done that, wouldn't it?

Or maybe it was just the sense of familiarity with Larry. He's like a half-dozen guys she's slept with—for no good reason, except that she wanted them at the moment. She thinks again of the tough way he held his cigarette, of the way he seemed pleased to announce that his father beat him. She liked all that. Cheap taste, she thinks. White trash.

White trash. She remembers that this was what Al called her, Al, the roommate of Derek's whom she'd slept with first, who seemed to understand how Lottie felt about herself before she did. White trash: he made a joke of it. Of everything. Of sex.

Al. He was a biochemist. He'd disappear for two or three days at a stretch, running experiments that had to be continuously monitored, and then Lottie would answer the knock on her door at two in the morning, or four in the afternoon, and he would be standing there grinning, his fly unzipped, his penis hanging out.

He called his penis Al too. "Al would like to go swimming," he'd say, nudging her with it. He embarrassed her. She felt he was irreverent. She wanted love and sex to be elegant, and Al was not elegant. She misunderstood him too. She thought his long absences, his seemingly cavalier attitude, meant he didn't care for her.

When Derek asked her out during one of Al's experiments, she was glad to go. Derek was a poet; he had long, carefully combed blond hair. He wore Brooks Brothers shirts in pale colors that reminded silly Lottie of Gatsby. By the time Al reappeared, it was over. He walked in on her and Derek, actually, embracing in the kitchen. "Well, all my friends!" he said. "What's for dinner?" Was that the response of an elegant person? Lottie thought not, at the time.

Years later, long after Lottie was divorced, he'd looked her up when he was at a conference at the University of Chicago. He was married by then, to another biochemist, and they were both teaching at Cal Tech. He had a good life, a nice life, he told Lottie. He showed her a photograph of his kids, taken by a jewel-blue pool in a sunlit California backyard. They squinted into the bright light. There were palm trees behind them.

Later in the evening, drunk, they mildly kissed for a while. Al got teary about the past. He said he'd loved her then. He asked her why, how it could have happened that she'd chosen Derek.

Lottie was teary too. For what? For her youth, over before she felt it? For all the wrong choices she'd made? For her tiny pool-less apartment across from the el in this gray and frigid city? "Oh, Al," she cried. "I had such a cold heart, you wouldn't believe it."

In his kindness, Al had protested. "You only think it was cold, Lottie," he said, and they both had a good cry and swore they'd stay in touch and so forth, which they didn't do, of course.

And ain't this your cold little Lottie revisited? Lottie thinks now.

"I should lock the door," she says aloud. And she goes back into the dark front hall and flips the little knob on the lock to the right. Closing the barn door. She thinks about Larry again. Elizabeth's husband. His kiss. Why had she let him in? She licks her lips. Her mouth still tastes faintly of cigarette. She goes into Ryan's bathroom, puts a half inch of toothpaste on his worn, frazzled-looking toothbrush, and scrubs her teeth. The new filling on her tooth twinges, just slightly, and after Lottie spits out the toothpaste, she bites down hard on it, to feel it again.

She comes back into the dining room and stands in the doorway, surveying the mess she has sometimes thought of as welcoming. I should do a little work, she thinks. Dutifully she sits down.

Then suddenly she stands up again. She goes upstairs and puts on her running shoes, then comes back down, gets her keys, and goes outside.

Though she is walking, she slowly traces the pattern of right and left turns she usually makes when she runs. The streets are emptied, and she walks on the smooth asphalt instead of the brick sidewalks, so she won't have to think about where she's putting her feet, the bumps and sudden gaps in the brick. It's ten-thirty by now, and there aren't many lights on downstairs in the big wooden houses. Lottie usually runs earlier, midevening, when kids are still playing in the streets on certain blocks, when people are on their porches or in their yards, and lights are just coming on in the living rooms, the kitchens, you can catch quick glimpses of all the variations of family life. Tonight everything seems desolate to her.

A light rain is beginning to patter in the leaves above her, and Lottie feels a drop or two. She stops in front of a lighted window on Hilliard Street, one of those many-paned windows that reach from the floor to within a few feet of the ceiling. A couple sit on a couch with their backs to Lottie, their heads and shoulders rising above the curved frame of the couch. Each head is bent forward— they are apparently reading—each lost in whatever universe his book holds. They sit about three feet apart on the couch, infinitely companionable, it seems to Lottie, but separate. How does this happen? How do you get that? she wonders.

She hears footsteps approaching in the distance, voices, and she makes herself move on. She passes a young couple, the girl talking that idiotic young talk: "I was like, *duh*, you know. I mean, I was like, so out of it, then. When I think of it now, I'm like, wow, was I ever so young?"

Yes, my dear, you were. You, like, are.

At the corner, Lottie stops. She's been headed for the river, but the rain is falling harder now. She turns and walks back up Hilliard on the other side of the street. At the window she pauses again. The woman's head is lifted now; she is turned to look at the man. She sits, impassively staring at him, and Lottie stands outside, staring at her, getting drenched. She's aware of this, suddenly, the absurdity of it, and she starts to walk again, quickly this time, in the direction of her mother's house. She's like some creature from outer space, she thinks. Some Martian, reading her books, staring in through windows, trying to figure out what it means to be human. *What is this thing, called love?* She jogs a little, humming, then slows again to a fast walk.

And after all, how can you tell, how can you know? Maybe what looks like peace in the living room is anything but. She stares at him with love, Lottie had thought. But why not hate? Or a sort of shocked indifference: you look up from a book that's full of feeling and importance to you and encounter a face, a self-contained and alien face, reading its book. Maybe you think, *Who is this person whom I live alongside of? For whom I feel this sudden nothing?* A couple live together happily for twenty-five years, and then the man runs off with a woman exactly the age his wife was when she married him. They live together unhappily for twenty-five years, and when she dies, he's besotted with grief. "Besotted," Lottie says aloud.

Lottie remembers that one of her closest friends, the editor who'd endured her obsessions about Jack, told her she'd been married for seven years to a man who wanted to live close to the earth, who rejected civilization, filthy lucre. She said that for all that time she bought into it, absolutely. They built their own house, on difficult rocky land miles from anywhere. They had no electricity, no running water. They used a wood-burning stove for heat and to cook on. Diane had kept goats for milk. She made cheese, she put up quantities of vegetables and fruits each harvest season. She sewed all their clothes.

And one day she walked the four miles down to the highway and hitched a ride to Denver, and it was over. She said if anyone had asked her the day before whether she would ever think of leaving, she would have told the person he was out of his mind.

The lights are off downstairs at Elizabeth's house, but her bedroom windows are glowing through the old, parchment-colored shades. Lottie thinks of that marriage, the way Elizabeth described it in her letter to Cameron: steady, full of devotion. Can that be true? And if it is, does it matter that Larry has affairs? Does it matter that Lottie has almost slept with him the day after he's returned for Elizabeth?

Who can know about anyone else's marriage, really? Maybe Jack and Evelyn weren't so happy, even when she was whole. Maybe when he played the clarinet, it drove her wild, she went through the house, slamming doors; and he pretended not to notice. Played louder, in fact. Maybe every now and then he wished she'd get a job, *get a life*. Maybe he came home sometimes and saw the carefully addressed invitations to the carefully orchestrated dinner parties stacked on the little burled maple table in the front hall, waiting to be mailed; and wished he'd married a different kind of person.

As she reaches into the dining room to turn off the light on her way upstairs, Lottie suddenly thinks of a passage she read a long time ago in *Anna Karenina*, a passage about how arbitrary our decisions about marriage, about whom we should love, are. It connects to all this, somehow, to everything she's been thinking about. She squats by the stacks of books on the floor and finds *Anna Karenina*. She flips through the pages until she comes upon it.

But it isn't quite what she was thinking of. It isn't apt. It describes a moment when two minor characters have gone for a walk to collect mushrooms. She is sure he will propose; and he has decided that he will, today. And there comes a moment as they move toward each other when it seems this will happen. But it doesn't. And then, because it doesn't at this moment, it becomes clear to both of them that it never will.

Puzzled, Lottie puts the book down. She turns off the light and goes upstairs. She's wet, and cold. Her bedroom window is open, and a raw breeze is blowing in. She shuts it and peels off her clothes. Water has beaded on the floor in front of the window. She wipes it with a T-shirt, puts on her robe, and goes down the hall to the bathroom.

She lets the hot water pelt her back, not even soaping herself. She turns and feels it beat against her breasts—the sensitive, radiated flesh—against her belly. She looks down. Her wet pubic hair is pulled to a point between her legs by the water, like the point of an old-fashioned valentine heart. The water makes a jittery dotted line down from it. She leans her head back, shuts her eyes, and lets the water strike her face, puddle in her open mouth.

Then she moans aloud suddenly, opens her eyes. She's remembered: she first thought of the passage from Tolstoy not when she was pondering the mysteries of decisions and feelings in marriage, in love; but earlier, when Lawrence—Larry—kissed her. When she, or he, or the moment itself, decided that they wouldn't sleep together. They wouldn't ball each other. Thinking of the difference between that trashy scene and the beautiful, sad passage in Tolstoy, Lottie twists her head back and forth sharply. Then she reaches down and pushes the stiff knob above the faucet. The shower stops; after a second the water courses out of the faucet. And Lottie stands there wet and shivering, watching the thick silver ribbon of water divide and splash over the tops of her feet.

CHAPTER 10

The next morning is dry and hot, and Lottie sleeps late, not wanting to wake into the memory that waits behind her dreams. She's sweaty and tangled in the sheet when she does open her eyes, and she lies for a moment staring at the ceiling. Though the window is closed, she can hear children yelling in the street. A window somewhere slams shut. And already Lottie is going quite carefully over the evening before, calling up each element of her own participation in it, remembering the real excitement she felt, playing her shabby game with Larry. She conjures an image of Jack—his lined, gentle face—to shame herself more, to increase her own guilt; and then feels this, abruptly, as the shabbiest behavior of all. She cries out, and unwinds herself from the sheet. Her problems, even her self-disgust, are purest self-indulgence, she thinks. After all, Jessica is dead, Cameron is mourning.

She's naked; she dresses quickly. In the bathroom mirror, her hair is crazed—flattened, a tangled wild wedge shape. She smiles at her own ugly reflection. "Just so," she says. She brushes her hair, rubs it with a wet washcloth to restore its even curliness. She brushes her teeth and is suddenly aware that her tooth is sore, it aches slightly.

The house is still as she moves through it. Outside, the cicadas whir. No breeze. Lottie is sweating as she stands in the kitchen and waits for the water to boil. She turns on the radio, but then turns it off quickly. Churchy music, holy-sounding sopranos.

She didn't look out her bedroom window upstairs; she hasn't gone to the front of the house down here; and so it isn't until she steps off the porch to retrieve the paper from where it lies on the walk that she notices that Cameron's car is gone. She stops, and then she walks down to the curbside with her hands on her hips. She looks stupidly up and down the street—as though she might be mistaken about where she parked it, as though it might have moved on its own in the night and she might discover it in some other spot. Her pulse has quickened. She takes the steps two at a time on her way back into the house. Her bare feet thud. She is angry, a reasonless, pulsing rage. Cameron came for the car! he came for it without bothering to get in touch with her, and she is pissed off at him. She imagines his impassive face, his self-containment. Her hands fumble with the phone; she makes a mistake. "Fucking rotary dial," she says, starting over. That he didn't leave a note! That he didn't call her!

She gets through. The telephone rings, and then goes on ringing, in his apartment. She imagines its empty beauty and order, the phone ringing and ringing in the open space, and she is more angry by the second.

And then she realizes: the machine is off. The answering machine. The bastard came home and turned off the machine. She slams the phone down and stands in the dining room for perhaps a full minute. She has begun to talk to herself. "Okay, then. It was definitely Cam. He was here. Maybe he did leave a note. Say he did. Where? Where would he put it?"

She spends some time looking on the few surfaces left on the first floor, mostly in the kitchen and among the papers on her worktable. Of course there's no note. She drains her cup and sprints upstairs. She puts on shoes, gets her purse, then comes back down and leaves the house.

For the second day in a row, she drives through the morning air to the South End. Today she barely notices anything. That consciousness of detail which descended on her yesterday—perhaps because she was so full of the thought of Jessica's death?—is gone. She's aware only of anger, and under it, the possibility of something

196

gone wrong. She feels as she did the first few times Ryan was very late for a curfew, a rage intensified by the helpless edge of worry. She prefers the rage, she dwells in it and pushes the worry under. Blindly, unintentionally, she cuts someone off on Storrow Drive. He pulls in behind her, then careens into the passing lane, cuts her off in return. Lottie brakes, slows down. She drives more carefully along the sparkling river and then across Back Bay. A post-breakfast crowd is milling around in the courtyard of the homeless shelter on Cam's block, and Lottie has to creep by them where they spill obliviously out into the street. One of them turns and socks her car as she brushes past him. Lottie can't be bothered protesting. She drives to the end of the block and parks. She doesn't see Cameron's car on the side street where he usually leaves it, or in front of his building. She takes the stairs up two at a time again for the first flight, then slows for the next three. She hammers on his door, and then, while she's waiting, goes to get the key from the top of the electric box. She knocks again: again no answer. She opens the door and carefully closes it before she calls Cameron's name. No need to risk waking Prince Charming downstairs again.

Her voice echoes in the room. Her eyes sweep the big space. Her note is gone. There's a wine bottle on the counter that separates the kitchen area from the rest of the room. She crosses the room, touches it. Recorked, half gone, and an empty wineglass in the sink.

She checks the bathroom. Empty. She steps quickly to the bedroom door and stops in shock. Blood! splotched everywhere on the bed and floor. And then she sees: not blood, but roses. Rose petals. She steps over the threshold. The bed is slightly rumpled—lain on, rather than slept in—and across its surface the broken roses and their stray petals lie, a brownish-red color. A running stain of damp on the wall shows where they hit first. The shards of curving glass lie scattered on the bed, crunch underfoot now as she steps across the room. She sits on the bed.

She's talking aloud again, nervously swinging her eyes around the room. "Okay, he was here. He was here. He turned off the machine. He picked up his car. So? So. So. So. So. So he's at work, maybe. So you call."

Of course, she can't remember the number at the bookstore. She calls information, then the store. Maeve answers. She says no, Cameron isn't there.

"Shit," Lottie says. She punches her leg.

"What? You still didn't find him?"

"No. And you haven't heard from him either?"

"Unh unh. But you know, he's like, never in on Saturdays anyhow. So it doesn't mean anything. It's the day he always visits your mom."

"Ah!" Thus the car, Lottie thinks. "So you think he's out there?"

"Well, really, who am I to say? But you could sure try anyhow."

"Yes. Well, thanks, Maeve."

"Yeah, let me know."

"Okay."

Lottie calls information for the South Shore Nursing Home. Nothing. She and the operator fool around a bit and finally find it: the South Shore Elder Care Community. It takes three different connections there, long waits each time on a dead-sounding line, before Lottie gets the nurse in charge of her mother.

She's out for a drive, the nurse says. Yes, with Mr. Reed. They're usually back by lunch.

Lottie looks at her watch. Almost ten. She's pretty sure she knows how to get there. She can make it by ten-thirty, ten forty-five if she doesn't get lost.

"What time is lunch?" she asks.

"She usually goes in to the eleven-thirty seating. Occasionally later on the days your brother visits, depending on how long they're out for their little spin."

"Yes. Well, look. If you see him—Mr. Reed, that is—could you tell him I'm coming out? I'm his sister. I'm Mrs. Reed's daughter. Could you tell him I'm on my way?"

"Well, Miss Reed." Her voice is nippy. Lottie has affronted her. "If I see him, I will, of course. But you know, we're not a message center for visitors, exactly. And I can't guarantee I'll actually see him, in any case."

"Yes, of course, I know that. I only meant *if* you see him," Lottie answers, straining to keep her voice polite.

"Very good, then," the nurse says, crisply.

"Thank you." Lottie hopes the anger in her voice isn't audible.

"You're entirely welcome."

Lottie hangs up. She defames the nurse loudly as she gathers her purse and car keys from the various places she's dropped them. She returns Cameron's key to the electric box and hurries back down the stairs.

But everything seems to work against her need for speed. She gets trapped in the maze of one-way streets near Cameron's house and has to make the same circuit past the same winos several times, looking for a way out that will give her access to the expressway going south. They watch her blankly twice. The third time they're ready; they call loudly to her: "Darling, you need a driver. Let me drive your car for you, baby." Laughter. It was ever thus, Lottie thinks.

Once on the road, she realizes she isn't going to make it to Scituate unless she gets some gas. Within five minutes of getting on the highway, she is pulled off it, waiting to have the tank filled. The gas station attendant, a former member of the third world, moves at third world speed. He practices his English on Lottie. "You are driving to the south?" he asks while the pump whines. "You are working on your job?" He has to return to the office to get change when Lottie hands him a twenty, and on his way, he stops to take someone else's order and start that pump going, chatting with that driver too. All this is done with such a beneficent smile on his face that Lottie can't even take the satisfaction of being surly to him. When she drives away, though, she lets her tires squeal loudly, and feels a mean pleasure in the noise.

Traffic is light in her direction. Lottie weaves in and out among lanes, driving too fast. She's thinking of the earlier visit to her mother this summer. The old woman didn't seem to know who Lottie was; she definitely was clueless as to Ryan's provenance—her face was blank as a baby's, looking at him.

She was clearly happy to see Cam, though. She kept up a kind of patter, senseless to Lottie, for the half hour they stayed; and Cam seemed able occasionally to wrest meaning from it, to offer a response that clearly smacked of conversation to her. She'd smile and agree, or ponder and disagree.

In the car on the way home they talked about her. Lottie admired aloud Cam's ability to translate her gibberish into something like language. He said he thought he could because he'd been there all along, he understood her patterns of speech, even though they'd slowly gotten more obscure.

Cam was driving, and Lottie was watching him while they talked. She'd watched him with their mother too, the careful civility with which he greeted the absurd, repetitive sentences, the polite attentiveness to every bit of meaningless drivel.

In the car she asked him, "So you've just forgiven her for everything?"

He looked over at Lottie. "What's to forgive, Lottie? You see the shape she's in."

"She slapped you around with some regularity when we were kids."

"She stopped when I was as big as she was."

Lottie snorted. "Just when stopping didn't count morally, I'd argue."

"Wait, are we talking about child abuse?" Ryan asked, leaning forward now.

"No. Not child abuse," Cam snapped back. He looked up at Ryan in the rearview mirror. "That kind of label is the least useful—"

"She drank too much," Lottie said quickly, her eyes moving back and forth from Ryan to Cam. "As you know, honey. And when she'd drunk a lot, she lost control." She redirected her voice to her brother. "But interestingly, only with Cam. She almost never hit me. Why do you suppose that was?" she asked.

Cameron shrugged. When he spoke, his voice was mild again. "After Dad died, I think she was scared of everything. Of life. Of managing on her own. She wanted me to be the man. To run things. And every time I behaved like a kid, I think it terrified her. It reminded her that she was alone." Lottie watched his impassive face, the noble profile. "Therapy speaks," he said, and smiled wanly.

Lottie turned to Ryan, in the back seat. "Cameron was all of twelve when Daddy died," she said dryly.

Cameron's lips pressed together. "I'm not justifying it, Charlotte. Just explaining it."

"Hey, no way you can justify it," Ryan said.

"Touché," said Lottie.

Cameron didn't answer.

"I used to feel so guilty," Lottie said. " 'Why him? Why not me?' Is that what they call survivor's guilt?" she asked.

Cameron shrugged.

"Actually, no," she said. "That's not even true. First I'd feel glad. 'Thank God it's him and not me.' That's what I really felt. I remember once or twice even laughing. While she hit you. Do you remember that, Cameron?"

"I guess so."

"Laughing!" she said.

"God, Mom," Ryan said.

She looked back at him. "I suppose it was a kind of nervousness. But *then* I'd feel guilty. But really, guilty because I was so glad not to be the one. To have escaped. That's what I can't forgive." She looked at Cameron and waited for a response, but there wasn't one. "Don't you think that's the worst thing she could have done to me? To make me glad for your pain? To make me complicit?" She watched his still face, his graceful hands on the wheel. His busy eyes flicked to the rearview mirror, then to the road ahead, to the car moving alongside him. But never to Lottie.

"Don't you think that's unforgivable?" she persisted.

"I don't know, Char." He was tired of this. "Yes, sure. It's unforgivable. Don't forgive her."

Lottie waited a minute, and then said, "Okay, you've convinced me. I'll forgive her."

Cameron had looked at her, then again back at the traffic. Finally he had smiled, his slight, composed smile. Lottie grinned back in gratified delight.

But the truth was, of course, that Lottie didn't forgive her mother. Helpless, hopeless as her mother was now, Lottie had only to remember a few of the details of her childhood, her adolescence, to call up her anger once more. Perhaps most wounding of all, though, were the memories of visits she'd made to her mother with Ryan when he was little, visits in which her mother had simply seemed uninterested in him. After the first one, made the Christmas when Ryan was a little over two months old—when they had stayed for three nights before moving on to Derek's parents for the same length of time—Derek had said he would never visit her mother again.

Lottie wouldn't have been capable of such a decision then, but the moment he'd said it, she felt a hateful assent. She was still nursing Ryan; she still lived in the constant memory of the sundering, transforming pain of labor, in the daily awareness of the ecstatic relief of the moment after birth. She still thought of Ryan in part as a physical expression of something she hadn't understood about herself, as well as a perfect and miraculous being. Her mother's indifference to him, to herself as a mother, struck Lottie as sharply as a blow.

And though Derek's position was a dead issue by the next year—they had separated by then—Lottie found herself more and more finding excuses not to make that trip back to Cambridge. After Derek had moved east again, she sometimes stayed for one night when she was bringing Ryan for his summer visit to his father, but her mother was even then so remote that as soon as Ryan was able to travel on his own, Lottie simply stopped coming east. For the last fifteen years or so, she had visited her mother perhaps once every three or four years, when business took her near Boston. Ryan hadn't seen her until this summer.

She had Cameron's reports in the meantime. And she wrote her mother the odd brisk and obligatory letter, the kind of letter some-one else might write to a great-aunt with money, someone she needed to be polite to. But her mother rarely responded. When she did, it was likely to be a Hallmark card—an embossed rose, a bunch of heart-shaped balloons floating in a cloudless sky—compliment-ing Lottie in childish rhymes on being a wonderful daughter. Cam-eron's fidelity to her over the years had made this distance possible; but also made Lottie feel a confused pang of guilt whenever she thought of him or her mother.

Now, turning off the expressway and beginning the slow weave through the little South Shore towns, she feels the same sense of dread she felt sitting in Cameron's car as they approached the nursing home on that earlier visit. Why can't she forgive her? Maybe in part, she thinks, because her mother's way of getting old, this retreat into alcoholic senility, is only the exaggeration of that earlier retreat into depression or despair or whatever it was that denied responsibility or the importance of her connection to Lottie and Cameron. Can this be it? that it seems, really, more of the same, and that Lottie simply can't allow herself to have sympathy for it? She is frowning, her jaw is tense as she drives along. She's aware again of the dim ache in her tooth. He's made this filling too big, she thinks.

It's just after eleven when she finally pulls into the lot outside the home and parks. The place is low-slung, brick, built, perhaps, in the late fifties. It reminds Lottie of a school, and she isn't sure for a moment why this is; but then she notices the cutouts of flower baskets taped to the windows of the wing she's headed for. They're identical in shape but decorated differently, with Magic Markers and glued-on glitter—like the uninspired art projects schoolchildren are forced to create to decorate their classroom windows seasonally. She has a picture of her mother then, bent intently as a kindergartner over her cutout, and she feels, momentarily, more pity for this imagined person than she was able to muster for her in the flesh on her earlier visit.

There's no one at the nursing station, so Lottie makes her way down the wheelchair-wide hallway to her mother's room, thinking she'll wait there for her and Cam to get back. The linoleum gleams. You can see in it the wide arcs of the buffing machine, you can smell the wax, mingled with other, sweetish odors. Glancing into the open doorways as she moves down the hall, sometimes seeing an old lady staring blankly back at her, or two of them sitting in silence watching television, Lottie remembers that her mother has a roommate too; and when she turns into her mother's room and sees the slumped figure in the chair by the window, she's so prepared for this roommate that it takes her several seconds to recognize her mother. The old woman is asleep, her head dropped forward, chin on chest. The back of her neck is painfully, vulnerably presented, and her knobbed, veiny hands clutch the wooden arms of the plastic-covered chair. There's no one else in the room.

Lottie goes in and sits on the bed. The TV set is on, a soap opera with the volume turned much too loud. A woman whose flesh is nearly orange is pleading to keep her baby over an ominous and swelling organ chord. Just as she fades out, Lottie reaches over and turns the set off. She looks back at her mother. Now that the television is off, she can hear the labored push of her breathing. She's thin, gray, dead-looking.

Lottie doesn't know whether her mother was ever a pretty woman. In the few photographs Cam has of her parents, and in others Lottie had seen of her mother as a young woman, she's attractive in a stocky, sexy way. But in Lottie's memories she is so inert, so phlegmatic except for her rage, that her appearance simply doesn't count. Asked to describe her then, Lottie would fumble. And in fact, asked what her mother was like, Lottie would be able to list only habits—she chewed Doublemint gum and smoked Chesterfields and kept spare packs of each in the top left-hand kitchen drawer. She drank Pabst Blue Ribbon beer. She collected glass and china figurines. She gave herself home permanents every few months, and after she'd had one, she smelled peculiar for a week or more. There was absolute regularity to her days. She did the wash, for instance, on Mondays. Other days were fixed for shopping with her wheeled cart, for cleaning house. When the children were young, even the meals were predictable: tuna casserole on Wednesdays, chicken pot pies on Saturday night, and so on. By the time they were teenagers, she didn't cook anymore, and Lottie and Cameron fixed what they wanted from what was in the freezer. That's what Lottie knows for sure. There are dim memories of her, happier, when Lottie's father was at home. And of a few fights that Lottie realized only later—actually, Cam told her—were about money, about the embezzlement scheme that went haywire. She can't imagine what her mother ever thought, except that she didn't like disruption; or what she looked like when she was younger, except that she was short and had, even in Lottie's earliest memory, gray hair.

Now, too, slumped in the chair, she has a quality of anonymity—smaller than she ever was, her hair recently, tightly permed in rigid, silvery blue waves whose artificial elegance makes her seem, simply, unworthy. She's wearing pilled synthetic slacks and a loose sweater. Her unpressed yellow blouse has stains down the front. The skin of her face is coarse and flushed, netted with spidery red lines from years of drinking. She wears no makeup, of course. Her feet, curled neatly under the chair, are encased in the odd, slipper-like shoes many of the residents wear. Easier to get them on, Lottie supposes, than shoes that fit tightly or lace up.

Lottie reaches over and touches one of her mother's hands. The skin is surprisingly smooth, soft to Lottie's touch. Experimentally, she strokes it.

"Mother," she says.

Her mother moans and swings her head up. Her mouth stays open. Lottie sees that her tongue is curled near the front of her mouth like a foreign object—a large, flesh-pink lozenge.

"Mother, it's Charlotte," she says.

Her mother's mouth closes. She smacks her lips and swallows. She blinks, and then her eyes unveil themselves, pale and lifeless. "It's Charlotte," she repeats without focusing.

"Yes, it's me, Mother."

The old woman looks at her with no sign of recognition, and then her eyes slip away.

Lottie touches her hand again, grips it. "Mother, I've come about Cameron."

There's no answer, no sign that the question has registered.

"Mother, did Cam visit you today?"

"Cam," she croaks. She frowns at Lottie.

"Yes."

After a long pause, she says, "Cam is . . . my son."

"I know. Was he here? Earlier? Was Cam here?"

She shifts in the chair, sits up a little straighter. "Of course he was," she says with sudden irritable energy.

"He visited you?"

"Yes. I said so," she wails. Her head bobs for a few seconds, and then she turns her face away and says, "Now don't keep at me."

Lottie feels a sudden embarrassment. She looks at the empty doorway, as though she might at any second be caught here, be asked to leave. Somewhere down the hall there's the rattle of dishes.

Suddenly her mother speaks, contempt thick in her voice. "He comes to visit me. Not you. No one comes to visit you."

A bloom of confusion makes Lottie momentarily speechless. Then she tries to remember Cam's example, his ability to revise what the old woman says. What can she make of it, this remark? Finally she says, "I know I haven't come to visit enough, and I'm sorry—"

"Well, that's the way," her mother interrupts. "I try and try, but I can't do everything. There's only so much . . ." She trails off.

"I know," Lottie says after a minute. "I haven't tried enough. And I'm sorry, Mother."

The old woman's head swings toward her. She squints at Lottie, then her eyes open wide. "You're not my mother," she says finally, with some indignation.

"No," Lottie answers. "I'm Charlotte."

There's no response. After a few seconds, her mother looks

205

away. She slides her feet forward on the shining linoleum, and then, as though she likes the sound, she slides them again, and again.

Lottie takes a deep breath and starts once more. She keeps her voice mild and pleasant. "Mother, did Cam say where he was going? Did Cameron tell you . . ." How to put it? "Did Cameron . . . was he going home when he said goodbye?"

"Home," she echoes. Her eyes wander to the open doorway.

"Yes. Did Cam . . . was Cameron on his way home?"

"You're not allowed to go home," her mother says. "You never are. It's not like that, but it could be."

"No, Mother, I meant Cameron." This is hopeless.

"Cameron takes *me* in his car. Not you."

"I know, Mother. I came in my own car."

"*You* don't have a car."

Absurdly, Lottie feels irritated. "Yes, I do, Mother. I have a car." I do too.

She looks sharply at Lottie, suddenly. "Do you have a car?" she asks.

"Yes. I drove here too. Just like Cam."

"Are you going home?" There's a startling access of energy in her voice, her face. Her eyes seem a deeper blue.

Lottie leans away from her mother. "I was asking about Cam, Mother," she says.

She looks blank.

"Cameron is gone. He left, right?" Oh, good, Lottie. Left, right: what's she going to make of that?

"I *asked* him to take me," she says, suddenly querulous. After a moment she says, "Are you going home?"

"I don't know, Mother. I'm trying to find Cameron."

"I'm trying too. I'm trying and trying. But you can only do so much. There's only so much, and they won't let you out. It could be, but it isn't. You see how they won't. They lock the doors. So how can I in the first place? But if you've got a car, you could give me a ride."

"Where would you like to go, Mother?"

"I'm going *home*."

"But this is your home now."

"I'm not talking about this," she says angrily. She starts to struggle up. "If you've got a car, you'd better take me."

Lottie rises quickly. "Mother, no. Listen, Mother. I'm staying here," she says. Before her mother can fully stand, Lottie puts her hands on the old woman's bony shoulders. She pushes gently and feels a few seconds' resistance; but then her mother seems to give up. She collapses back down, her head wavers on her stalky neck, her hands fall into her lap in resigned prayerful curves.

Lottie is murmuring to her, bending over her, stroking her mother's arm, the soft smooth flesh of her hands. "It's all right, Mother. I'm staying with you. Lunch is in a few minutes. I'm not going anywhere, Mother." She feels abruptly deeply ashamed, and somehow moved.

Her mother is staring up at Lottie. Her eyes are blazing with sudden furious life. "You don't know who you're talking to."

"Yes, I do," Lottie says gently.

"You do not."

"Yes, I do. You're my mother. And I'm Charlotte."

There's another pause. Then the old woman says, craftily, "I have a Charlotte."

Lottie sits down again, she bends toward her mother, brings her face close. "I'm Charlotte. I'm your Charlotte, Mother."

"Not you." She pulls her hand out from under Lottie's and swipes at the air between them, as though Lottie were an irritation, an insect bothering her. "I mean another Charlotte. That's just it. I need to talk to my Charlotte. Not you." She looks around the room. "My Charlotte."

"You can talk to me. I'm Charlotte."

"No, no no. You are not . . . you haven't got the right . . . *Charlotte*, for me." Her mother's breath is short for a minute; Lottie can hear it surging in her nostrils. She sees that her mother has a little beard, five or six long white whiskers that curve under her chin. "I am trying, but you just have not got the right, Charlotte." Her voice is rising in a muted wail, and Lottie is terrified she'll begin to cry. "I am trying and trying. I am trying and trying."

"Mother, it's okay. It's okay. It's okay." She pats and strokes her mother's hand, and the woman seems to relax back in the chair a little. "Mother," Lottie says gently, "would you like to talk to Charlotte?"

"Yes."

"I can talk to her for you, Mother. I know Charlotte. What

would you like me to say to Charlotte when I see her?"

"You know where Charlotte is?"

"Yes. I can take a message for you to Charlotte. I can write a message down for you." Lottie reaches into her bag, finds a scrap of paper with a partial list on it. She keeps fumbling. At the bottom, under a lot of junk, is a pen. "I can write a message, if you tell me what you would like to say. Tell me."

"Tell you."

"Yes, I'll write it down." Lottie holds up the paper, the pen. "And I'll give it to Charlotte. What would you like to say?"

Her mother looks at her, her mouth open as though she'd forgotten how to make words happen for the moment.

Lottie prompts, "You could begin: 'Dear Charlotte . . .'"

Her mother sighs with great effort. Finally she says softly, "*Dear Charlotte . . .*"

Unexpectedly, the tears spring to Lottie's eyes. She and her mother sit together in silence for a minute. Lottie looks up from the blurred paper. Her mother's face is blank. Lottie speaks, gently. "I wrote that, Mother," she says. "I wrote, 'Dear Charlotte.' What comes next?" She leans forward, supplicant. "What would you like to say?" What does she imagine? That she can somehow call up a message truly meant for her, as she is today? Not that, surely. But some vague sense of possibility, of hope.

"Dear Charlotte," the old woman repeats hesitantly. "Dear Charlotte, I am writing to you . . . so you can give it to the one, the one who's Charlotte." There's a long silence. Lottie is writing slowly. "That I had a Charlotte. But they will not let you. And I am trying. And I am trying . . ."

Lottie looks up.

"I am trying and trying. You can only do so much." The sense of strain is gone from her mother's voice. She's found the familiar track again. "You see how it is. I try, but they won't let you do a thing. It's not like that, but when Cameron comes, he should take me home. They just don't help you here, they just don't try."

Lottie lets the pen lie on her lap. She looks for a long time at her mother. "I wish I could help you, Mother," she says finally.

"I want my Charlotte," the old woman says expressionlessly, not looking at her.

"I know," Lottie says. She has an impulse to touch her mother

208

again, but she doesn't. She feels intimately chastised by all this. She is, after all, a stranger, isn't she? with no such rights. "I know," she says again.

And they sit that way, silently, until the nurse comes to get her mother for lunch. The old woman's eyes have closed again, her head has jerked and dropped. Lottie has watched her draw away into sleep, has thought about leaving but somehow hasn't. She's sat in the little square room with the two beds, the two chairs, and listened to the puff and mutter of her mother's dogged, regular breathing.

Now she follows the nurse's aide and her shuffling mother down the hall. The nurse's aide, a teenager, holds her mother's hand comfortably, as though they were schoolgirl friends. She calls her "Ella" and tells her the menu slowly and in great detail. She is so thorough that Lottie thinks of her as a kind of parody of a pretentious waiter explaining the day's preparations in some snazzy restaurant. Her mother gives no indication of hearing her, but she moves along without protest.

When Lottie says goodbye, the nurse's aide smiles and says a loud, seemingly corporate goodbye back, but Lottie's mother says nothing. She doesn't look at Lottie either.

It isn't until Lottie steps outside and the damp air brings her the odor of the sea, of grass, that she realizes how heavy the smells of Lysol and wax, of floral air perfume, in the home were. Walking back to the car, she is most aware of simple relief: to be out here, in this mild air, not that; to be free, to be free of her mother. Not to be the one who will visit her again next Saturday and the Saturday after that. *Never*, she thinks. Never again.

And then she is overwhelmed by a sense of loss that includes her father too, the few treasured images she has of him, the thought that she might, one day, have understood from her mother, from Cam, something about who he was. Her face tightens, she breathes slowly until she's in control of herself. Okay? Okay.

And then the question: Where to?

Home again, home again, she supposes. Such as it is.

Her pretend home. Her mother's real one.

The pretend Charlotte, the fake, goes to the real home. She smiles grimly and starts the car. "The real Lottie goes to her pretend home," she says. She drives on the narrow, curving roads, pondering the layers of confusion of real and imaginary. And what about being the unrecognized Charlotte taking dictation for an imaginary Charlotte whom *she* can't imagine; from a mother she knows is her own mother, but who has lost her motherness—if she ever had it—when she lost the ability to know "Charlotte"? Who is her mother anymore? As Cam asked in a different way, she thinks, when he asked what there was to forgive anymore.

It makes Lottie think of Jack, of course, of Jack and Evelyn. The question of who she was when she wasn't his old Evelyn anymore but was still there, still alive, and needed him and wanted his love and attention. Did he love Evelyn then? Or someone else? And if this Evelyn loved Jack, without being able really to know a Jack anymore, who was it that she loved? Who was it that made her cry out in joy—that Evelyn with cropped dark hair, drunkenly tilted in her wheelchair—when "Jack" came home each night?

And who is it that Jack loves now that that Evelyn is dead? Not her, surely, but perhaps some ancient Evelyn who contains a long-ago Jack too? The way her mother's idea of "Charlotte" contains everything lost to her: home, herself, memories of her husband, Cameron, Lottie—maybe even the happy thought of booze, the little jelly jars, the sticky circles they left everywhere.

What becomes of love when it stretches this way, to hold so much loss?

When Lottie held her mother, touched her, she felt for a few seconds what it might be like to love her as she is, she pitied her so. As she drives along, thinking of this, she feels she understands, perhaps, fractionally, what Jack talked about when he said he learned by holding Evelyn, by touching her, how to love her again in a different way. Lottie thinks perhaps she could be that kind of person too—it seems possible to her momentarily that she could learn to love that way, to reshape herself and her feelings.

But then she thinks of her relief when she got free, of her hunger to be gone. That mean eagerness to be solitary, insular, that rises again and again in her life.

She's on the expressway by now, approaching Boston; and she decides abruptly to get off at East Berkeley Street, to check Cameron's apartment once more on her way home. She signals and exits. She circles back to Cameron's building and parks.

She rounds the corner and goes into Cam's dark entryway. She begins the long climb up the concrete stairs again. Behind the door on the second floor a woman is crying steadily, a hopeless drone of despair that recognizes no possibility of comfort. Lottie stops momentarily, her own throat clotting. She remembers abruptly a little boy she saw on the train in Chicago one day, crying like this. He was black, he was maybe two and a half or three, and he was with his mother, who couldn't have been more than a child herself, seventeen or eighteen. He was sitting on her lap, and as Lottie watched, he began, simply, to cry. His mother was wearing a Walkman so she couldn't hear him—not that he made much noise over the clatter of the train anyway. But Lottie watched as the tears landed on the girl's hand, as she lifted it and looked at the drops; then she wiped the wet off on her jeans and looked out the window. She never bent to the little boy, she never said anything to him. And after five minutes or so, he stopped. He just stopped crying. Lottie had thought at the time she had rarely seen anything so terrible in her life; and the sound of this crying, which follows her as she climbs the stairs, brings the memory of it back to her. She has to stand for a minute or so outside Cameron's door to compose herself before she knocks.

She knocks several times, louder each time. There's no response, so once again she goes down the hall and gets the key. She lets herself in and again, absurdly, checks everywhere in the apartment for him, in case—she supposes this has to be the reason—Cam is hiding from her.

As she's standing in the bedroom doorway, the telephone rings. It knocks her heart, and she's almost breathless as she picks it up.

"Yes?" she says. "This is Cameron Reed's residence."

There's a startled silence. Then: "Is Mr. Reed there?" It's a woman's voice, a woman probably around her age. Not Elizabeth.

"No. He's not right now. Could I"—she reaches for the pad and pen by the answering machine—"could I take a message?"

"Well. Actually. When will he be in, do you think? When do you expect him?" The voice is cultivated, very New Englandy.

"I can't really say. I . . . This is his sister, and I don't really know his schedule that well. I could leave him a note."

"No. I think I'd rather not do that."

Lottie waits, but the woman offers nothing else. Finally Lottie says, "Well, I'm sorry not to be more helpful."

The woman says, "I have this other number for him. Maybe his work number? Do you think he might be there?"

"He might. It's probably his store. He owns a bookstore. But he wasn't earlier today. I'm not sure where he is at the moment, actually. He's had a kind of . . . crisis in his life. But you could try there, certainly."

She can hear the woman sigh. She says, "You're his sister?"

"Yes."

"And you know about . . . this accident he was involved in?"

"Yes. Who is this, please?"

"Oh, I'm sorry. I'm Dorothea Laver. I'm Jessica Laver's mother. You know, the girl . . ." She trails off.

Lottie experiences a sense of helpless shock that seizes her speech for a moment. Then she says, "Oh. I am sorry. I'd met Jessica. I was just so . . . so sorry to learn about her death."

"Well. Thank you. I appreciate that. Thank you. But you know, I was calling . . . You see, Mr. Reed had told the police I might call. I wanted just to talk to him, to ask him a few things."

"Yes, I talked to the police too, when they were trying to reach him, and they told me you might. Call Cameron." Lottie's talking too fast. She'd do anything to help.

"Did your brother . . . Did Mr. Reed, by any chance, talk to you about it? About the accident?"

"No. I haven't . . . actually"—she slows herself down, willfully—"had time to talk to him at any length about it."

"I see." Lottie can hear the woman's controlled breathing for a few seconds. "Well . . . I don't mean to be ghoulish, to make him dwell on it, or anything. Or to intrude on what must be very hard for him too. Just that it's, of course, it's much on my mind. I felt I needed to know . . . how it was for Jessica. And he was the only one with her, you know. And he did say. To the police. He wouldn't mind."

"No, I know that." Lottie is astonished at the woman's politeness, her graceful composure. Her concern for Cam and his privacy. Perhaps it's a form of shock, she thinks. It makes Lottie pity her even more than tears would.

"Well, maybe . . . you could tell him I called. I would appreciate that. And maybe I will leave him my number. It's . . . do you have a pen?"

"Yes. I've got one."

She dictated the number, and Lottie wrote it down. "And please, be sure to say that I don't blame him. That I understand completely that Jessica . . . well, perhaps you don't know this part, but she'd had a lot to drink, I'm afraid. That it was . . . that while it wasn't her fault, exactly . . ."

"Oh no!" Lottie cries. She feels undone at this. It's too much.

"But, genuinely, an accident. And I know that. I want to assure your brother I understand that. I simply don't hold him responsible, and that won't be any part of our conversation."

"I'll tell him that."

But Jessica's mother seems to want to go on, to keep talking. "Apparently she had a crush, I guess you'd say, on some boy in the neighborhood. Elizabeth—Mrs. Butterfield—do you know her?"

"Yes."

"Elizabeth said she thought it was possible Jessica was going down the street, maybe going to see him. She'd been writing a letter about him, to a friend, a letter we found in her room. So you see. And I had just wanted to ask Mr. Reed, to ask your brother, if he could tell. What she was doing out there. And to be sure she didn't have any . . ." Her voice pinched down. "Well. Pain." She cleared her throat.

"I understand. I'll leave him your number. I'll tell him all this."

"You're very kind."

"No. No, not at all."

"Well, thank you, then."

"Of course."

Lottie sits for a while on the bed. She's heartstruck for Jessica's mother; but, after several minutes, suddenly nearly breathless with anger too, at Elizabeth. For lying, for offering Ryan to this woman as the reason for Jessica's death. *He was not*, she wants to say.

But of course, she wouldn't have said that. She won't. How could she? And what would it matter to Dorothea Laver anyway? Maybe it's better, actually, for her to believe Elizabeth, that Jessica was outside because of her crush on Ryan, rather than to know that she was there at Elizabeth's bidding, carrying her tawdry message to Cam.

Suddenly it all seems so useless, so horrible. And Lottie is aware again, as she's been able to be only sporadically, that someone has died, that Jessica is dead.

She feels angry again at Cameron too. All this should be central to him. He should be helping this woman. Where is he? She writes a quick note on the pad and sets it down by the machine on the bedside table. She looks for a moment at the machine, turned off now, the dark dead eye of the message signal. She reaches over abruptly and flicks it on. The dot lights up, ruby. It begins to blink steadily. After a few seconds, she pushes the button for messages. The tape winds back for a long time, then clicks several times and begins. It's Elizabeth's voice, sounding hard and urgent. "Cameron. Cameron, this is Elizabeth. I just want to say to you—"

Cameron breaks in: "I'm here. It's me, Elizabeth."

There's a sharp intake of breath. Then: "You shit!" Her voice is low but holds great rage. "What the hell do you think you're doing?"

"I knew you saw me." Cam's voice is oddly buoyant—a kind of bitter exultance.

"Of course I saw you. Of course I goddam well saw you. I'm just thankful Lawrence didn't. What is wrong with you? How could you do such a thing?"

"I just wanted to see it. You with him. To make myself look at it."

"At us in bed?"

Lottie leans forward, toward the machine. Her heart is pounding.

"You with him, yes."

"What, you didn't believe me? You couldn't take my word? What is it with you? I can't believe it. I just find you . . . You are preposterous."

"Am I?" His voice loops higher. "I don't think so, Elizabeth. I don't think I'm the preposterous one. Not at all."

Elizabeth's voice, too, has risen, and now it drops again. She's nearly whispering. "Look, I wrote you. I told you. I explained everything. It's done. It's over."

Where was she, saying this? Lottie wonders. In the little hallway with the telephone table off the kitchen? Upstairs somewhere?

"I was concerned about you," Elizabeth says. "I was very, very nice. But I will not have you sneaking around my mother's house in the dead of night, do you get it? That's beyond the pale. Do you understand me?"

There's a silence. Lottie can hear Elizabeth's shallow, fast breathing. Her own mouth has dropped open.

"That's not a good way to talk to me, Elizabeth." Cam has made his voice calm again, but Lottie can hear the strain in it.

"How do you expect me to talk to you? There's no other way to talk to you."

"We need to talk reasonably."

"We could, if you knew how."

"I want to see you." He sounds almost tearful.

"*Absolutely* not."

"You just said if I behaved reasonably . . ."

"But you haven't. You've been absolutely . . . wacko! Nuts!"

"I need to see you." His voice is urgent.

"Cameron, look. There is just no way . . . Look. I *came* to see you. I wrote you a letter. I made every effort to end this thing kindly. Reasonably. And look what that produced: this. You! Crazy. Sneaking into my bedroom, for what?"

"I told you, to look at you."

"To look at me? That is nuts!" Her voice shrills, then she drops it again. "See? That's what I mean. That's absolutely crazy."

"I need to see you, Elizabeth." Lottie grimaces at his pleading voice.

"No! If you needed to see me, you could have. I was calling you. For hours yesterday. I came over. I already did that. Where were you? Yesterday, where were you? Hiding? I mean, Christ!"

"I was watching you." He's almost whispering.

There's a beat. "Don't tell me that. That's too sick."

"It's true."

"When I came to your place, Cameron, yesterday morning, where were you?"

"I was out then."

"Out! Where?"

"I was out all night. Christ, Elizabeth." There's some percussive sound behind him, he's hit something. "Think about it, will you? I killed someone. And then you . . . you pretended I was sort of . . . some acquaintance. A distant friend, or something. So, yes, I was out. I was out. In the first place I was with the police for about

215

four hours. I had my blood taken. I must have sat in the emergency room for . . . And then I just lost it. I walked around awhile. I thought I'd get the car. I was there, at your house, when I realized I didn't have the keys; I didn't know where I'd left them. For a while I just sat in the car. I watched your windows. When it was light, I took all the change from the car and went to Mass Ave. I had some coffee. I waited awhile. Then I came back. The car was moved by then. Your shades were up. I thought I could get in touch with you, I needed to see you. I went back to Mass Ave and I called. I got him. I called again after a while, and I got Emily this time. So I had some more coffee, I walked around, I came back to your house, I don't know, I went back. I must have called four, five times." He ends, exhausted.

"And then hung up?" she says, after a second.

"I only wanted to talk to you, Elizabeth. I had nothing to say to him, or to Emily."

"I knew that was you."

"In the afternoon I came home. I slept."

"So you *got* my letter."

"No."

"No, what? Did you get my letter?"

"No; Charlotte has your letter."

"That's ridiculous! Why would Charlotte . . . ? This is absurd. Why would Charlotte take my letter?"

Lottie shifts on the bed.

"She did."

"Why?"

"Ask Charlotte. I just know she took it."

"That's absurd. It's preposterous. How do you know that?"

"She left me a note. She said she had it. She wanted me to call her. I don't know. Maybe she took it so I'd call her."

"That's crazy."

"What difference does it make anyway?"

"Because, Cameron. Look. I explained everything to you in the letter. I think you should—"

"It's self-evident, isn't it, what you wrote in the letter? You said goodbye, right?"

"Cameron, I explained to you—"

"You said goodbye. You told me to kiss off. You said, in effect,

that if I came for you, I'd find you in bed with someone else, right?"
His voice cracks. After a few seconds he says, "And I did, and you
were."

"Jesus Christ, Cameron, Lawrence is not *someone else*. He's my
husband."

"Remember what you said when you gave me the key, Elizabeth?" His voice has dropped, suddenly. It is gentle, urgent. He is
desperate, wooing her. *Don't*, Lottie thinks. "Do you remember?"

There's a silence.

"Do you? Do you remem—"

There's a light click, then the quick empty fizzing of blank tape
for a few seconds, and then the machine turns off. No more of this.
And no more messages. He must have turned the machine itself off
completely just after they finished talking.

Lottie sits on the bed for a minute, staring through the open
doorway into the light-filled room beyond. She finds herself wondering if he played the tape back for himself before he turned the
machine off. If he listened to himself and to Elizabeth, to the venom,
the desperation, in their voices. She wonders what else they could
have talked about after the machine stopped taping. Where could
they have gone from where they were?

She sits motionless, unsure of what to do next. She thinks about
calling Cameron at work again, but then thinks, *why?* He's gotten
her messages. Probably every one. And chosen not to respond. He
might even be there. Or driving around. Or watching Elizabeth
again. The point is, there isn't any need, anymore, to worry. He has
rarely sounded so alive as he does in this telephone conversation
with Elizabeth. What was it Larry said about him last night? That he
was full of life.

But not a kind of life Lottie has sympathy for. She feels dis-
tanced from him. For the last day and a half she has thought of him
as mostly focused on Jessica, on the accident, on her death and his
responsibility for it. For Lottie—and for the Cameron she's been
imagining over these hours—the news that Elizabeth was abandon-
ing him was incidental. Sad. Awful, even. But, in the balance, not
that important.

And of course, that's not the way it is for him in reality. In
reality Jessica's death for him is . . . what? Something he'll think
about later? Something that just intensifies his feelings about Eliza-

beth? She can't imagine it. But clearly what he is focused on now is Elizabeth, only Elizabeth.

Lottie hears again Dorothea Laver's quiet, apologetic voice. *He's not even thinking about your daughter.*

She looks around the room at the scattered darkening roses, their curling petals. A thick curved shard of the broken vase lies by her feet. Abruptly she remembers Ryan turning, sweeping the glassware and tins off her mother's table, marking, she supposes now, his own powerlessness in the matter of Jessica's death, of death itself. The coincidence of the violent ceremonies seems remarkable to her momentarily.

And then she remembers how readily she'd knelt to help Ryan, how pained she'd been by his pain. She stands up. *Not this,* she thinks, and picks her way back across the room. At the door, she stops and looks once more at the running stain on the wall, at the splotches of bloody rose drifted over the bed. *Not this time,* she thinks. *Not me.*

CHAPTER 11

As soon as Lottie turns left onto Storrow Drive and the river comes into view, she has that curious uplifting of the spirit you get when you start out on a trip, which she had, in fact, when she came east earlier in the summer. There's some heartbreaking adagio on the radio by—she thinks the pontificating announcer said Schubert. The white sails of a gaggle of boats tilt their way east across the river basin, and the silver maples leap and flare in the breeze, and suddenly Lottie could sing. She feels she's been put on earth to experience this, to see this.

She knows that what she is feeling, at least in part, is relief. For the last day and a half when she's thought of Cameron, what she's really been thinking of is *herself as him*—what she would be doing if she were he. Because, she sees now, she thinks of herself as *like* him, she thinks of his crazy desperation for Elizabeth as like things she's felt. She thinks of the accident—the dead girl—as something she might have done in that desperation.

The revelation that what he's been feeling and thinking is so much not what she expected, is so different from what she might have thought or felt—this, combined with Dorothea Laver's muted politeness and the frightening image of him making his way through Emily's cavernous, darkened house: these have set Lottie free. He is himself, and she is here, *not him*, driving her car along the river. To her right, the beating oars of a cluster of long narrow boats catch the light suddenly, as the wings of a flock of birds will sometimes do when they all turn at once in the sky.

Harvard Square is jammed with traffic, and Lottie has to move slowly through it. She's so gracious to jaywalkers that she infuriates the guy behind her, who leans on his horn to encourage her to get into the right spirit. As she approaches the gourmet sandwich shop near Porter Square, she remembers Ryan and their comradely lunch on the back stoop the day before. She parks and goes in.

The place isn't as full as she expects. She looks at her watch and is surprised to see it's one-thirty: the lunch hour is mostly over. She realizes she hasn't eaten yet today. While the young man behind the counter—who might be moving underwater, everything happens so slowly with him—fixes her expensive sandwiches, Lottie has a cup of coffee and a brownie in the little back room. She has to shift the chewy cake to the left side of her mouth, away from her sore tooth.

There's one guy sitting alone back here, smoking what smells like a Gauloise and reading a paper; and there are eight or ten people gathered around several tables they've pushed together in the corner, having a meeting of some sort. It is orderly in the extreme. They raise their hands to make their announcements; gatherings are planned and signed up for months ahead of time.

They are wearing Earth shoes; two of the men have beards, the women have on peasant blouses and ethnic jewelry. Their goodness, their worthiness, are apparent. "Terry and Felice are going to have a potluck the week before Thanksgiving to plan the Christmas events, and they need to know how many are coming. A show of hands." With her face bare of makeup—not even washed, she remembers!—Lottie probably looks like a potential member. Yes, a woman catches her eavesdropping and smiles warmly. Someone else speaks of the need for visits to Naomi in the hospital, and some time is taken working out a good rotation. There's a discussion of the Christmas "events"—are there too many? not enough? It's noted that it is a tough season to get through. There are moans of agreement.

These people are Lottie's age or maybe just a little younger. She is incredulous and, she notes, slightly jealous, even while she knows she wouldn't be able to sit through a whole meeting like this. But to fill your life with such harmless happiness seems remarkable to her. Who cares if it's makework? There is something to be said for the sheer mad organization of it. Does your group have a purpose? she wants to ask. Are you concerned with some greater good? Or are you, say, a volleyball team with social life appended? They are still at it when she leaves to get her sandwiches from Mr. Thorazine.

She pulls up in front of the house and looks at it. The porch sags, she sees this clearly as if for the first time. And without the shutters the neighboring houses have, the house itself looks blank-eyed, a pale woman with no makeup. Still, it will sell. It will all take care of itself. It will sell, and this part of her life will be gone, finally. And she will be nothing but glad. She thinks of her mother again, her mother and her yearning for home. Is it this building, this street, she yearns for? Somehow Lottie doubts it. It's probably finally as abstract as the pang Lottie can sometimes feel when she hears the word "mother."

Lottie suddenly remembers a moment of seeing her home just this freshly once before: when she'd come back from college in final defeat. Seeing it and thinking, *No*. She'd yearned for it while she was away, she'd convinced herself it was the right thing to do, to leave college, to come home and save more money before she tried it again. But stopped then in front of the house, having hauled her suitcase up from Harvard Square, she couldn't believe how cheap it looked, how little and shabby. Somehow it wasn't the *home* she had in mind.

That night her mother had made a meal, she remembers, and they sat together at the kitchen table to eat, as they hadn't, it seemed, in years. Chicken and mashed potatoes. Her mother had a glass of beer by her place. They ate in silence. Neither of them really knew what to say. That her mother was glad she'd come home was clear. Lottie can't remember her own feelings; perhaps she didn't have any.

But then somehow Lottie's mother started talking about Cameron, about how "high and mighty" he was. Her mouth had shaped a bitter curve. "He always thinks so well of himself, he's always trying to be what he's not." And then her voice had warmed. "That's not the way you are, Charlotte. You're more down-to-earth." She said a number of other things, all meant to make Lottie feel allied with her—but what Lottie was feeling was a growing sense of shocked clarity: her mother had wanted her not to make it! She had seen Lottie as less than Cam! Lottie had remembered then all the small things, mostly things not done, that had made it harder for her to get out, to go. All the ways in which her mother had insisted, somehow, that Lottie was hers. That to have ambition, to want out, was to be "high and mighty," *to think well of yourself.* Oh, why not? she wants to cry out now on behalf of that younger Charlotte.

At the end of the meal, her mother piled the dishes in the sink, saying she'd do them the next day. Perry Como was on; she wanted to watch. When Lottie didn't join her in the living room within a few minutes, she called out, "I hope you're not doing those dishes in there, Charlotte. I said I would, and I will—in the morning." The height of graciousness.

Lottie had sat for a while at the table, thinking in a variety of befogged ways about what she should do next. For so long she had simply wanted to be where she was. Now she saw she couldn't stay, and a void seemed to yawn in front of her. Life. Lottie hadn't a glimmer of an idea about what came next.

And now, twenty-five years later in her car in front of the house, she has something of that same feeling. Bridges burned, it seems. Decisions to be made. She sighs. She can hear what she assumes is Ryan's radio faintly from the back of the house. There are little kids on bikes pedaling in big looping circles behind her in the wide street. She opens the door and heaves herself out of the car. She walks slowly up the front stairs, and then through the empty rooms to the back of the house. The back door is open, and through the rusty and paint-dotted old wooden screen door, she sees the dappled sunlight as blotches of lighter green in the scraggly yard. She pushes the door ajar.

Ryan is almost next to her on the ladder—it startles her—painting the window to his bedroom.

"You look starving," Lottie says, holding up the white paper bag with the sandwiches in it. "I have lunch."

He starts down. "I actually ate a couple of hours ago, so I'm not. Starving. But I'll take some coffee if you want to make it."

When he comes in, Lottie is already at the sink, rinsing out the coffeepot. She puts the kettle on to boil. "Why didn't you make coffee?" she asks.

"I did. It was horrible," he says. "Hey, where did you *go*? I thought you were sleeping late. Then I thought you were really sleeping late. And then I thought you must be dead, and I checked on you and you weren't even there."

"The Cameron chase again. I found him."

"Oh. How *is* he?"

"Well, I didn't talk to him, actually. But I know he's okay, which is the main thing."

"But where has he been this whole time?"

"Oh, out and around. A little crazy, as you might suspect." She thinks of his voice on the telephone. "But he seems to be back to the normal routine now." She spoons the grounds into the paper filter. "He visited Mother today." This is true. It sounds normal, and it is true.

But Ryan is barely listening. "Well, good," he says. "And I found out about the service. Jessica's service."

"And?"

"And it's tomorrow, at twelve-thirty. I wrote it all down. Elizabeth came over and told me. She wants you to call her when you get in. Like, now."

"Thanks."

"She said it was very important, quote unquote."

"Okay. I will in a bit."

"I just deliver the messages."

He goes into his room. Lottie hears him washing up. He comes back bent forward from the waist, his hands and face dripping. He uses three or four paper towels to dry himself.

"You look as though you're just about done out there," she says. "True?"

"When I finish these windows. I figure a second coat tomorrow, and that's that. Unless you want me to do any more inside."

"I don't think so, hon. There are a few more things I can do. But we're not about to start anything radical."

"That's what I thought. So. I've been trying to decide whether I want to go directly home, with you, and *then* come back east and visit Dad; or stop to see him on the way to Chicago."

"Well, I don't know exactly when I'll be heading back to Chicago." The water is starting to boil. She's glad to have to turn her back to him.

"Oh."

223

"Of course, you can go on ahead of me. I'm sure Jack will have no problem with that." She pours the water into the grounds, watches it begin to dribble through.

"I don't think so, actually. I mean, no insult intended, it's just that it is his house, you know. I just . . . I don't know. I'd rather you were there."

"There's a room all set for you. All your stuff." She turns around now and rests her buttocks against the sink.

"No. I know. It's just, you know. The car and all. And . . . well, I'd just be more comfortable."

"I understand."

"So. So I guess I'll go to Dad's for a week or so. That's about what he's been talking about, lengthwise." He gets a cup out of the cupboard and comes to stand by the pot. The dripping has slowed. He looks at Lottie. His face seems vaguely fearful to her. "Think you'll be heading back by then?"

"Yes," she says lightly.

So that's when she'll do it. Good. And then she'll see. She imagines her return: she imagines Jack, absurdly, standing as he was, in the driveway with the old dog, watching her approach, just as he watched her depart.

Well, whatever happens, she says to herself, Ryan deserves some time in Chicago. He deserves to see his friends, to move in with his books and trophies and yearbooks and sports equipment and old letters and homework; all the stuff he's religiously saved all his life with an avidity and affection that has always startled Lottie.

Together they watch the last drops filter through. Then Lottie lifts the paper cone and grounds, still dripping a little, and throws them away.

Ryan pours a cup and sips it, carefully. "Okay. So that's set. I'll call Dad in the next day or two, then. Let him know."

Lottie watches him for a moment. "You going to work some more?" she asks.

"Mm-hmm."

"I think I'll come out and help you, hon."

"You're supposed to call Elizabeth."

"I got the message, thank you. I *will* call her, later."

"Okay." He shrugs.

"I'll go change into painter's stuff," Lottie says.

224

"Fine with me," he says, and heads, carefully balancing his full cup, toward the back door.

While Lottie is upstairs, though, Elizabeth comes over. Lottie hears her in the hall, calling, the way she did earlier in the summer.

For a second or two, Lottie thinks of not answering, simply hiding. She doesn't want to hear about Cameron's midnight visit. She doesn't want to defend taking Elizabeth's letter, or to talk about what Larry—Lawrence—was doing over here for so long last night. She doesn't even want to discuss the lies Elizabeth has told about Jessica and Ryan, about Cameron and Jessica.

But somehow she's been implicated in all this; somehow there is this scene to play out too. And then, she tells herself, she *will* be finished. "I'm up here," she yells back.

She hears Elizabeth come to the foot of the stairs. "Shall I come up?"

"*No*. No, I'm changing. I'll be right down."

She takes her time, carefully folding the clothes she's removed. Finally, carrying her paint-dotted, worn-out running shoes, she starts down the stairs.

Elizabeth begins to talk before Lottie has reached the landing. "Charlotte, listen, you have *got* to do something about Cameron. I came over earlier. I've been frantic. I need your help."

Lottie raises her hand, as if to ward this off, to slow Elizabeth down. "This stuff is between you and Cameron, Elizabeth. Whatever's going on is strictly between you two. There's nothing I can do—that I'm going to do." Lottie sits down on the stairs and starts to put one of her shoes on.

Elizabeth is silent. Lottie ties her shoe, not looking at her. Then Elizabeth says urgently, "Char, please," and Lottie lifts her head. Elizabeth's eyes are glistening. "You've got to listen. He's gone crazy, Charlotte. He sneaked into the house last night. I . . . In the middle of the night, I woke up. I heard a noise, and there he was. Just standing there, in the bedroom. God! Looking at me! At Lawrence and me. I was terrified."

"Of what, exactly?" Lottie's voice is calm. She slips her other foot into its shoe.

"What do you mean? Of everything! Of him, for one. Of what in God's name he was doing. Of Lawrence's waking and seeing him, and . . . who knows? A fight? I mean, what did he *want*? What if

225

Lawrence had seen him?" Elizabeth's hands are in motion all this while, the silver bracelets glinting.

"What *did* he want?"

Elizabeth stops. She stares at Lottie. "How can you be so calm? I find this . . . This is very irritating, Charlotte. Your response. This is crazy, his behavior. And you know it. He's out of control."

"What do you think he wanted?" Lottie repeats. She bends to tie the other shoe.

"How would I know? I called him, actually, this morning, and for once he answered the phone, and I asked him just that. And he said some ridiculous thing about wanting to make himself *look* at it. At us. Jesus."

"Well, so that's what he wanted." She pulls the bow tight.

Elizabeth's face changes, watching her. She says, "Charlotte, you think this is crazy too. Don't tell me that you don't. This is absolutely nuts."

Lottie gestures back toward the kitchen. "I have some stuff I have to do now, Elizabeth. Do you want to come out and talk to me while I paint?"

"*No*," Elizabeth says. "Charlotte, look. What I would like is for you to get him under control. I have one more day here to get through, just this service tomorrow, and then I'm gone. And I'm just terrified. I'm really scared."

"That Lawrence will find out."

"No!" she wailed. "No, not even that. Lawrence is gone, I told you that. I mean, that's the point, really. I'm alone now. I'm alone and I'm terrified."

Lottie stands up. She's on the third step. She's taller than Elizabeth up here. She likes the feeling. "Elizabeth, I'd like you to try to understand that I haven't got a prayer of *controlling* Cameron, as you put it. I can't even get in touch with him. And if he's hurt or angry, or whatever . . . I don't know, maybe he has a right to be. You've treated him shabbily. You've been a real shit through this whole thing. No one else has mattered, not Cam or Jessica or even Ryan, for God's sake. You've lied to everyone around you. Telling Jessica's mother she went out to moon over Ryan."

Elizabeth's face is livid, suddenly. Her hand rises and rests on her bosom, the carefully painted nails set wide apart.

"Oh, that's the least of it, of course," Lottie says, disgusted with herself. "I mean, that can't hurt Ryan, really. Or anyone, I suppose, for her to think that. But you've just been so damned . . . self-serving, at every turn."

Elizabeth turns away. She draws a slow breath and exhales loudly. Then she says, in a small voice, "There's a lot at stake for me, Char."

"And not for Cameron?"

She looks directly at Lottie. "This is my marriage. It's my life. It's my children's life."

"Isn't it possible, just possible, that he sees this as his life? That he sees his life, in fact, as—preposterously, of course!—of equal importance to yours?" Lottie smiles a harsh smile.

Elizabeth is shaking her head. "Somehow he has to know, he had to know, that it was a fling. It was a summer romance. We never talked about the future, I never lied to him. If he thought otherwise, he deluded himself. Himself."

"Well, then. I think he may have deluded himself. What a pity."

"That tone is hardly helpful, Charlotte."

Lottie snorts, a bitter laugh. "Let me say, Elizabeth, that I feel no obligation to be helpful to you. I was helpful to you with your husband." She pauses for a second; she's aware of a flush rising to her face. "Your little soirée. And then I found out that you'd led him to believe Cameron and Jessica were somehow involved. And I still kept my mouth shut, which was asking a lot. Or doing a lot. Unasked. So the idea that I now have any further obligation to you just . . . boggles my mind. For God's sake." Lottie comes down the steps. "And now I have to go help Ryan, if you don't mind."

"I do mind." Elizabeth is standing in the way.

"Well, that's too bad, then." Lottie moves to step around her, but Elizabeth steps sideways.

"No; you need to listen to me for just a minute. What I'm telling you is important. Charlotte, listen!" Her voice shrills.

Lottie moves past her, crosses the dining room. Elizabeth is walking directly behind her. "You have to talk to him. Listen. I'm warning you, he's dangerous, Char." Her voice rises as she speaks.

As she's stepping toward the screen door, Lottie looks back at Elizabeth.

"He is; he's dangerous. Charlotte, in San Francisco—listen to me!" Her voice rips, and she grabs Lottie's elbow. Her fingernails dig in, and Lottie cries out. Through the old screening, she sees Ryan rise and turn to look in at her, confused, and then start to move up the steps; but freeze in the dappled sunlight when he hears Elizabeth, behind Lottie, begin to cry—a raw, gasping sound.

"In San Francisco I had . . . to get a restraining order. Do you understand what that means? I had to go to the police." She releases Lottie; she covers her face. "I had to tell them he meant to hurt me. That he wouldn't leave me alone." Lottie has turned to watch her. "Oh, God."

Lottie stands motionless, feeling imprisoned, trapped. After a minute Elizabeth's body stills, she wipes at her eyes. When she speaks again, her voice is whispery, but under some control. "He followed me, everywhere I went. For two whole days. And then he broke in. He was yelling outside. I locked everything; all the windows too. I thought he'd have to go away if I didn't answer. But he broke the glass, he broke in. Do you understand? He . . . pushed me around, he was yelling. He was there for four or five hours. I don't know. He wouldn't leave, he wouldn't let me use the telephone. And when he fell asleep, I sneaked out. Out of my own apartment. I had to get the police to come back to my own apartment, to get my thesis. To get my thesis." She laughs suddenly and wipes her eyes again with the back of her hand. "Can you believe it? My thesis—it was my life at that point. And I thought he would destroy it. I thought he wanted to destroy my life. I thought he would want to hurt me so badly that he would tear it up. The main thing on my mind was my fucking thesis." Elizabeth steps to the counter and peels off a paper towel, wipes her face with it and blows her nose. "I had to stay with friends until he had left town. He wouldn't leave me alone." She and Lottie stand for a moment, not looking at each other. Then she speaks again. "And now he's doing the same stuff again. The same thing. Charlotte, I don't want to call the police. I don't want to get him into trouble. I mean, it seems so risky for him, with Jessica's death and all. You've just got to help me."

Lottie looks out the screen door. Ryan has sat down; she can see the top of his head just above the stoop. She looks back at Elizabeth. "I just want to ask you," Lottie says, "why you ever would have started up again with him this summer after all that. I mean, what were you thinking of?"

Elizabeth lifts her hands. "Oh, Charlotte, you saw the shape I

228

was in. I wasn't thinking, I was just reacting. Grabbing. Someone who loved you that much . . . wouldn't you?" Lottie doesn't answer. "I needed him," Elizabeth says. "And how was I to know? I mean, that was *years* ago. We're grownups now. I never could have imagined anything . . . that he would be so . . . unchanged."

Lottie's elbow is smarting, throbbing. She holds it up, turns it to look. On the soft white flesh just above the joint are three raked red stripes.

"Oh, I'm sorry, Char," Elizabeth says quickly. "I didn't mean . . ."

"What do you want me to do?" Lottie says, dropping her arm.

"I don't even know, really. I've just got to get through tomorrow morning, and then we're gone. I've got reservations, plane reservations, for all of us in the early afternoon."

"Does he know Larry is gone?" Lottie asks.

"No. I don't think so. And I sort of implied he wasn't going till next week. I said I would see him then—Cameron. I promised. Just to placate him. And I think he believed me. But he's called and hung up a couple of times today. I'm sure it was him. Still, I don't think there's any way he could know we put Lawrence on the plane. Unless he followed us to the airport, for God's sake." She laughs. "And I watched for him, can you believe that? Checking out my rearview mirror. It felt like some . . . *movie.*"

"There's really nothing I can do," Lottie says. "He hasn't called me back. Not once."

"I know, I know. I called him for a whole day and night before I got him. But I don't know, I just have the feeling, Char, that if you could stay in touch with him, just keep him calmed down . . . Part of it is how he *feeds* on himself. He's so alone. . . ."

"Okay, I'll try. I'll do what I can." Lottie gestures, a gesture she wants Elizabeth to read as dismissal.

But Elizabeth needs more from Lottie. She shakes her head. "He's a thug, really, Charlotte. A gangster, emotionally."

Lottie raises her head. "Nobody around here looks very attractive at the moment."

"But this is just . . . another dimension, really. I mean, you wouldn't sneak into someone's *house.* You wouldn't hurt someone."

Lottie feels almost dizzy—shocked that Elizabeth has thought

229

she meant herself. Her mouth actually opens slightly. And then she smiles, grimly. "Okay, fine, Elizabeth. I'll try to call him, all right? It's what I've been doing anyway. But I'd like you to go now, more than anything."

"But you'll talk to him? You'll stay in touch?"

"I'll try to get in touch. Period."

"No. With *me*, I mean."

There's a long silence. Lottie says, finally, "I'm not going to call you, Elizabeth. You can call me, if you like."

"Well, thank you, Char. I mean it."

"I know," Lottie says, and she turns to go outside.

As she opens the screen door, she can hear that Elizabeth has started to walk to the front of the house. Lottie steps outside. Ryan is standing at the bottom of the porch steps, immobile. Lottie raises her finger to her lips, and they wait. The front door closes, distantly.

"God, Mom!" he says.

"Yeah." Lottie sits down—crumples, really—on the top step. "Ohh." She puts her face into her hands. "*Oh, Lord.*"

"What'll you do?" he asks.

After a long moment Lottie lifts her head. "I'll call him," she says. She sits staring out at the yard for a minute. "I'll try to be sure he stays out of trouble." She looks up at Ryan. "That Elizabeth has no reason to call the police."

She pulls herself up and goes inside. The house is dark, and when she shuts her eyes and listens to the phone ringing in the bookstore, she sees the whirling afterimages of the light patches she's been looking at in the jungly yard.

Maeve answers again. "Oh yeah, hi! He's here! Didn't he call you? I told him to."

"No. Not yet. He seems okay?"

"Completely normal. For this place anyway. You wish to make chitchat? I can connect you, via my magic buttons."

Lottie says no, just to say she called.

Ryan has come in while Lottie was dialing. He's been standing in the kitchen doorway through the short conversation. After Lottie hangs up, he says, "God, this is so crazy, Mom."

"I know. Quite the mess, hey? We should be ashamed, is what I think."

"It's not your fault, Mom."

Lottie smiles. "Well, technically I suppose you're right."

"It's not."

But Lottie is thinking, oddly, of a moment in the therapy with Megan. The therapist had been trying to get the girl to articulate what bothered her most about her situation, and she had abruptly cried out, "The whole thing! I had a perfectly nice life, and they took it and made a big fat mess out of it."

Now she says to Ryan, "Let's just go outside and paint, honey."

Through the afternoon, they work nearly silently together. Twice more Lottie comes into the relative cool of the house and calls the bookstore; twice more Maeve says Cam is there, in his office.

They finish the windows at about five. When they come in to clean up, Lottie notices the sandwiches she bought earlier. She'd forgotten them. After Ryan has bathed, they have them for dinner. Lottie doesn't eat much—she's determined to run tonight.

While Ryan does the few dishes, Lottie calls the store again. Cameron's gone home, someone says. She calls the apartment, and he answers. She's almost surprised at how much the same he sounds, as though she should be able to hear all he's been through in his voice. "I've called you a whole lot," she says. "I've been worried about you."

"I know. I'm very sorry, Char. It's just I've been upset. Too depressed, really, to talk to anyone."

Lottie has no choice but to accept this fiction. She asks him how he's doing now.

His voice is calm, his usual flat tone. He says he's fine, really. He just needed some distance on everything.

She asks him if he got her note, his wallet, the message from Jessica's mother.

He says yes. He asks her if she has the note from Elizabeth, and she tells him she does.

Then she says, "I heard about Elizabeth's husband . . . coming back. That must be hard."

"Yes," he says. And then: "You met him?"

"Yes," Lottie answers. "Last night. He seemed like a perfectly reasonable guy, I guess. It's hard to say, we were all on such good behavior." She has a quick flash of Larry, leaning forward over her, his tongue coming fully into her mouth. "But it must be very tough for you."

"It is. But it's her decision." He sounds reasonable, accepting. "Yes."

"Will you see them again?" he asks. Lottie thinks she can hear a tightening in his voice.

"I imagine," she says quickly. "There was some talk of a drink after dinner."

"I see. Sounds very sociable."

"It's not, really. But I think everyone's trying to pretend it is."

"Until he goes, I suppose."

"Yes. Right. I suppose that's the point, really."

They talk for a few minutes more. When there seem to be no more lies to be told, they say goodbye.

Ryan has finished with the dishes while Lottie was talking. He's come into the doorway again and stood listening to the conversation. Now, as she hangs up, she looks over at him.

He seems embarrassed suddenly. He shrugs. "So," he says.

"So. Lies, all lies," she says.

"You can't help it sometimes."

"Still," she says.

"I'll use the phone upstairs, if I can," he says. She's confused. "I'm going to call Dad," he explains.

"Oh, right. Fine," Lottie answers. And then she says, "Wait, no. I'm going to run anyway. Let me change, and then you can talk wherever you want."

Upstairs, she quickly peels off the paint clothes, the worn shoes; and puts on shorts, her flattening bra and a T-shirt, heavy cotton socks and her good shoes.

Ryan is back in his room when she comes downstairs. She goes to his doorway. He's sprawled on the bed, reading Calvino. His big bare feet twitch ceaselessly as though in rhythm to some internal music. "The coast is clear," she says.

Lottie goes outside and stands on the porch, breathing deeply. The air is still hot, and heavier now, damper than it was. It's beginning to be dusky. She stretches for a few minutes on the packed dirt of the front yard, feeling the pull in her muscles pleasurably.

She starts off slowly up the hill, a lazy jog. She weaves down it through the ladylike streets, past the public elementary school, past the summer-empty dorms. On Garden Street, a few cars have begun to have headlights on. Lottie is running now, kicking up behind, breathing hard, but she doesn't feel the sense of strength that usually comes to her. She turns down Berkeley, where there isn't much traffic, cuts down to Ash. The sky above the river is still light, a mild regretful golden color. Lottie pumps through the sultry air, feeling her legs, her whole body, as heavier than usual, the result, she supposes, of not running for a couple of days.

At the bridge, she turns to come back instead of making the longer circuit across the river and around. She runs back along the riverbank, then cuts across a narrow strip of park to Sparks Street, a slower uphill rise than Ash. The houses are tiny at first, then grander and grander; then, at Huron, begin the shift back again. The air feels thick and sour in her lungs. She visualizes it: not clean enough to feed her blood, not enough oxygen in it. Exhausted, panting now, she walks the last block. Her tooth hurts, her arm stings a little where Elizabeth scratched it. She feels betrayed by her body, peculiarly upset, though she knows this is unreasonable, that there are quite specific reasons it hasn't worked as well as usual tonight. But its failure wounds her. She counts on its strength, its health, the egocentric joy she feels using it.

Ryan is sitting on the front porch. As she turns into the walk, he says, "I want to go out. I'm bored."

"So go." Lottie's voice is hoarse; she's still breathing heavily.

"No, c'mon. You come too. Get cleaned up or whatever, and let's get out of here."

She looks at him. Is this charity? Some need of his own? She can't tell. "I'll be twenty minutes, at least," she warns.

"I can wait," he says.

Lottie goes upstairs. She's aware of hurrying as she showers and quickly applies makeup in the misty mirror. She finds some Mercurochrome among Richard's drugs and belatedly daubs the stripes on her arm. Naked, clutching her damp running clothes, she opens the door to the bathroom. Richard's door is open too, no light on: she's alone up here. She walks boldly down the hall, her damp feet making a wet squeak with each step. She pulls on a sundress and underpants. She slides her feet into sandals. It's getting dark by now, but she doesn't turn on any lights. She has to hold the banister coming down the stairs.

233

They decide to go to a café only a few blocks away, on Mass Ave, but Lottie wants to take the car anyway. "This is ecologically unsound," Ryan says. He's in the passenger seat, jumping stations, and Lottie feels a nervous irritation pinch her.

"So what?" she says.

He sits back and looks at her. "Hey, it was a joke."

Inside the café, Lottie and Ryan both order beer. Ryan seems to feel responsible for the conversation, and Lottie is content to let him talk—about school mostly, what courses he thinks he'll take.

At one point she says, "It was smart of you to pick a school as far away from me and Dad as you could."

He looks startled. "That wasn't why I picked it. That had nothing to do with it."

"Really? I've always thought it was."

"Mom, you can't believe the number of things in my life that have nothing to do with you at all. At all. It's like you always feel guilty or something: *you caused this, you caused that.*" He shakes his head. "I went to Stanford *(a)* because I got in and that impressed the hell out of me about myself, and *(b)* because Loie Griffith was going there."

"Loie Griffith? That anorexic shrimp? That . . . peanut of a girl?"

"Love is blind," he says.

She sighs. "Ain't it the truth."

They each drink and sit back. The waiter goes by, and Ryan signals him. He asks for chips or pretzels, something to eat. Then he says, "Do you think Uncle Cam is . . . well, dangerous?"

"I don't know, hon. He *is* such a humorless guy, finally."

"What does humor have to do with it?"

"It just does. Believe me, it does."

"That's ridiculous, Mom. What could possibly be funny in this situation?"

"I don't know. I mean, of course, really nothing is. I don't mean that kind of humor, I guess. Just . . . I guess I don't think you can forgive yourself for anything—much less forgive anyone else—if you can't somehow let go of . . . what? The *gravity* of everything? Something like that."

He frowns. He drinks some of his beer from the heavy mug and sets it down with a *thunk.* "So you do think he's dangerous," he says after a minute. The waiter comes back with a cellophane bag of pretzels and sets it in front of Ryan. "Oh, thanks," he says.

Lottie is pondering it. She thinks of Cam as she's seen him a few times in adolescence—enraged or in despair. Out of control. She thinks of his calm on the telephone with her. She thinks of the picture Elizabeth painted of him in San Francisco. "I don't know if he's dangerous or not," she says. "It appears I don't really know much about Cam."

"How can you say that? You grew up with him." He's dumped the bag out on the table, and Lottie reaches across and takes a pretzel.

She laughs. "Neither of us grew up at all together. We didn't even begin until after we'd stopped living together." She chews the pretzel, frowning. "Nobody grows up in a home such as ours. You just wait to be done with it, and you hope you'll have the opportunity to grow up later."

He seems struck by this and is silent for a moment. Lottie looks at him. He's beginning to have a line, a kind of permanent frown line, across his forehead.

Suddenly he says, "Yeah, you're right, in a way, I think. I mean, I really think I didn't grow up at all till I got to England."

Lottie is startled that he has so misunderstood her remark; but then just as glad, really, that he's missed the bitterness in her point. She asks him about England, and he talks about it. Then about his feeling of being too American there—sort of a sweet, dumb person. "Like Goofy," he says, and imitates Goofy's laugh.

"What was Goofy, anyway?" she asks after a minute. "A dog?"

"Yeah, a dog, I think." He makes a face at her. "What does it matter, Mom? Why are you always asking questions like that?"

"Am I? Like what?" Lottie is surprised.

"Oh, I don't know. I can't explain. You have a very . . . tangential brain, let's say." Someone has started the jukebox, soupy music. Someone like Percy Faith. Yes. "A Summer Place." "But actually, that's really kind of how I felt. Doglike. They were all, you know, elegant, cynical—the Brits. Very articulate. And I was this doglike, eager person. I thought things mattered that we were talking about. Doglike. Yes. And that's really how they treated me. I mean, while being quite puffickly civil. And I kind of reacted by getting even worse. Even more 'Amurrican,' or something like that, there." He pretended to swagger in his seat. And then his face opened, painfully. "But I have to say, it was the first time I thought of that stuff, that I saw myself in those terms. And it changed me. It did make me grow up—a lot—to face this sort of version of myself."

"So now what?" Lottie asks after a minute.

"What do you mean?"

"Well, what do you do with this information?"

"Fuck if I know." He grins. "Go back to school. Hang out. Have some brews. Let the river of time wash over me." He sobers. "I don't know. I'm not very happy right now, I guess. And this thing with Jessica. It feels like, in a way, the same stuff."

"What do you mean?"

"Aaah, I don't know. I just . . . proceeded through, you know. I proceeded through. I didn't ask myself anything. *Why*, for example. Aside from the basic. I've been pretty, well, rapacious, I guess you'd have to say, this last year. In England too. I think I was"—he lifts his shoulders—"using sex, or something. To make me feel better." He's speaking slowly, thoughtfully. "Like I had some control, or something. Anyway. I didn't look at myself doing it at all. And now all of a sudden I have to. And it's like seeing myself again. Like in England. Seeing myself. And I'm glad for it, I suppose. But I also wish it had never happened." He's been twirling his glass on the table. Now he looks up at Lottie quickly. "I mean, of course I wish Jessica's dying had never happened. But I mean also that I'd never had to see myself."

"To grow up."

"I suppose." And then he suddenly seems embarrassed. "Of course, I'm so very grown up now. I'm sure that's what you've been saying to yourself all summer long, right, Ma? How grown up I am?"

There's a painful quality to this. He's really asking her. She reaches a little way across the table and smiles. "On alternate days, darling, of course. At least as frequently as I'm grown up." Almost simultaneously, they finish their beers. Lottie looks at her watch. "We should get back, honey. I want you to call Cam for me, to be sure he's still there. Being good." She waves to the waiter.

"What am I supposed to say?"

"Say you're looking for me. Maybe ask him if I'm there, or if he knows where I am, or something."

As they're walking out, he says from behind her, "How did you get so good at being devious, Mom?"

"It's in the genes," she says. "Look at my dad."

Back at home, while Ryan calls Cam, Lottie stands grinding her teeth in the front hall, feeling the pain in her filling as familiar, almost comforting.

Ryan sounds natural and relaxed. "Mom's not there, is she? I wanted to know if I could take the car." He pauses, then says, "Okay, thanks," and hangs up. Lottie steps into the room. "He says you might be having a drink with Elizabeth. Otherwise he doesn't know."

She looks at him a long moment. "You're pretty good at this devious stuff yourself," she says.

"Hey, they're my genes too," he answers.

Lottie laughs, but she's also oddly touched by this. She crosses to the bottom of the stairs. "I'm going to head up, sweetie," she says. "Don't stay out too late. We've got the service tomorrow."

"I'm not going anywhere tonight anyway."

"Oh! This is a first."

He looks sheepish. "Well. You know, it seems like it might be good—I don't know—just to be around."

"Nothing's going to happen, honey."

"Whatever you say, Ma."

"Sleep tight."

"You too."

Lottie reads for a while before she turns out the light. But she doesn't fall asleep right away. She's restless. She gets up twice to look out the window at Elizabeth's. Her light is on until very late, a flickering, dim glow through the leaves outside. She hears Ryan too, several times, walking around downstairs.

Just as she's falling asleep, she imagines it clearly: Cam moving into Elizabeth's room the night before, the dark shape that's Elizabeth on the white bed turning away from Larry's humped form, lying suddenly awake on her back with just the sheet over her. She lies very still; she's hoping only that he hasn't come to hurt her, to hurt Larry. Cameron stands there a long time. His breath is ragged but regular. He sees they are naked. It is four-thirty. Light has begun to incandesce in the white things in the room: the sheets, the clothing heaped in a pool on the floor. He remembers how it felt to lie in this bed next to her, to get up and move through the darkened house on his way out at this time of the night—of the morning. He remembers how it felt to fuck her when the pressing need for silence made them wilder, as though it were some equivalent to moaning aloud, to crying out. He watches the sheet rise smoothly and fall again across her breasts; he watches Larry turn slowly away from her, move his legs, the shadows shape-shifting. He is his breathing imagination, frozen and made to see it—and Lottie is Cam, she feels his murderous heartbeat flutter in her rib cage, seize her breath; and she wakes to a sense of her true self.

She lies in the dark for a few minutes, and then she gets up and pulls a pair of jeans on, tucks her T-shirt in. She picks up her sandals and carries them down the dark stairs with her. Her purse is in the dining room. She goes outside and stands on the front porch. The porte cochere light is on at Elizabeth's, but all the house lights are off. There are no cars except her own parked on the street. She thinks of Cam, walking quietly up the driveway, turning his key in the locked door. Suddenly she is remembering her own craziness each time Evelyn had another stroke. The calls, the nighttime drives down the dark alley with the headlights off so no one would spot her. If she'd had the key, if he'd been sleeping with Evelyn, mightn't she have wanted to look?

What had her drives been if not the same old thief-in-the-night routine? Who is she except Cam's sister? While others are grappling with the Grim Reaper, Cam and she apparently are destined to sneak around.

"It's in the genes," she'd said to Ryan. And for a moment Lottie smiles in the dark at the idea of some kind of nature-versus-nurture argument about herself and Cam. *Is* it perhaps a genetic predisposition? The son and daughter of the thief succumbing to their chromosomal fate?

Or maybe it was simply being raised in a house so bland, so emptied of emotional valence, that it was inevitable they'd be Peeping Toms of the emotions. Sorrow? I want to *look.* Love? I want to be a fly on the wall.

She disgusts herself. Cam disgusts her. But he is her brother. And she, it appears, is her brother's keeper.

Lottie gets in the car, starts the engine. Once again she makes her drive through the empty Square, along the dark, glinting river. Here and there in the South End, as she approaches Cam's part of it, she sees shadowy figures moving on the streets. At a stoplight she rolls up her window, locks her door, and reaches over to lock the others.

Cam's car is on the street. She parks behind it and turns off her engine. She slides across the seat to peer up at his windows. There is a light on dimly somewhere deep in his apartment. She watches, but no one moves in the windows.

For a while she sits in the silent car. She sees the hulked, monster shapes of what she thinks is earth-moving equipment parked behind a chain-link fence under the expressway. Suddenly a tiny light flares among them, orangy, and goes out. A match, she tells herself. Someone is there, lighting a cigarette. A homeless person, most likely. She is straining. She thinks she sees figures moving among the backhoes, the bulldozers, a flicker here and there in the shadows. She focuses so hard that they suddenly take on an entirely different aspect; they seem to waver, then disappear, like the images in heat shimmers. Lottie squints, she tries harder, but they've been swallowed by darkness, her eyes can't pick them out. It seems to her she's imagined them, her whumping heart the only evidence that something, someone was there. Though she's unaware of it, she makes a noise in her throat, a caw of fear.

She sees a lone car swishing by on the expressway, going south. She thinks of her mother, asleep in the nursing home; or awake, perhaps. It didn't matter, did it? Either way, since everything she has to live through must have the same reasonless quality of dream life to her. She thinks of Jessica's mother then, of Dorothea Laver— how she may wake in the morning and for a second or two, before she remembers, feel whole and right, as though the terrible thing might only have been a nightmare, just a neurological event in her dreaming brain.

She looks up again at Cameron's window. She's done everything she can, hasn't she? He's here, Elizabeth is there, presumably sleeping soundly. Why should she be the only one awake, worrying?

She knows this is pointless. But she sits for a long time in the locked car anyway, looking as blank and still as an animal in a trap, waiting, in case something should happen.

CHAPTER 12

It seems initially that all of Jessica's high school class has turned out. Groups of people that age stand clustered together on the steps of the church; there are long embraces being shared as Lottie and Ryan pass through the narthex, and Lottie hears weeping behind her. Once she and Ryan are seated, though, she looks around and realizes that there are many more young women here than men. And that a good number of them are wearing white—the effect is almost like that of some mass ritual wedding.

Ryan has shaved this morning, and a lemony smell rises off him. Lottie looks over at his face. His eyes are skittering back and forth, taking it all in. He looks like a frightened animal. She leans back against the hard pew and lets her own eyes blur, looking around the room again. The men's summer sports coats are spots of pastel color—mostly pale blue—and the flowers mounded in front of the pulpit make hectic splotches. Everywhere, too, are the glistening wood colors—blond and walnut—of long, American girls' hair, streaking down their backs in smooth, flat panels. You can hear, scattered through the room, the shallow insucks of air: people sobbing quietly. Lottie's tooth throbs with her pulse.

There's a portrait of Jessica propped on an easel just below the pulpit—probably her high school graduation photo. It isn't precisely unretouched, and the sense of skylike roil behind her is clearly false, the backdrop in some artist's studio. Still, it catches something in Jessica's face that draws Lottie's attention, something she would have had no way of noticing, given the nature of her encounters with the girl: a sort of eagerness, but with an edge, a determination. "What's next?" she might be asking. But even more important than that, Lottie thinks, maybe also, "When?" Lottie is oddly touched by this. She wants to see Jessica as having, in some sense, begun to shape her own little life—it's too pathetic to think otherwise—and the Jessica in the photograph might have.

Ryan fumbles with the program, opens it, pretends to read. Looking over his shoulder, Lottie sees that they're listening to a prelude by Bach. The pews fill in, slowly. Ryan and Lottie have arrived a little early because she was worried that she might not be able to find the church. But it was easy. Three high white spires towered visibly over the center of town even before the approaching road opened onto the green, and she had only to circle the little park once to locate the Congregational church—the largest of the three.

Inside, it feels even more huge. The windows rise tall and narrow in a row on each side, the clear crazed panes palsying what would otherwise be the trees' slow drag in the light wind outside. There's a balcony above and a little behind Lottie and Ryan, and she can hear from the thumps and creaks that it's filling up also. Looking directly overhead, she sees the immense dazzle of a chandelier suspended high above them all.

Lottie glimpses a familiar head of hair out of the corner of her eye. She glances in that direction and sees that Elizabeth has arrived. She and the children are walking slowly behind an elderly woman with a cane. Elizabeth is holding little Emily's hand, and the boys are behind her in matching navy-blue blazers, white shirts, and ties. Elizabeth has on something darkly vibrant, striped. Lottie can see only the top of Emily's head, the brownish-red hair the color Elizabeth's was in youth. Elizabeth stops by a pew four or five rows in front of Lottie but on the other side of the center aisle. She gathers the boys toward her with her arm—Lottie sees the gleam of one of her silver bracelets—and they move ahead of her into the pew. When she sits down, she bows her head forward immediately, as if in prayer.

Finally the music ends; it begins again, with the organ unstoppered. Everyone rises, and in their midst Lottie can see the preacher and several others, these without robes, walking down the aisle, producing a muffled thunder on the bare wood floor. They step up to the chancel, and when the processional stops, the minister moves forward into the pulpit and blesses the congregation, says a brief prayer. They all sing a hymn together, they sit down. The smothered sobbing in the room has intensified. Someone opens a window with a loud squeal, then another. Lottie turns slightly and sees that it's an elderly man with a long pole, the kind her teachers had used to raise the enormous windows in her grammar school.

Now several of the girls in white move toward the chancel from various places around the room. They gather in a group of five directly below the pulpit. Lottie can hear one of them hum a note; together, audibly, they fill their lungs. And then they begin to sing, a cappella, a sweet, slow version of "My Bonnie Lies Over the Ocean." Even Lottie feels her throat clog as their voices mourn, "Bring back, bring back, O bring back my bonnie to me." They stop a moment after the last chorus; and then launch into "Yesterday." These seem odd choices to Lottie, though there's a painful poignancy to them. She looks on her program. It says, under the song titles, that Jessica sang with this group in high school. They're called the Minute Maids.

When they're finished, two of the girls mount the stairs to the chancel, while the rest disperse. Behind the pulpit, one sits down and drops from Lottie's sight line. The other steps forward and sets a paper down on top of the immense Bible in front of her. Her eyes sweep the congregation—she looks frightened—and she begins.

She has a soft, little-girl voice, whispery as Jackie Kennedy's. She talks about how she and Jessica used to go into Harvard Square by train together in high school, how Jessica would always pretend to be someone other than herself. She'd change her voice, she'd sometimes actually fake an accent. She'd walk differently. She'd be loud and boisterous, or painfully shy. The girl's voice trembles, and she bends her head; she seems to be smoothing the paper. Then she looks up again, her lips tight and determined as she begins to speak once more. She says she wasn't able to do anything of the kind, that she was always the straight man, setting things up for Jessica. But once she asked Jessica how it was possible for her. "And she told me that it wasn't as if she was acting at all. What she said was, 'They're all me, really.' "

The girl pauses. She looks over their heads. "When I heard that Jessica had died, I thought about that, about how she didn't even get to be who she was going to be, but even so, there was so much to her. And I wanted to say today, 'Jessica, we'll miss all of you.' "

She steps back a little, and then the other girl stands up and slings a guitar around her neck. She tunes it for a moment, and over the notes, you can hear people blowing their noses, the pews creaking. Lottie glances over at Ryan. He looks miserable.

The girls sing "Amazing Grace," their two voices in a tight, yearning harmony that comes as close as anything audible to heartbreak.

Then the minister stands in the pulpit again and leads them in the Twenty-third Psalm. He says a long rambling prayer, talking about Jessica, naming the members of her family—there are four or five siblings, apparently. He looks down at the front rows on Lottie's side of the aisle as he speaks. Lottie wonders which of those heads looking back at him is Dorothea Laver's; whether she's let herself weep or cry out her anguish yet. Lottie thinks about her voice on the telephone again, tries to understand what it must feel like to be her. For a fraction of a second, she tries to imagine the void and hurt of somehow losing Ryan. And then stops herself. It is unimaginable.

She looks at him again, at the reddened patches on his cheek and jawline, the set of his face. He is frowning, trying to understand something too. His face is earnest, attentive. And private. Whatever he is thinking is his own. He is, of course, lost to her, but in the way he should be. In the way Lottie still has not worked out her acceptance of, she realizes.

They have another hymn. Then several other people speak in turn—a teacher, a friend from college, who talks about Jessica's struggle to figure out what she wanted to do with herself.

Ryan sits, riveted, and Lottie wonders what he's getting out of this, whether he's getting anything. For a moment—she can't stop herself—she thinks again of the way they looked in bed together. Then she thinks of what she told him about her father's funeral—how unknown he'd still been to Lottie after everything was said. Cameron had cried, she remembers now, and that had horrified and

243

fascinated her. Cameron never cried, not even when their mother hit him. Sometimes, yes, tears came up and glittered on the lower rims of his eyes; but then his face would redden violently and— Lottie thought of it this way at the time—it was as if his eyes *swallowed back* the tears.

But he had cried when their father died, even though their father had been gone from home for four years then, and Lottie had understood finally that Cameron had loved their father, in spite of his being a criminal. She had envied Cam, she remembers. Partly because at that age she would have liked the drama of being the one weeping; but also for the feeling that made him weep, which Lottie, who remembered so little of her father, couldn't share.

And then she thinks of Evelyn again, of her death, a year ago now. Her service had been held in a big church in Hyde Park, and Lottie could easily have gone: no one would have known who she was except for the only couple who saw Lottie and Jack together socially, Jack's closest friends. But it had never occurred to her. Instead she stayed at home and tried to keep busy that afternoon. She'd done load after load of wash, filling the apartment with the smell of soap and bleach. She and Jack hadn't yet discussed what Evelyn's death would mean to them.

Now she finds herself looking again at Ryan and wishing earnestly that she had done what he is doing. That she had gone—come late, left early, sat in back—and listened to them talk about Evelyn. Jack had told her that the children had all taken part in it, that Charley, who had been fourteen when Evelyn had her first stroke, had talked about her eloquently; that Matthew had read scriptures. Jack had asked Megan to read one of Evelyn's favorite poems. Friends had spoken too, Lottie remembered his saying. He had not. Lottie had asked him what poem Megan read, and she looked it up later. It was by Elizabeth Bishop; it was about a moose that stops a bus on a highway in the night. She had liked it too—she found it funny and austere—and it made her think she understood something about Evelyn that she hadn't known before.

Now, oddly, tears for that service she hadn't gone to, for the lost opportunity to know more, perhaps, of who Evelyn might have been, come to her eyes. She fumbles in her purse for a Kleenex and finds an old one, wadded and shredding, which she unfolds a corner of to blow her nose.

Ryan grips her arm momentarily in sympathy, assuming, Lottie supposes, that she's weeping for Jessica. Let him, she thinks. Soon enough he'll learn that you can mourn for any loss at any funeral; that there comes to be a general sense of sorrow and loss in life which can be released by the ceremony even of someone you didn't know.

To her surprise, though, Lottie can't stop crying—she weeps through the rest of the service, like any of the young women in white around her—and it occurs to her just as they're hearing the benediction that she's also weeping for herself, for what she finally lost when Evelyn died.

At the time, she had wept for Jack, for them all, but felt for herself only a kind of hungry happiness. For her, it was over at last. Evelyn's long dying, yes, but also her own standing always outside, looking in. What she's feeling now, though, as the minister speaks of corruptible bodies being changed, is her own sense of loss; is how much she loved having Evelyn there, how much she loved the yearning that resulted. She had accused Jack of needing Evelyn, but it seems to her that what she understands at this moment is that she needed Evelyn too, that she misses the potency that Evelyn's existence, her life, gave to her own love for Jack, and his for her. "Wouldn't you love to have it back?" Lottie had asked him, talking about their secret, dark love together. And now Evelyn's death has beckoned them both into the light. What Lottie has a confused sense of as she weeps is that she needs to leave behind a part of her own life, a part that loves the dark, that always chooses what's temporary, what's thrillingly marginal—the hotel, the car, the secret meeting—and try instead to try to build something permanent out of the quotidian, out of daily life. Out of everything that's most fragile and mortal and corruptible.

On the way out, she feels a touch on her shoulder. Elizabeth. There's no one she'd less like to talk to, but Elizabeth stays close behind her as they slowly shuffle toward the doors, flung open now on the church steps and the sunlit town green beyond.

On the steps, Elizabeth embraces Lottie abruptly, she thanks her for what she's done. Lottie raises a dismissive hand, shakes her head, but Elizabeth insists. Then she tells Lottie they're leaving, as soon as they get back from the reception in the parish hall. "Everyone's packed and ready, so we can just put stuff in the car and take off. Mother will return it to the leasing company for us, and that will be that. What I did on my summer vacation." She smiles, wryly.

Little Emily presses against her, whining, and buries her face in her mother's side. Elizabeth encircles her with one hand, puts the other hand out and grips Lottie's arm. "So this is goodbye, Charlotte. But I hope, maybe . . ." She looks hard at Lottie, perhaps noticing now that she's been crying. "Well, Chicago and Minneapolis aren't so far apart. That's what I'll count on," she says firmly, cheerfully.

Lottie turns away to where Ryan is waiting for her at the bottom of the steps. Then forces herself to look back. "That's not going to happen, Elizabeth," she says quietly. "The Chicago-Minneapolis thing. I hope everything works out for you, but I don't won't to hear about it either way, all right?"

Elizabeth stares and raises her hand, but before she can say anything, Lottie turns away into the crowd moving raggedly down the steps.

She lets Ryan drive back. She sits on her side of the car, watching the pretty New England scenery float by. Through the woods, she can see the regular rhythm of tract housing. Then the trees open out onto an office park. She's thinking of Jack, of Evelyn. She rouses herself: this is selfish, she thinks. She looks over at Ryan, at his sober face. The sore-looking patches from shaving make him look young to Lottie. Young, and more vulnerable than he usually does.

"Well, what do you think you learned?" she asks him abruptly. "Anything?"

He shrugs. "No. Well, I don't know. Maybe. Mostly that a lot of other people cared a lot more about her than I did. It made me think, though."

"About what?" she asks.

"Oh, it's pretty egocentric, I guess, but really about what anyone could say about me." He looks over at Lottie. "If I died." He grins ruefully. "Not much," he says.

"Well. Honey, come on. You're just starting to be who you are."

He's looking back at the road, still smiling slightly. Then he says, "I guess I'm just having a kind of pre-life crisis, then."

Lottie laughs, delighted.

"What about you?" he asks after a while.

"What? What about me?"

"You were crying. You seemed affected."

"I wept for general mortality," she says. "No. Well, yes and no. I was being egocentric too, really. I wept for myself. The bell was tolling for me."

"Really? Do you think about that? About dying?" He looks over. "I mean, I know you did when you were sick. But. Well, I just wonder."

"I haven't so much, I guess. I did then, a lot, of course. Cold-sweat thoughts, sometimes. And I worried terribly about you, about how you'd do. But since then I've led the kind of life where you don't have to, much."

"And what kind of life might that be?"

"Well, unattached, primarily, I guess."

"But you're attached now."

Lottie is speechless for a beat or two. Then she says, "I seem to be, yes."

"You are," he announces firmly; and she wonders what he's noticed, what he's guessed at. He smiles at her. "So maybe you're in a pre-life crisis too."

"Ah, pre-life, pre-death." She makes her voice tough. "It's all the same kettle of fish. Ball of wax."

"Tub of chicken," he offers.

She laughs and looks out the window again.

"This reminds me," he says.

"What?"

"Oh, I was just thinking of this course I took, this biochemistry course? Freshman year, it was required. And there was this section called Sex and Death. The point being that where you have parthenogenesis, you know, before you have sex, animals don't ever die. They just go on splitting forever. They're immortal. But once you get two different sexes coming together to make a third creature—to make life—there's also death."

"Well, there you have it."

"I suppose." They're coming to the parkway now, slowing down for the light. "Still," he says as he downshifts, "there are always accidents. Deaths in both worlds that have no connection to that issue. I mean, paramecia must get squashed sometimes, or devoured, or what have you. And then in our universe too. I mean,

247

Jessica—her death wasn't connected to sex at all."

"Mmm," Lottie says.

They begin to move through the network of streets toward her mother's neighborhood. The air feels dry, Lottie realizes. Dry and hot. "Are you going to work at all today?" she asks him.

"I haven't decided. I have so little to do, it's like I could finish in a couple of hours anytime. Maybe I'll call the weather guy and see if it's supposed to rain again soon." They stop at a light. Suddenly he turns to Lottie, grinning. "Remember when you used to telephone the weather guy, Mom? And play that game?"

"Yes," Lottie says. She's grateful to him for calling it up. She would dial the service while Ryan watched, and then repeat the odd detail—"Sixty degrees tomorrow, yes, partly sunny"—and laugh, more and more hysterically at each additional element. She would begin by faking the laughter, of course, but Ryan would inevitably start really laughing, and then she would laugh genuinely too; until by the end of the forecast, they'd be in tears over the final repeated details. After she hung up, he'd say, "Do it again, Mom," and that in itself would set them both off once more.

Ryan parks the car aimed in the wrong direction on their side of the street. As they come up the walk, they are arguing about whether this is a ticketable offense. Suddenly Lottie sees that the door is open. She stops. They left it locked, of course, when they went to the service. As she mounts the front steps, her heart is pounding. She steps into the empty hallway and freezes, looking around, ready for anything. But then Cameron calls from the kitchen. "Charlotte?"

"Oh, Cam, it's you," she says, and feels, for just a few seconds, relief. But as soon as he comes out from the dining room doorway, she sees that this is bad, this is trouble. He looks disheveled, frantic. He's moving too fast; Lottie can see perhaps a little too much white in his eye. His hair is uncombed, he looks ill.

He smiles at Lottie and Ryan, a tethered, false rictus that terrifies her. "All dressed up. Where ya been?" he says in his small, pressured voice.

Before Lottie can think of a lie to tell, Ryan says, "Jessica Laver's funeral."

He turns his harsh smile on Ryan. "There must have been a fair crowd, no?" Ryan starts to answer, but he rides on: "Seems like everyone I know and love was there. If you'd asked me, I'd have gone with you."

Again Ryan begins to speak; he's saying Cameron's name. This time Lottie interrupts. "It didn't occur to us. Ryan had his own reasons for going—he knew Jessica. And I wanted to be with him. It had no connection to you, Cam."

They stand in a little circle in the empty front hall. Outside the open door, the huge sycamore stirs, sighs in the wind. Cam is staring at Lottie, then his eyes flick to Ryan, then to the living room windows, then back to Lottie. "Well, you look very nice, both of you. Very nice," he says finally. He seems to mean this.

"Thank you," Lottie says.

"Thank you," Ryan echoes.

"It's over?" he asks. Before they can answer, he walks quickly to the living room windows and stands staring out.

"The service? Yes," Lottie says.

She follows him into the room, willing herself to move slowly. His nerviness seems volatile and dangerous, and Lottie is aware of wanting to pull against it. "Elizabeth was going on to the what-d'you-call-it. The reception, whatever. We didn't."

"She's alone?"

"Elizabeth and the *family*, I should have said." She watches him from the side, his strong, harsh profile, his quickly shifting eyes. "Why don't we sit down?" she says. "You're making me nervous."

He laughs, a mirthless bark, but when Lottie sits in one of the chairs facing the windows, he sits too. He looks at Lottie now; he's smiling again. "I called her this morning and got Emily," he says. "I talked to Emily. Emily and I had a little chat. She said Elizabeth's leaving. After the service. Elizabeth's leaving town."

"Ah!" Lottie says. She's frightened suddenly.

"And what I'm wondering, Charlotte, is if you knew that, that Elizabeth was leaving." Lottie doesn't respond. "And if you knew that, why you wouldn't have told me. Why you would have led me to believe something distinctly other than that."

In her peripheral vision, Lottie can see Ryan shift his weight slightly. He's still standing in the hall, watching her and Cameron.

"I did know it," Lottie says softly.

"What?" Cameron's voice is sharp.

249

"I said I knew it. And I thought that she had a right to go. Unmolested, as it were."

"Charlotte." He shakes his head. He smiles sadly at Lottie. "That was wrong of you. That makes me very angry."

"What part was wrong?" she asks.

"It was all wrong," he says. He has leaned forward, and the smile is gone. "To lie to me. To think it's right that she should go. To think that what I am about is . . . molesting Elizabeth. Wrong. All wrong."

"Well, I disagree with you, then. Obviously. I did what I thought was right."

"Right for who?"

"*Right*. More abstract than that."

"There is no abstract right, Charlotte." He shakes his head again.

There's the sound of a car door slamming somewhere outside, and he turns quickly in his chair, half rises. His head moves, small tugs left and right. He looks feral. He stills finally and sits back down. There's a long silence.

Lottie says, "Would you like some coffee?"

He looks at her. "No. Thank you."

Lottie gets up. Elizabeth won't be here for another fifteen minutes at the soonest. "Well, I would," she says. "Ryan? You?"

"Umm. Sure," he says, and starts to move toward the kitchen.

"No, no," Lottie says. "I'll do it."

She goes back out to the kitchen and puts some water on to boil. She gets out the paper filter, the grounds. She makes herself move slowly, calmly, through this ritual. She can hear the stillness in the living room, though once Cam speaks and Ryan answers, something about the service. Someone is up once too, walking around, but Lottie forces herself to stay in the kitchen, to watch the brown drops fill the glass pot.

When she comes out, she is carrying two mugs. She hands one to Ryan, who's sitting now on the arm of one of the old chairs. She sits down again in her chair. Cam is watching her steadily. She looks back, keeping her gaze level. "Are you sure?" she asks. "That you don't want any?"

"Quite sure," he says.

"What's your plan?" Lottie says at last. Absurdly, she has tried to make her voice conversational, and he hears that. He smiles. As if in response to this, Ryan shifts his weight.

Cameron looks over at him. "Your mother's funny, Ryan."

"Unh huh," Ryan says. "I know. I like Mom."

"At the moment," Cameron says, "I do not." His face falls, then—in a way that shocks Lottie—it grows flaccid, his eyelids seem to thicken, lines pull, as though he's stepped into a more powerful gravitational field. She sees that he's exhausted, near the end of something. She wonders how much he's slept since Jessica died; whether he's slept at all.

"What *is* your plan, Cameron?" she asks again.

"Oh, Charlotte, come on."

"No, I'm curious."

He stares over at her coldly. "I'm here. I'm waiting. Clearly I'm going to try to stop her. Is that a plan?"

He's waiting for an answer, so she lifts her shoulders.

"If it is, that's my plan. To hold on to what I love. Wouldn't it be your plan?"

"I might execute it differently."

"I think you might." His voice is heavy with something ugly.

"What do you mean?"

"Oh, come on, Charlotte. When have you ever tried to hold on to something you love? When have you ever worked at love? You think love is something that happens to you—a feeling."

"And what do you think it is?"

"What you choose. What you do. How you live."

"Grace versus works," Ryan says.

"Thank you, Ryan," Cameron says. He shuts his eyes. "Grace versus works. It'll do."

Lottie meets Ryan's eyes across the room and feels a welling of gratitude. He understands, then. He knows they have to keep Cameron distracted. Distracted and talking. And then she realizes what *her* plan is. She realizes that she's decided against her brother here too. That she will try to guarantee Elizabeth's departure. That what she is choosing, what she is doing, are in the service of everything she's been struggling against in her own life since she and Jack married.

"I don't think 'versus' is correct," she says.

His eyes snap open. "What?"

"I don't think it's grace *versus* works."

"Oh, Char. The philosopher of love. No doubt you've solved it all this summer with your research."

"I've thought about it."

"Fine." He turns slowly in his chair to watch a couple of kids walk past, their sharp voices carrying back long after they've passed the window. They're talking about money, it seems.

"You need them both, surely," Lottie says. He looks almost confused as he stares at her. "I mean, you can't work at it if there's not a sense of—occasionally anyhow—of grace. In love, after all, there are two. Two people. If you're working at it alone, you're working *on* the other person."

"And that's what you think I'm doing?"

"Elizabeth wants to go, Cameron. She wants to work on her marriage. You can't make her love you through *works*. *Love-works*. Whatever you want to call it."

"I don't need to make Elizabeth love me. She does love me."

"Yes, of course she does. But she loves Lawrence too, and that's where she wants to turn her energy."

"But that's because *he's* been working on her. She's a very vulnerable person. Very easily swayed. I understand Elizabeth. I understand how important all those conventional aspects of life— all the status things—are to her. They always have been. But they're not what she wants, really. And now maybe it's *my* turn. To work on her again. To remind her of what she really wants."

They sit in silence for a minute. Cameron's fingers are dancing nervously on the arm of his chair. Lottie looks at Ryan, who's sunk farther down in his chair.

She says, "You know, I'd be furious if someone said that of me."

"Said what?"

"Said that they knew what I *really wanted*. Implied that they understood me better than I understood myself." Abruptly she remembers that this is what Larry has said about Elizabeth too, and she stops too quickly, her mouth a little open.

Cameron looks at her. "Because you understand yourself so very well, no doubt."

Ryan stirs a little at his tone, and Lottie glances quickly at her son, then back at Cam. "You know," she says, "I have a letter for

you. From Elizabeth. Maybe it would be good for you to read it."
Lottie starts to get up, but he raises his hand.

"I don't need to read it."

"Come on, I'm just going to go up and get it. I think you should." She stands.

"I'm not going to, Charlotte."

"Why not?"

"Because. Because I know what it says. And it's not news. And it's not interesting. And it's not relevant."

"Cameron, it's what Elizabeth wants to say to you. What could be more relevant than that?"

He shakes his head, looks sideways down the street out the window again.

"I think you should read it, Cam."

"Why?" He looks sharply back at her. "Have you? Have you read it, Charlotte?"

"Yes. I have."

"How perfectly extraordinary," he says. He turns to Ryan, as though to ask him to comment.

Over his shoulder Lottie sees Elizabeth's big rental station wagon pull up the driveway. It stops with the tail just visible, sticking out under the porte cochere around the side of the house. Lottie begins to talk loudly. "All right, yes. I read it. I was worried about you, for God's sake." What she is thinking is: *Don't slam the doors. Don't, for Chrissakes, slam the doors.* "A young woman had died—do you remember that?—and I was assuming you might be upset." Lottie strides across the room, turns, strides back as she talks, like any bad actor trying to invent stage business, trying to call attention to herself. "I came to your apartment, and you weren't there. I had no idea where you were! What you might be doing. I was very worried. I was worried you might have killed yourself, Cam!"

He grimaces.

"And then I was worried that if the letter was in any way a rejection, a rebuff, that it might make you worse. Might make everything worse." Lottie is standing directly in front of him now. She points at him. "You would have done exactly the same thing, Cameron. Exactly. Or I hope you would. You would have tried to protect me. Or a friend. Or whoever. You would have read the

253

letter. You would have taken it with you just the way I did."

She lets a silence fall. No sound from outside. Just the trees, a very distant honking. Surely Elizabeth has made it into the house by now, Elizabeth and the children.

"Because it might have caused me to despair? Because what was in the letter might have caused me to despair, Charlotte?"

"Yes," she says. She sits down again, on the edge of her chair, and tries to keep her eyes intent on his.

"But you'd like me to read it now. Why is that?"

"Because. You're being ridiculous. Arrogant. As though she had no will or choice in the matter. As though your will, your choice, were all that mattered."

"My will and hers are one."

"They are *not* one. I know that."

"By reading my mail."

"By talking to her. By listening to her, which is more than you've done."

"You can't tell me she talked to *you* about me."

There is such contempt in his voice that Lottie feels stung. After a few seconds she says, "That is what I'm telling you. She talked to me many times."

He smiles, slightly. "I can promise you, Charlotte, that she didn't tell you anything that really mattered. That you know nothing, you understand nothing, about what really went on between us."

"Oh, you'd be very surprised, very surprised, at what I know." Lottie's voice is shaking, but she couldn't have said whether this is something that has happened to her or something she's willed to keep his attention.

"I don't believe you," he says.

"You should."

He lifts a dismissive hand and starts to turn his head, to look out the window again.

Quickly Lottie says, "She told me about a time you made love in an alleyway. Or a passageway, I guess, really." He looks back at her, his mouth slightly opened. "In Central Square," she says. "It was raining. You were standing up." His face is so drained, suddenly, that she feels a horrible pity for him; but she goes on. "She told me you cried when you first made love again."

Lottie keeps her eyes on his face, but in the corner of her vision she can see one, then another, figure moving around the back of the car. Then they're gone.

"But why would she? Why would she talk to you?" His voice is whispery and cracked. He isn't quite looking at Lottie.

"Because. I don't know. Because it made the whole thing more romantic to do so, maybe. It jacked it up. And that's what she wanted, I think. She wanted romance, something to take her mind off the fact that her husband was leaving her. Seemed to be leaving her. Something to make her feel alive." Lottie lifts her shoulders. "She was bored. She told me that too. And lots of other things. Things about that time you went out to San Francisco, for example. Which is not so very different from this, really, is it?"

He stares at Lottie.

"Is it?"

"Yes, it is different." His voice sounds hollow.

"How is it different? You went out there with the same argument, as I recollect it from that visit you made to me in Chicago on the way. That you knew what was best for you and for her. That what you wanted had to be what she wanted, whether she knew it or not." Elizabeth's bright dress flickers across the street, but Lottie doesn't shift her eyes. She hopes Emily has told Elizabeth that she talked to Cameron, she hopes that Elizabeth by now understands she has to get out of here, fast. She hopes they are loading the car, but she can't shift her eyes to check without signaling Cameron. "And you were willing to smash a few things up, then, in order to hold on to her. Weren't you? Weren't you?"

He doesn't answer. He's just watching Lottie now.

"She told me about what you did in San Francisco. That you broke in. That she called the police."

"Mom . . . ," Ryan says.

Lottie looks over, sees that he thinks she's gone far enough, or maybe too far. The skin around his eyes looks white. But Lottie has wound herself very tight with this conversation; at some point she's stopped pretending outrage and has come to feel it. She looks back at Cam. "You've always claimed you had this understanding of love, this capacity for it that I don't have. Stupid little Charlotte, who settles for what she can get. And you're so noble, so high and mighty. But not above really hurting someone, really doing damage,

255

are you? Are you?" The sound of Lottie's breathing fills the room for a minute.

"Even Mother," she says, the thought suddenly occurring to her. "Even your great devotion to her. How good you are. How patient. But you can't stand her, really, can you? It's just that same myth you make about yourself. Cam the noble, Cam the good. Cam the romantic. But that's *it*. It's all about yourself. It's all lies. Because you're the only one who counts. You never really even see the others.

"So if I kept it from you that she was leaving, why should that be the least bit surprising? Why shouldn't I have wanted to help her get away? Why shouldn't I have kept my mouth shut about her going?" Lottie's voice is loud and hard. She has gotten up again, and now she's standing close to him, standing over him, really. He is sagging in the sagging chair, his head tilted back, looking up at her with what might be shock mingled with some renewed surge of fatigue.

Then several things happen at once.

There is the sound of someone starting up the front steps. Cam convulses and spins: Richard Lester. And behind him, across the street, the engine revs and Elizabeth's car begins to slide backward down the long driveway.

Cam pushes himself up out of the chair awkwardly, sideways. He slips back somehow, and Lottie grabs at him. He's saying "Fuck," "Bitch," something like that; he shoves her. She feels the blow in her breast, her rib cage, and falls, hard, against the arm of his chair. He has made it nearly to the doorway when Ryan grabs him with both arms, a kind of tackle-cum-embrace.

"No!" Cam shouts. "God!"

Later Lottie will remember how odd their noises were as they fought. Grunts, little cries. She's struggling up. Richard Lester stands behind them in the doorway, filling it with his bulk, his mouth slung loose.

And Cam hits Ryan. Lottie hears it rather than sees it. She feels herself moving forward too slowly, as in a dream. Ryan has let go of Cameron, he's holding his face. "*Jesus,*" he's saying. Richard is there. Lottie is yelling something, and Richard is holding Cam now, he has grabbed him from behind. He encircles Cam, who is trying, jerking this way and that, to swing his body free.

256

Lottie takes the last step and hits him, hits him as hard as she can, face, neck, shoulder—not punches but bludgeon blows with her fists, raining down on his head, on the bones of his body, beating and then slapping him over and over. She's shrieking at him, wildly and senselessly; and then someone grabs her from behind—Ryan—and they all stop.

There is gasping silence, and Lottie begins to cry. Between wails, she cries out, "You shit! What's wrong with you? You're his uncle, you bastard! What's wrong with you?"

CHAPTER 13

This is one of those situations you find yourself in, Lottie thinks, that you would swear could not happen to you. They're all outside—her ex-husband, their son, the wife who's replaced her, and the baby—sitting on the pretty deck behind Derek's condo. They are all behaving wonderfully, their mild, pleasant voices floating out over the lawn, spiked now and then with polite laughter. Lottie has coffee, the others are drinking beer. Carol is nursing the baby. So far no one has asked about Ryan's eye, but it isn't really conspicuous yet. A little pink, a little puffy. Tomorrow it may be closed up, it may have begun to darken.

Carol turns to her suddenly—they've been talking about rugby, which Ryan played in England—and says, "You look exhausted, Lottie. I wish you'd think about staying over. There's loads of room."

"Oh no, but thanks," Lottie says. She's appalled at the notion. "I really don't mind the drive back. And I have a lot of work still to do. Packing up, that kind of stuff."

The baby shudders, suddenly, and falls away from Carol's body, making a wet, smacking sound with its mouth. Carol bends her head, raises her hand to her blue-veined breast, and helps the baby reattach itself. A girl, named Genevieve.

Ryan and Derek have continued to talk, and now Carol and Lottie sit quietly and listen. Lottie's tooth is aching, gently but steadily. She looks out over the backyard. Though the condo is only a few blocks from Yale, it feels like a country estate. It's in an old mansion, divided up into six or seven spacious apartments. Derek and Carol have the back of the first floor and two rooms on the second. The ceilings are absurdly high for the size of the rooms; the apartment is cool and dark. Everyone shares the use of this back-yard, Derek told Lottie and Ryan as he showed them around. There is a woman out there now in a portable webbed aluminum chaise, sunbathing. A breeze puffs against Lottie's face, and she closes her eyes. Ryan's voice, Derek's, seem distant and unconnected to her. She wishes that she were that woman on the lawn; any woman but herself.

All Lottie had said to Derek on the telephone was that it would be better for her, more convenient, if she could bring Ryan to him right away, today. Something in her voice must have given her away; he responded with the instant sympathetic cooperation that we employ when we're called to help in emergencies. *Of course that was fine. There were a few things he'd need to rearrange, but easily done, easily done.*

She'd said they would arrive before dinner. No, she wouldn't stay. Well, just for coffee, then, but she had to get back.

Lottie couldn't have told anyone, she couldn't tell herself, how or when she'd decided on this course of action. There had been the horrible long seconds of silence after all the violence was over, when Lottie, still weeping—wailing, really—was aware only of being over-whelmed by confusion and sorrow. They were all frozen in their positions, as though they'd spun off from each other in the chil-dren's game of Statues—as though each of them had been assigned to hold this posture indefinitely.

Ryan moved first and broke the spell. "God, it's bleeding," he said. He held his hand up in front of his face and looked at his palm. Lottie stopped and looked at him too. A narrow stripe of red streaked sideways down the back of his hand from between two fingers, over his knuckles, toward his wrist. Where had it come from? Then she saw that his nose was streaming with red.

Richard began nervously talking about medicines—he had

something, he said—and disappeared. Ryan turned and walked back toward his room, his head held up and back awkwardly. Lottie noted that Cam had sunk abruptly into a chair. She heard Richard panting audibly up the stairs, then the rattling of prescription bottles. She alone seemed unable to assert some will over her body; later she would describe this moment as being like those strangely peaceful nightmares you have every now and then of being dead, floating somehow above the activity of others, unable to find a way to intersect with it.

Richard stumbled down the stairs toward her, hurtled past to the back bathroom, clutching something. Lottie looked stupidly after him, she looked again at Cam, who had slumped back and was gazing blankly at the ceiling, and she made her choice. She followed Richard to Ryan's bathroom.

By the time she had made sure Ryan was all right, by the time Richard had succeeded in stopping his nosebleed, the only thing Lottie clearly knew was that she wanted to get Ryan out of here, away from what she thought of as this *mess*, her mess. When she came back to the dining room to call Derek, Cam was gone, which didn't surprise her. It just seemed irrelevant.

And now, only a few hours later, here she sits on Derek's deck, watching his second wife's nipple slide in and out of their baby's mouth and making polite chitchat. What's wrong with this picture? Find the hidden wounds. But no one else seems to feel them. Carol has been attentive, Derek avuncular, as though Lottie were a dear old friend—no, perhaps a relative—who needed looking after. She is clearly the only one who sees all this as strange. She looks over at Ryan, who's sitting forward with his elbows resting on his knees, listening with careful attention to his father. Lottie has a sense of herself as a sour presence among them.

"Is there more coffee, Carol?" she asks.

Carol starts to struggle up.

"No, no," Lottie says. "I can get it."

"There's almost all of a fresh pot, right out on the counter," Carol says, relaxing. "You really can't miss it."

Derek has started to rise now too, but Lottie holds out her hand. "I know where the kitchen is," she says. "I'll manage, thanks."

She goes back in through the French doors, into the sudden deep peace of the living room. This was probably the study—the library—in the mansion in the old times. It's richly paneled, and tall walnut bookshelves line two walls of the room, bookshelves full of the bright splotches of paperbacks, as well as the hardcovers. Many Penguin books, she notes, remembering how their orange spines always dominated the bookshelves she and Derek had while they were married.

She goes into the kitchen—really just a galley built into a corner of the dining room. Everything is modern, white, clean. It's an invented space, made cleanly from Sheetrock. The outer walls of the dining room, though, are original and must have been part of a sun porch: they are all glass, many-paned. Outside, sitting in sepa-rated splendor on a sloping bed of bark chips, are four or five young rhododendrons, several of them still wearing their plastic garden tags.

She pours herself another cup of the coffee. It's percolator cof-fee, and Lottie doesn't like it much, but she's fueling herself for the trip back. She opens the refrigerator to find some milk, and is instantly unnerved by the abundance. Three bottles of wine lie on their sides, cooling. There is the half gallon of milk Lottie reaches for; and another, unopened half gallon behind it. There are fruit juices in thick glass jars—pink, orange, a lemony pale yellow. In the bin at the bottom of the space, flattened green leaves press upward against the clear plastic lid, as though trying to escape. There are two pint containers of fat strawberries, a big bowl of what looks like potato salad, and innumerable smaller bowls, with lids or plastic wrap on them. There is a curved platter that holds frosty-looking green grapes.

Lottie pours the milk into her coffee, returns the cardboard carton to its shelf. Does Ryan stand drinking from jars and cartons in front of the open refrigerator here? She takes a quick pleasure in the idea that he does not. And then shames herself: what virtue is there, after all, in running the kind of house where that's acceptable? Where wet towels lie on chairs and couches? Where books and papers fill half the bed? Who, after all, would not like this abun-dance, this neatness?

And perhaps she's wrong to assume that this is all Carol's handi-work. Maybe Derek shares now. The baby, after all, is in day care part time, Carol has said. She's gone back to work, Lottie recalls, something vaguely social-servicey. Sociable cervix, they call such women in training hospitals. She wonders if Carol knows this term.

As she's approaching the open French doors, she hears Ryan mention Cameron's name. She halts. But he's only talking about the house, his grandmother, the work he's done this summer.

In the car on the way down here, she had looked over and noticed the swelling, the faint discoloration. "You're going to have a shiner," she said to Ryan. "What will you tell your father?"

"The truth?" he suggested.

Lottie had sighed. "Yes, I suppose so."

"You'd rather I didn't?"

"No, you should. It's just . . . Well, I don't know."

"What? Tell me, what?"

"Oh, just that he's always seen my background as so . . . seedy. Not that it didn't appeal to him, in some way. But this will not. Appeal."

And then, as they drove along, she had pondered momentarily why her instinct so frequently was to lie. When she'd first met Jack, before she knew how important he was going to be to her, she'd told him that both her parents were dead, killed in an accident. Later, when she'd had to revise this ("Well, not quite dead," she'd begun sheepishly), she'd tried to explain to him why she'd lied earlier. And there were some perfectly good reasons for the lie: it was shorter, easier, she didn't have to get into her childhood with someone who might not care about it, her mother might as well have been dead to her. But the deepest reason—and Lottie knew this—was that she used the lie to push away the chaos of her life. And even if the lie was itself chaotic—an automobile accident! how awful!—this was a chaos Lottie controlled, not one she was a victim of.

Now she wonders what Ryan will say when they ask—and surely they will ask. She looks down at the table she's standing next to. There's a photograph in a silver frame of the baby, only hours old, it seems, wearing one of those white watch caps they put on them now right after birth. And there are two pictures of Ryan, one as a toddler, grave and concentrated on something above the camera, one in a baseball uniform at nine or ten. Lottie has never seen either picture before. It's startling somehow. He is theirs too, Lottie thinks. He has a separate life with them.

When she comes out, Carol has switched the baby to the other breast. Lottie sits down again in one of the sun-faded director's chairs.

"You found it—good!" Carol says. She smiles warmly at Lottie. She's a pretty woman, tall and blond. Lottie has met her only twice before. She's just beginning to be not-young-looking, to have smile lines—to appear, in repose, a little tired from some angles. Lottie guesses her to be in her early thirties now. She seemed a child to Lottie the first time they met. Afterward, in a moment alone with Derek, she had said, "What is it you're trying to prove? That you're immortal?" She thought she'd been joking, but perhaps her voice was harder than she intended, or perhaps it was a joke he was tired of. "Oh, Lottie, give me a break," he'd said.

But Ryan likes Carol, and Lottie's grateful for this. What's more, she can understand why. What's not to like? And she seems to have softened Derek over the years, mellowed him, which must make Ryan's life easier too. Watching Derek now, sitting on the deck's railing, holding forth, Lottie muses that he hasn't changed much. He's one of those tall, slender, precise-looking men who seem to stay young through orderliness, through sheer willpower. He must be fifty now, Lottie thinks. She remembers that his birthday is in December. She remembers a party she once had for him, a party from which he disappeared and didn't return until the next morning.

He's talking about a robbery, a mugging that occurred on the street only a few blocks from their house. "The guy did everything they told him—gave them his wallet, a ring, a jacket—and they beat him up anyway."

"He's lucky to be alive," Carol says. "Lottie?"

Lottie looks over, startled. Carol's holding a plate of crackers and cheese out to her. Lottie takes one. When she begins to chew, she's aware, again, of the tooth. She winces, sets the rest of the cracker in her saucer, beside the cup.

Though the tale of the mugging was brought up as a cautionary note for Ryan, a warning about being careful on the street, Derek is expanding on it now, turning it in another direction. He's talking about how the university is challenged by the encroachment of the ghetto. He says it's never defined its connection to the town, and that's contributed to social problems. Carol talks about Columbia, where she went to college. She rarely went out alone at night, she tells them. Ryan laughs and begins to relate a story about having fallen asleep on a lawn at Stanford one night and not waking up until the sky began to pale.

A long silence falls. Lottie senses they are waiting for her to leave so they can talk more personally. The door will shut, Derek will turn to Ryan and say, "So, good buddy, how *are* you?" and their visit will truly begin. She looks at her watch and stands up. "I should be getting on the road," she says. "I'd like to be back before dark. My eyes, you know." She taps her cheek and smiles ruefully.

"More carrots, Ma," Ryan says.

"And speaking of carrots," says Carol, rising too. She slings the baby up to her shoulder. "Can't I give you a snack or something for the road? You've eaten next to nothing. You must be starving."

"Oh no, thank you," Lottie says. "Actually—the truth is—I've got a tooth that's bothering me. I just got a new filling, and I think it's too big."

"Lottie and her teeth," says Derek, with grim satisfaction. There's a pause that recognizes their long-ago intimacy.

"Well, you know," Carol says, "I still have some great postpartum meds. Do you want a little painkiller, just in case? If it gets worse tonight, you won't be able to get a dentist. You'll be in trouble." She is frowning in genuine concern. Genevieve is reaching toward something behind Carol now, calling.

"Oh no, it'll be all right. I think."

"Are you sure? I mean, I got a whole bottle of something quite terrific, and I took just one or two. Please let me give you a couple. Even if you don't use them, you'll know you have them, and you won't need to start panicking if it feels like it's getting worse."

"Well . . . okay. Thank you, yes. Maybe that would be a good idea," Lottie says. Maybe I'll take just a little nibble as soon as I get into the car, she thinks. Seat belt on, lock my door against the fabled mugger, nibble on some lovely drug.

Carol has handed the baby to Ryan. Now she disappears into the house. Ryan holds the baby up. She's swimming in the air and his face is lifted to look at her. She squeals, she chews her fist, she drools on him.

"Bull's-eye!" he says. "Bull's-eye, you little twerp." He swings her against his side and wipes his cheek off. Derek stands watching him with a pleasure so naked Lottie looks away. She senses his wish to say something, that he would say something if she weren't here. She bends down, picks up her purse, and starts back into the condo too. She's stepping across the threshold when she hears Ryan say behind her, "She's wet, Dad. Should I change her?" There's something excited about his question.

"Sure; head upstairs. Carol will show you where her stuff is."

And so it's Lottie and Derek who go out the front door together and stand awkwardly in the semicircular drive. Their shoes bite and crunch on the gravel each time they shift their weight.

"I'm sorry," Derek says. He gestures at the house. "I probably should have changed her myself. But I was pleased he asked, you understand. I'm sure he'll only be a minute."

"Or two," Lottie says. "He's never done it before, to my knowledge." Her tone is sharp, but he doesn't appear to notice.

"Well, Carol will help him."

"Yes," Lottie says.

After a moment, she tips her head back to take in the whole house. She's about to comment on it, when he says, "It's a great feeling, starting all this up again."

Lottie glances over at him. He's smiling at her confidentially. "I'm sure," Lottie answers.

"It feels like an opportunity—I don't know—I suppose to do it right this time."

"You can only do the best you can, anytime." Lottie's aware of a quick, burning anger that comes through in her tone.

"You know what I mean, Lottie. We screwed up, with Ryan."

She turns away from him. "I'm proud of Ryan," she says. "Of how he turned out. Of who he is."

"Of course. I didn't mean . . . I'm terribly proud too. Of him. And, really, of all you did in raising him. Maybe that's my point. I had so little, really, to do with all that. Genevieve, she's a new chance, a new start."

As though you could sweep away what you'd been, what you'd done, Lottie thinks. All she says, though, is, "She is lovely."

Derek leans back against her car, folds his arms. And then: "Do you and . . . is it Jack?" Lottie nods. "Do you ever think of starting again? Another kid?"

Lottie is shocked by the question. She says, "It isn't possible," in a cold, flat voice. Though it is possible, as far as she knows, just unthinkable. They've taken every precaution against it.

Carol appears, suddenly, on the front porch. "Oh, you're out here!" She's breathless, smiling. "I went out back." She sweeps down the front steps. She's barefoot, and Lottie crosses quickly to the foot of the front stairs so she won't have to step out on the gravel. "I'll tell Ryan. I'm not sure he knows you're waiting for him."

She extends her hand to Lottie. "Here," she says. "Percocet. They're very strong, really."

Lottie reaches out her hand and feels the heat of Carol's as she drops the sticky pills into her palm. "Thank you," Lottie says. "I think I may, in fact, use one tonight."

"Oh, I'm glad to give you *something*," Carol says. "I'll go in and send Ry down. Drive carefully," she flings back, already dashing into the house.

Lottie opens her purse and tucks the pills into the little zipper pocket inside.

Derek walks over to her. "I'm sorry, Lottie, to have been so . . . carelessly rude," he says.

"Oh, it's fine," Lottie says. "It's not an *issue*. I mean, we wouldn't have wanted to *start over*, as you put it, anyway. Just starting is complicated enough for us, thank you very much." She laughs. Let him think she's being brave, putting the best face on it. Whatever. God, the nerve of the man!

"Still, it was insensitive, at best. Please forgive me."

"Don't be silly. Of course I do." But Lottie has kept her tone cool. They walk slowly, side by side, over the noisy gravel in the direction of Lottie's car. Neither looks at the other. The silence lasts just too long.

Derek says, "Do you have a dentist in Cambridge?"

"I'll go to the guy I got to put the filling in. Maybe he can just file it down, or something."

"Well, it's good you have the Percocet."

"Yes, I'm very grateful."

The woman who'd been sunbathing out back emerges from around the side of the house, wearing a robe and carrying the chaise, folded up. She waves to Derek and goes up the porch steps. The door slowly closes behind her. "Apparently she's never heard of cancer," Lottie says.

266

She's only been trying to change the subject, to be funny, but Derek must hear it as snide; or else as a reference to her own illness. He lets a little audible puff of exasperated breath out from between his tightened lips. "I'll get Ryan," he says. "I know you need to go, Lottie. It was good to see you." He extends his hand, and they shake.

But Ryan is already coming out the door, holding the baby, who now wears only a diaper and rubber pants over it. She sits, potbellied, swaying with every step Ryan takes, on his arm. He looks pleased with himself. He looks paternal, Lottie realizes.

Derek pauses in the doorway, lifts his arm slightly, and Lottie lifts her hand too, in farewell. He goes in.

She turns to Ryan, to Ryan and Genevieve. "I'm on my way, lovey," she says.

"Okay, Mom. I'll call you in, like, four or five days." He bends toward her.

She has to stretch over the baby to kiss his cheek, smelling the sweet talcy smell Genevieve exudes, the smell Ryan had as a baby too. Lottie touches the baby's silky arm, as though she were touching Ryan then, she remembers it so well. "Sounds good," she says.

"In Chicago, right?" he asks. He looks sternly, perhaps apprehensively, at her.

"Well, try there first. I'll probably be there by then." She opens the car door. "And how will you come?"

He shrugs. "Bus, I guess. It's the cheapest."

"Oh, don't worry about the expense, honey."

"Oh, really? You'll pay?"

"Sure."

"All right! Great. A plane, then, for sure. I'll see if they can get me up to Hartford."

Lottie is sitting in the car. She is looking up at him, her tall blond son with the bald baby perched so naturally on his arm. He has jutted a housewifely hip out to support her. "You look nice with that baby," she says, and smiles. "It's like gazing into the future."

"Me? With a baby? But I hear you have to have sex first, Mom."

"Yes." She laughs and closes the door. "Nasty sex. Born into sin, we are. Into sin, into death, as we know."

He takes Genevieve's little paw, then, and pretends to be dancing with her, spinning around once, twice. She squeals. He is asking her, "*Were* you born into sin, Genny, into sin and death?" When he stops, she laughs, a short burble that is pronounced "Clegh."

"Understand, I'm in no *rush* to be a grandmother," Lottie says. "I just feel like one, looking at you."

"And I'm in no rush to make you one," he says. "As you might have known. But it's worth remembering, Mom"—he points at her—"that I'm in control of your life from now on. I make *you* be things: a mother-in-law, a grandmother. A great-grandmother." He looks at the baby. "She is pretty cool, isn't she?" He puts his hand on her head—it covers her skull entirely—and strokes it gently.

"At least pretty cool." Her voice is very cheerful, very final. She starts the engine. "Okay, darling," she says. "Have a wonderful time here, and try to forget everything that ever happened in Cambridge. And I'll see you soon."

Ryan reaches down and touches her arm.

She smiles up at him again and then backs out of the parking space. When she stops for one last look at them as she reaches the street, he is waving and talking to Genevieve, concentrated more on the baby than on Lottie's leaving, and she feels a pang of completely muddled emotion that makes her eyes blurry, her throat dry. In her confusion, she drives for too long down Whitney Avenue. What's more, she senses at the first corner that she has turned the wrong way. But she needs gas in any case, she sees. She can get instructions at a station and start again.

She begins a slow meander through residential streets, trying to guess where the commercial center of all this might be, where the gas stations are. Gradually the neighborhood is perceptibly rougher. She's at the edges of the ghetto, then in it. But Lottie is thinking of Ryan, Ryan with the baby. How right that seemed, how topsy-turvy that it was Derek's child. And yet, of course, why shouldn't it be?

She would have liked to hold Genevieve, she acknowledges to herself now. If it had been anyone else's child but Derek's, she might have asked to. She thinks again of his rude question about her having a baby, and feels once more her rage at it; then, oddly, at what he's chosen in having Genevieve. It seems to her somehow a denial of responsibility for what *is*, for what he already has: Ryan.

But that's not true, and she knows it. He has been completely reliable in his love for Ryan for some time now.

She thinks of what she said to Derek—that starting has been

hard enough for her and Jack. That, anyway, was the truth. She thinks of Megan; and feels a flash of pain that makes her face pull tight. Megan is, after all, what *she* already has. She remembers the girl's silence in therapy when Lottie asked her what she could be to her; she remembers the way she'd joked about that with Elizabeth. But what would Lottie have answered if Megan had asked her that question?

On her right now, there is the sprawl of a blasted-looking project, squat and barrackslike. For a moment Lottie thinks the whole thing is empty, abandoned. There is cardboard here and there in a window, and there has been a fire in one of the buildings—black streaks rise on the brick above each boarded window. But then she sees children in a corner lot, little children, jumping and yelling, playing on a stack of discarded, dirty mattresses.

There's a group of men on the corner ahead. She is going to ask them where she is, but they stare at her with such unreadable blankness as she approaches that she doesn't; she drives on. She rolls up her window and switches on the air conditioner.

She comes out onto a wide street with stoplights, cars whizzing past. The street sign on the corner has been removed from its bracket. Lottie takes a right, arbitrarily. She passes several gas stations, but they are deserted. She looks at her watch. It's six-thirty. Six-thirty Sunday night, and these streets have the deserted air of a postcolonial city. She passes a group of adolescent girls walking together. Even through the closed windows she can hear their raw, high voices.

The street is gentrifying slightly; showing, anyhow, signs of commercial life. There are stores—closed now, on Sunday evening, but viable-looking. Then a Dunkin' Donuts, a Chevrolet lot. Lottie feels reassured. She sees, several blocks ahead, the bright primary colors of a gas station sign. She opens her window again; the hot air strikes her arm and the side of her face. Her tooth hurts.

The man in the service station is elderly and soft-spoken. He slowly and carefully cleans Lottie's windshield, and she feels a tender kind of gratitude to him. He tells her she's drifted pretty far from the turnpike entrance. She's closer to the Wilbur Cross Parkway here, if she just keeps going.

Lottie uses the ladies' room nervously—the door won't lock, and the walls are covered with the unreadable hieroglyphics of urban graffiti. There is no toilet paper. When she leaves the station, she follows the old man's advice and continues down Dixwell Avenue. She passes between shopping malls on either side of the road. The lots are even now half full. Ugly vistas of commercial success, she thinks. Not much better to look at, finally, than the empty shells of failure in the ghetto.

Then she is thinking of Ryan again. She sees his swollen face and feels ashamed. How, after all, can she fault Derek for denial—for pretending—when she has apparently spent the summer in a kind of waking dream? Her mind goes back to the fight with Cameron, to the ecstatic and vicious release she felt pounding and slapping him. She remembers the nagging swirl of Elizabeth's skirt in the edge of her vision, the way Cameron's face had lifted in contempt for her and her life's choices. She sees again the dark line of blood on the back of Ryan's hand.

The green and white sign to the Wilbur Cross looms ahead, and she signals. She's thinking of all this, and of how she'd yearned after what Elizabeth and Cameron seemed to have. Then she's thinking of Jack—just of how he looks, then of the moment in the hotel when she felt such tenderness for his gangly nakedness. She flips her visor down against the bright, low sun. Her tooth is really hurting now. This qualifies as an out-and-out toothache. She pulls her bag over to her, fishes blindly in the zipper pocket, and pulls out a Percocet. She holds it up, visually records its size, and puts it between her front teeth. She bites down. A little piece crumbles off and lands on her lap or on the floor, but there's a bitter tiny chunk in her mouth too. Lottie swims her tongue in her mouth until she's generated enough saliva to swallow it. She holds the Percocet up again. She must have eaten about one third.

She pushes her bag into the middle of the passenger seat again, she adjusts the visor a little more. She reaches into the open pocket below the radio for her sunglasses. And then she realizes: she's heading into the sun. She's taken the wrong turn again; she's going west.

CHAPTER 14

We lie to ourselves about such things. We say they were meant to happen. We let them thrill us, shake us. Lottie does: *I'm going to Jack*, she thinks, and feels a light-headedness, an excitement, that makes her hands tremble on the wheel, that quickens her breath.

But of course Lottie has read Freud too. She knows very well that this kind of mistake is like a slip of the tongue, that it reveals intention more than destiny—that this is the more reasonable way to speak of it. So later what she will say is that she was so afloat in her confusion about what she had done that she missed the first two exits where she might have turned back. And that by the time she reached the third, she had consciously made a decision to drive on. She will speculate that if she hadn't been someone who drove so much to make a living, it might not have happened. If the car itself, the breaking open into four lanes, the green and white signs, hadn't somehow signaled *beginning* to her, maybe the reality of the distance to be covered would have been too daunting.

She will speak, too, of how pretty the Wilbur Cross is for that old stretch, pretty in a way that American highways used to be— winding, barely wide enough, with trees growing in the median strip and little hillocks rising on either side, giving way to sudden mild vistas. It could be said—she'll say it herself—that this, too, might somehow have helped.

And she will feel, but not say so often, that maybe if she hadn't hit Cam, to whom she would have to return; if he hadn't been held by Richard Lester, whose sounds she would hear in the night; if the same sprung chairs hadn't been waiting in the same vague, unwelcoming circle, if the angle up the street to Elizabeth's house with its glimpse of the porte cochere hadn't been there—if she hadn't had the sense that she would be returning to the sordid scene of a crime, a terrible and ugly accident she had some responsibility for: maybe then she would have turned around at the first exit, or the second. She will always know that some part of it, too, was running away.

But she will also always believe that it was the thought of Jack that made her make the mistake in the first place, and she will privately take that as a sign of her destiny, her fate, adolescent at heart that she is. *White trash* she'll call herself, when she thinks of it this way.

For whatever the reasons, then, Lottie drives on. The sun sets, gold and then pink in the clear western sky ahead of her. In the twilight it leaves behind, she can still see the muted shapes of everything, but other cars begin to turn their fierce silver lights on. Once or twice, unbidden tears begin to slip from Lottie's eyes, though she could swear this is happiness she's feeling. She winds into heavier traffic as she passes the last, expensive shore towns in Connecticut, as the houses thicken up in New York and become more suburban. Her heart is swishing steadily in her ears, and her tooth throbs to its rhythm.

Jack, she is thinking. Not that she's trying to imagine him in terms of what his response will be to her, particularly—that seems dangerous. But his physical presence. A gesture: his clenched fist and grimace of pleasure when a musical passage he loves begins on the stereo. His slow, widening grin when she says something that surprises or amuses him. His distinctive smell, soapy and salty, and how she wears it after sex. The ease with which he carried her up the stairs one night when they were alone in the house. The way he walks in winter, his coat open, no scarf.

She remembers facts about him, parts of his story that she loves. That he grew up in a small town in western Ohio with four brothers. That his father was the high school principal. That every night there was a meal on the table. His father sat at one end, his mother at the other. There was attention, as evenly distributed as food, passed up and down.

That his mother was an island of calm, unflappable in spite of her sons' wildness, their fights, their broken limbs, their pranks. Though once his father had criticized her for something—no one could ever remember what it was, it had seemed so harmless: maybe they could eat a little earlier, maybe the boys should take on some chore for her—and she had lunged forward suddenly and bit him. Her teeth had pushed through fabric and skin, and his father had cried out in shock and pain. Jack couldn't remember whether he had been present or not: it was one of those memories that are retold so often, every detail made so familiar, that everyone feels he must have been there.

His father had driven himself to the emergency room and lied about the accident. He said he'd been wrestling with one of his almost grown sons and it had gotten out of hand. They cleaned him up, put a stitch or two in the deepest holes. It scarred him, though, Jack said, a curve of little white marks across the flesh of his shoulder. She didn't like to see him without a shirt on after that, even at the beach. It must have been emblematic to her, Lottie thinks now, of a moment when all that love failed her. When she felt as trapped as an animal, suddenly, and fought for something vital in herself that she couldn't have known until that moment she cared about.

She didn't like them to joke about it, but they did, of course. Later in her life she would sometimes be able to laugh too, he said. The first time she did, they all applauded her, having understood without speaking of it that this meant that she'd finally forgiven herself.

Lottie has always envied everything about this story. The peace, the order. The encircling applause. The sense of violence as aberration. Now she thinks, too, of the powerful control his mother must have exerted on herself much of the time: the revelation that perhaps it took great effort to achieve the kind of family Jack had had. The extraordinary fact that to someone it was almost always worth that effort.

What else does she know about him? That he played in a band in high school—all of his brothers did when they came to be an age when their parents would let them, each a different instrument.

They traveled in a radius of one hundred fifty miles or so to high school proms, to roadhouses, to private parties. The permanent members of the band were older, men who taught school in town or worked in banks. They would drive around in a car belonging to one of these men, crammed in, five or six of them usually. Jack had his first drink on the road with them, his first cigarette, his first sexual experience—with an older woman who followed him outside during a break. "Older," he'd said. "It occurred to me much later that she was maybe twenty-five or so."

Lottie has seen a studio photograph of him at that age, holding his clarinet. He'd paid for the picture himself; he had thought, then, that he might become a musician. In it he's wearing a dark suit, his hair is pomaded wetly back. He is unbelievably long and skinny, but there's a sense, too, of something knowing, something hungry about him that stirred Lottie when she held the photograph, even all those years afterward.

The excitement of those days had folded into Jack's love of music, even into his love of dancing. Once when they were moving together to a swing-band tune at a hotel ballroom in Chicago, he'd bent over Lottie and whispered, "Care to dance?" and when she'd said yes, they walked straight off the slick floor to the front desk and rented a room.

She's in New Jersey now, on route 80, floating on the Percocet. She can still feel the pain, a light, steady throb from under the tooth, actually, but it seems almost to be happening to another Lottie, another Charlotte. Dusk has deepened into near-dark along the highway, but there's still a light cast to the sky. The dark moving shapes of the trees are silhouetted against it. The needle teeters at around 72, 73. Lottie feels invincible. She asked for directions when she crossed the George Washington Bridge, and she has made every connection, feeling a peace and accomplishment simply in driving: in making this curve, in signaling so politely to change lanes. Traffic was heavy around New York, but it has cleared out now, and she takes comfort in the distant taillights ahead of her, the headlights that move up from behind and then sweep past. Others on ordinary errands. Or, like her, hastening home, mending rifts.

Lottie turns the radio on. She thinks of the music she listened to on the way out east, when she thought she was leaving Jack. It seems another universe. But what has changed?

She thinks momentarily of his big house, the handsome rooms—too many, too much. Of Megan's closed face across the dinner table.

But love is something you choose to do.

Cam said that.

Nonetheless.

I have changed, she thinks. I can do it. I can.

She finds another oldies station but tires of it quickly. They seem to specialize in white boys—Ricky Nelson, Frankie Avalon. She pushes the Seek button, settles on the first clear station, a call-in show. They're discussing the effects of crack cocaine on kids in the ghettos. There's an expert, of course, full of statistics. His voice is nasal, nerdy. Lottie would put money on it, he's never done drugs. Crack is cheap, he says. It's highly addictive, it's the beginning of the end. She thinks of Ryan, of finding dope in his jeans pocket when he was fourteen or fifteen, of trying to decide whether to confront him. She'd talked to Jack about it.

He said she had to.

"But *I* smoked dope, Jack. I *don't* disapprove. In the abstract."

"He's not abstract, Lottie. That's the point." His concerned face, the lines deepening. His light eyes on her.

The calls start now on the radio. Gradually the tone of the show changes. Nobody is forcing these kids to use it. Nobody's excluding them from the American dream if they just get off their asses and go to work. The talk show host is on the callers' side. Maybe addicts deserve their fate.

Lottie changes the station. She finds some soft rock, then an Elvis retrospective: the Las Vegas years. She turns the radio off. The Percocet isn't making her sleepy at all. Just somehow tranquil, in absolute control. Practicalities begin to occur: she's left everything behind. She'll have to go back for her computer, her books and papers. Her clothes. She moves through the house mentally. She packs everything up. Then she starts again, rearranging. Then: did she lock the door when she left? Should she call Richard? Might he be worried? Cam?

Cam. God. She doesn't want to think about him. And suddenly she's aware of the pain again, sharper this time. She fishes in her purse, swallows the rest of the pill.

Just over the line into Pennsylvania, she stops to use the toilet in a rest area. The foyer is half filled with milling weekend travelers heading home. Heavy people—why are people in rest areas so often heavy? she wonders. Several of them have bright, painful-looking sunburns. Still, there's something pleasurable in the bustle, the sense of being in motion among them. We're all *going* somewhere. But it's more than that. Lottie wishes there were someone she could tell. *I'm going back.* She'd like to say it aloud. *I'm going home.*

In the bathroom, she splashes water on her face, wipes it with the rough, stale-smelling paper towels. When she comes out, she's aware of the aroma of coffee and thinks for a moment of having a cup. But then, she tells herself, she'll just need to stop again sooner.

She goes into the little front room off the lobby, full of vending machines, and sees that, as she'd hoped, one of the machines dispenses No Doz along with other over-the-counter drugs. There's another woman in here, buying candy. After Lottie's bought her No Doz, she watches this woman dropping quarter after quarter as though she were feeding a giant slot machine, pulling the handle, which releases, with a heavy thud each time, a huge Milky Way. She does this six or seven times.

After she leaves, Lottie buys a candy bar too. She may get hungry. At the last minute, she gets a can of Coke also. Handy to wash down whichever drug she needs to take. She drives to the pumps and has the tank filled. Might as well, even though it's still got some gas left.

On the road again, it's truly dark; the sense of sky is gone. Lottie's been driving an hour or so when she realizes she's hunched over the wheel, that tension is radiating from her jaw through her whole body. She makes herself sit back. Her leg aches. She adjusts the seat. She tries the radio again. There are several religious services in progress now, a lot of country music, a replay of a Democratic debate. She finally settles on some static through which she can faintly hear sweeping orchestral music. It may be Brahms; but then suddenly a bit of melody makes her think it's the sound track to the movie *Giant*, something she wouldn't have said she'd known.

The road lifts and drops. The terrain here would be different if she could see it. She remembers it from the trip east: hilly, and beginning to be farm country. The cars around her have thinned out, just an occasional light ahead or behind, and Lottie is aware of the glow from the dashboard. She thinks of Jack again, driving on the straight section roads of the Midwest in his adolescence, the way the lights would have reflected up on the tired faces of the older men in the band.

Where was she when he was that age? Eight, ten, running wild, a wiry, small girl with scabs on her knees who still liked to boss the other kids around, who didn't realize that her day as leader, as queen of the block, was almost over. In a few years, she would be wearing the wrong skirts, long and straight and too tight. She would have on too much makeup, she would sport a ponytail with spit curls, her nails would be a frosty pink. And five or six years after that, long after she thought she'd put both of those Charlottes behind her, Derek's mother would look at the dress she was wearing as she came down the curving staircase in the White Plains house and say crisply, "I think something a little less revealing would work better at the club, Charlotte."

Derek: he'd smiled openly up at Lottie from behind his mother. He'd liked the idea of her discomfiting his parents, making his mother and her friends nervous as they tried to have bridal showers and ladies' lunches for her. That was part of the point of Lottie—of Charlotte—for him. She thinks of him now, tall, blond-going-to-gray, his face pulled tighter, more skeletal in age, instead of pouching into deep tired lines, as Jack's does. His comment comes back: that he has the chance to do it right this time.

She smacks the steering wheel. Here's what bothers her. Not just what that suggests he feels about Ryan, but the arrogance in assuming he has control. Sure, you might do it right, she should have said. Or you might make a whole new and incredibly inventive set of mistakes.

She should have said no such thing.

The music has changed by now on the radio. It is more sprightly but even less clear. Lottie turns it off.

She's in trouble, she's in trouble, with this tooth.

If she hates Derek so much, it must be that she hates herself as she was with him. And that is true. It makes her angry that she let herself be fooled so readily by his ease, his smoothness. His wardrobe. Al had tried to warn her. "Think of it, Lottie," he'd said. "What does it mean that he's nominally the only humanist in the house, and he was the last one to realize you were human?"

She smiles at this until she remembers her tough answer, something like: "It doesn't seem to me that fucking me is the same thing as recognizing my humanity." Al didn't try again.

He'd come to their wedding, though. He'd gotten staggeringly drunk and fallen asleep in a kneeling position, with his head resting on the seat of a chair in the anteroom to the men's and ladies' johns. Lottie had passed him several times, and it pained her to see him there, his wide ass presented to all who passed this way. She had a sense, by this time, that marrying Derek was a mistake, but she seemed to be in the grip of a kind of inevitability constructed of invitations, and tickets for the honeymoon, and elaborately boxed silver-plated presents. A little drunk herself, she'd bent over Al once, asked him please to get up, please not to kneel here anymore. He moaned. She started to cry then, holding his head. Thinking of it as something precious, something dear, thinking drunkenly and sentimentally of Al as truer, sweeter than anyone she would ever know again.

Lottie has started to hum, a little moaning hum that intensifies with each breath. She's in real pain, she realizes. She finds another Percocet, bites part of it off, swallows it down with some tepid Coke.

Is she sleepy? She doesn't know. The earlier Percocet has made her feel alert somehow; but also strangely peaceful. This is worrisome, this peace. This might be sleepiness in another guise. She opens the box of No Doz and takes one of those.

Pills, pills. That secretarial job she had in the hospital when they first moved to Chicago. The doctors dumped their sample meds into canvas carts that sat at the ends of the hallways, and Lottie, who was going to night school then too, had developed quite a little appetite for sample Dexedrine. She never even noticed the strength of the pills she took when she picked up the packets, when she swallowed them. All she knew was that it let her stay alert, it made her snappy and nervy. During this period she began to fight back when Derek was sarcastic to her, when he disapproved. And that changed her, permanently. Even after she quit the hospital job for a job at Roosevelt, where she could take courses for free, she remembered the way she could be when she was on Dexedrine, and she made that part of herself—never to be passive again, never to let him get away with it.

His eager look, asking her if she and Jack didn't think of having a child. She could have slapped him. "We have a child," she should have said. "We have several children." Really, though, wasn't it that she found something unseemly about his wish to have everything that a young man, newly married, would want? He should understand he can't have it all anymore. Isn't there an age, after all, when you ought to settle for a little less?

In the dark, she is abruptly appalled at herself. She doesn't believe this; she, too, is greedy for everything. Like Derek.

Like Cam. At the thought of Cam, she feels again the rage that rose in her, hitting him. She sees his head, bowed under her fists.

What was it he'd said to her? That she'd never worked at love? But had he? Had he?

His face that time in Chicago, so closed, so sure. That couldn't have been love. And the way he looked the night they stripped the wallpaper, when he spoke of their parents so bitterly. His clear contempt for her too. How angry he is! How shut off. What did Elizabeth say? He *feeds* on himself. She thinks of his voice on the tape, so urgent, so lost in his own way of seeing things. He lied to himself about forgiveness, about love. He needed to think of himself that way. She said to Ryan that she didn't know him. But she does, doesn't she? He's like her; she has that same rage, that coldness. It's just that she doesn't lie to herself as much.

But *has* she ever worked at love? As the names of towns rise up on the signs under her lights at the side of the road and then pass away, she thinks of lovers. The faces, the sex, the places where she had fights, where she kissed someone. She didn't try very hard, not often. Maybe once or twice, when it really mattered.

But what is this, this long drive to Jack, if not effort, work? If not for love? She's even grateful in some way for the pain. She's glad that it's costing her this much to come back to him.

In the dark stretches ahead of her lights, the road is silvery now in the moonlight, the sky has lightened once more with deepest night. She passes a sign for Mount Ronan.

Mount Ronan! She did a story here once. She lived here for a couple of days. This was a town famous for an abortionist. He was known for safe work. He'd done hundreds of women; Lottie herself knew several who'd made the pilgrimage. He'd kept a few motels and a couple of small-town restaurants alive for years. She'd gone to interview him in the late seventies, a couple of years after Roe versus Wade. Lottie remembers him now. A handsome little white-haired man—Norman Rockwell could have used him as a model doc—living in a perfect white clapboard house with a front porch. He sat on a wide courting swing with Lottie while they talked. He'd retired by then; he couldn't earn enough money in a standard gynecological practice to make working worthwhile.

He'd bragged to Lottie over lemonade about how well-trained his nurses had been, how clean his practice was. Lottie had asked him finally how it could have gone on for all those years without people in the town knowing.

"Oh, they knew," he said. "Just if they didn't want to know, they didn't have to. If you're careful, if you do good work, then nobody ever has to know, even if they *do*, you see what I mean." That was the angle she took in the article too—the complicity of upright people when public policy is bad.

How strange. She hasn't thought of it, of him, in years. All that stuff she did on the road, the interviews, the research. A part of her life that's gone from her.

She can't stand the pain under her tooth. She turns on the radio again and finds another call-in show. They're talking about self-esteem, this group. She concentrates on listening. She tries not to think, not to feel her pulsing jaw. There is another expert on, someone who has apparently developed just the right amount of self-esteem. There is the host, who seems to have an overabundance of it; there are the pathetic callers, trying for the soupçon that a moment on the radio will provide. This is why Freud hated America, she thinks; and he didn't even know about call-in shows.

A woman calls who has been rebirthed; another new beginning, thinks Lottie. Like Derek's, only from the other side. The woman speaks of her reexperience of vulnerability, of the loving support of her group, her leader: their soothing touch as she emerged—whatever that could mean—correctly this time.

Of course, this can be helpful, the expert says with condescension in his voice. *For the likes of you*, is the suggestion. In general, though, because the trauma, the shaming, the damage to self-esteem comes later, it's usually better to focus on issues that occur later in childhood.

Lottie imagines her mother after giving birth, her mother holding a reddish bundle that is Lottie. Or perhaps Cameron. She might have been a loving mother to an infant; there is no way to know. *Charlotte, Cameron*: these romantic names. Surely they mean that she wanted something for them, something from them.

And suddenly Lottie has a memory of her mother sewing, work-ing on a costume for Lottie, a wide net skirt set with red hearts: Lottie was to be the Queen of Hearts. For Halloween? For a school play? She can't remember. But she was on a chair in the dining room, the sun was streaming in, her mother knelt beneath her. She tapped Lottie with a yardstick when she wanted her to turn—she couldn't speak; her mouth was full of pins. She tapped Lottie over and over, on the belly, the hip, the buttocks, a little hard rap that Lottie felt as the knock of her heart in love. Because she had loved her mother so much then: the bent graying head, the sharply parted hair, the whitish scalp, the intermittent hard rap.

It *had* happened every now and then; Lottie remembers it now. It must have been like an awakening for her mother. What could have caused it, what could it have been? Her mother would have a project, suddenly. The television would not be on when you opened the door. Instead her mother would be humming somewhere in the house. She would be busy. There would be the smell of something cooking, of laundry being ironed, of wallpaper paste. The clickety-clickety of the sewing machine. What would it have felt like, Lottie wonders, to be her mother? To be so at the mercy of chemicals swimming in your brain.

Lottie can't imagine, really. She only knows what it felt like then to be the child, slowly to learn to distrust what she loved most about her mother. She'd grown to dread the days that were different, because you couldn't believe in them. Because they preceded the inevitable return to silence and inertia. Later she would be sarcastic in describing those moments. "She must have been getting ready for the Pillsbury Bake-Off," she would say. "Competing for Mrs. America, no doubt."

The man with self-esteem has completely faded by now, and Lottie presses the Seek button again. She lets it make its cycle four, five times, sometimes stopping it and trying to listen to a fading signal for a while. The only clear station has a religious service on, a black preacher whose organist punctuates every sentence with a vibrating chord. The congregation shouts over it, over the preacher too. They are all far gone; it's like strange music, repetitive, ecstatic.

After a while Lottie tires of it and turns it off. She drives in silence with the pain.

Jessica. The service. Lottie was surprised when the preacher read the lines about man passing away, the place thereof knowing him no more. Why would he speak such lines? she had wondered. Such cruel lines. Of course, she knows that it was to emphasize how ephemeral earthly life is, the difference between everything mortal and everything connected to God. But to read this to a grieving mother! Dorothea Laver's voice sounds in her head, calm, slow, full of apology.

Maybe in grief you want such lines, though, maybe you cherish the absoluteness of loss, the sense of your own pain as the only connection left. Wasn't that really what Dorothea Laver had called Cam for? For Jessica's last words, if there were any, yes. But also for the confirmation. She wanted him to say, I was there and I saw she was dead. She is dead. Over and over. *She is dead. She has died.* The paradox that as long as we still feel the pain of that, as long as we're able to lacerate ourselves with the fact of loss, we still feel some connection. When the pain fades, so, finally, does the person. And the real loss, which begins exactly then, isn't felt anymore. A betrayal. The way things are, and must be.

Jack had never had that with Evelyn, of course. She was dead, she had died, but the place thereof continued to know her. A version of her. He had told Lottie that the first stroke eliminated a lot of short-term memory and, for a while, speech and her ability to walk. But as she began to recover some of that and they began to be hopeful, he realized that a whole layer of her personality had disappeared. She knew him, she knew the children, but she was childlike, her judgments and responses were shallow. He said that he felt enraged at her stupidity sometimes during that period, at her impulsiveness. And it was during this time too—almost a year and half— that he most wished she'd died.

After the second stroke, she was so reduced that he could only feel pity, sorrow. And he finally learned to feel love for the person she had become.

And now his pain. Now that Lottie has learned to feel love.

She thinks of the weekend he spent in Boston, of how unwilling she was to hear about his pain, to talk about it. She makes herself go carefully over the details of their time together, of their lovemaking, their fight. Her face, in the light of dashboard instruments, moves constantly—winces, frowns, is agonized—as the images play through her mind. She makes little noises and finally, hearing this, stops herself.

This is it—her finger points at the dark road ahead: she couldn't bear to be at the mercy of his feelings anymore, of his sorrow. In her experience, she realizes, either you're in control or you're at the mercy of someone else, you're lost. She had felt that, a kind of living death, with Derek. Somehow he set the terms—because Lottie had still been Char Reed when she met him. Because she was trying to get to be who he was, trying to get to be like him. Low self-esteem, no doubt about it.

Now, suddenly, she sees, she feels, that it is this same Char Reed she has been dragging after herself all along, even into her marriage with Jack. Even now, driving back to him. She has felt changed, over and over in her life. She has marked the changes: Char to Charlotte to Lottie. Char Reed to Lottie Gardner. She has reinvented herself once, twice, three or four times, shed the past like a snake shedding a useless papery skin. *Rebirthed* herself. She smiles grimly in the upward light of the dash. Didn't she and Cam talk once about that very thing?

She has felt the old lives fall away: her mother, the enclosing house, Derek and her struggle to catch up. Like shedding lovers, Al and Derek and Avery and all the others. She has seen herself as a different person each time, spinning free into the false promise of a clean slate, a fresh start. She hasn't been willing to acknowledge the refining of a self that has never changed, that has been there through all the choosing, the grabbing, the discarding: the needy, frightened girl who chooses quickly and quickly throws things away, because she cannot bear to be chosen. To be discarded.

Even now. Even this trip, this romantic gesture, this *gift* she is making of herself: isn't it, really, another way of setting the terms, of insisting on a shape?

This is what Lottie is thinking.

But this isn't what Lottie is thinking either. Because one clear thought passes into an opposite and equally clear thought. The contradictions pile up. She is tired, she is in pain. There is just a jumble, finally. The sense of false understanding, of confusion and vulnerability at the core; all of it driven by the steady and growing pain from her tooth.

She's in Ohio now. She'll need some gas soon. Her headlights sweep an exit sign with the symbol of a motel on it—a bed. She begins to signal. A bed. This is what she needs. She'll take a whole Percocet and stop this pain. She'll sleep, she'll wake free of pain to a new day, a new start. The end of these morbid thoughts.

There are two motels to choose from, but Lottie is suddenly so tired, so hungry for the pill she imagines will release her, that she pulls, without thinking of comparing them, into the one on her side of the road. It's a Days Inn, like a dozen she's checked into before, all of it familiar: the shape of the plastic key holder in her hand, the cheesy chandelier in the lobby, the drive around to the unlighted parking lot in back, the sudden sense of country air as you step out of the car. The same concrete staircase to the same balcony girdled by the same spare, wrought-iron rail.

In the bathroom under the fluorescent light, she fumbles in her pocketbook, finds a whole Percocet, and takes it. She checks to see how many are left. One and almost a half. She washes her face. She comes out into the room and tries the television, sitting on the foot of the bed to change stations. There's only snow and noise. She peels back the covers and lies down. She holds herself, making a gentle mewing, rocking from side to side. As soon as she feels the Percocet start to work, she turns the light off.

Pain wakes her, a solid pressure, no longer throbbing. It owns her before she remembers where she is, what she's doing or why. She touches the tooth with her tongue. The gum below responds. She can feel that it is swollen, hard. She moans aloud.

When she slides the curtain back, the sky is a pale, dirty gray. In its watery light, she squints at her watch. Four-thirty. She goes to the bathroom and uses the toilet. She rinses her mouth with water that tastes wrong, that tastes of iron, Lottie thinks, or some other mineral. She takes a No Doz and another half of a Percocet. Her face is starting to swell along the jawline, but even so she can't believe how little it has changed. She looks tired, older, puffy, but you can't see the vise of pain her head is gripped in. She drinks another glass of water, warm this time, hoping this will dissolve the pills faster. She imagines them floating in her stomach, a little white circle and an approximate half circle. She is trying very hard to imagine anything but the pain. She shrugs her sweater around her shoulders, slides into her sandals, grabs her purse, her car keys. At the door she looks around. Nothing else is hers. There's no sign of her having been here except for the rumpled bed.

The air outside smells fresh, and Lottie stops for a moment on the long balcony. She's looking over the parking lot to a line of trees, black against the whiter sky. She recalls the freshness of the sea air outside her mother's nursing home, the abundance of floral odors inside. Manufactured air. She thinks of her mother, of her own feeling that perhaps she could call forth from that leftover husk something that was meant for herself, some sense of what she'd meant to the woman who once lived inside those bones, that flesh. Of who she'd been to her. Apparently, she thinks, you will have to live without that knowledge.

She starts the car and drives to the gas station next door. While the attendant fills the tank, she goes inside and buys some coffee from a machine in a lobby not unlike the one in Pennsylvania. There's no one else in the restaurant. The dining room here is closed, corded off. A lone worker, wearing a jaunty uniform hat, is moving behind the aluminum steam counter, setting things up.

The sky is a lighter gray when she comes out. She pulls back onto the local road, then the access road, then the highway. She opens the coffee and sips at it. It's too hot. She sets it carefully on the flat console between the two front seats. After a while she tries the radio again. Anything to escape the sense of enclosure with this pain. There is a lot of silence, a lot of fierce static. She finally gets a country music station and turns it up, loud.

She tries to sing along, guessing at the rhymes. She's bad at this, never imagining "hand" and "ring," for instance, would work. But she concentrates hard, listening intently, visualizing the singers. She's able to drink the coffee after a while. She holds it in her mouth briefly before each swallow, and its warmth soothes her swollen gum for a few seconds. The sky slowly lightens behind her, a gassy yellow. She looks at the speedometer. She's going almost eighty. She brings it back down to seventy-five. When the country music finally fades, she jumps stations for a while again. She's driving through flat gray terrain—fields, farmhouses. Here and there she passes a farmhouse with breakfast lights glowing in a downstairs window.

She's hungry too. She finds the candy bar in her purse and breaks off a piece. She chews gingerly on the left side of her mouth, finally allowing a sugary nugget just to dissolve slowly. When it's gone, she breaks off another piece.

Gradually all that's been grayish in the world around her takes on color—green, mostly—and the sky is bright in the rearview mirror. The sun bursts over the horizon behind her. She's humming steadily. When she can't stand it anymore, she eats another half a Percocet. She has one half left now. It is six-fifteen.

She tries to force her mind to focus on something outside herself. She thinks of Carol, giving her the pills. A nice woman. Of Ryan with the baby. The sudden sense it gave her of being pushed aside. The way it will be. Taking her place in line.

Lottie has escaped this. Escaped thinking about it. Even with the cancer, she never allowed herself to dwell on it. She made plans, she exercised. She swore she wouldn't die.

She and Cam have escaped it.

No, not Cam. He said—it's true he said—that he, like her, had mothered himself; but he has also somehow been able to care for their mother. He remembers their father. He lies to himself about where he is, but he has known very well all along where he came from, where he's going. Lottie is the one who thinks of herself as *sui generis*, her own mother. And even her own child: hasn't she used Ryan's childhood as her own? Lottie the paramecium. Divide and conquer. Be there, in every generation. "Immortal Lottie." She smiles grimly through the very mortal pain in her skull.

The dead girl. The accident. Jessica.

It is Jessica, it is Jessica and Cameron and even Elizabeth who have brought her here, to this place, this moment. She feels, suddenly, that she owes them something, something she can't repay.

And now, in a strange kind of penance, Lottie makes herself think of exactly how it was, the car turning into the driveway in the rain. Jessica—drunk, pretty Jessica—stepping forward. She makes herself imagine Cam, thinking only of Elizabeth, only her, on the drive over, *how certain he must have been that he could get control again, that he could win her back.* How lost in that thought.

She even makes herself imagine Elizabeth, where she would have been, phoning Cam, how she would have felt. She thinks of Larry and Emily and the children somewhere else in the house, Elizabeth hearing them, Elizabeth wanting to be safely with them again. Elizabeth choosing Jessica as the way to get what she wanted.

And Jessica, so eager to help, to be part of it. Jessica waiting outside for Cam to come. Lottie sees it, she makes herself see it all: Jessica on the dark lawn, the headlights, the girl lifted up, falling back. Lottie's hands gripping the wheel jerk convulsively; she cries out and hits the horn by mistake. Its honking sounds faint, distant, under the noise of the rushing car, and Lottie presses it now, again and again, thinking of Cam, of Jessica; thinking of herself and Jack and Evelyn and Ryan.

When she stops, her heart is racing, her tooth is pulsing agonizingly to its beat. The fertile green fields roll by outside, and she listens to her own ragged breathing and wipes the tears that are sliding down her cheeks. She can't tell, anymore, why she's crying: grief, pain, exhaustion, the otherworldliness of the drug state she's in, her fear of what's to come. Whatever. She's undone by it, by all of it.

She needs to blow her nose too, and has nothing to do it with. Absurdly, this adds to her sorrow. Sniffling, wiping at her face with her bare hands, she drives on and on, with the sun rising slowly behind her in the east, flooding the world around her with pale light.

Lottie does return, as she left, to an oldies station. It's all she can get in Indiana, and she leaves it on as she passes the steel mills, then as she descends into the city, crosses it—long after the point when the music and lyrics are swallowed by static; because she can't hear it anymore: she's lost in her pain. In Indiana she had actually pulled off the road, stopped the car and bent over, desperately feeling on the floor and under the seat, under both seats, for the little bit of Percocet that had broken off when she bit it the evening before.

In the city, instead of going home, she drives directly to her dentist's office on the near North Side. There are two people reading magazines in the waiting room, two people who look up as Lottie comes in, and then, startled, keep looking at her—at her rumpled, slept-in clothes, at her smeared, swollen face, at her halting walk, the result of stiffness after the long drive.

When she opens her mouth to explain herself to the receptionist, she begins to weep, and this works better than anything else could have. The receptionist, a Wagnerian blonde who has—today as always in Lottie's experience—an impeccable thick mask of makeup on, rises magnificently from her desk, comes around to Lottie, and engulfs her. She sweeps her directly into an exam room. Within less than a minute the dentist is there. Lottie opens her mouth and points. He reaches in with several instruments and adds to her agony momentarily. She groans, screeches, and then, with a searing jolt, the filling is off. Her mouth fills instantly with salty fluid. She is crying still, but in such relief! such happiness!

"What a mess, Lottie," the dentist says. She can't answer.

"Open wide," he says. He applies cotton wadding. He pulls it back out, stained. He holds it up in his tweezers. "This is your life, eh?"

Lottie laughs. This is why she comes to this dentist.

The receptionist—Georgia is her name, Lottie remembers now—comes in with a damp washcloth. Gratefully Lottie accepts it. She covers her face and wipes it thoroughly. She is talking now, talking and laughing in shaky joy, trying to explain about the tooth, the trip. "God, what a relief!" she says finally. "I can't believe it. I feel as ecstatic as I did when I gave birth."

The dentist is busy with instruments on his little tray table. "This is going to cost you almost as much too," he answers.

It's midafternoon when she gets home. There's no car in the driveway, and the house is still when the door swings in. She calls. No one answers. And then Bader appears around the corner from the living room, his hindquarters swinging recklessly for a creature as arthritic as he is, his mouth hung open in joy. He has trouble even walking toward her, he's so happy. He tries to jump up on her, and Lottie quickly squats to spare him. He's beside himself, licking her face, turning in circles. Trying, as she anthropomorphizes it, to offer her the equivalent of an embrace. In the end, he's too excited; he simply falls over with a gentle thud.

"That's right, lovey," Lottie says, and she holds him down, dropping to her knees. She pats him for a long time, speaking gently to him, scratching his ears, rubbing his muzzle.

As soon as she rises, though, he scrambles up too, his long nails scratching on the stone of the foyer. He pants as he follows her through the house. She calls once again at the foot of the stairs. Jack's at work, of course. Megan must be at school. Or with friends.

288

She goes into the kitchen, takes a banana from a bowl of fruit, and eats it quickly. Her mouth is still numb on the right side. She pours herself a glass of orange juice, then has another banana. The kitchen is messy, she notes. There are dishes in the sink. The counter by the toaster is sprinkled with crumbs. Two pizza boxes bent in half are leaned against the trash can. *I'll do it later*, she thinks. *Just a little rest, and then I'll do it.*

Before she goes upstairs, she gives Bader a dog biscuit to distract him, but when she turns at the landing, he's followed her to the stairway. He's looking up at her, bereft.

In the shower, Lottie hears him start to howl. Even so, she stands under the warm spray for a long time. She shampoos her hair, she soaps herself thoroughly, massaging herself slowly with the washcloth—her aching legs, her swollen feet. When she gets out, he's still at it. *Aroooo*, the mad call of dog love. Wrapped in a towel, she goes to the top of the stairwell and looks down. He's heard her and stopped. He's looking back up at her.

"*Stop* it, Bader," she says. "I know you have, but stop it anyway." He looks away in shame and lies down slowly.

Lottie goes back to the bedroom. She dries off, puts on a T-shirt and some bikini pants, and gets in bed.

Bader starts again. For a while she lies there, thinking he'll stop, drifting every now and then into the near sleep of strange images—the unfolding dark road, Jessica floating up and back, her mother's empty face, Ryan, injured. Bader does stop briefly once or twice. But then, slowly at first—a tentative pain—and then more whole-heartedly, in all-out yearning, he starts again.

Lottie gets up. Frantically she snatches the bedspread from the bed, drags it trailing behind her to the stairs and down. The old dog is standing up. His tail slowly begins to swing as he sees he's done it, he's brought her back to him. She strides by him, heads for the living room. She flops down on the couch and sloppily yanks the bedspread this way and that to cover herself.

Bader has followed her in. He noses her once or twice. "No," she says. "I'm sleeping." But she has to sit up once more to throw the pillows off the back of the couch, and then to arrange the bedspread again.

Finally she falls into a deep sleep on the couch. And Bader, content at last, lies down exactly below her, as close as he can get to her on the floor, resting his head on one of the pillows she's discarded.

And that's the way Jack finds them when he comes home from work.

CHAPTER 15

It's three days before the arrival of all their sons home from graduate school and college for the Christmas vacation, and Lottie is
outside early this morning, walking Bader. She has been waking
early for the last several days, with lists of things to do to get ready
for the holidays taking shape in her mind; though once she's up and
starts to write them down, the lists are always surprisingly short.
Certainly not worth waking at five-thirty or six o'clock for.

It's just nervousness, she thinks. She's anxious about how it will
all go. She feels responsible.

It's snowed heavily the night before, and the city seems especially hushed under the white blanket. No one has shoveled the
sidewalks yet, so Lottie and Bader are out on the plowed street. He
has stiffly preceded her down their own snowy driveway, awkwardly lifting his paws with each step to try to keep them dry. And
he's ahead of her now, here and there marking the snow heaped up
against the cars with an unsteady, short spurt.

He stops suddenly, nosing a dark shape in the street. Lottie,
getting closer, can see that it's a cat, that it's dead. She bends and
yanks Bader away by the collar. He tries to return, but she scolds
him and he shuffles off, his head drooping in a weary acceptance of
blame.

Lottie stands helpless in the street for a moment, looking down at the animal. It's been hit by a car, clearly, but it's unmarked. It's a pale orange. Its mouth and eyes are open in the surprise of death, and Lottie can see its pointed, perfect white teeth. It's got a plastic flea collar on. It's someone's pet. She bends over, grabs the cat's tail, and pulls it to the edge of the plowed street, against a snowbank. At least it won't get hit again here, and maybe its owner will be able to find it and claim it. Its body is completely frozen, stiff as a piece of wood.

She trudges after Bader, her bare feet cold in her fur-lined boots, a long coat on over her nightgown. Her breath plumes from her nose, and she can feel the cold pinch the flesh of her nostrils. There's no one else out at this hour. Behind their vast white lawns the houses seem remote and small, almost like miniatures. Doll houses.

Her own house is still eerie with sleep when they return. Lottie can hear and notice, as she never does in the daytime, the hum and tick of all the machines that keep them alive and comfortable. She hangs her coat on the coat tree and pries her cold, wet boots off. Bader's nails click on the polished floor ahead of her, leading her to the kitchen. In its murk, she changes the water in his dish and gets him a dog biscuit from the shelf in the broom closet. Then she goes back into the hall and slowly climbs the carpeted stairs to the bedroom.

Jack's flesh shudders when she touches him, but she pulls herself close under the covers, presses herself against his furnaced skin.

"God! Returned from the Antarctic," he says.

"Bader and I."

"Mmm. Just don't put your hands on me."

"But that's what I want to do."

"Well." He turns. "With surgical precision, then."

They each shift a bit toward the other. "Lovely hand warmer," she says.

"Should have had one with you on your walk."

"I like it attached."

He opens his eyes. "What time is it? Do we have time?"

As if in answer, they hear Megan, the slam of the bathroom door down the hall.

"There it is, the cold shower in person," she says.

292

Jack laughs. "The saltpeter in the mashed potatoes."

After a minute she says, "Do you know someone around with an orange cat?"

"No. Why?"

"There's one outside. Dead. Hit by a car."

"Oh. Too bad." He's looking at her, and suddenly his eyes change. "No wonder you're up here trying to seduce me."

"What do you mean?"

"You're the only person I know for whom death is an aphrodisiac."

She slaps him lightly on the shoulder. "Not fair." She sits up, throwing the covers back. "It probably is for everyone else too. Just I admit it." She gets up, puts her robe on this time, her slippers, and pads silently across the room, the dark hall, and down the stairs to fix breakfast.

She is thinking about what Jack said. He has pointed out the pattern to her: that she met him indirectly as a result of her cancer, that Evelyn's death gave him to her at last, that Jessica's death brought her back. They've talked about all of it, occasionally even joked about it, as they just did. But Lottie isn't entirely comfortable with the jokes yet.

She turns on the kitchen lights. She puts on water for coffee and sets the table. She brings a carton of orange juice, a loaf of raisin bread, the butter and jam, and a bowl of fruit to the table. All this is for Jack and herself. Megan won't eat anything. She claims now to find the thought of food before noon appalling. She sits with them because Jack makes her, but all she has is coffee, black.

Megan is somewhat easier with Lottie now, but this is partly because she's withdrawn from Jack. She's done with him, it seems, as Ryan is done with Lottie. But Megan needs to have her departure noticed. She's making trouble. She's fallen in love with a man several years older than herself, who plays guitar in some kind of rock band—though the other instruments in this band are a cello and a trombone, which raises questions of the band's viability for Lottie. Megan is refusing to apply to colleges because it's her plan to go on the road with the band next year. She and Jack have fought almost daily for several months about this. Now she's angry because she's discovered that if she does go on the road, Jack won't give her any money. All she's asking for, she said the night before in a tone that held unfathomable contempt for his rigidity, is whatever allowance he'd give her if she were at college. What is his problem?

This discussion took place in the living room. Lottie had stood up and left when it started to get rancorous—nearly right away—but she could still hear their voices from the kitchen.

"It's in the nature of some experiences that you pay for them yourself," Jack said. His voice sounded calm and reasonable, but Lottie knew he was deeply upset. He wasn't used to fighting with Megan. He would probably never get used to it. And then she would be gone.

"Why? Why is it"—and here Megan changed her tone to mock her father—"*in the nature of some experiences?*"

"Because it is. Because a family-supported rebellion is a thoroughly half-assed thing."

Lottie shut the door as Megan started to yell. And standing there in the kitchen, Lottie thought of two things simultaneously. First, that her experience the summer before—the experience that had brought her back to Jack—had been paid for by everyone but herself. By Jessica, by Cameron and Elizabeth. Even by Ryan. And second, that she felt a kind of dark, shameful glee at these fights between Jack and Megan, at his discovery that Megan could be difficult for him too. She concentrated on the first thing. She began to speculate on it as she went about her business in the kitchen, waiting until they were through fighting to emerge.

Lottie never takes part in these discussions. Mindful of Megan's having said she doesn't want another mother, she lets Jack handle all of it. At night, in bed, he talks to her about it, though, and she comments and commiserates. He has been through a stage when he really thought Megan would come around, that he could just insist and she'd finally do what he wanted her to do. Now he's mostly resigned. He still struggles with her, hard, but really, he's simply waiting for her to leave. In part, so she can come back to him sometime later.

They're both waiting for her to leave, then; and Lottie feels some relief that Jack has joined her in this. It seems a turning into their life together. And who can say for certain whether Megan began to pull away so hard because she sensed their turn to each other? or whether they began to turn to their life together because Megan began to pull away? It has happened. It is happening.

They've talked, actually, of selling the house. Not next year—the kids will probably still be coming home en masse, as they are for Christmas this year. But maybe a year or two after that. It's possible, of course, that they won't in the end. But their daydreaming about it from time to time has made Lottie feel easier about the house too. It isn't what *has to be* anymore.

In any case, whether they move or not, they're going to be alone soon. Megan may or may not go to college, she may or may not be on the road, but she will leave, eagerly and bitterly. And Lottie, as it turns out, will apparently be the least important factor in that decision. Sometimes, actually, Megan allies herself with Lottie now. She'll turn to her occasionally in the midst of some argument and say, "Why does he have to always be right? I mean, why do you put up with it?"

They will be alone.

Although it's also true that Lottie's begun again to go on the road a bit herself, researching a new book she's started. It's about emergency room medicine.

She decided on this project over the day and a half she was in Cambridge when she went to retrieve her belongings. She flew out in mid-August, only a few weeks after Jessica died and she'd come back to Jack. She stayed in a fancy hotel in Cambridge for the one night she was there. She couldn't bear the thought of staying at her mother's again, and as it turned out, that wouldn't have been possible anyway. The bed was gone. The rooms were completely empty. Cam had cleared everything out of the house except for her stuff and Richard Lester's room. As Lottie walked through the bare spaces, every noise she made—footfall, breathing—seemed amplified. Cam had left her clothes in their neat piles upstairs, and he'd set her papers down carefully on the floor of the dining room. He'd reclaimed his own books, Lottie noted, but there were eight or ten of hers still here—ones she'd brought out from Chicago, as well as the ones she'd purchased over the weeks of the summer.

Lottie had a liquor box with her, and now she sat down on the bare floor in the dining room and began to go through the stacks of papers in preparation for packing them up. Here were her notes on Donne's poems, on Turgenev's stories. Here was the napkin with the comment about exhibitionism she'd jotted down in front of Elizabeth so long ago. Here was a scribble she'd made early in the summer on the paucity of twentieth-century love stories. *Wonder why not?* she had noted. *It still orders our lives—amidst all this chaos, machinery. Abandonment. Casual betrayal.*

Sitting there on the floor with this paper in her hand, Lottie realized abruptly that she wouldn't do this article, that she had nothing clear to say about this topic. She set the paper down. To do it right, she'd have to be able to write fiction; because what love offers, she thought, is a narrative thread. It gives things a beginning, a middle, and—as Twain had seen so clearly—an end. And Lottie had neither the ability nor the wish to write a story.

Still, she was careful with everything; she sorted it all, stacked it—even the napkin. She packed it all carefully into the liquor box, and on the way back to the hotel, she stopped the cab at the post office to mail it, along with the boxes holding her computer and printer, to Jack's house.

That night Cam came over to her hotel for a drink: Lottie had arranged this by phone several days before from Chicago. They sat outside on a wide brick terrace overlooked by the wings of the hotel, by the rows and rows of identical windows and curtains. The lamps were slowly being switched on in the rooms. Lottie was tense. She focused immediately on the house—a safe topic—and Cam seemed willing to go along with her.

He was about to list it with a real estate agent, he said. Their mother had finally been declared incompetent. They talked about money, about how to proceed. "Are you going to see her?" he asked.

Jack had asked this too, before she left. "No," she said. "It's too much like just looking at her to see her. She gets nothing from it. And it's horrible for me."

He nods. "She still knows me."

"She should. You've been very good to her."

Someone on the other side of the terrace dropped a glass, and for a few seconds everyone was quiet. Cam looked in that direction, then back at Lottie. He didn't seem the least uncomfortable with her. It became clear it would fall to her to say something about what had happened between them, if anything was to be said.

"Have there been any . . . repercussions?" she started. "Of the accident? For you?"

"How do you mean?"

How did she mean? *Have you stayed awake at night thinking about it? Have you heard from Elizabeth? Has anything made a dent in you?* "Just whether all that . . . whether your life is any different on account of it, I guess."

"Not really." His voice was chilly. Or not chilly, just flat. Expressionless. He wasn't going to tell her anything of any real importance to himself. Why had she thought he might?

He shrugged and smiled just slightly. "I got a notice that I passed my blood test."

"Your blood test?"

"Yes, the one I took that night?"

Lottie frowned.

"In the emergency room. I spent most of that night, the night Jessica died, sitting in the emergency room waiting to have my blood drawn. While every knife fight and . . . kidney stone in Cambridge got treated first."

"Oh, that's right," Lottie said; and once again, just for a moment, she felt how different his experience of those days had been from hers. "I forgot about that." After a long silence, she said abruptly, "I'm ashamed of myself for the scene we had." She had rehearsed this line. This was what she'd decided she needed to say to him.

"You needn't be," he answered.

Lottie waited, but he added nothing. She looked at him. He was so self-contained, so handsome. He was all she could ever know about her family, and she would never know him.

In her dream that night in the hotel, Cam appeared to her. The dream was strangely connected to the last radiation treatment she'd undergone for cancer, when they threaded rods through her breast and filled them with radioactive material. They'd kept her in isolation for more than a day that time, with a sign on her door that warned everyone away. Lottie had felt like an alien, a mutant, some science fiction creature. When Ryan visited, he had to stand in the hallway to talk to her, looking homely and frightened. He was twelve then, and his legs and nose were far too big for the rest of him.

In her dream, Cameron, like Ryan in life, was standing on the other side of a wide room from her. She knew this to be an emergency room, in the way we know these things in dreams. It was full of equipment, mostly the ordinary machines that fill ordinary lives—televisions, answering machines, Xerox machines, computers. But somehow it was clear to Lottie that their purpose was to read your blood, your heart. There were beeps and clicks, amber and green lines making words on the screens. It seemed to be through these machines that Cameron was speaking to her, but she couldn't read the words or understand the noises, hard as she tried. Lottie was herself partially just such a machine in the dream, but full of a human straining, to understand, to speak. Her own cry woke her.

Lottie couldn't have said exactly how everything connected, but somehow, in the plane on the way back to Chicago, she decided that she would write next about emergency rooms. Once she returned, she spent four days sitting and making notes in a waiting room at Cook County Hospital, watching the bits of high drama that jolted quickly past—the accidents, the overdoses, the family fights, the spiking fevers; as well as the ordinary, slower misery and pain of people who waited, who had no other source of medical care. The ceaselessly wailing child with an earache. An old woman with a foot so swollen Lottie couldn't see her toes. Again and again while she sat there, Lottie imagined Cameron in a setting like this: polite, cooperative with his police escort, nothing showing in his face or bearing of the reality of what he'd done.

She is excited about this project, and so is her publisher. It has everything, they've agreed. Dramatic episodes, an angle into the social and medical ills of our time, a commentary to offer on what's going wrong with American medicine. It's also become part of the joke about death with Jack—how perfect for her to have access to this never-ending stream. How perfect for him that she does.

But what is perfect for Lottie, too, is going away, being *on the road*. She's picked hospitals in two big cities besides Chicago to study, and in three small towns. She has made two trips this fall, one to Seattle and one to southern New Mexico, and before both of them she has felt the familiar hunger to be gone, to be alone; and then, once she's out there, the yearning solitary pleasure in the anonymity and isolation of the trip.

And when it's over, each time the coming home again.

* * *

Jack had waked her that summer afternoon she'd fallen asleep on the living room couch after her long drive home. He was bending over her and gently touching her swollen cheek.

"Lottie? What's going on? What happened to you?"

Lottie opened her eyes and fought off her thick sleep, untangling the bedspread and trying too quickly to tell her tale: the tooth, the girl who died, the drive through the night, the funeral, the fight with Cameron. She had to back up again and again and start over, filling in the missing elements. Finally she began to weep as she was talking—out of fatigue, out of confusion and effort. "Oh, don't look at me!" she moaned. "I'm so ugly." Lottie cried as a child does, great hiccuping intakes of breath between her wails, her short sentences. "And I wanted so much. I tried so hard. I drove the whole way thinking of it, of how it would be. And then my tooth. But then I saw I was just like him. Like Cameron. The whole drive. I was trying so hard to be different, to love you. And it was just like him. Except I didn't kill anyone. But I could have. I might as well have. And now I have to have *root* canal," she wailed.

Jack had eased onto the couch with her as she wept, sitting and then stretching the length of his body out next to hers. He was stroking her face, wiping the tears away, murmuring comfort. At last she stopped, and they lay next to each other.

"Don't look at me," she whispered after a minute.

"I love to look at you," he said. "My hollyhock." His hand rested gently on her swollen jaw. "My half a hamster."

Lottie laughed, and choked. She turned quickly to her side, coughing, curled against the back of the couch. Finally she lay still. Jack had raised himself on an elbow behind her.

"You almost killed me, Jack," she said, hoarsely. She cleared her throat.

"With kindness," he said.

"Regardless."

They lay cupped together for a while, looking up at the trees moving behind the panes of the windows above them, listening to Bader's snorts and whimpers in sleep on the floor. Lottie slept a little too, and then woke, momentarily feeling Jack's arms and legs as part of her.

They roused themselves. Lottie went upstairs to wash her face and put makeup on. She came back in Jack's bathrobe, rolling up the long sleeves. He was in the kitchen, wiping the counters. He was apologetic about the mess. Lottie insisted on helping him. She wiped too, she scrubbed. She ran the disposal. She put the pizza boxes in the garbage, and then, because they wouldn't fit, she climbed in and stood on them until they went down. She unloaded the clean dishes from the dishwasher, rinsed and loaded up the ones in the sink. She swept the kitchen floor.

Jack, meanwhile, set the table, cleaned the stovetop, and fixed them dinner—poached eggs, in honor of Lottie's tooth. They sat across from each other at the kitchen table and ate them, and then drank wine, talking, until all the color drained from the room and twilight filled it.

Jack was speaking about the weekend he'd come out to visit—only the weekend before, Lottie realized with a little shock. "I was going to win you back, Lottie. I was going to give it everything I had. But I didn't have a chance. You were wild; that was your agenda. If I didn't want to let you bite me, it meant I was trying to destroy you somehow."

"I know, I know, I know, I know," she said apologetically. She drank some wine. "And look at me now. I couldn't bite oatmeal."

He laughed.

A little later, when the room was truly dark, he asked, "What does this mean, Lottie?"

"What?"

"This," he said. "You. Here." His hoarse voice seemed to fill the darkness. It thrilled Lottie.

"It means, I think, that I'll pretend I can do it."

Jack was quiet. His shirt was a pale blur across from Lottie. Finally he said, "Well, that's fine, Lottie. That's all I ask, I think. That's what we do, isn't it? Like a story we tell ourselves. And then, with luck, it comes true."

The refrigerator hummed steadily. Outside somewhere, a car honked. The kitchen was dark and still and smelled of cleansing powder. Lottie wanted to see Jack. She reached over to the little lamp hanging on the wall by the table and turned it on. Suddenly he was there, startling—alarming, even—in his reality, his otherness. And yet exactly as she'd known he would be. Exactly as she'd been seeing him in her mind's eye.

And sometimes it still happens that way, when she returns from a trip or when she comes on him unawares. Just as now, turning in her bathrobe from the snowy view outside the window, she feels the shock of pleasurable surprise, not just that he is there in the kitchen doorway when she didn't hear him coming; but that he is as she expected him to be: the graying shock of hair, the goodness in his lined face, the cat-colored eyes that lift now and meet hers across the dim, winter-lit room.

Sometimes, though, it takes a little longer, and then Lottie feels the way she did that afternoon in the first seconds after she woke from her dreamless chemical sleep on the living room couch. She knew she was nowhere she was supposed to be, and Jack's face, while dear to her—she knew that too—was not instantly familiar. It was in some ways like the feeling we all have on waking in a strange place—but more intense, more deeply disordered. Perhaps more like the confusion recovered stroke victims report feeling in the first moments after it happens: when am I? why is this? what is the being living through this moment?

And then everything shifts slightly and takes on shape and meaning, just as it did that day. And with a great effort, Lottie gathers herself together and begins to tell her story.